HE WAS LOUIS XIV, KING OF FRANCE,
fought over by exquisite, glittering women. But there was
one he had not yet possessed—and she was the one
woman he wanted.

SHE WAS THE FABULOUS ANGÉLIQUE
a woman risen from the gutters of Paris to the giddy
heights of power and position in the King's Court.

Angélique knew Louis was irresistibly drawn to her beauty,
yet all his mistresses were also beautiful, and he discarded
them like toys. That, Angélique could never bear. She knew
she must find ways to keep the King's passion for her
aflame!

Here is the tremendous novel of seventeenth-century Versailles, the most fascinating period in French history.

The Novel Bookshop

5116 - 50th Avenue
Innisfree, AB TOB 2G0
Ph: (403) 592-2209

Angélique and the King

by Sergeanne Golon

Translated by Monroe Stearns

A NATIONAL GENERAL COMPANY

*This low-priced Bantam Book
has been completely reset in a type face
designed for easy reading, and was printed
from new plates. It contains the complete
text of the original hard-cover edition.*
NOT ONE WORD HAS BEEN OMITTED.

ANGÉLIQUE AND THE KING
*A Bantam Book / published by arrangement with
J. B. Lippincott Company*

PRINTING HISTORY
*Lippincott edition published May 1960
Bantam edition published November 1961*

2nd printing .... June 1966	6th printing ..... January 1968
3rd printing .... May 1966	7th printing .... June 1969
4th printing .... July 1966	8th printing .... February 1970
5th printing ..... October 1966	9th printing .... April 1971

Translation by Monroe Stearns

*Bantam Books are published by Bantam Books, Inc., a National
General company. Its trade-mark, consisting of the words "Bantam
Books" and the portrayal of a bantam, is registered in the United
States Patent Office and in other countries. Marca Registrada.
Bantam Books, Inc., 666 Fifth Avenue, New York, N.Y. 10019.*

Contents

🌿 🌿 🌿

Cast of Characters: 1

PART ONE: The Court   7

PART TWO: Philippe   149

PART THREE: The King   269

Cast of Characters

The time of action in this novel is roughly 1667 to 1675.

The following is a list of the principal characters. Those marked with an asterisk are known more or less prominently to history, but memoirs of the period indicate that almost every person mentioned here in connection with the Court of Louis XIV actually existed, as did the events and politics.

ANGÉLIQUE. Born Angélique de Sancé, of a family of the minor nobility in Poitou, she first married Comte Joffrey de Peyrac of the Palace of Gay Learning in Toulouse, by whom she had two sons, Florimond and Cantor. Joffrey was condemned to death at the stake by Louis XIV on a trumped-up charge of sorcery. Angélique, reduced to beggary, became a member of the Paris vagabonds whose headquarters were the Court of Miracles in the Saint-Denis quarter. Later, under the name of Madame de Morens, she opened a chocolate shop with David Chaillou whereby she made a great deal of money which she invested shrewdly and became extremely rich, and friendly with literary Parisian society. Having been in love with her cousin Philippe since they were both children, she more or less blackmailed him into marrying her, thus gaining a position in the high nobility of the realm of France.

BAKTIARI BEY. The ambassador to France of the Shah of Persia.

BARBE. The nurse of Angélique's children, a friend from her days of poverty.

BARCAROLE. Queen Marie-Thérèse's dwarf, and a friend of Angélique's from her Court of Miracles days.

BINET. Louis XIV's wig-maker and hairdresser, introduced to the monarch by Angélique, whose coiffeur he had also been.

BONTEMPS. Louis XIV's confidential valet.

* BOSSUET (1627-1704). One of the most famous preachers of all time. His funeral orations for "Madame" and for the Prince de Condé are among the world's classics of oratory. Louis XIV made him a Bishop and entrusted the education of the Dauphin to him.

CANTOR. Angélique's younger son by Joffrey de Peyrac.

* COLBERT (1619-1683). First an apprentice in a draper's shop, Jean Baptiste Colbert subsequently entered the French War Office. He became Comptroller of France in 1665. Under his supervisoon the country's revenues doubled. He greatly stimulated French industries, established foreign colonies, and encouraged trade. Possibly his greatest achievement was the creation of a powerful French Navy. In many ways he founded a whole new epoch in France.

* CONDÉ, Prince Louis (II) de (1621-1686), was known as "the Great Condé." In the civil wars of the Fronde, the details of which are among the most complicated of all political struggles, he fought against the Royal Party successfully until finally defeated by Turenne in 1658. The following year he was pardoned and entered the military service of the then unified France, winning many campaigns. A brilliant strategist and sincere patron of the arts, he was one of the greatest men of his time.

DE GESURES. High Chamberlain of Louis XIV.

DUCHESNE. Steward of Louis XIV.

FLIPOT. Angélique's lackey. A friend from her Court of Miracles days.

FLORIMOND. Angélique's older son by Joffrey de Peyrac.

* FOUQUET (1615-1680). Comptroller of France from 1659 to 1661, when his extravagance, maladministration and dishonesty were revealed by Colbert. Tried unfairly, he was sentenced to life imprisonment in the fortress of Pignerol. He was a deadly enemy of Joffrey de Peyrac, Angélique's first husband.

GILANDON. The surname of two impoverished spinsters

Angélique employed as ladies-in-waiting or chaperones.

* GRANDE MADEMOISELLE, Mademoiselle de Montpensier (1627-1693). The daughter of Gaston d'Orléans, Louis XIII's brother and the son of Henri IV; hence the first cousin of Louis XIV, against whom she fought in the wars of the Fronde. Later pardoned, she lived at Louis XIV's Court, where she fell in love with Lauzun.

GREAT COESRE (Wood-Bottom). A legless, loathsome cripple who reigned as King of the Paris underworld in the Court of Miracles, and was once a protector of Angélique.

JAVOTTE. Angélique's maid. One of her friends from her Court of Miracles days.

JOFFREY DE PEYRAC, Comte de Toulouse. Angélique's first husband.

* LAUZUN, Péguilin de (1632-1723), a Gascon soldier and minor nobleman, a favorite of Louis XIV and an old friend of Angélique. History testifies to his romance with Mademoiselle de Montpensier (La Grande Mademoiselle), Louis XIV's cousin.

* LA VALLIÈRE, Louise de (1644-1710), mistress of Louis XIV from about 1660 until she was completely supplanted by Madame de Montespan in 1674. Known as "the little one," she was shy and retiring, but was famous for her winning personality.

LA VIOLETTE. Steward and valet of Philippe du Plessis-Bellière.

LESDIGUIÈRES. A young priest employed by Angélique as supervisor of her sons' education.

* LOUIS XIV (1638-1715), King of France from 1643, when his father, Louis XIII, died, leaving the government in the hands of his widow Anne of Austria and Cardinal Mazarin. In 1660 he married Marie-Thérèse of Spain, and after the death of Mazarin early the following year, took the reins of the kingdom into his own hands. He became something of a despot, but raised France from anarchy to a world power through his skillful employment of ministers and militarists

wiser than he. His Court was so brilliant, and he stimulated art and literature to such a degree that he ranks among the greatest monarchs of history and probably deserved the title of "Sun King." His character is best expressed in his famous remark: *"L'état c'est moi"* ("I am the State").

* Louvois (1641-1691). Minister of War under Louis XIV, and son of Le Tellier, Chancellor and Secretary of State. A ruthless militarist, he was largely responsible for the efficient organization and operation of the French Army, and many of his measures still obtain in it.

* Madame (Henriette d'Angleterre), daughter of Charles I, sister of Charles II of England, married to Philippe, Duc d'Orléans, brother of Louis XIV, to whom she bore two daughters.

Malbrant. Fencing-master of Angélique's sons. An old man, he was nicknamed "Swordthrust" because of his preoccupation with all kinds of swordplay.

* Marie-Thérèse, daughter of Philip IV of Spain and Queen of Louis XIV of France from 1660 to her death in 1683.

* Molière (Jean Baptiste Poquelin) (1622-1673). Probably the greatest of French playwrights. One of his finest plays, *Tartuffe* (1664), referred to in the novel, was a bitter satire on religious hypocrites. His play watched by Angélique and Philippe was probably *The School for Wives* (1662).

* Monsieur (Philippe, Duc d'Orléans) (1640-1671), brother of Louis XIV and founder of the existing House of Orléans.

* Montausier (1610-1690). A Huguenot who fought on the royal side in the wars of the Fronde, and was later made a Duke and served as guardian of the Dauphin from 1668 to 1679. Austerely pious and brusque, he is thought to be the model for Molière's *Le Misanthrope*, but he was also a patron of literature.

* Montespan, Athenais de (1641-1707), born a Mortemart of Poitou, was married to a minor Gascon noble, Pardaillan de Montespan. In 1668 she became Louis

XIV's mistress, and ruled as uncrowned queen of France.

* NINON DE LENCLOS (1616-1706), a Parisian courtesan of great and lasting beauty, famous for her wit and her influence over the great of her time in art, literature and politics.

PARAJONC, Philonide de. A *"précieuse,"* or bluestocking intellectual, of Paris. In the reign of Louis XIII the *"précieuses"* held literary salons in an attempt to refine the somewhat crude manners of that time. Their efforts, however, were often more affected and silly than inspirational. They indulged in artificial, "poetic" language, and by the time of this novel were considered passé.

PHILIPPE, Marquis du Plessis-Bellière, Angélique's second husband, was one of the great nobles of France, dearly beloved by Louis XIV, whose Master of the Hunt he was, as well as a Marshal of France. Handsome, but cold and something of a misogynist, he bitterly resented having to marry Angélique, whom he abused on their wedding night at his Castle of Plessis.

RACAN, Gaspard de. Tutor to Angélique's sons.

RAKOCZY. An exiled Hungarian prince and revolutionary.

ROGER. Angélique's steward or majordomo. Like most others of his profession at that time he was a Swiss.

* SCARRON, Françoise (1635-1719), was married first to the deformed but highly respected poet Scarron, who died in 1660, leaving her in great poverty. She was befriended by Madame de Montespan, who engaged her as governess for the children she bore the King.

* SCUDÉRY, Madeleine de (1607-1701). A french novelist prominent in society and in literary circles. Her most famous work, *Le Grand Cyrus,* gives a fine picture of the French aristocracy of the period.

* SÉVIGNÉ Madame de (1626-1696). A famous wit of the period of the novel, best-known for the brilliant, charming letters she wrote her daughter, who lived in Provence, about life in Paris and in the Court of

    Louis XIV. These are valuable source material for 17th Century social history.

SOLIGNAC. High Chamberlain of Queen Marie-Thérèse, and a leader of the Brotherhood of the Holy Sacrament, a zealous, puritanical society devoted to correcting loose morals.

THÉRÈSE. Angélique's maid, and a friend from her days of poverty.

VIVONNE. Brother of Madame de Montespan and an Admiral of the French fleet.

Part One

The Court

🌿 🌿 🌿

chapter 1

ANGÉLIQUE could not fall sound asleep. Exciting visions of the thrilling events the next day would bring danced through her head. She was like a child on Christmas Eve.

Twice she had got up and struck a flint to light the candle so that she could feast her eyes again on the two costumes that lay on chairs near her bed—one for the next day's royal hunt, the other for the festivities that would follow it.

The hunting costume really pleased her. She had sent the tailor precise instructions for giving the pearl gray velvet jacket a masculine cut that would set off the delicate curves of her youthful figure. Her huge cavalier's hat was of white felt, and ostrich plumes cascaded over it like a snowdrift. But what delighted her most of all was the stock. Of the very latest style, it would, she fully expected, attract the attention and excite the curiosity of the great Court ladies.

After making several turns about her neck the yards of starched linen were fastened into a big knot. The ends, intricately embroidered with seed pearls, fanned out like the wings of a butterfly. The idea for it had come to her just the night before. For an hour she had posed before her looking glass trying on at least ten of the loveliest cravats that the draper of the Golden Casket linen shop had brought her, before she finally decided to tie one in an even more dashing style than the cavaliers themselves. She knew that a woman's face does not show off to best advantage above the severe lines of a riding habit's collar. This billowing white wave beneath her chin would give the whole outfit a feminine touch.

Back in bed, she tossed and turned. She thought of ringing for a cup of verbena tea to soothe her into

sleep, for a few hours of sleep she must have in order to
face the heavy schedule of the morrow. In the late morning the hunt would meet in the forest of Fausse-Repos.
Like all the other guests of the King who were coming
from Paris, Angélique would have to start out very
early to meet the parties coming from Versailles at the
crossroads of Les Boeufs at the appointed time. There,
in the heart of the forest, were stables to which the
aristocrats sent their saddle horses long enough in advance so that the mounts would be completely fresh for
the long chase after the fleet stags. Earlier in the day
Angélique had seen to it that her precious Ceres was
sent there with two grooms. She had paid a thousand
pistoles for that pureblooded Spanish mare.

Once more she arose and lit the candle. There was
no doubt about it, her ball gown was a total success—
flame-colored satin with a cloak more lustrous than
clouds at sunrise, and a bodice embroidered with tiny
pink mother-of-pearl flowers. For jewels she had chosen
pink pearls. They would dangle in clusters from her ears,
and a string of them was to entwine her neck and shoulders in three great strands. A tiara in the form of a
crescent moon would adorn her hair.

All these she had got from a jeweler she fancied because he entranced her with his tales of the warm seas
that once had bathed these pearls, the intricate bargain-
ings by which he had acquired them, the long travels
they had made sewn into packets of silk that passed
from Arab trader to Greek to Venetian. He could quin-
tuple their value in her eyes simply by his skill in making
every pearl seem fabulously rare, as if it had been secretly stolen from the gardens of the gods.

In spite of the fortune it had cost her to possess these
treasures, Angélique had never had one of those agoniz-
ing second thoughts that so often follow a vain and
wildly extravagant purchase. She gazed at them ecstatically as they lay in their white velvet cases on her bedside table.

She had an insatiable sensuous desire for all the exquisite and precious things of life. This was her venge-
ful compensation for the years of hardship she had

known. Thank heaven she had put an end to those early enough for her still to have time to deck her youthful beauty in gorgeous jewels and lavish gowns, to surround herself with beautiful pieces of furniture, rich tapestries, ornaments fashioned by artists of the first rank.

Everything about her gave the impression of costliness but also of discrimination, displaying the simplicity of true sophistication without a trace of vulgarity.

She had lost none of her zest for living. This was a constant wonder to her, and she secretly thanked God that her trials had not broken her spirit. She still had the enthusiasm of a child.

She had seen far more of life than most young women of her age, yet had been less disillusioned by the world. And like a child she could still get a wondrous excitement out of little things. If you've never known what it is to be hungry, how can you savor the taste of a piece of warm fresh bread? And once you've walked barefoot over the cobblestones of Paris only at last to own pearls like these, how can you doubt that you're the happiest woman in the whole wide world?

Once again she blew out the candle, and sliding down between the soft iris-damasked sheets, she stretched out, thinking: "What a joy to be rich and beautiful and young . . . !"

She did not add: ". . . and desirable." Such a thought caused her to remember Philippe. A dark cloud passed over the face of her radiant happiness. She heaved a sigh from deep in her breast.

"Philippe!"

How she despised him! She recalled the two months that had gone by since her second marriage—to Philippe, Marquis du Plessis-Bellière—and the outrageous way in which she had been constrained by it.

The day after Angélique was received àt Versailles, the Court returned to Saint-Germain. She had had to go back to Paris. Naturally she thought it her right to live at her husband's hôtel on the Faubourg Saint-Antoine. But after she had finally made up her mind to go there, she found the doors shut against her. The Swiss majordomo answered her protests by saying that his master was following the King and the Court, and that he had no instructions about her. She had had to go to her own Hôtel de Beautreillis, which she had owned before her marriage. Since then she had been living there, waiting for another invitation from the King that would allow her to take her proper place at Court. But none had come, and she was beginning to get more and more worried about being ignored.

Then one day Madame de Montespan, whom she met at Ninon de Lenclos', said to her:

"What's happened to you, my dear? Have you lost your mind? You've not replied to three invitations of the King's. Once you had a fever. Then some stomach disorder made you dizzy. Or else a pimple on your nose so spoiled your beauty that you did not dare appear. The King does not like such shabby excuses. He has a horror of people who are always ailing. You are going to displease him."

That was how Angélique discovered that her husband, whom the King had asked to bring her to various entertainments, not only had failed to tell her of the invitations but had made her look absurd in the King's eyes.

"At any rate, I warn you," Madame de Montespan concluded, "with my own ears I heard the King tell the Marquis du Plessis that he wanted to see you at Wednesday's hunt. 'Try to see,' he said rather wryly, 'that Madame du Plessis-Bellière's health does not compel her to neglect us. Otherwise I shall have to take it upon myself to advise her by letter to go back to the country.' In other words, you are on the brink of disgrace."

Angélique was astonished, then furious. It did not take her long to weave a plan to unravel this web of deception. She would go straight to the meet and confront Philippe with the inescapable fact that there she was in person. If the King happened to question her, she would tell him the truth. Why not? In the presence of the King, Philippe would have to confess.

With the greatest of secrecy she had had her new costumes made, had sent her mare ahead, and scheduled her departure in her own coach for daybreak. And now dawn would soon be there, and she would not have had a wink of sleep. She forced herself to shut her eyes, dimiss all thoughts from her mind, and glide softly into slumber.

Suddenly her little griffon dog Arius, which was curled up into a ball under the counterpane, shivered, then sprang up on all fours and began to make hoarse sounds in his throat. Angélique caught hold of him and nestled him to her under the bedclothes. "Shh, Arius, be quiet!"

The tiny animal continued to growl and tremble. For a second or two he stayed quiet, then leaped up again yapping sharply.

"What's the matter, Arius?" Angélique was irritated. "What's going on? Do you hear a mouse?"

She covered his muzzle with her hand and strained her ears to catch what it might have been that disturbed her pet. Yes, she detected a sound, so barely perceptible that she could not tell at once where it came from. It was like a hard object slipping over a highly polished surface. Arius kept up his muffled growling.

"Quiet, Arius, quiet!"

Oh, would she never get to sleep!

Suddenly behind her closed eyelids Angélique had a vision of dark hands emerging as if from ancient memories—the filthy, horny hands of the Paris thieves that in the thick darkness of night press against the panes as they silently slice through them with a concealed diamond.

She sprang up in bed. Yes, that was what it was. The sound was coming from the direction of the bay window. Robbers!

Her heart was pounding so violently that all she could hear was its dull thudding.

Arius wriggled away from her and began yapping again. She caught him and covered him up to stifle his barks. When she was finally able to strain her ears once

more she had a distinct impression that there was someone in the room. The window slammed. "They" had
penetrated.

"Who's there?" she shrieked, more dead than alive.

No one answered. But footsteps were approaching
from the alcove.

"My pearls!" she thought.

She thrust out her hand and seized a fistful of jewels.
Almost at once the suffocating weight of a heavy blanket
descended upon her. Sinewy arms wrapped themselves
around her, paralyzing her. She yelled into the thick
folds of the cloth, squirming like an eel until she had
freed herself.

Catching her breath, she screamed. "Help! He-l . . ."

Two thick thumbs dug into her throat, strangling her.
Great crimson bombs exploded before her eyes. The
frantic yipping of the dog grew dimmer, farther and
farther away.

"I am going to die," she thought. "Strangled by a
housebreaker! This is too insane! Philippe! Philippe!"

Everything went black.

As consciousness returned to her, Angélique felt something round slip through her fingers and fall on the
flagstones with a click.

"My pearls!"

Numbly she leaned over the edge of the pallet on
which she was lying and saw the strand of pink pearls.
She must have kept it clutched in her fist while they
were carrying her off and bringing her to this strange
spot.

Angélique ran her smarting eyes over the room. She
was in a kind of cell into which the hazy light of dawn
was slowly seeping through a little barred gothic window, dimming the yellow glow of a guttering oil lamp in
a niche above her. The furnishings consisted of a rude
table and a three-legged stool, and the wretched cot
made of a square of wood on which had been laid a
horsehair mattress.

"Where am I? Whose hands am I in? What do they
want of me?"

They had not stolen her pearls. Her bonds were gone, but the coarse blanket still lay on top of her thin pink silk nightgown.

Angélique reached out and picked up the necklace. Mechanically she put it around her throat. Then she changed her mind and slipped it under the scratchy bolster.

Outside a silvery bell began to tinkle. Another answered it. Angélique's eyes lit on a small wooden crucifix hanging on the white-washed wall, a sprig of boxwood stuck behind it.

"A convent! I am in a convent."

She could just distinguish the faraway tones of an organ and voices chanting psalms.

"What is the meaning of all this? Oh, good God, how my throat hurts!"

For a moment she lay prostrate, her thoughts in a turmoil, hoping she could persuade herself that she was only having a bad dream and that at length the ridiculous nightmare would pass and she would awake.

The ringing sound of footsteps in the corridor made her sit up again. A man's footsteps. Perhaps her kidnapper's. Ah! She would not let him go without first dragging an explanation out of him. She had seen plenty of highwaymen and had no fear of them. If necessary, she would remind him that Wood-Bottom, the king of the underworld, was a friend of hers.

Whoever it was stopped outside her door. A key turned in the lock, and the person entered. For a moment Angélique was dumbfounded at the sight of the man who stood before her.

"Philippe!"

The appearance of her husband was the last thing she expected. For the whole two months she had been in Paris Philippe had not visited her a single time, not even paid her a formal call or otherwise remembered he had a wife.

"Philippe," she repeated. "Oh, Philippe, what a relief! Have you come to rescue me?"

An uncustomary frigidity in his glance chilled the emotion with which she had greeted him.

He stood stock still by the door, stunningly handsome in his high white leather boots and his dove gray doe-skin tunic with its silver braid. The curls of his scrupulously dressed blond wig trailed over his collar of Venetian lace. White plumes flowed over the brim of his gray velvet hat.

"How is your health, Madame?" he asked. "Good?"

It was as if he were greeting her in a drawing room.

"I . . . oh, I don't know what's happened, Philippe," Angélique stammered. "Someone attacked me in my bedroom. They carried me off and brought me here. Who could have done such a thing?"

"I shall be glad to tell you. It was La Violette, my steward."

Angélique was too astonished to speak.

"It was at my orders," he added obligingly.

The truth burst upon Angélique. She jumped up.

Still in her nightgown, she ran barefoot over the icy flagstones to the window and gripped the iron bars. The sun was rising on a fine summer's day. The King and the Court would hunt the stag through the forest of Fausse-Repos, but Madame du Plessis-Bellière would not be among those present.

Beside herself with rage, she turned on Philippe. "You did this to keep me from appearing at the royal hunt!"

"How quick you are!"

"Don't you know that His Majesty will never forgive me for this towering insult? He will send me back to the country."

"That is exactly what I hope he will do."

"Oh, what a . . . a *fiend* you are!"

"Indeed? Well, this is not the first time a woman has honored me with that title."

Philippe laughed. His wife's rage seemed to please his saturnine temperament.

"Not such a fiend as that, after all," he said. "I am going to have you confined in this convent so that you may find a new life through prayer and abstinence. God Himself can find no fault with that."

"How long must I be a penitent?"

"We shall see . . . We shall see. A few days at least."

"Philippe, I . . . I actually believe I hate you."

He laughed louder than ever, his lips stretched back over his fine white teeth in a cruel grin.

"You are responding beautifully. It makes changing your plans worth while."

"Changing my plans! Is that what you call it? Break into my house . . . kidnap me! And to think that when that monster was strangling me, it was you I called out to for help!"

Philippe's laughter turned into a deep frown. He came close to her to inspect the bruises that spotted her throat.

"Damn! The rascal went a little too far. But I rather imagine he found his work cut out for him. He's a fellow who does only what he's told. I instructed him to be as subtle as possible so that he would not attract the attention of your household. He got in through the gate at the end of your garden. Never mind, next time I'll tell him not to be so rough."

"So you think there will be a next time?"

"So long as you refuse to be tamed, yes. So long as you toss your willful head and give me insolent answers and look for ways to disobey me. I am the Master of the King's Hunt. I am used to handling ferocious bitches. They always end licking my hands."

"I would rather die," Angélique said savagely. "You would rather kill me anyway."

"No, I prefer to make you my slave."

He fixed his hard blue eyes on her so penetratingly that she was forced to turn away. The duel promised to be a deadly one, but she had experienced others like it. She faced him defiantly again.

"You expect too much. What methods do you intend to use to get your way?"

"Oh, I have plenty of little ways," he said, pouting. "Lock you up, for example. How would you like to have your visit here extended? Or else, I could separate you from your sons."

"You would not do that."

"Why not? I can also cut off your food and reduce you

to a bare subsistence diet, compel you to beg me for bread to keep yourself alive."

"Now you are being silly. My fortune belongs to me."

"All that can be arranged. You are my wife. A husband has absolute power. I am not so stupid that I can't find a means of having your money put in my name."

"I will defend my rights."

"Who will listen to you? I recall you used to have a facility for getting the King's ear, but after your social blunder of not putting in an appearance today I am afraid that will not do you any good. Now, on that note I shall depart and leave you to your meditations. I must not miss the unleashing of the pack. Is there anything else you would like to say to me?"

"Yes. I hate you with all my heart and soul."

"That is nothing to what you will do. Someday you will pray for death to deliver you out of my power."

"What are you getting out of all this?"

"The sweet pleasure of revenge. You have humiliated me so deeply by forcing me to marry you that I could cheerfully see you weep and implore my mercy and turn into a half-crazed wretched creature in rags."

"What a charming picture! Why not the torture chamber while you're at it—brand the soles of my feet with red hot irons, the rack, thumbscrews . . . ?"

"No, I shall not go that far. Perhaps I derive a certain pleasure from the beauty of your body."

"Indeed? Who would ever guess it? You certainly do not show it."

Philippe had almost reached the door. He turned toward her, his eyes half-closed.

"So you are complaining about that, eh, my dear? What a happy surprise! Have I disappointed you then? Haven't I made a costly enough sacrifice on the altar of your charms? Have you so few lovers to worship you that you need a husband's devotion? So far as that goes, I had a distinct impression that you were rather loath to perform the duties of your wedding night. But I could have been mistaken."

"Get out, Philippe, let me alone." With terror Angé-

lique watched him come toward her. She felt naked and
defenseless in her filmy nightgown.

"The more I look at you, the less I want to leave,"
he said.

He clasped her to him, pressing her close against his
body. She shuddered, her throat too tight to release the
nervous sobs that choked her.

"Let me go, let me go, I beg you."

"I love to hear you beg."

He lifted her like a wisp of straw and let her
drop on the nun's pallet.

"Philippe, have you forgotten we are in a convent?"

"So? Do you think two hours in this sanctimonious retreat have endowed you with a vow of chastity? You
do not need to stand on ceremony, I have always got a
delicious sensation out of raping nuns."

"You are the lowest creature I have ever known."

"Your love talk is hardly the sweetest I have ever
heard," he said, stripping off his baldric. "You should
spend more time in the drawing room of the lovely
Ninon. No more affectations, Madame. You remind me,
quite happily, of the duty I owe you, and I intend to
perform it."

Angélique shut her eyes. She had ceased to resist
him, knowing from experience what a struggle would
cost her. Passively she endured the humiliating and repulsive embraces he forced upon her painfully as a kind
of punishment.

All she had to do, she reflected, was behave like ill-
mated women—and, Lord knows, their name is legion—
who endure their obligations by thinking of their lovers
or saying their rosary while they suffer the attentions
of the pot-bellied old man their greedy father has bound
them to.

Such, obviously, was not the case with Philippe. He
was neither middle-aged nor pot-bellied, and it was
Angélique herself who had wanted to marry him.
Well she might repent of that now, but it was too late.
She would have to learn to accept the master she had
given herself to.

What a brute he was! For him a woman was only a

thing to be crassly pursued for the gratification of his physical desires. But he was a lithe, muscular brute just the same, and in his arms it was hard for her to let her thoughts wander to someone else, or to say her prayers. He charged to the attack like a seasoned warrior under the command of lust. The thrill of battle, the thirst for slaughter had long accustomed him to do without any tenderness.

Nevertheless, as he released her he made a slight gesture that she later believed she must have imagined. Placing his hand on her smooth upturned neck at the very spot where the gross fingers of the steward had left their livid traces, he had let it linger there for a moment as if in a slight caress.

Then he stood erect, surveying her with a mean sneer. "Well, my pretty, it would seem you are growing wiser. Just as I said you would. Soon you will be cringing. Meanwhile I wish you a pleasant stay within these thick walls. You can weep and moan and curse as much as you like. No one will hear you. The nuns have orders to bring you food, but not to let you set your foot outside this cell, and they have an excellent reputation for being efficient jailors. You are by no means the only unwilling boarder in this convent. Enjoy yourself, Madame. Perhaps this evening you will hear the hunting horns of the King as they pass by. I shall order them to blow a fanfare just for you alone."

Then with a burst of mocking laughter he was gone. How hateful his laughter was! He knew only the laughter of revenge.

Angélique remained motionless under the rough, heavy blanket on which lingered the masculine scent of jasmine water and new leather. She was tired and listless. The strain of the night, the vexation of the quarrel, the demands of her husband had sapped her energies. Overpowered as she had been, she had no more strength of her own. Her body lapsed into a deep state of blissful relaxation.

Unexpectedly she felt sick at her stomach. The sour

taste of bile was in her mouth, and sweat broke out on her forehead. She struggled for a moment against this rebellious sickness, then fell back on the pallet more dispirited than ever.

That touch of faintness betokened the symptoms that for a month she had tried to ignore. Now she had to face the facts. The dreadful wedding night at Plessis-Bellière, which she could not think of without flushing with shame, had borne fruit. She was pregnant. She was carrying Philippe's child, the child of that man who hated her and had sworn to torture her with his revenge until he drove her insane.

For a moment Angélique felt so defeated that she was tempted to give up the struggle and succumb. If only she could sleep! Sleep might give her courage again.

But this was no time for sleep. It was already late in the morning. She would have aroused the King's displeasure and be forever banished from Versailles, even from Paris.

She sprang up, ran to the door and pounded with her fists on its thick wood panels until her knuckles were raw.

"Open the door," she shrieked. "Let me out!"

Now the sun was flooding the cell. At that very moment the King's hunting party would be gathering in the Cour d'Honneur. The carriages of his guests would be filing through the Porte Saint-Honoré on their way from Paris to join them. Angélique alone would be absent from the grand rendezvous.

"I must be there! I must be there! If the King turns against me, I am done for. Only the King can keep Philippe in line. I must get to the royal hunt, cost what it may!

"Did not Philippe mention that I could hear the hunting horns from my window? This convent must be near Versailles. Oh, I have got to get out of this place!"

But long as she paced the cell, she could find no solution.

Finally she heard the dull echo of wooden shoes clomping down the corridor. She froze tensely, full of sudden hope. Then she stretched herself out again on her pallet and feigned an attitude of not having a care in the world.

A key turned in the lock, and a woman entered. She was not a nun, but apparently a servant. She wore a linen bonnet and a corduroy gown, and she was carrying a tray.

The visitor growled a surly "Good-morning," and began unloading the tray on to the table. It was a skimpy meal—a jug of water, a bowl from which rose a faint odor of beans and bacon grease, a round loaf of bread.

Angélique watched the servant closely. Perhaps this woman would be the only contact she would have with the outside world for the entire day. She would have to take advantage of this meeting.

The servant did not seem to be the usual fat, clumsy peasant type that generally cleans up around a convent. She was young and almost pretty. Her big black eyes were full of fiery spite, and she had a way of rolling her hips under the corduroy skirt that said a great deal about her previous employments. The practiced eye of Angélique was no more mistaken about that than she was when she heard the oath the girl let out when she carelessly let a spoon slip off the tray. There was not a shred of doubt in Angélique's mind that here was one of the most amenable subjects of the Great Coesre, king of the underworld.

"Hello, Sister," Angélique whispered.

The woman whirled about. Her eyes popped as she saw Angélique make the gesture of recognition that was a password among the beggars of Paris.

"For God's sake," the girl exclaimed when she recovered from her astonishment. "For God's sake! If I'd thought . . . They told me you were a real Marquise. Well, you poor kid, so you got caught by those dirty bastards of the Saint-Sacrement gang too? No luck, eh? Well, who could ever make a living with those vultures?"

She sat down on the foot of the pallet, drawing her gray woolen shawl provocatively across her breasts.

"Six months I've been in this hole! Don't mind if I giggle, it's as good as having a square meal to see you.

It takes my mind off my troubles. What neighborhood did you work?"

Angélique made a vague gesture. "A little bit here and there—everywhere."

"Whose doxy were you?"

"Wood-Bottom's."

"The Great Coesre! By God, you must have been well taken care of. For a novice you certainly got to the top fast. And a novice you certainly must have been. I never laid eyes on you before. What's your name?"

"Beautiful Angel."

"Mine's Sunday. They gave me that name on account of my specialty. I only worked Sundays. I got the idea of doing that because I don't like to be the same as everyone else. It suited my work too. I just strolled up and down in front of the churches. My God, all those men so stiff and pious when they went in must have had plenty of time to think things over while they were saying their prayers. A nice girl after Mass—why not? When they came out, I had my pick of clients. What a racket all those sanctimonious old wives raised! Anyone would think I was making everyone in Paris skip Mass. They just about killed themselves trying to get me arrested. They even went to court to get me locked up. Hell must make a lot of money out of the rent those old prudes pay there. Just the same, they won out. That's why I'm here now, with the Augustines of Bellevue. It's my turn to sing vespers tonight. But what about you? What happened to you?"

"A pimp wanted me to move in with him to save money. I was supporting him; he forced me to turn over all my earnings to him. To hell with it! He couldn't make me. But he took his revenge by sending me to a convent till I changed my mind."

"It's a hell of a world," Sunday sighed, raising her eyes to heaven. "He must be a regular old miser. I heard him arguing prices with the Mother Superior. He wouldn't give her more than twenty *écus*. That's what the Saint-Sacrement gang pays to keep me under lock and key. All you get to eat for that is peas and beans."

"The bast . . . ," Angélique exclaimed, hurt to the quick by that last bit of information.

Was there ever anyone more repulsive than Philippe! And a miser to boot! Paying no more for her than for a common streetwalker!

She grasped hold of Sunday's wrist. "Listen, you've got to get me out of here. I have an idea. Lend me your clothes and show me a gate that will let me out into the countryside."

The girl bluntly refused. "Nothing doing. Why should I help you escape when I can't get out myself?"

"This is different. The nuns know you. They would catch you and bring you back at once. No one has seen me close up except the Mother Superior. Even if they run across me in the corridors I can tell them some story or other."

"You're right at that," Sunday admitted. "When you arrived you were all tied up like a sausage. And it was the middle of the night too. They brought you straight up here."

"You see, I have a good chance of making it. Hurry up, hand me your petticoat."

"Not so fast, Marquise," the girl growled. " 'Everything for me and nothing for anyone else' seems to be your motto. What good is this doing poor little Sunday, forgotten here behind all these bars by everyone? Perhaps an even deeper dungeon yet for me, eh?"

"What do you say to this?" Angélique darted her hand under the bolster and brought out the string of pink pearls. She held them up to the light.

The shimmering splendor of their sunrise tints dazzled Sunday. She let out a long whistle.

"Those must be fake, Sister," she whispered.

"No. Just weigh them in the palm of your hand. Here, take it. It's yours if you'll help me."

"You're joking."

"I give you my word. With that you'll have something to use to set yourself up with all the clothes and trappings of a princess when you get out of here."

Sunday was letting the string of princely pearls slide from one hand into the other.

"Well, have you made up your mind?"

"I'll do it. But I have a better idea than yours. Wait, I'll be right back." She slipped the necklace into the depths of her skirt and went out.

It seemed to Angélique that she was gone for an eternity. Finally she rushed in out of breath, a bundle of clothes under one arm, and a bucket hanging from the other.

"That poisonous old Mother Yvonne got hold of me. Whew! I could have killed her. Now we have to hurry, because milking time will soon be over, when the country women come to get milk at the convent farm. You are going to put on these dairymaid's clothes, take this bucket and your little pillow, and go down the ladder from the pigeon roosts. I'll show you how. Once you're in the courtyard you can mix with the others and go out with them by the entrance. Just be sure to keep your milk well balanced on your head."

Sunday's plan was easily effected. Less than fifteen minutes later Madame du Plessis-Bellière was walking along the dusty road intent on reaching Paris, which she could glimpse through the bright haze far away in the valley. She was clad in a short red and white striped skirt. Her bosom was confined by a black bodice. In one hand she carried the shoes that were too big for her, and with the other she steadied the bucket of milk that wobbled dangerously on the cushion atop her head.

She had reached the courtyard just as the novices of the convent, who had milked the cows, were finishing the distribution of the milk to the women who would carry it to Paris and its suburbs. The old nun who checked the roll had asked who the latecomer was. Angélique put on her simplest manner and answered all her questions in her Poitou dialect. Since she insisted on contributing several *sous* that Sunday had generously advanced her, she had been given her milk and allowed to depart.

Now she had to make haste. She was halfway between Versailles and Paris. After considering the matter she decided that to go directly to Versailles would be foolish. How could she appear before the King and the

Court in a peasant's striped skirt? It would be better
to go to Paris, get into her fine clothes, summon her
coach and dash into the forest after the hunt.

Angélique walked fast, but she felt as if she were
making no distance. The sharp pebbles hurt her bare
feet, but when she put on the heavy shoes she stumbled
and lost them. The milk kept splashing over her, and
the little pillow kept slipping.

At length a tinker in a cart going toward Paris caught
up with her. She signaled him to stop.

"Could you take me along with you, friend?"

"Indeed I could, sweetheart. Give me a little kiss
and I'll take you all the way to Notre Dame."

"Don't count on it. I'm promised to a boy, and I keep
my kisses for him. But I'll give you this kettle of milk
for your youngsters."

"All right, all right. It's a swindle, but climb aboard,
girlie. You're as sensible as you're pretty."

The horse trotted right along. They were in Paris by
ten o'clock. The tinker took Angélique straight to the
riverbank. She sprinted to her hôtel, where her porter
almost fell over backward at seeing his mistress disguised as a peasant fresh from the country.

Since morning, she learned, the servants had been
baffled by the mysterious happenings in the house. To
their consternation at finding their mistress vanished
was added their astonishment at having the valet of
Monsieur du Plessis-Bellière, an insolent giant of a man,
appear and demand all the carriages and horses of the
Beautreillis establishment.

"All my horses! All my carriages!" Angélique echoed.

"Yes, Madame." Roger, her steward, appeared on the
scene to confirm the story. He lowered his eyes, as
shocked to see his mistress in her white bonnet and
black bodice as if he had seen her stark naked.

Angélique's spirits revived. "What difference does it
make? I'll get a friend to help me. Javotte! Thérèse!
Hurry up! I need a bath. Get my riding habit ready.
And fix me up a picnic hamper with a good bottle of
wine."

The clear tones of a clock counted off the twelve strokes of noon. Angélique jumped.

"God knows what excuse Philippe will have invented to explain my absence to His Majesty! That I have taken physic and am lying in bed in the agonies of nausea? That would be just like him, the beast! And now, with no coach and no horses, how will I ever get there before sunset? Damn Philippe!"

chapter 2

"*D*AMN Philippe!" said Angélique again as she crouched to stare out of the coach window at the deeply rutted road over which the shabby vehicle was slowly making its way.

As they penetrated deeper into the forest, the roots of the huge oak trees writhed out of the mud like fat green snakes knotting in the very middle of the road— if indeed this little gulley of muck could be called a road. It had already been churned up by the wheels of the carriages and the hooves of the horses that had just passed over it.

"We'll never get there," she groaned, turning to Philonide de Parajonc beside her.

The old intellectual casually picked up her fan and poked with it at her wig which a shattering jolt had disarranged. "Don't argue with fate, dear," she said gaily. "Even the longest journey has an end."

"That depends on how you travel and where you want to go and when you want to get there," said Angélique with some spirit. "If you are trying to catch up with a royal hunt that you ought to have joined six hours ago, you have some reason for getting into a rage. I would even try walking if I thought I'd get there in time to hear the hounds called off. If the King notices my absence, he will never forgive me for this final insult."

A violent jerk made the carriage creak ominously and threw them against each other.

"A plague on this dump cart!" Angélique exclaimed. "It's as rickety as an old fish barrel. The only thing it's good for is a bonfire."

Mademoiselle de Parajonc bridled. "I grant you my little flying pergola may lack the splendor of the magnificent carriages in your stables, but it seems to me you

29

have been rather fortunate in finding it at your disposal
today, particularly since your good husband thought it
amusing to remove all your horses to some mysterious
hiding place only he knows about."

Angélique sighed again.

Where were her own royal purple whips with their
golden stocks and their crimson tassels? And she had
been so overjoyed at the thought of at last being invited
to a royal hunt in the woods around Versailles!

She had pictured herself arriving at the meeting place
of the guests of honor drawn by her own matched team
of ebony horses, and escorted by her three lackeys in
their livery of blue and daffodil yellow and the coachman and the postillion in red leather boots and plumed
hats. She could hear the envious whispers: "Whose carriage is that?" "Why, it's the Marquise du Plessis-Bellière's. You know, the woman who . . . You seldom see
her, her husband keeps her hidden away. He's a tiger for
jealousy. Still it looks as if the King had found out
about her . . ."

She had made such careful preparations for this fate-
ful day, resolved that nothing would stop her. Once
she had got one toe inside the door of the Court, she
would plant both feet there so solidly that Philippe,
try as he might, could never dislodge her from it. All
eyes would be turned on her beauty, her queenliness,
her incomparable charm. She would struggle and push
and cling like a barnacle to this world of her dreams,
just as all the other ambitious parasites did. To hell
with reticence or modesty!

Mademoiselle de Parajonc snickered maliciously behind
her fan. "I don't have to be a sibyl to guess what you're
thinking. I can see the light of battle in your eyes. What
redoubt are you planning to storm—the King himself, or
your husband?"

Angélique shrugged. "The King? He is already spoken
for and well gaurded. He has the Queen, his legal wife,
and an acknowledged mistress in Mademoiselle de la
Villière, and plenty of others. As for my husband,
what makes you think I should want to capture an objective that has already surrendered to me? Is it consist-

ent, to use one of your own expressions, for two married persons to be interested in each other once the knot has been tied? How terribly bourgeois!"

The old spinster clucked. "I can't help thinking your charming Marquis is rather interested in you just the same." She passed her tongue over her thin lips with relish. "Tell me all about it again, dearest. It's one of the most delicious stories I've ever heard. Is it really true there wasn't a single horse in your stables this morning when you wanted to start for Versailles? And half your servants vanished too? Monsieur du Plessis must have tipped your domestics very handsomely. And to think you had not the faintest suspicion! He was slyer than you this time, my sweet."

Another bump jostled them. Javotte, the little chambermaid, sitting opposite them on the narrow jump seat, was catapulted forward so that she crushed the golden gauze bow which held Angélique's riding crop to her sash. The frothy loops were torn to shreds. Out of sheer frustration Angélique slapped the girl and ordered her back to her precarious seat, where she crouched whimpering.

Angélique was sorely tempted to apply the palm of her hand with equal violence to the heavily rouged cheeks of Philonide de Parajonc, who she could see was glorying in her mortification. Still it was this elderly bluestocking to whom she had fled in desperation when, thanks to Philippe's despicable trick, she could see no other way out of her dilemma than to borrow a carriage. And besides, Philonide de Parajonc was a good neighbor and a fairly intimate friend.

Madame de Sévigné was in the country. Ninon de Lenclos would have come to her aid, but her reputation as a courtesan had made her persona non grata at the Court, and her coach might have been easily recognized. Angélique's other woman friends in Paris would either be at the hunt themselves, or if not, too jealous to give her much hope of help from them. Mademoiselle de Parajonc was the only one she could turn to.

Even so, frantic with impatience as she was, Angélique had had to wait while the old maid fluttered

about trying to get into her sadly old-fashioned best
gown. And while the maid with nerve-wracking slow-
ness combed out the tangles of Philonide's best wig.
And while the coachman cleaned the spots off his livery
and shined up the varnish of the battered carriage. At
last they had got on the road. But what a road!

"Oh, this—this trail!" Angélique groaned. Once more
she peered out into the dim tunnel of branches and
tree trunks through which they were passing, hoping to
glimpse a clearing in the dense woods.

"You'll only catch a chill," Mademoiselle de Parajonc
remonstrated like an old nannie. "It will spoil your
complexion, and that would be a shame. What kind of
road did you expect? You can blame the King for making us traipse through the mire in places like this. Once
upon a time nothing but herds of oxen went through
here on their way to market from Normandy. That's
why they call it the Ox Road. Our late sovereign Louis
XIII used to come here to hunt, but he never dreamed
of making all the fine flower of his Court be dragged
over these ruts. Louis the Chaste was a considerate
King, simple and sensible."

She was interrupted by a deafening creaking of the
carriage and more terrific jolting.

The vehicle listed dangerously. Then something
scraped against the boulders in the road, and a wheel
came off, throwing the three passengers on top of one
another.

Angélique was at the bottom of the heap, on the
side of the missing wheel. Her first thought was one of
despair for her gorgeous hunting costume, crushed now
under the weight of Mademoiselle de Parajonc and
Javotte. She did not dare budge to disentangle herself,
for the window had been shattered and all she needed
now was to get cut by splinters of glass and arrive
drenched in blood.

The other door opened and Flipot, the young lackey,
thrust his foxy face at her. "It ain't too bad, Marquise," he panted.

Angélique was in no condition to rebuke him for his

disrespectful tone. "Is the old dungeon still in one piece?"

"It is," Philonide answered cheerfully. She liked nothing better than such animated divertissements. "Saucy boy, give me a hand and help me out of here."

Flipot yanked with all his might. With the help of the coachman, who had succeeded in calming the two horses and had unharnessed them, the two women and the servant girl were soon standing in the muck of the road. They had got off without a scratch, but their situation was no less painfully hopeless than before.

Angélique controlled her desire to burst into oaths. Getting angry would not help matters. This was the end! Now she not only would never get to the royal hunt, but never never never would she be able to return to Court. The King could hardly be expected to forgive this last refusal of his invitation. Should she write to him, or throw herself at his feet, or try to get Madame de Montespan to intervene for her, or the Duc de Lauzun? But what excuse could she give? The truth of the matter, that the carriage was wrecked, would seem a very flimsy pretext—it was what everyone used when embarrassingly late.

She sat down on a stump, so overwhelmed by these gloomy thoughts that she did not notice a small band of horsemen approaching.

"Hey, here comes somebody," Flipot whispered.

In the silence of the forest the only sound was that of the horses approaching at a walk.

"Merciful God!" murmured Mademoiselle de Parajonc. "Highwaymen! We are lost!"

Angélique raised her eyes. The deep shadows of the forest road did nothing to improve the menacing aspect of the newcomers.

They were tall men and lean and swarthy. Their eyes were dark and their black mustaches and beards were of a style that had not been encountered for years in the Ile-de-France. The braid on their faded blue uniforms was tarnished, and dangled unsewn. The feathers in their hats drooped scrawnily. Their coats were tat-

tered. Still almost every one of them wore a sword. At
the head of the troop were two jolly looking fellows
carrying ornate banners that were nonetheless torn and
full of holes. They had obviously seen service in many
hot battles.

Some of the band marched on foot carrying pikes and
muskets. These passed by the overturned coach without giving it a glance, but the first rider, who seemed
to be the chief, stopped before the women huddled together with their servants.

" 'Sdeath, my fine friends, God Mercury, who protects
travelers, seems to have deserted you most shamefully."

Unlike his companions, he seemed well enough fed,
but the loose-hanging folds of his tunic indicated that
he too must have lost a good deal of weight. When he
lifted his hat, his sunburned face was jovial.

His singsong accent betrayed his origins at once.
Angélique smiled sweetly at him, and mustering her
charm, said: "You must be from Gascony, sir."

"You don't miss anything, do you, oh lovelist of forest
nymphs? Now, what can we do for you?"

"Sir," she said quickly, "you can do a great deal for
us. We were supposed to join the King's hunt, but we
met with an accident. There's no question of trying to
get that old coach going again, but if some of you would
take my companion and me with you to the crossroads
of Les Boeufs, we would be very much obliged to you."

"The crossroads of Les Boeufs? We are going there
ourselves. Jove, everything will turn out all right!"

A quarter of an hour later the horsemen, who had
lifted the women up behind them on their mounts, arrived at the meeting place.

At the foot of the hill of Fausse-Repos the glade appeared, thronged with carriages and horses. The coach-
men and lackeys were rolling dice as they waited for
their masters to return, or drinking in the nearby tavern which had never known such a windfall before.

Angélique caught sight of her groom. She jumped to
the ground. "Janicou, bring me Ceres!"

The man ran off toward the stables. A few moments

later Angélique was in the saddle. She guided the animal out of the crowd, then dug her spurs into its flanks and darted off toward the forest.

Ceres was a noble animal, her gleaming golden coat well deserving of her name of the goddess of summer. Angélique loved her only for the richness of her beauty; she was too self-interested to be genuinely fond of pets. But Ceres was gentle, and Angélique liked to ride her.

Angélique turned off the path and spurred the animal up the steep slope of a little rise. At first the mare stumbled in the thick carpet of dead leaves, then recovered her footing and galloped up the hill. At the crest the trees still hid the view. Angélique could see nothing in the distance. She cupped her hand to her ear. From far away she could distinguish the baying of hounds in the east, then the note of a single horn which the other horns took up in chorus. She recognized the notes of the "to water" call, and smiled.

"The hunt's not over, Ceres my pet. Now, top speed! Perhaps we will save our reputation yet."

She urged the mare into a gallop along the ridge of the hill, guiding her among the dense trees and under their gnarled leafy branches and over their moss-covered roots. The wild tangle of this deep part of the forest had scarcely been disturbed for years except occasionally by single hunters, or poachers with crossbows on their shoulders, or by outlaws. Louis XIII, and Louis XIV in his youth, had roused these ancient druidical oaks from their centuries-long slumber. The fresh breeze of the dazzling Court had dispersed the dank mists; the perfumes of the great ladies had dispelled the dank scent of rotting leaves and mushrooms.

The baying of the hounds drew nearer. The stag they were chasing must have succeeded in crossing the stream. It was not admitting defeat and was continuing its flight even though the dogs were at its heels. It was coming toward her. The horns blew again to rally the hunt.

Angélique proceeded more slowly, then stopped again. The thud of galloping hooves drew closer. She emerged from the screen of trees. Beyond her a gentle slope led

down to a grassy valley, at the bottom of which a swamp
glittered in the sunlight. Roundabout her on the other
side the forest still raised its dark screen, but here she
could see the sky streaked with sooty gray clouds through
which the pale sun was slowly sinking. The approach
of twilight thickened the haze over the landscape, blot-
ting out the dark blues and greens of the deep-summer
trees.

Suddenly the massed baying of the hounds broke forth
again. A brown shape leaped from the skirt of the woods.
It was the stag, a young one with scarcely a prong on its
antlers. The reeds on the marshy edge of the stream
shook as it galloped past. The pack of hounds descended on the trail of the stag like a torrent of red
and white. Then a horse emerged from the coppice
carrying a huntress in a scarlet habit. Almost at the
same moment the riders broke into the open from all
directions and dashed down the grassy slope. In an instant the peaceful rustic glade had been invaded by the
wild rout joining their cries to the frenzied baying of
the hounds and the whinnying of the horses, the shouts
of the huntsmen and the glorious fanfare of the horns
sounding the "view halloo." Against the dark backdrop
of the forest the gleaming garments of the lords and
ladies shone like sunset clouds, and the rays of the
sinking sun sparkled on their golden embroideries, their
buckles and plumes.

But in one last supreme effort the stag managed to
break out of the lethal circle. Darting through a gap it
was rushing again toward the shelter of the thickets.
The shouts now were cries of disappointment and frustration. The mud-streaked hounds grouped again and
set off once more on the chase.

Angélique spurred Ceres gently forward and began to
descend the hill. It seemed just the right moment for
her to mingle with the crowd.

"It's no use following," said a voice behind her. "The
animal can't last much longer. Crossing that bog will
only mean you'll get spattered up to your eyes. Believe
me, lovely stranger, you'd better stay on this side. It's

a sure bet the keepers will come back to this clearing to leash up the dogs, and then we shall be clean and fresh to present ourselves before the King."

Angélique turned around. She had no idea who the gentleman was who had just ridden up to within a few feet of her. His pleasant face smiled out from under a full powdered wig, and his costume was elegant. To bow to her, he removed his hat covered with snow-white ostrich feathers.

"Damned if I've had the pleasure of meeting you, Maddame. I couldn't have, for I would never have forgotten such a face as yours."

"At Court possibly?"

"At Court?" he protested. "Hardly. I live there, Madame, I *live* there. You could not have passed me by unnoticed. No, Madame, don't try to fool me. You have *never* been at Court."

"Ah, but I have, sir." Then after a brief pause she added, "—Once."

He began to laugh. "Once! How delightful!" He drew his blond eyebrows together in thought. "When was it? At the last ball? No, I don't recall you there. And yet . . . It's improbable, but I would bet you were not at the meeting at Fausse-Repos this morning."

"You seem to know everyone here."

"Everyone? That's right. I'm in a good situation for that. You have to remember people if you want them to remember you. It's a principle I have tried to adhere to since my early youth. My memory is faultless."

"Then in that case will you be my mentor in this society I know so poorly? Tell me the names. For instance, who is that huntress in red who was riding so close to the hounds? She rides marvelously. A man couldn't gallop any faster."

"How right you are! That's Mademoiselle de la Vallière."

"The King's favorite?"

"Ah, yes, the favorite," he said in a knowledgeable tone she could not immediately understand.

"I did not know she was so accomplished a huntress."

"She was born on a horse. In her childhood she used
to ride the most spirited horses bareback. Just look at
her floating over that jump like a cloud."

"You seem to know Mademoiselle de la Vallière very
well."

"She is my sister."

"Oh," Angélique choked, "are you . . ."

"The Marquis de la Vallière at your service, lovely
stranger."

He took off his hat and brushed its feathers against
the end of his nose mockingly.

Feeling slightly embarrassed, she moved away, and
spurring her mare, descended toward the floor of the little valley. The mists were thickest there, hiding the
pools of stagnant water.

The Marquis de la Vallière followed her. "Wait a moment. What could I have said to offend you? Hark,
they're calling off the hounds not far from here. Monsieur
du Plessis-Bellière will have taken out his knife and
slit the stag's throat by now. Have you ever seen that
gentleman perform his supreme function as Master of
the King's Hunt? It's worth seeing. He is so handsome,
so elegant, so perfumed it's hard to believe he can even
use a knife. Well, he can handle a blade as if he had
been raised among the sheep-shearers of the Paris
slaughterhouses."

"As a boy Philippe was famous for killing wolves he
hunted all by himself in the forests of Nieul," said Angélique with simple pride. "The country folk used to call
him 'The Bane of the Wolves.' "

"Now it's my turn to say you seem to know Monsieur
du Plessis very well."

"He is my husband."

"Well, for heaven's sake, this *is* funny!"

He burst out laughing with the calculated and yet
apparently spontaneous laughter of the witty courtier
who is at home anywhere. He must have practiced that
laugh as studiously as one of the King's own actors.

Then quickly he broke off and repeated with concern:
"Your husband . . . ? So you are the Marquise du Plessis-

Bellière? I have heard about you. Didn't you . . . good heavens, didn't you offend the King?"

She stared at him horrified.

"Ah, there is His Majesty now," he exclaimed suddenly. Leaving her in the lurch, he galloped off to meet a group that was emerging into the clearing. Angélique quickly recognized the King among his courtiers.

His conservative costume was in contrast to that of the other nobles. Louis XIV liked to dress casually, and it was said that whenever he had to put on his robes of state, he took them off again just as soon as the ceremony was over. When he went hunting he refused, more than at any other time, to deck himself out in laces and furbelows. Now he was dressed in a brown cloth riding habit, modestly embroidered with gold thread at the buttonholes and on the flaps of the pockets. His huge riding boots encased his legs in black up to the groin. He was as inconspicuous as a country squire.

But after one look at his face, no one would confuse him with anyone else. The dignity of his gestures, which were nonetheless studiously graceful, and his serene expression gave him a truly royal bearing regardless of the occasion.

In his hand he held a light wooden wand tipped with a boar's hoof. This had been solemnly given him before the start of the chase by the Master of the Royal Hunt, and was intended primarily for pushing aside branches which might impede the sovereign on his swift course. For centuries it had also been a symbol of honor and dignity and played a large part in the ceremonial of the hunt.

Beside the King rode his favorite in her red habit. The excitement of the hunt had lent a rosy glow to her thin face, and disguised its sallow pallor in which there was no true beauty. Nevertheless Angélique perceived in it a delicate charm that aroused a secret pity in her. She could not explain this feeling, yet it seemed to her that Mademoiselle de la Vallière in spite of her secure position was not of sufficient stature to dominate the

Court or be secure in it. Around her Angélique recognized the Prince de Condé, Madame de Montespan,
Lauzun, Louvois, Brienne, Humières, Madame du Roure,
Madame de Montausier, the Princesse d'Armagnac, the
Duc d'Enghien. At a distance she glimpsed "Madame,"
the dazzlingly beautiful Princess Henriette, and, of
course, "Monsieur," the King's brother, and beside him
his inseparable favorite, the Chevalier de Lorraine.
Others she saw too, whom she knew less well. They all
were stamped with the same brand of distinction, self-
assurance—and greed.

The King was watching impatiently a little footpath
that wound into the woods, from which two horsemen were emerging at a walk. One was Philippe du
Plessis-Bellière, who, like the King, was carrying a light
wand of gilded wood ornamented with a stag's hoof.
His garments and his wig had hardly been ruffled by the
hunt.

At the sight of his handsome figure Angélique's heart
swelled with anger and apprehension. What would
Philippe's reaction be when he caught sight of her,
whom only a few hours before he had left quivering
in a convent-prison? Unconsciously she tightened her
grip on the reins. She knew Philippe well enough to
know that he would not make a scene in the presence
of the King. But afterward . . . ?

Philippe was curbing his white horse to keep pace
with his unhurried companion, an elderly man with a
tanned face, and a pointed gray beard in the style of
the previous era. It seemed to emphasize the slow pace
he was keeping in spite of the obvious impatience of
the King, and made him appear almost sullen.

"Old Salnove thinks His Majesty has made him gallop
long enough," said a person next to Angélique. "The
other day he kept complaining that in Louis XIII's
time there didn't use to be so many hangers-on getting
in everyone's way, slowing up the hunt, making everyone ride all day long."

Salnove had been the late king's Master of the Hunt,
and had taught the present monarch the rudiments of

that sport. He did not like to see its traditions violated. It was anathema to him that anyone should treat a hunt as merely a Court game. Louis XIII would never have had a lot of petticoats getting in his way when the fancy took him to go on a hunt in the forest. Salnove never missed a chance to call that principle of hunting to his pupil's attention. Even now he could not grasp the fact that Louis XIV was no longer the chubby-cheeked little boy he had once hoisted into the saddle for the first time. Out of loyalty and affection the King kept his father's old mentor still in his post. Philippe du Plessis was the Master of the Hunt in fact, but not in title. He demonstrated that distinction when he was almost up to the King, by giving the Marquis de Salnove the insignia of the wand with the stag's hoof.

Salnove took it from him, and according to the ceremonial, received from the King's hands the wand with the boar's hoof which he had given the King at the start of the hunt.

The hunt was at an end, yet the King asked: "Salnove, are the hounds tired?"

The elderly Marquis was puffing with genuine exhaustion. All who had actively participated in the hunt—courtiers, whippers-in and servants—were drooping.

"The hounds?" Salnove shrugged. "Yes, of course. Why wouldn't they be?"

"What about the horses?"

"The same."

"And all for two stags too young to have antlers," said the King drily.

He glanced at the crowd that surrounded him. Angélique sensed that regardless of his imperturbable and inscrutable expression he had nevertheless observed her presence and recognized her. She withdrew a little.

"Very well," said the King, "we shall hunt again on Wednesday."

His announcement produced an astonished and anxious silence. Many of the women were wondering how they could ever get themselves into a saddle again just the day after tomorrow.

The King repeated a little louder: "We will hunt the day after tomorrow, Salnove. Is that clear? And we want a ten-pronged stag this time."

"Sire, I completely understand," replied the Master.

He bowed very low before he withdrew, but said loud enough to be heard by the guests: "What gets me is all this worry about the dogs and horses being tired, and never a thought for the humans."

"Monsieur de Salnove!" Louis XIV was calling him back. And when the Master of the Hunt stood again before him, "Understand that in my realm true huntsmen are *never* tired. That is the way *I* understand it."

Salnove bowed low again.

The King moved out to lead the colorful procession of courtiers resolutely keeping their chins up and their backs straight as they rode homeward. What else could they do?

As he passed Angélique, the King signaled for a halt. His impassive eyes were upon her, yet he seemed not to see her. Angélique kept her head high, reminding herself that she had never betrayed any fear she felt and resolving not to weaken now. She returned the King's stare. Then she smiled at him.

The King winced as if he had been stung by a bee. His cheeks colored. "Why . . . it is Madame du Plessis-Bellière, I believe," he said loftily.

"Your Majesty is gracious to remember me."

"Indeed, it is more gracious of you to remember us," replied Louis XIV, calling the attention of his entourage to her singular indifference and independence. "I trust you are in good health again, Madame."

"Thank you, Your Majesty. My health has always been good."

"In that case, how does it happen that you have ignored my invitations three times now?"

"Sire, forgive me, but I never received them."

"You astound me, Madame. I personally informed Monsieur du Plessis of my wish to have you with us at the Court entertainments. It seems unlikely that he could have been so absentminded as to forget to tell you."

"Sire, perhaps my husband considered that a young woman should stay at home and ply her needle, rather than be distracted from her humble duties by the splendor of your Court."

As if rehearsed, every plumed hat turned along with the King's toward Philippe, who, frozen with impotent rage, sat his white horse like a statue.

Sensing the situation, the King, with his knack for extricating a group from an embarrassing moment, burst out laughing. "Oh, come, Marquis, I cannot believe your jealousy is so keen that you would stoop to conceal from our eyes the lovely treasure you possess. It seems to me you risk the sin of avarice. I shall forgive you this time, but I command you to look well to the happiness of Madame du Plessis. As for you, Madame, I do not wish to encourage you in your course of wifely insubordination by congratulating you for disobeying the edicts of so autocratic a husband, but your spirit of freedom does please me. Pray, do not restrain yourself from taking part in what you so graciously call the splendors of the Court. I can guarantee that Monsieur du Plessis will not reproach you for doing so."

Philippe took off his hat and holding it at arm's length made almost too extreme a gesture of obedience to the King. Angélique noticed the smiles stealing over the mask-like faces of the courtiers, who only a few moments before had been panting with eagerness to tear her into a thousand pieces.

"Congratulations!" Madame de Montespan said to her. "You have a genius for getting yourself into awkward situations, but you certainly know how to get yourself out of them. You're as good as the mountebanks on the Pont-Neuf with their escape-tricks. From the looks of the King I thought you were going to have the whole pack on your heels. The very next second you made yourself out a spunky prisoner overcoming a hundred obstacles, even prison walls, just to accept the King's invitation, regardless of what it might cost you later."

"If you only knew how right you are!"

"Oh! Tell me everything!"

"Perhaps. Some day."

"Really! Is Philippe truly so dreadful? What a shame, and he so handsome . . ."

Angélique put an end to the conversation by spurring her horse into a gallop. By a winding road the hunters, the hounds and the squires were descending the slopes of Fausse-Repos, while the horns kept sounding behind them to guide those who were bringing up the rear. Soon they came upon the crossroads crowded with carriages.

At last everyone was free to dash for his own coach. The huntsmen, who were dying of thirst, called to the vendors of lemonade who followed the Court wherever it went. But night was falling, and there was just time for them to drain one goblet of the refreshing beverage, for the King was in a hurry to return to Versailles. Already the torches and lanterns had been lit.

A coach grazed Angélique as it turned.

"What are you doing?" Madame de Montespan called out to her through the door-window. "Where's your carriage?"

"I don't have one. It turned over in a ditch."

"Climb in with me."

A little further on they picked up Mademoiselle de Parajonc and Javotte and like everyone else set their thoughts on Versailles.

chapter 3

*A*T THAT time woods closely surrounded the
castle. As the hunting party issued from them it appeared quite close by on a little hill, its windows flashing like shooting stars as the torches behind them moved
from one room to another.

There was great bustling about. The King had let it
be known that he was not going to leave for Saint-
Germain that evening, as he had previously intended,
but would stay on at Versailles for three more days.
Now instead of packing up, accommodations for the
King and his household and all the guests had to be
prepared; the horses had to be properly stabled, and
banquets had to be got ready.

The entrance court was so crowded with vehicles and
soldiers and grooms that the coach had to stop outside.
Philippe jumped out of the left hand door of his coach,
Angélique by the right hand door of hers. The Marquis
strode off at once toward the palace without paying any
attention to the women.

"Monsieur du Plessis-Bellière must doubtless be hurry-
ing to the quarry," said Mademoiselle de Parajonc, as
if she knew all about it. "Take care you don't miss the
ceremony."

"What do you intend to do?" asked Angélique.

"Sit down on this milestone and wait till I see someone I know going back to Paris. I am not one of the
King's guests, remember. You trot along, darling. All I
ask is that you come to see me and tell me everything
about life in the courts of the sun."

Angélique promised. She kissed the old maid and left
her there in the night mists wrapped in her old-
fashioned cloak and pink-ribboned bonnet, her wrinkled

white face beaming with childish delight at having been
so near the Court on this never-to-be-forgotten day.

Angélique herself crossed the rim of the magic circle
and began her ascent toward the elect.

"In the courts of the sun," she repeated to herself as
she made her way through the bustle to the center of
the gathering.

This was close to the central building of the castle,
in the third courtyard, which was called the Court of
Stags. In spite of the general disorder, the select persons
who were entitled to join the King during the quarry
were being carefully segregated. Angélique was stopped
by a Swiss guardsman with a halberd, and a master of
ceremonies politely inquired her title. As soon as she
had given her name he let her pass, even guided her
attentively up the staircases and across the splendid
rooms to one of the balconies on the second floor which
overlooked the Court of Stags.

The courtyard was lighted by countless torches. The
pink brick wall of the palace over which flickered
feathery shadows glowed like a brazier; the intricate
tracery of the balconies and the cornices, and the gold-
leaf sconces gleamed like many-colored embroidery on
a robe of purple velvet.

The horns sounded a grand fanfare.

The King advanced to the center balcony with the
Queen beside him. The royal princesses, the princes,
the highest ranking noblemen surrounded them.

Out of the depths of the night came the baying of the
hounds as they approached up the hill. Two whippers-
in appeared out of the shadows at the iron-grilled gate
of the courtyard and entered the brightly lighted circle.
They were dragging some sort of bundle from which
dripped blood and gobbets of guts. It was the quarry,
composed of the intestines of the two stags that had
been killed, wrapped in the freshly flayed hide of one
of them. Behind these two came other trainers in red
livery, keeping the pack of greedy hounds from snapping at their heels with long whips.

Philippe du Plessis-Bellière descended the staircase

to meet them. In his hand was the wand with the stag's hoof. He had had time to change into a dazzling hunting suit, red also, but trimmed with forty golden buttons across, and twenty up and down, its two pockets. His yellow leather boots had red heels with silver-gilt spurs.

"His leg is as shapely as the King's," remarked someone near Angélique.

"But he walks with less grace. Philippe du Plessis-Bellière always strides as if he were setting out to battle."

"Don't forget he's a Marshal too."

The young man stood at attention, his eyes fixed on the King in the balcony. The King gave a signal with his own wand.

Philippe handed his insigne of office to the page behind him. Then he advanced toward the lackeys and took their dripping burden into his own hands. The gorgeous embroidery and laces of his silk coat were immediately drenched in blood. With magnificent unconcern he carried the quarry to the center of the courtyard and there laid it down before the crescent of hounds, whose yapping and baying rose to the pitch of fiendish howls. The whippers held them back with savage lashes, yelling, "Down, you! Down!"

At a signal from the King, they were released. They sprang on the bundle with snapping jaws, their sharp teeth gleaming in the torchlight. The dogs, kept tied up day after day and fed on raw meat, were like escaped wild beasts. The men who trained them now fought with them like gladiators in an arena.

Philippe stood nearest to the savage horde armed with only a riding crop. From time to time he struck at them casually when they got into fights and seemed ready to devour one another. Soon the beasts would separate, growling but subdued. The cool temerity of the Master of the Hunt, standing so straight in his gorgeous, blood-drenched costume, his blond head so arrogant and his laces and jewels so sumptuous, added a strange and fascinating dimension to the barbaric scene.

Torn between disgust and a passionate excitement,

Angélique could not take her eyes away. Everyone
there was, like her, hypnotized by the spectacle.

" 'Sdeath," murmured a throaty male voice near her,
"to look at him you wouldn't think he had the strength
to crack an almond or pull petals off a daisy. I must
say, I never in my life saw a huntsman who dared go so
close to the trophy for fear of being attacked."

On the pavement of the Court of Stags there now were
left only the well-gnawed bones of the carcases. The last
whipper-in stuck his pitchfork into the pile of remains
of a stag's belly, and called the dogs to follow him out.
The horns sounded the last phase of the quarry, then
the call to quarters. Everyone began leaving the balconies.

At the entrance to the brightly lighted rooms the irrepressible Péguilin de Lauzun was putting on an act
like a barker at a carnival. "Have fun, ladies and gentlemen. You have witnessed the most extraordinarily stupe-
fying spectacle ever seen in this world—Monsieur du
Plessis-Bellière in his role as tamer of wild beasts. You
have shuddered, gentlemen. Ladies, you have trembled.
How would you like to be she-wolves and be tamed by
so gentle a hand? And now the wild beasts are subdued. The gods are content. Nothing remains of the
stag that this very morning was belling so gloriously in
the depths of the forest. Come, ladies, gentlemen, let's
dance!"

Actually no one was dancing yet, for the King's or-
chestra of twenty-four violins had not yet arrived from
Saint-Germain; but gaily dressed, deep-chested musicians
were strutting around the great hall on the ground floor
of the castle, blowing trumpets. These military fanfares
were intended to stimulate the appetite. Stewards of the
kitchen began to pass among the guests offering them
silver trays laden with flowers and dainties and fruits.
Four huge tables covered with damask cloths were being
set with platters of silver-gilt and gold, and chafing
dishes, piled with such mouth-watering delicacies as
partridges in aspic, pheasants surrounded with fruits
and vegetables, roast kids, pigeon pies, cassoulets of rice
and ham. In the center of each table was a great bowl of

autumn fruit, around which were grouped bowls of figs and melons.

Angélique was feasting on a poached quail and a mixture of salads that the Marquis de la Vallière had brought her. She sipped at a glass of raspberry wine. The Marquis kept insisting that she take some rosolio also, which he called "the liqueur of sportiveness." A page brought them two glasses to the window alcove where they sat chatting. It floated her into ecstasy.

Once her appetite and her wonder at the scene were appeased, her thoughts turned to Mademoiselle de Parajonc sitting on the milestone in the damp mists of the evening. The least she could do for her old friend was to take her some leavings from the royal banquet. Hiding under the voluminous folds of her gown a cake studded with almonds and two fine pears, she slipped out of the crowd unnoticed. Hardly had she stepped outdoors than she was hailed by Flipot carrying her cloak, a cape of heavy satin and velvet that she had left behind in Philonide's carriage.

"So there you are! Could the coach be repaired?"

"As if we cared! When it got dark, me and the coachman just walked out to the highroad and hitched a ride on a wine cart going to Versailles."

"Have you found Mademoiselle de Parajonc?"

"She's over there." He waved toward the lower courtyard where lanterns were bobbing. "She was talking with some other one of your girl friends from Paris. I heard her say she could take her back in her rented coach."

"That's good. Poor Philonide! I suppose I ought to buy her a new carriage."

To make sure, she had Flipot lead her through the unimaginable tangle of coaches and carriages and horses and sedan chairs to the spot where he had seen Mademoiselle de Parajonc. When she caught sight of her she recognized the "other one of your girl friends" as Madame Scarron, an impoverished but worthy young widow who often came to Court as a petitioner in the hope of eventually getting some little job or other that would relieve her eternal poverty.

Both of them were stepping into a public vehicle
that was already crowded with other insignificant persons, many of whom were also petitioners. They were
leaving just as they had come; the King had announced
that he would hear no petitions that day—tomorrow
after Mass.

Some petitioners were staying on, resigned to sleeping
in a corner of the courtyard or in a stable in some neighboring hamlet. The rest were going back to Paris, where
they would have to get up at dawn to catch the barge
from the Bois de Boulogne and then cut across the forest to reappear pertinaciously in the King's antechamber
clutching their petitions in their hands.

The public vehicle started out before Angélique could
reach it and before she could attract the attention of her
two friends. They were thrilled at having spent a day at
Court, where they knew everyone, although no one knew
them. They were like bees swarming around the queen
of the hive, making honey out of the smallest incident
that came within their reach. They "knew the Court"
better than many women whose high lineage automat-
ically admitted them to its circle, but who lacked experience and were unfamiliar with the involved protocol, the prerogatives that rank or favoritism earned,
the patronage of the King or of a grandee.

Angélique put her cloak about her shoulders, and
gave the cake and the pears she had stolen to the young
lackey.

While she was returning to the ballroom, not even
the bright scenes around her could distract her mind
from Philippe. Any minute now she would find herself
face to face with him. She could not decide how to behave. Should she be furious? Or nonchalant? Or repentant?

At the threshold she stopped to try to spot him, but
she could not see him. Catching sight of a table where
Madame de Montausier was sitting with some of her
friends, one of whom was Angélique's acquaintance
Madame du Roure, she went to join them. Madame de
Montausier looked at her in amazement, then, rising,
informed her that she could not sit at this table where

there were only those ladies privileged to ride in the Queen's carriage and dine with her.

Angélique excused herself. She dared not sit at any other table for fear of being driven away again, and decided to leave to find her room by herself.

The lower floors were given over to quarters for the courtiers. Just outside the royal apartments huge reception rooms were being made ready. In contrast, the attics were divided into many little rooms crudely partitioned off and reserved for servants principally, but where many a great noble would be happy to find rest on a night like this. Here too was a swarm of activity as people rushed from cubicle to cubicle dodging the trunks and portmanteaus that the servants were lugging in. Ladies driven frantic in their attempts to dress were shouting abuse at servants who darted back and forth carrying their voluminous ball gowns. The chief worry of the guests was how they could ever squeeze out of the doors of their "closets" and through the narrow corridors.

The blue-uniformed quartermasters assigned to the distribution of rooms were just finishing writing the names of the occupants on the doors. The guests followed on their heels emitting groans of disappointment or little shrieks of delight.

Flipot hailed Angélique. "Psst! This way, Madame." Then he added disgustedly: "It's not much like your own big bedroom. How can people live like this in the palace of the King?" All his dreams about the luxurious life of the nobility had been shattered.

Javotte appeared, her cheeks flushed. She seemed worried. "I've laid out everything you will need, Madame. I haven't forgotten a thing."

Progressing a little further, Angélique discovered the cause of Javotte's anxiety. It was La Violette, her husband's valet. His mouth fell open, and he stared at Angélique as if she were a ghost. Could this be the same woman whom only a few hours earlier he had rolled up in a blanket like a sausage and carried off to the good sisters of the Augustine Convent at Bellevue?

"Yes, it's I, you scoundrel," Angélique shouted at

him. Her anger flared. "Out of my sight, you wretch. Murderer! Do you know you almost strangled your master's wife?"

"Ma—Madame—Madame la Marquise," stammered La Violette, lapsing into his peasant dialect, "it wasn't my fault. Monsieur le Marquis . . . he . . . he . . ."

"Get out of here!"

Shaking her fist she hurled at him a fine string of insults she remembered from the dialect of her childhood. It was too much for La Violette, who gave way before her onslaught. Almost trembling, his shoulders drooping, he squeezed past her toward the door. There he ran into the Marquis.

"What's going on here?"

Angélique looked him straight in the eye. "Why, good evening, Philippe," she said.

He turned on her the look of a blind man. Then suddenly she saw his features contort and his eyes open in an expression of astonishment and confusion that soon changed into fear and little by little into despair.

She could not keep from turning around as if to see some demon leering behind her. She saw only the swinging leaf of the folding door on which one of the quartermasters had written the name of the Marquis in white chalk.

"That's what I owe you!" he exploded, striking the door with his fist. "That is the affront I owe you. Disrepute! Ignominy! The loss of the King's favor! *Disgrace!*"

"Why, how is that?" she said. He must be out of his mind, she thought.

"Don't you see what is written on that door?"

"Of course. It's your name."

"Yes, my name. Indeed it is my name." He grinned. "And that is all."

"Did you want them to put someone else's there?"

"It's what I have seen there for all the years and in all the residences in which I have followed the King, and that your foolishness, your . . . your idiocy make me want to see erased now. It's the 'Reserved for . . .' The 'Reserved for'!"

"Why?"

" 'Reserved for' the Marquis du Plessis-Bellière," he said between his teeth, white with anger. "That phrase signifies the special guest of His Majesty. By it the King shows his friendship as if he himself were standing on the sill to welcome you."

The gesture with which he described the narrow, crowded little attic room restored Angélique's sense of humor.

"I think you're getting far too excited about that 'Reserved for,' " she said, trying to keep from laughing. "One of those quartermasters must have made a mistake, don't you think, Philippe? His Majesty has always held you in very high regard. Weren't you appointed to bring the King his night-light this evening?"

"I was not," he said. "There's proof enough of the King's displeasure with me. That extraordinary honor was taken away from me hardly a moment ago."

His loud tones had drawn the occupants of the neighboring rooms into the corridor.

"Your wife is right, Marquis," interposed the Duc de Gramont. "You are wrong to be so pessimistic. His Majesty himself took pains to explain to you that if he asked you to relinquish the honor of bringing him his night-light this evening, it was only to do something for the Duc de Bouillon, who was put out at having been obliged to surrender his office to the Prince de Condé during supper."

"But the 'Reserved for'?" roared Philippe, pounding on the door again. "That slut there is responsible for my loss of favor."

"How can I be to blame for your damned 'Reserved for'?" shouted Angélique, whose anger was also rising. "You displeased the King by refusing his invitations, by your late arrival . . ."

Angélique's words stuck in her throat. "How dare you blame me for that when you . . . you . . . All my carriages, all my horses . . ."

"That's enough out of you," said Philippe sternly, raising his hand.

She felt her head bursting. The flames of the candles

fluttered crazily in deep blackness. She put her hand to
her cheek.

"Come, come, Marquis," said the Duc de Gramont.
"Don't be so brutal."

Angélique had never before endured such a humiliation. To be struck in front of all the servants and courtiers in a sordid household quarrel! She blushed with
shame up to the roots of her hair. She called Javotte
and Flipot, who dashed out of the room in astonishment, one carrying her undergarments and the other
her cloak.

"So," said Philippe, "go to bed when you wish and
with whom you wish."

"Marquis! Marquis! Don't be coarse," intervened the
Duc de Gramont once more.

"My lord, even a woodcutter is master in his own
hut," replied the furious nobleman, shutting the door
in the face of the spectators.

Angélique broke a passage for herself through them
and escaped, pursued by their insincere expressions of
pity and their ironic smiles. An arm thrust out from a
door caught hold of her.

"Madame," said the Marquis de la Vallière, "there is
not a woman in Versailles who does not envy you the
license your husband has just given you. Take the boor
at his word and accept my hospitality."

She broke away, irritated. "Please, sir . . ."

The one thing she wanted was to get away as fast as
possible. As she descended the great marble staircase,
tears of vexation glistened in her eyes. "He's a fool, a
mean, shabby good-for-nothing disguised as a great
nobleman . . . a fool . . . a fool!"

Nevertheless, she realized, he was a dangerous fool,
and it was she herself who had forged the chains that
bound her to him. She had given him the incontro-
vertible rights that a husband has over a wife. Determined to revenge himself on her, he would show her
no mercy. She could imagine the unspeakable satisfaction he would derive from his determined efforts to
humiliate her and make her his complete slave. She knew
of only one weak point in his armor—his devotion to the

King which was neither love nor fear but rather a single-minded, unwavering loyalty. She would have to play on this relationship. If only she could make the King her ally, get from him a permanent place at Court, little by little maneuver Philippe into a dilemma in which he would either have to displease the King or cease provoking his wife. But what happiness would she get out of that? Only the happiness of which, in spite of everything, she had dreamed in the stillnesses of the forest of Nieul, when the full moon rose above the white turrets of the little Renaissance castle as she prepared to consummate her wedding night. What a bitter disappointment! What a wry memory! So far as he was concerned, everything had turned to ashes in her mouth.

She felt unsure of her charm and her beauty. Not to be loved as a woman is to feel utterly forlorn. Would she be able to finish what she had begun? She knew her own weakness—to love him and at the same time to want to hurt him. In her driving ambition, her resolute determination to rise above her misfortunes she had forced him into the alternatives of either marrying her or exposing himself and his father to the wrath of the King. He had chosen to marry her, but he would never forgive her. Through her own fault the spring from which they both might have drunk invigorating draughts had become polluted, the hand which she might have given him in tenderness now was a thing of horror to him.

Angélique gazed at her own white hands with sad regret.

"What damned spot would you have out, my beautiful Lady Macbeth?" The voice of the Marquis de Lauzun was close to her ear.

He bent over her. "Where is the blood of your crime? Why, how cold your little paws are! What are you doing here on this draughty staircase?"

"I don't know."

"Abandoned? And with such lovely eyes? What a crime! Come along with me."

A little group of ladies joined them, Madame de Montespan among them. "Monsieur de Lauzun, we have been looking everywhere for you. Take pity on us."

"It is very easy for you to arouse pity in my heart. How may I help you, Mesdames?"

"Take us to your house. The King had you build a hôtel in the hamlet. Here we don't even have a right to a flagstone in the Queen's antechamber."

"But aren't you the Queen's own ladies-in-waiting, just like Madame du Roure and Madame d'Arignys?"

"Yes, but our usual rooms have been torn up by the painters. They are putting Jupiter and Mercury up there . . . on the ceiling. The gods have chased us out."

"Cheer up. I will take you to my hôtel."

They went out into the fog which had become thicker and thicker, imbued with the dank odor of the forest. Lauzun summoned a linkboy and guided the women down the hill.

"Here we are," he said, stopping before a heap of white stones.

"Here? What is this?"

"My hôtel. You are quite right that the King ordered me to build one, but the first stone has yet to be laid."

"You are not very funny," hissed Athenais de Montespan in a rage. "We are chilled to the marrow here in this muddy rubbish."

"Be careful you don't step into a hole," Péguilin warned them. "There's been a lot of digging around here."

Madame de Montespan stalked off, stumbled several times, and twisted her ankle. She burst out into oaths again, and all the way back to the palace kept hurling epithets over her shoulder at the Marquis that would have done credit to a guardsman.

Lauzun laughed again when the Marquis de la Vallière, who was passing by, shouted to him that he would be late for "the nightshirt." The King had gone to his bedroom, and the nobles were supposed to be there when the chief valet handed the nightshirt to the Grand Chamberlain, who passed it to His Majesty. The Marquis de Lauzun left the ladies abruptly, but not before he had offered them his hospitality again . . . in his bedroom which was "somewhere way up there."

The four young women, followed by Javotte, returned to the crowded ballroom, where, to use an expression of Madame de Montespan's, "the floors were creaking under the weight." After a long search they found the inscription of honor on a little low door: "Reserved for the Marquis Péguilin de Lauzun."

"Lucky Péguilin!" sighed Madame de Montespan. "What difference does it make if he's the biggest fool in the world so long as the King treats him as a favorite. When you stop to think of it, he has a very average figure and indifferent looks."

"But his good qualities make up for that," said Madame du Roure. "He is very witty, and he has something that makes a woman, once she has been with him, never leave him for another man."

Such was doubtless the opinion of young Madame de Roquelaure, whom they found in the bedroom in quite scanty attire. Her maid had just finished helping her into a nightgown of lawn embroidered with lace and designed to conceal none of her charms. After a moment of confusion she recovered herself to say graciously that since Monsieur de Lauzun had invited his friends there, she would indeed make them welcome. Cooperation was the least one could show in such unusual situations as turned up during a stay at Versailles.

Madame du Roure was delighted. She had long suspected that Madame de Roquelaure was Péguilin's mistress, and now she was sure of it.

The room was no wider than its window, which opened on the woods. The curtained bed, which the servants had just made up, filled it entirely. When everyone was inside, no one could budge. Fortunately, due to its tiny size, it was warm. The fire in the little fireplace crackled cheerily.

"Ah," said Madame de Montespan, pulling off her muddy slippers, "let's get rid of the last of that damned Péguilin's practical joke."

She rolled down her mud-spattered stockings, and her friends did likewise. All four of them sat down on the flagstones in their widespreading skirts and toasted their toes at the fire.

Lauzun returned, accompanied by one of his noble
friends, who helped him undress. Lauzun and Madame
de Roquelaure went to bed. Once the curtains were
drawn, no one paid them the slightest attention.

Angélique started thinking of Philippe again. How
to humble him, how to vanquish him, or at least how to
escape his revenge and prevent him from ruining the
future she had so painstakingly planned for herself?

The day would come when his stupid tricks like hiding the carriages, would give way to more dangerous
patterns of behavior. He knew indeed how to perform
them—through her sons or through her own freedom. If
the inhuman fancy should strike him to torture Florimond and Cantor, as he had already done her, how
could she protect them? Fortunately the two little boys
were safe at Monteloup, where they were growing strong
and healthy running around the countryside with the
peasant children of Poitou. Their fate was of no immediate concern to her. She told herself that she was
being foolish to plunge herself into such imaginary
terrors during this, her first night at Versailles.

The fire was getting too hot. She asked Javotte to
hand her two fire-shields of daintily decorated parch-
ment. One of them she offered to Madame de Montespan. The beautiful young woman admired her little
traveling case of red leather lined with white damask
and bound in gold. Inside, separated by partitions, were
an ivory night-light, a bag of black satin containing ten
candles of virgin wax, a hollow bodkin to hold pins,
two small round mirrors, and a larger oval one set with
pearls, two lace nightcaps to match a delicate linen
nightgown, a gold case holding three combs and another
one for brushes. These last were little masterpieces of
tortoise-shell enhanced by gold filigree.

"I had them made from the tortoise-shell that comes
from the tropic seas," Angélique explained. "I can't
stand horn or hoof."

"I see," sighed the Marquise de Montespan enviously.
"Ah, what wouldn't I give to have such beautiful things!
I suppose I might have had them, if I hadn't had to

pawn my jewels to pay off my gambling debts. If I
hadn't done that, how could I have put in an appearance at Versailles tonight? Monsieur de Ventadour, to
whom I owe a thousand *pistoles*, will be waiting for
me. He's a charming man."

"But haven't you been appointed Maid of Honor to
the Queen? That must have brought you some perquisites."

"Pooh, it's a trifle! My clothes alone cost me twice as
much. I spent two thousand *livres* for the costume I
wore in the ballet of *Orpheus* Lully composed that was
given at Saint-Germain. Oh, but it was lovely! My costume especially. The ballet was the same as always. I
was a nymph, with all sorts of ornaments representing
the things that grow around a woodland spring. The
King was Orpheus, of course. He opened the dance with
me. Benserade mentions it in his Court chronicle. So
does Loret, the poet."

"Everyone has been talking about the attention the
King has been paying you," Angélique remarked.

The feelings that Madame de Montespan had aroused
in her were somewhat mollified. She envied the flashing
radiance of her charm and the brilliance of her conversation, even though her own beauty was quite com-
parable. Both of them were from good families in Poitou. Yet beside Athenais de Montespan Angélique felt
inferior, in spite of her gift for easy repartee, and she
was often silent in her company. She was aware of how
alluring the young marquise's conversation was; no matter how she exaggerated anything, her voice was so
trained and modulated that people believed her before they were appalled. This eloquence of hers, in
which nature and art were so subtly combined that even
a cynical observation drew admiration, was a talent in
her family. It was called "the Mortemart speech."

The family of Mortemart de Rochechouart was an impressive one. Angélique de Sancé, who knew all the
genealogy of Poitou, was always impressed by the mag-
nificence of the traditions that clung to that great house.
Long ago Edward of England had married one of his

daughters to a lord of Mortemart. The present Duc de
Vivonne had the King and the Queen Mother as god-
parents.

In the deep blue eyes of Madame de Montespan could
be divined the proud and perhaps foolish motto of the
family:

> Before the sea produced the earth
> The waves of Rochechouart had birth.

But none of those traditions had protected her from
arriving in Paris poor as a churchmouse, without any
possessions other than an old carriage, and from struggling before her marriage with all the hateful obstacles
of poverty. Prouder and more sensitive than anyone
believed, the girl had often been reduced to tears.

Better than anyone else Angélique knew the humiliating problems with which the lovely Montespan had
wrestled. Time and again since she first knew the family,
she had had to pacify their irascible creditors, and lend
sums that she knew she would never see again and for
which no one would dream of thanking her. Angélique
derived a certain pleasure from putting the Montespans
under obligation to her. Often she asked herself why
she kept up such an unrewarding friendship, arguing
that on the one hand Athenais was fundamentally a
sweet person, and on the other that she ought to have
the good sense to have nothing more to do with her.
Still the girl's vitality bewitched her. Angélique had always liked people who were bound to be successful, and
Athenais was one of them. Her ambition was as boundless as the sea whose origin her family claimed. It was
better to follow her and ride on the crest of her wave
than to try to oppose her.

For her own part Athenais found it convenient to
have so generous a friend whose fortune was secure
thanks to good investments, a friend as well whom she
could see without losing caste. In spite of her beauty
Angélique did not overshadow her.

In response to the allusion her friend had made to

the King's favor, Madame de Montespan's face, which had seemed careworn all evening, relaxed a little.

"The Queen is good and pregnant. Mademoiselle de la Vallière is just beginning to be. It's a propitious moment for attracting the King's attention," Athenais said with a sparkling smile in which there lurked a suspicion of mischief. "Oh, Angélique, what are you getting me to say, or even to think! I would be stricken with shame if the King wanted to make me his mistress. I would never again dare appear before the Queen, she is such a good woman!"

Angélique was not taken in by this protestation of virtue. There were certain dimensions of Athenais' character that astonished her, such as her ability to dissemble when she was torn between hypocrisy and sincerity. Her piety, for example: frivolous as she was, Madame de Montespan never missed Mass or any other devotion, and the Queen would repeat to anyone who cared to listen how pleased she was to have so devout a lady-in-waiting.

"Do you remember," said Angélique laughingly, "the visit we made with Françoise Scarron to that fortune-teller named Monvoisin? Even then you wanted to ask her whether you'd succeed in getting the King to fall in love with you."

"Nonsense!" said the Marquise, with a gesture as if to brush aside such a whim. "Furthermore I had not then been appointed to Her Majesty's suite, and I was looking for some way to get advancement at Court. The old woman told us nothing but lies."

"She said all three of us would be loved by the King."

"Even Françoise?"

"Oh, I forgot. Françoise's destiny was the most glamorous of all. She would marry the King!"

They laughed together. "Françoise Scarron, Queen of France!"

"Oh, how unhappy I am," Athenais sighed suddenly. "Can you believe that I owe my carriage-maker eighteen hundred *livres* for the saddle and bridle he made for me to use today. I hope you noticed how lovely the leather is. I had him touch it with gold leaf so that it would look like real embroidery. It was magnificent!"

"For eighteen hundred *livres* . . ."

"Oh, it's not an enormous debt after all. I'll just turn up my nose at Gaubert's complaints and tell him he'll have to wait along with his fellow-creditors, the tailor and the draper and the jeweler. But that unbearable husband of mine has ordered a pair of diamond earrings that my heart is set on, and if I don't pay up tomorrow the jeweler won't deliver them. Did you ever hear of such a meddling husband? He doesn't know how to hang on to his money. He gambles—lord, how he gambles! I can't make him listen to reason. And such extravagant notions! I can see that I shall end my days just like my old aunt the Duchesse de Bellegarde. You remember. She's not one of my family, I'm glad to say. Her husband got furiously jealous of her—he's seventy-five and she is only fifty-five—and shut her up in his castle, took everything away from her to the point where she had to cut up her sheets to make clothes. That's the reward I'll get for marrying him. All the Montespans are touched somehow."

Angélique, whose cheek was still smarting from the slap Philippe had given her, did not find these tales of Madame de Montespan very amusing. Her expression delighted the mischievous young woman.

"Now don't go having gloomy thoughts again. You hold your Philippe with stronger reins than mere conjugal affection. They say you let him rummage freely in your commercial treasure chests."

At Court Angélique wished to be the Marquise du Plessis-Bellière and nothing else. The reference Madame de Montespan made to her maneuvers in business set her teeth on edge.

"Well, don't you worry about whether or not I'll allow myself to be locked away," she said testily. "If I am, you'll have plenty of time then to think about what you have lost. If you were smart you would help me find a place at Court instead. For instance, you could tell me of some vacant position I might acquire."

Athenais raised her arms to the heavens. "My poor

child, what are you thinking of! An empty place at Court? You might as well try to find a needle in a haystack. Everybody is on the alert for one, and even when he has the price ready, he can hardly get one."

"Still you succeeded in becoming Maid of Honor to the Queen."

"The King himself appointed me. I used to make him laugh when he came to Mademoiselle de la Vallière's. His Majesty thought I would amuse the Queen. He is very solicitous about his wife. He was so insistent on my being with her that he was discreet enough to pay what I couldn't of the fee. You have to have a patron, and there is none like the King himself. Just think a little of whom you could get. Or else you could invent something for your own good and show it to His Majesty. It would be examined by the Supreme Council. If you could have it introduced into the Parlement, then you would be sure to get it."

"That sounds quite complicated and hard. What exactly do you mean by 'inventing something for my own good'?"

"Well, I myself don't know. You have to use your imagination. Wait, here's a recent example. I know the Sieur du Lac, majordomo of the Marquis de la Vallière, joined up with Collin, the Marquise's butler, to ask permission to collect two sous an acre on all the vacant land between the township of Meudon, near Saint-Cloud, and the hamlet of Chagny, near Versailles. It was a happy inspiration because now that the King has selected that region for his palace, everyone will buy up the land there. And how were these vacant lands secured? The bill was recommended by Mademoiselle de la Vallière, and the King signed it immediately. He has never refused her anything. The Parlement was compelled to approve it. Those two insignificant little commoners will end up with their coffers bursting with gold. Furthermore it's a trait of our favorite to play fairy godmother to her servants. She never says no to them. Then the King began to be bored with the horde of petitioners she presented to him. The most outstanding is her own brother, the Marquis; he's got a real genius for petitioning. You could consult him advantageously. He'll give you good advice, I'm sure, because, as I have noticed, he is not wholly indifferent to you. And while you are waiting I might present you to the Queen. You could speak to her. Perhaps you would attract her interest."

"That's just what you can do," said Angélique with spirit. "And I promise you I'll find something in my 'commercial treasure chests' to appease your carriage-maker."

The Marquise de Montespan did not disguise her delight. "Agreed. You're an angel! You'd be an archangel if only you could get me a parrot. Yes, one of those big tropical ones you import. You know, one with red and green feathers. Oh, I'm dreaming!"

chapter 4

*A*S DAY broke, Madame de Montespan yawned and stretched. She had continued to gossip with Angélique by fits and starts, since the limited space in the room hardly allowed them an opportunity to stretch out and rest.

Behind the curtains of the great bed they heard two bodies turn over, yawn too, and then a tender murmuring.

"I imagine it would be a good idea to go downstairs," said Athenais. "The Queen is about to call for her Maids of Honor. I want to be one of the first to answer so that I can go to Mass with her. Are you coming?"

"Perhaps it's not an auspicious moment for me to be presented to Her Majesty."

"No, it would be better if you waited until we came back from the chapel. You stand in the passage. But first I must show you the best spots to see Their Majesties and, if possible, be seen by them. It's a tricky business. Come down with me. I will show you a little retiring room near the Queen's apartments which the Maids of Honor use to tidy themselves up and also as a meeting place. Have you anything to wear except your riding habit?"

"In my trunk. But I'll have to lay hands on my lackey so that I can send him for it into my husband's room."

"Wear something simple for the morning. After Mass the King receives his petitioners and then goes into conference with his Ministers. This evening, I think, there will be a play and a ballet. Then you can trot out your best jewels. But now, let's get going."

The air outside the room was cold and damp. Madame de Montespan tripped down the staircases oblivious of the draughts that swirled around her beautiful bare shoulders.

"Aren't you freezing?" Angélique asked.

The Marquise dismissed the question with a gesture of indifference. She had acquired a courtier's endurance in putting up with the worst kinds of inconveniences—heat and cold in rooms that were either open to the four winds or stifling hot under the blaze of thousands of candles, the fatigue of standing for hours, sleepless nights, the weight of the brocaded gowns laden with jewels. A robust constitution, the continual excitement, and particularly the endless entertainments kept sophisticated women like her going. Without being aware of it they were actually heroic, even to the point of welcoming their torments.

From her days of scanty rations Angélique had retained an extreme sensitivity to cold. She could hardly do without a cloak, and she had a huge collection of them, all very handsome. The one she wore now was made of alternate bands of velvet and satin whose colors blended into a blue-green tonality. Its hood was trimmed with a veil of Venetian lace which she could pull down over her face when she did not wish to be recognized.

Madame de Montespan left her at the entrance of the Banquet Hall, where the Swiss guards stood as motionless as statues, each in a starched ruff and holding a halberd. Nothing in the palace seemed yet to have awaked to life, even though the bright morning light was seeping into the dim salons. The balconies and galleries gaped in the gloom like huge storied grottoes, suggesting that they might be filled with gold and precious stones. Most of the candles had guttered out.

"I'll leave you here," Athenais whispered as if awed by the silent solemnity that pervaded these usually boisterous rooms. "Over there is a dressing room where you can sit while you wait. In a little while the courtiers who help the King to rise will put in an appearance. His Majesty gets up early. I'll see you soon."

As Athenais moved off, Angélique opened the door her friend had pointed out. It was almost a secret door, concealed by being covered with the same tapestry as the walls.

"Oh, I beg your pardon!" she said, closing it quickly.

She would never have suspected that a hideaway so tiny that it could not accommodate a sofa might still be put to such a romantic use. "Strange," she thought, "I didn't imagine Madame de Soubise had so handsome a bosom. Why do you suppose she hides such allurements?"

Needless to say, her companion was not Monsieur de Soubise. Angélique was sure of that. At Versailles no one paid any attention to infidelity; indeed any show of affection between husband and wife would have been considered utterly plebeian and in poor taste.

Angélique had no recourse but to wander through the enormous empty rooms. In the first she stopped, the Ionic Room, so called because of the twelve columns supporting its cornice. Here the light was strong enough for her to admire the grace of the white shafts rising into the shadows and unfolding into curls like ripples on a calm dark sea. The gold of the lofty ceiling, divided into squares by heavy ebony beams was still hardly visible, but out of its cavern darted the gleams of the crystal prisms of the chandeliers like fairyland stalactites suspended on invisible threads. Three sets of mirrors on the wall reflected the windows through which the early morning sun was now streaming.

Leaning against the marble window casing she looked out toward the park, awaking too from its night's slumber. The terrace that stretched away from the palace in an unbroken expanse of grassy lawn was as smooth as a tide-washed beach. Further off rose wisps of mist draping the tops of the well-pruned elms. Their trunks seemed the towers of a phantom city within whose blue-white walls lay magic gardens embroidered with flower beds and sequined with pools of dark green water on whose surface glided silvery swans.

As the sun rose higher it flashed from the mirror-smooth basins of the great fountains that stretched into the horizon—the Fountain of Latona, the Fountain of Apollo—all the way to the golden ribbon of the Grand

Canal into which emptied the streams of the marshland
roundabout, where beyond the reach of human eye
dwelt wild ducks and teal.

"A penny for your thoughts, Marquise," whispered
the voice of an invisible male.

Angélique stared about her, as startled as if the marble statue that confronted her had broken into speech.

"Tell me your dreams, Marquise."

"Who . . . is it?"

"It is I, Apollo, god of the beauty which you have
been so gracious to share with me this early morning
hour."

Angélique gasped.

"Chilly, isn't it? You wear a cloak, but as for me, I
am quite nude. For, as you might guess, a marble body
has no warmth."

Angélique peered behind the statue. She saw nothing
but a heap of multicolored garments lying on the floor
by the pedestal. As she bent down and touched it, it
sprang up like a frisky kid, whirled on its toes, and
coming to rest revealed a tiny gnome-like face peering
out at her from deep within a hood.

"Barcarole!" exclaimed Angélique.

"At your service, Marquise of the Angels."

The Queen's dwarf bowed low before her. No taller
than a seven-year-old child, his poor little deformed body
on its twisted legs diverted attention from the sweet intelligence of his face. A cap of scarlet satin trimmed
with bells and baubles fitted closely over his skull, and
his tightfitting doublet was also of parti-colored black
and scarlet satin, but bare of bells and other ornament.
There was lace at his cuffs, and he carried a miniature
sword.

It had been a long time since Angélique had seen
him. He had the manners of an aristocrat, and she told
him so.

"That's true," Barcarole said smugly. "If I had the figure for it, I could match any one of the fine lords who
strut about here. Ah, if only our good Queen would let
me snip off these bells from my cap, how truly happy

she would make me. But she maintains that in Spain all jesters wear bells, and that if she couldn't hear them jingling, she would be even more homesick. Fortunately my two companions and I have an unsuspected ally in the King. He can't stand us. When he comes to see the Queen he never misses a chance to chase us out with his stick. We keep out of its way by turning somersaults that make all our bells jangle like mad. Then when he is deep in some intimate discussion we shake our rattles so that he can't hear what's being said, and that puts him into a bad humor. Finally the Queen takes notice, sighs, but only says one of our bells has come unsewed and we should go and get it fixed. Soon we shall venture to obtain another privilege."

"What will it be?"

"A wig," Barcarole answered, rolling his eyes till only the whites were visible.

Angélique laughed. "You're putting on airs, *Monsieur* Barcarole."

"I want to get ahead, rise in the world," the dwarf said matter-of-factly.

Under his pose of a mature man, she could detect the irony of melancholy. "It's good to see you again, Barcarole. Let's have a little talk."

"Aren't you worried about your reputation? They'll start telling tales about us. What if your husband challenged me to a duel?"

"You have a sword, haven't you?"

"Why, of course. Nothing is impossible to a valiant soul. I'm going to flirt with you, Madame. Just keep looking out the window. Anyone who passes by will simply think we are admiring the gardens and never suspect I'm pouring out a heart's devotion to you."

He skipped over to the window and flattened his nose against the pane like a child. "What do you think of this place? Pleasant, isn't it? Ah, Marquise of the Angels, you may be a great lady now, but you still haven't forgotten your friendship with the Queen's jester!"

Angélique kept her eyes on the gardens, but she laid her hand on the dwarf's shoulder. "The memories that bind us to each other are not such that they can be forgotten, Barcarole." Softly she added, "Would that they might be!"

By now the sun had melted the mists. The day would be cloudless, as bright and fresh as if it were springtime. The green leaves of the elms gleamed like emeralds, the clear water of the fountains reflected the deep blue of the sky, the flowers danced with a thousand colors. The dozens of gardeners who had gone to work with their rakes and wheelbarrows were lost in the vast expanse of the esplanade.

Barcarole was speaking in a low voice. "Sometimes our Queen worries when she hasn't seen me all day long. That's because her favorite dwarf has gone to Paris to pay homage to another Majesty, whose subjects are not permitted to forget him—the Great Coesre, Wood-Bottom, King of the Underworld. He hasn't many subjects left like us, Marquise of the Angels, who can swell his purses with money to the size of melons. I think Wood-Bottom is pretty fond of me."

"He is fond of me too," said Angélique.

She conjured up the impressive face of Wood-Bottom. Who suspected the clandestine strolls the lovely Marquise du Plessis-Bellière, masked and dressed inconspicuously, sometimes took to the very end of the Faubourg Saint-Denis? Every week her house-servants, whom she had chosen from among her former underworld companions, brought to his lair baskets of fine wines, chickens, and roasts.

"Never fear, Marquise of the Angels," Barcarole murmured, "we know how to keep a secret. Just don't ever forget that you will never be alone in danger . . . not even here." He turned and with his stumpy arm made a sweeping gesture that embraced the whole splendid room. "Here! In the palace of the King, where everyone is more alone and more in danger than any place else on this earth."

The first courtiers began to appear, hiding yawns behind lace cuffs, their wooden heels clicking on the mar-

ble floor. Servants were carrying piles of logs and starting fires in the tremendous fireplaces.

"The 'old woman' will be along any minute. Look,
there she is."

Angélique caught a glimpse of a woman of inde-
terminate age wrapped in a hooded cloak. On her gray
hair she wore a peasant's starched coif made of fine
lawn. Some of the nobles bent their knee slightly as she
passed, but she seemed not to see them. She continued
on her way with majestic serenity.

"Where is she going?"

"To the King. It's Madame Hamelin, his old nurse. She
still keeps her privilege of entering his room in the morning before anyone else at all. She draws back the curtains and kisses him in bed, asks if he's slept well and
how he feels. They chat a bit. All the while the great
of this world are fidgeting outside the door. After she
leaves, no one sees her the rest of the day. Who knows
what secret room she spins away in? She's a bird of
night. And every day princes, cardinals, ministers of
state gnash their teeth at seeing this humble little person from the back streets of Paris favored with the Monarch's first smile of the day, and often getting his first
indulgence."

On the heels of the nurse came three doctors in the
black gowns, full white-ringleted wigs and peaked hats
that signified their high calling. One by one they felt
the King's pulse, inquired after his health, exchanged a
few Latin words among themselves, and departed.

Then came the great First Entrance—the princes of
the blood. As they bowed low before him, the King got
out of bed. The Grand Chamberlain handed him his
dressing gown which the First Lord of the Bedchamber
had been holding ready. His Majesty retained the right
of putting on his long-hose himself. Then one of the
high dignitaries knelt to fasten on his garters.

The act of presenting the royal shirt was the per-
quisite of the First Nobleman of the Realm, and there
was a wait while he strode proudly into the room at
the head of the Second Entrance—the high nobility and

specially authorized lords. When the King was in his
shirt, the First Lord of the Bedchamber handed him
the right cuff, and the First Lord of the Wardrobe handed
him the left.

Then came the Third Entrance—dukes and peers—
jostling one another as with many low bows they un-
folded the King's knee-length waistcoat, brocaded like a
field of flowers tossing in the wind.

The Master of the Wardrobe exercised his privilege
of fastening the King's jabot, but the Lord of the Neck-
cloths was permitted by right to adjust it, and did so.

The Fourth Entrance was composed of the Secretaries
of State. The Fifth was the Ambassadors. The Sixth, in
crimson and purple, was the Cardinals and Bishops. Little by little the King's bedchamber filled up.

The King glanced at the company, bowed to each,
and made a mental note of the absentees. He put several
questions to them to inform himself on the latest gossip,
and seemed amused if any gave him a witty answer. And
the Elect of Paradise—in terms of Versailles—thinking of
the simple mortals condemned to wait outside the
golden gates, tasted the inexpressible joy of being able
to gaze upon the King in his dressing gown.

Angélique watched file past all those sanctified for
entrance into the holy of holies.

"We are the souls in Purgatory," laughed one of the
women near her. They were decked out in all their
finery, striving to be in the front row when the King
and Queen returned along this passageway from the
chapel.

The Marquis du Plessis-Bellière had been one of the
Second Entrance. Angélique waited to be sure that she
saw him go into the Royal Bedchamber. Then she
dashed up to the attic, taking pains not to lose her way
in the labyrinth of corridors which reeked of orris root
and candle-grease, and were full of confusion.

La Violette was humming as he polished his master's
swords. He offered to lace Madame la Marquise's stays,
but Angélique put him out unequivocally. Without

waiting to go in search of Javotte or some chambermaid,
she dressed herself as well as she could. Then she ran
back and arrived in time to see the Queen's procession
go by.

The Queen had a red nose, in spite of the powder
with which she had covered her artfully made-up face.
She had wept the whole night through, for the King, as
she tearfully confided to her intimates, had not come
near her—"not even for one little hour." This was an unusual occurrence, for the King always was scrupulous
about keeping up appearances by slipping into his wife's
bed for at least "one little hour." Quite often he even
remained there all night, but at least he always paid her
a visit. The La Vallière had inflamed his passions in her
role of Diana the Huntress the previous day.

The Queen's retinue merged with that of La Vallière
as they approached the chapel together. Marie-Thérèse
held her head high, though her Hapsburg chin trembled
with the sobs she was suppressing. The favorite bowed
low before her. When she rose again Angélique saw the
hunted look in her soft blue eyes. Here in the glorious
light of Versailles she was no longer the huntress, but
the doe at bay. Angélique knew she had been right; the
royal favor was ebbing, if it was not already gone.
Marie-Thérèse had small reason to fear her. Not far
away were rivals ready and much more formidable.

Presently the King returned from the chapel and went
out into the gardens. He had been told that some of the
scrofulous from nearby had heard of his stay and had
gathered behind the gates in the hope of receiving the
royal touch. The King could never refuse to bestow
this miraculous gift. There were not many of them, and
the ceremony was soon over. Then His Majesty moved on
to receive the petitions of the troopers in the Salon of
Diana.

A young man in the King's suite pushed through the
crowd and bowed before Angélique. "His Majesty wishes
to remind Madame du Plessis-Bellière that he fully expects her presence at the very start of the hunt tomorrow."

"My thanks to His Majesty," she said, taut with emotion. "Pray tell him that death alone will prevent me from being there."

"His Majesty does not require so much. But he has made it clear that if you should be prevented, he would like to know the reason."

"You may assure him he shall, Monsieur de Louvois. That is your name, isn't it?"

"It is indeed."

"I should like to speak with you. Would that be possible?"

Louvois seemed astonished, but he said that if Madame du Plessis would remain in the corridor, he could perhaps join her as soon as the King retired to his conference room after receiving the petitions.

"I shall be waiting. Meanwhile, please assure His Majesty that I shall be at the hunt tomorrow."

"No, you shall not," said the voice of Philippe in her ear. "Madame, a wife owes obedience to her husband. I never gave you permission to appear at Court. You came here against my will. I now order you to leave and returned to Paris."

"Philippe, you are absurd," Angélique replied in a voice as low as his. "Absurd, and not very subtle either. It is to your advantage for me to appear at Court. What right have you to torment me so?"

"You tormented me first."

"Don't be childish. Let me alone."

"Only if you leave Versailles this minute."

"No."

"You shall not go to the hunt tomorrow."

"Go I will!"

Louvois had gone back to the King's suite and so had not heard their argument, but their neighbors looked at them mockingly. The domestic quarrels of the Plessis-Bellières were becoming famous. Next to them, pretending to be looking in another direction, was the young Marquise de la Vallière with her supercilious, bird-like profile.

To escape being laughed at, Angélique burst out

with, "All right, Philippe, I'll leave. Let's not discuss it
any more."

She crossed the corridor and took refuge in one of
the great rooms where there were fewer people to observe her. "If I had a place at Court," she kept saying
to herself, "I could depend on the whim of the King,
not on that wild man's."

How to get this grant, and as quickly as possible, was
her immediate problem. That is why she had seized
upon Louvois while he was talking to her. Her businessman's imagination was at work. She remembered that
when she had started her five *sols* carriage trade in
Paris she had been told about Louvois, a great courtier
and politician and the owner of the franchise to operate the mail coach and baggage vans between Lyons
and Grenoble.

This was certainly the same Louvois. She had not
thought him so young, but she did not forget that he
was the son of Le Tellier, Secretary of State and Chancellor of the King for the High Council. She would
make a business deal with him and try to enlist his
support and his father's as well.

The Marquis de la Vallière was tacking from group to
group, looking for Angélique. Her first maneuver was
to disappear. Then she changed her tactics. She had
heard a good deal about this Marquis de la Vallière,
having been very much on the alert for mutual ac-
quaintances who could tell her about him. He knew the
Court better than anyone else. She might learn a great
deal from him.

"I don't think the King was very hard on you for
being late to the hunt yesterday," he said when he met
up with her.

"And is that why you dare pursue your little intrigue
with me?" she thought. She forced him into conversation, but when she spoke to him about a place at Court,
he laughed pityingly.

"My poor little girl, you must be out of your mind.
You would have to kill off not one but ten persons to
create a vacancy for even the most insignificant post.

Don't you know that all the offices of the King's and the
Queen's bedchamber are sold only by quarters?"

"What does that mean?"

"That one gets them for only three months. After
that they are put up at auction. It annoys the King, for
he is all the time seeing new faces in positions where he
would prefer to have persons who know the ropes.
Since he does not want to part with Bontemps, his
chief valet, at any cost, he must be continually helping
him not only to buy back his place but even to pay for
his right to buy it back. That makes others disgruntled."

"Lord, how complicated! Can't the King assert himself and put an end to these weird transactions?"

"He has to try to keep everyone happy," said the Marquis de la Vallière, with a gesture revealing that so far
as he was concerned such strange customs were as un-
avoidable as the changes of the seasons.

"How do you yourself get around them? People say
you are very well provided for."

"They exaggerate. I hold a position as Lieutenant of
the King, which as far as pay goes is one of the smallest.
With four squadrons to equip and maintain, and my
rank to uphold at Court, I would never manage if I
didn't have some ideas of my own . . . And now, my
lovely Marquise, I must leave you, for I suspect the King
will want to return to the gardens very soon."

Louvois returned. As he passed by her he bowed
slightly and whispered that much to his regret he had
been obliged to attend the King during a second audience, following which it would be a pleasure for him
to devote a few moments to her, for after that he would
have to serve the King at table and would not have
another moment for her.

Angélique agreed resignedly. She was beginning to admire the young King's capacity for work. He had not
gone to bed until three o'clock in the morning, but he
was up and at Mass at six, and ever since had been at-
tending to his business without stopping.

As he prepared to leave her, Louvois steered her toward a young man, so wretchedly dressed that he seemed

out of place in that elegant assemblage. His powdered
wig and his lace jabot, both of which seemed unaccustomed articles of dress to him, made his tanned
face appear even darker. He bowed stiffly.

"Yes," he said, confirming Louvois' introduction, "I
am the envoy from Ile Dauphine." [1]

The weight of a hand on Angélique's shoulder just
then made her jump. She looked up to see a dark-clad
person whom, try as she might, she could not place.
A low, hoarse voice, full of authority and uncompromising, echoed in her ears. "Madame. You must give
me an opportunity to speak to you about that matter
at once."

"About what, sir?" Angélique asked.

Suddenly she remembered that this was Monsieur Colbert, the new Comptroller, and member of the Supreme
Council.

Colbert led Angélique by the hand to a corner of
the balcony outside. On the way he signaled to one of
the clerks he had with him to bring him the contents
of a large black velvet sack in which were a number of
ledgers. He drew out one with a yellow binding.

"Madame, I think you know that I am neither a courtier nor a nobleman, but a tradesman—a draper. Now,
thanks to the business we did together, I have learned
that although you are a noble you are also a businesswoman. To come to the point, it is as a member of the
merchants' guild that I approach you for advice."

He was trying to give his little speech a light touch,
but he did not have the art to do so. Angélique was in-
censed. When would people stop throwing her chocolate
business up to her!

She pursed her lips, but then, looking at Colbert, she
saw that in spite of the frosty air his forehead was beaded
with perspiration. His wig was askew and he had obviously hurried his barber that morning. Her antagonism
melted. Why should she be difficult?

"I was indeed in business," she said, "but in nothing

---

[1] Subsequently renamed Madagascar.

so important as your enterprises, sir. How can I help you?"

"As yet I do not know, Madame. Perhaps you can tell me. I discovered your name on a list of shareholders in the East India Company. What held my attention was that I was aware you are one of the nobility. Hence you are in an unusual position, and since your business prospered, I thought you might enlighten me on certain details I am lacking about the operation of that company."

"My Lord Minister, you know as well as I that that company, just like the Society of One Hundred which imitated it and in which I also had five shares, traded with the Americas. Today the shares are not worth a penny."

"I am not speaking of the value of those shares, which as a matter of fact are no longer quoted, but of the profits you made, whereas everyone else lost money."

"My only real profit was that I learned you don't get something for nothing. I paid through the nose for that lesson. The whole business was run by thieves. They expected stupendous gains from doing nothing, whereas any results from business in those distant lands are always the fruit of hard work."

The hard lines that lack of sleep had carved in Colbert's face softened into a kind of smile that was expressed more by his eyes than by his lips. "What you have just told me is rather like my own motto: 'Nothing without work.'"

"The harder the effort, the sweeter the task," Angélique quoted at him quickly, raising a finger. "Application makes work play."

The smile spread across the face of the cold Comptroller, making him almost pleasant looking.

"I see you even know the wording of my report on the said company," he said. "I wonder if any other of the shareholders took the trouble to read it."

"I wanted to know what a person of your great experience would think. The undertaking seemed so logical and to have such a potential."

"But how did you imagine such an undertaking could

succeed?" the Comptroller asked quickly. Then he resumed his dry, monotonous manner as he enumerated the secret possessions of Madame du Plessis-Bellière, alias Madame Morens: "A whole share in the ship *Saint John the Baptist,* armed with twelve cannon to trade and bring cocoa and pepper and spices and precious woods from Martinique and Santo Domingo . . ."

"Correct," said Angélique. "I had to keep my chocolate business going."

"You put the pirate Guinan in command of it."

"I did."

"Were you unaware when you took him into your service that he had previously worked for Fouquet, who was then in prison? Did you think of the serious consequences of such action, or did Fouquet advise you to do it?"

"I never had occasion to talk with Fouquet," Angélique said. "I believe he was a dangerous man because his great wealth gave him power. He abused it. But, to give the devil his due, he knew how to choose his associates. Sheer chance brought me Guinan. He was an excellent seaman and a good trader. He was in hiding then, greatly concerned at having lost his patron. I thought he was the only one who could rescue my investments after the collapse of the East India Company, in which I had confidently sunk a lot of money. Then I took him into my employ. I have a horror of messes. Furthermore I was inspired by an example from on high."

"What do you mean?"

"The King. He punishes those he deems guilty, but he is not one to let a man of talent slip out of his grasp. In my own modest way I employed the pirate, but I was ready to give him up to the King if he demanded his services."

She had spoken with spirit, but she finished with a disarming smile. Nevertheless she was far from feeling comfortable. Colbert had been a bitter enemy of Fouquet, and he had slyly set the trap in which Fouquet had eventually been snared. Everything the former Comptroller had done was now exposed.

"That boat you sent to trade in America, why didn't you send it to the Indies?" Colbert asked bluntly.

"I thought of it. But a single French boat wouldn't have been able to carry it off, and I could not afford several."

"But your *John the Baptist* sailed to America without accident."

"There was nothing to fear from the Barbary pirates. They give a single ship no chance to get beyond the Cape Verde Islands. If it is not asked where it's bound as it sails, it will be when it returns."

"What about the ships of the Dutch and English East India Companies which are not molested?"

"They sail in flotillas. Twenty or thirty ships of considerable tonnage leave Liverpool or The Hague together, and accomplish their purpose."

"Why don't the French do likewise?"

"Sir, if you don't know, how in the world do you expect me to? Possibly it's a matter of temperament, or of money. For instance, how could I alone equip a fleet? The French need a revictualing station halfway on the long route to the East Indies."

"At Ile Dauphine, for instance?"

"Yes, providing the military or any other government authority has nothing to do with administering it."

"Who would manage it then?"

"Why, men accustomed to dealing with new lands in trade and commerce. I mean merchants!"

Angélique had been speaking forcefully, but suddenly she started to laugh.

"Madame, we are discussing a serious matter," said Colbert.

"I am sorry, but I couldn't help thinking of an ultra-sophisticated nobleman like the Marquis de la Vallière in charge of such a station among savage tribes."

"Madame, do you doubt his courage? I know for a fact that he has given many proofs of it in the King's service."

"It's not a question of courage, but of just what he would do if he landed on a beach there and saw a horde of stark naked savages descending upon him. He would butcher half of them and make the rest slaves."

"Slaves are a staple of trade. They can amortize an entire investment."

"I won't deny that, but it's not a good way to establish factories and found an industry in a country. You could say it's the methods the French use that block their success and get them massacred every so often after they have settled in a place."

Colbert gave her a not unappreciative look. "Devil take it, if I relied on . . ." He scratched his stubbly chin. "I have learned more in these ten minutes than in many sleepless nights spent poring over those damned reports."

"Sir, my advice is subject to caution. I listen to the recriminations of the merchants and the sailors, but . . ."

"You can't overlook what they say. Thank you, Madame. You would do me a great favor if you would consent to wait a half-hour for me in the antechamber."

"I can bear up for just about half an hour," she said.

She returned to the antechamber, where the Marquis de la Vallière informed her with malicious pleasure that Louvois had asked for her and then had gone to luncheon.

Angélique checked her gesture of disappointment. It was just her luck. She was especially eager for an interview with the young Minister of War to ask him for a position at Court, and now thanks to her unexpected meeting with Colbert, who had done nothing but talk about maritime trade, she had missed her opportunity. She had no time to lose. Who could tell what fiendish notion was even now germinating in Philippe's brain? If she resisted him too openly, it would not be at all beyond him to have her locked up. Husbands had absolute authority over their wives. She had to get firmly rooted here before it was too late.

Angélique almost stamped her foot with rage and disappointment. They doubled when she heard the courtiers say that His Majesty was postponing his audiences till the next day and that everyone might as well leave.

Just as she reached the exit, Colbert's clerk accosted her. "If Madame la Marquise will please follow me. They are waiting for her."

The room into which she was escorted had graceful proportions but it was less spacious than any of the salons. The only thing about it that was overpowering was the lofty ceiling which seemed to open on an Olympian expanse of blue and white clouds. At the two windows heavy draperies of dark blue silk embroidered with gold and silver fleur-de-lis matched the upholstery of the high-backed armchairs and the three footstools placed along one wall. Like all the other woodwork of Versailles this was appliquéd with gesso garlands and fruits and vine-leaves, which glistened dazzlingly under a brand new coat of gold leaf painstakingly applied to each excrescence of the moulding. The harmony of the dark blue and the gold gave the room a majestically sumptuous atmosphere. Angélique took it all in at a glance. It was definitely a man's room.

At the far end of the room Colbert was standing with his back toward her before a table made of a single slab of marble supported by gilded bronze legs that ended in lions' paws. On its opposite side was the King.

Angélique's mouth dropped open.

"Ah, here is my informant," said the Comptroller, turning. "Pray draw near, Madame, and tell His Majesty of your experiences as . . . as—well, a privateer in the East India Company. They throw great light on certain aspects of the situation."

With the courtesy he showed every woman, even the most humble, Louis XIV rose and bowed to her. In confusion Angélique recalled that she had not yet paid him due respect. She sank into a deep curtsy, cursing Colbert as she did so.

"I know you are not in the habit of joking, Monsieur Colbert," said the King, "but I never expected that your reporter of *viva voce* news from the sailors would appear under the guise of a lady of my Court."

"Madame du Plessis-Bellière is nonetheless a very important stockholder in the Company. She equipped a vessel with guns and intended to trade with the Indies, but she had to give it up and turn her efforts instead toward America. She is going to tell you the reasons for her change in plans."

"To tell the truth, sir," Angélique said, "I am sorry that you attached such importance to my story. It is true that I have investments in maritime trade. My manager of these investments frequently complains to me of the difficulties of his job, but I myself know no more about such matters than I do about farming, even though my tenants tell me long tales of woe about their poor harvests."

Colbert turned all the colors of the rainbow. "Is your little farce quite finished?" he exclaimed. "Just now you were talking to me in a highly informed manner, but now you are masquerading. Are you afraid to speak up before the King?"

The King had sat down again. He trusted his Comptroller and waited patiently for some enlightenment on this interview which still astonished him. He kept watching Angélique with a sober, perspicacious eye. She could read in his glance the cautious, fathoming wisdom that characterized most of his decisions. It was so unusual to find such a quality in a twenty-seven-year-old monarch that even yet few veteran diplomats were aware of it.

Like him, Angélique had changed from youth into maturity within a surprisingly short time. Still she had retained all the intuitive impressionability of the young. Between herself and the King she sensed the rapport of two quite realistic minds.

"I know Your Majesty has no liking for eccentricity. And it does seem to be unconventional for a lady of your Court to be involved in such things as commerce and shipping. I am afraid . . ."

"You need not fear our displeasure. Nor should you try to please us by wandering from the truth," said the King rather severely. "If Monsieur Colbert thinks your information can help us, it is not up to you to determine whether we take it well or ill. Pray speak out, Madame, and concern yourself only with the fact that it is your duty to serve our interests."

He did not ask her to be seated, in order to make clear to her that she was no better than her associates who, no matter what their age or station, might never sit in his presence unless he especially asked them to do so.

"So your ship gave up trading with the East Indies in spite of your desire to send it there and in spite of the profits you hoped to reap from its voyage. Most privateers, it must be acknowledged, have done the same. It is the reason for their reluctance to trade with the East that is still obscure to me."

Angélique began by describing the hazards presented by the Barbary pirates who swept the seas between Portugal and the coasts of Africa. For centuries their whole source of income had come from pillaging ships without convoys.

"Are you not exaggerating the danger of these pirates, Madame? I have heard many tales of voyages to the Indies made by French vessels sailing alone and less well armed than yours. Yet these returned in glory from such odysseys without complaint of anything untoward beyond such storms as were to be expected. I have here reports of their voyages, including their dates of sailing and of returning. Since others can do it, why do you make out that your ship could not?"

"Because it is a merchant ship, Sire. Compare the total amounts of tonnage and you will solve the mystery. Most of the ships that have been reported to you are warships, even though they may call themselves merchant vessels. They know they can escape the pirate galleys by their very speed. They leave their home ports with their holds practically empty and return in the same condition. Indeed they do escape the pirates and complete their voyages, but such an expedition is impossible on a commercial scale. A ship of heavy tonnage, laden to the gunwales with goods, is incapable of outdistancing the swift Algerian or Moroccan galleys. It's like a fat bettle attacked by ants. Often the guns can't find the range. Nothing is left but to repulse the boarders if possible. That is why, thanks to the sailors of the *Saint John the Baptist,* my ship has twice escaped the

pirates. But not without bloody battles both times—
once in the Gulf of Gascony, the other in the Atlantic
off Africa. Half my sailors were either wounded or killed.
I gave up . . ."

Colbert's face showed his satisfaction, and his admiration. Seldom had any matter been so clearly explained
to him.

The King was thinking. At length he said, "So it is a
matter of convoys?"

"Exactly. That's the way the Dutch and the English
manage."

"I have no love for those nations, but it would be
foolish for us not to borrow what is good from our
enemies' strategy. See to it, Colbert. From now on when
big merchant ships are sailing, they will be convoyed
by warships . . ." Angélique's doubtful expression
stopped him. "Well, Madame, is there something about
this plan that strikes you as imperfect?"

Irony lurked in his voice. Louis XIV could not bring
himself to take seriously the advice of such a pretty
woman. But Angélique did not yield.

"I believe, Sire, that Monsieur Colbert has not got out
of all his difficulties. Frenchmen do not like to travel in
groups. Each wants to go his own way. Some are ready to
put to sea just when others cannot find the money for
guns. Even the largest stockholders have yet to find a
means for negotiating the necessary agreements that
would make these important armadas possible."

Louis XIV leaned his hand hard on the table. "Now
they shall do so at the King's order."

Colbert hesitated a moment, then said: "Madame, this
may be incorrect information, but let me say that two
years ago when the Montevergue expedition was setting
sail for Ile Dauphine you could have asked for the
benefit of its protection on a voyage to the Indies."

"Your information is correct, sir, but we couldn't
reach an agreement, and I do not regret it."

"Why is that?"

"I did not wish to become involved in an expedition
that was doomed to failure."

The King colored slightly in spite of his self-disci-

pline. "Are you unaware that I ordered that expedition
to set out for the very purpose of giving assistance to
the launching of the East India Company and establish-
ing a port of call on Ile Dauphine?"

"It was an excellent idea, Sire, and such a port is indispensable. But the ships that set out were in a shocking
state of disrepair. They had been carelessly examined.
Their captains thought only of easy conquests, and disregarded the fact that the port where they would have
to put in is no Garden of Eden, or that they would have
to go at least fifty miles into the interior of the island
to get drinking water, or that the natives are very hostile. In short, those gentlemen were brave but imprac-
tical, even Monsieur de Montevergue, their leader. They
rushed headlong into the disastrous situation in which
they are right now."

The King's eyes were cold. There was a heavy silence
after Angélique had spoken. She was terrified at
what she might have said, yet she had spoken frankly
just as the King had told her to do.

"How does it happen, Madame," he said at last, "that
you alone knew of the disastrous situation that awaited
Monsieur de Montevergue in Ile Dauphine? His second
in command landed at Bordeaux four days ago. He was
at Versailles this morning. He had strict orders not to
talk to anyone before he had seen me. I suspended all
other business until I had interviewed him. He has just
left."

"Sire, it was no secret to seafaring men. During those
two years foreign ships putting in at Ile Dauphine have
frequently out of pity taken aboard the victims of that
expedition ravaged with scurvy or wounded by the
natives, and brought them back home."

Louis XIV stared at Colbert. "So it need not have
taken Monsieur de Montevergue two years to send me the
first report I have had of his expedition when he knew
I was impatient to have it."

"There would have been the devil to pay if I had had
to wait two years to learn the fate of my ship!" Angélique said.

"Hah!" exclaimed the King. "Do you mean to say,

Madame, that your system of communications runs more smoothly than that of the King of France?"

"In certain ways, yes, Sire. Your Majesty can communicate only by direct means. Two years is not too long for the same ship to go and return, not counting the time that officer had to remain at Ile Dauphine until he was rescued. Things happen differently with merchants. I made a bargain with the Dutch East India Company that when one of its ships passed mine we would exchange information."

"The Dutch again!" said the King humorously. "It would seem that for their own convenience French privateers enter into bargains that are close to treason against the realm, and consider them perfectly normal."

"Treason is too strong a word, Sire. Are we at war with the Netherlands?"

"Certainly not! But this is something that annoys me more than I can say, Monsieur Colbert. That France, *France*, do you hear, has to play second fiddle on the seas to those herring-fishermen!

"In the time of my grandfather, Henri IV, the French navy had a glorious name. Its strength was so great that the English, the Dutch and even the Venetians would borrow the French flag to sail in the Mediterranean. It assured them protection because of the 'understandings' between France and the Sublime Porte."

"There were more than a thousand ships in the Mediterranean fleet alone then," said Colbert.

"And now?"

"Fifty vessels with from twenty-four to one hundred twenty guns. All five classes of ships armed the same way—frigates, fire-ships, flutes, galleys. It is a shame, Sire."

The King leaned back in his armchair, and began to ponder the matter, his eyes on a spot far away. His thick, flowing brown hair, which he wore in natural style, was silhouetted against the blue upholstery on which was embroidered a gold crown surrounded by fleur-de-lis.

"I do not intend to ask you the reasons for our having come to this pass," he said after a while. "I know

them only too well. We have not finished correcting
all the evils that so many years of civil disorder brought
upon us. I was still very young when I began to cast
my eyes on all the diverse parts of my realm. Not un-
seeing eyes, but the eyes of the master. I was deeply
touched to find no one who did not need my help.
There was disorder everywhere. I resolved to be patient
and attack the most urgent matters first. The years went
by. The swollen rivers have now returned to their banks.
Now is the time to see to the Navy, Colbert."

"I shall devote myself to it, Sire."

The King had risen. The Comptroller bowed and
began to back out of his presence, stopping every three
steps to bow again.

"One word more, Colbert. Do not take amiss what I
am about to say to you, but lay it to the interest I have
in you and the friendship I bear you. Now that you
have been given the high functions that are yours, we
should be pleased to see you take greater care of your
appearance and your manners."

The Comptroller's hand went to his chin. "Forgive
me, Your Majesty. Pray consider how little time I have
apart from what I devote to you. I stayed up most of
the night reading that report of Montevergue. Besides,
I did not know that Your Majesty was remaining at
Versailles, and I had to leave home in a great hurry."

"I know your devotion to me is to blame, Monsieur
Colbert. Far be it from me to force you to waste time
on ribbons and laces except to increase their manufacture. But no matter how modest you yourself may be,
you should be proud of the high place you hold. The
honor of the throne and its prestige in the eyes of the
world can suffer from lack of elegance on the part of
those who are close to it. It is not enough to be, one
must also seem. Take note of that, if you please, and
. . . talk it over with Madame Colbert."

The smile of the King softened what could otherwise
have hurt. The Comptroller bowed again and withdrew.
Angélique, who had begun to feel terribly tired and
was starving, started to follow him.

The King called her back. "Please remain, Madame."

He was watching Angélique closely. "Will you be at the hunt tomorrow?"

"Sire, I intend to be indeed."

"I shall speak to the Marquis so that he may help you keep your good resolutions."

She breathed a sigh of relief. Her smile widened. "Under those conditions, Sire, I am sure I can be present."

At this moment the First Gentleman of the King's Command, the Duc de Charost, appeared. "Will His Majesty be present at the banquet, or does he wish to be served in private?"

"Since there's going to be a banquet, let us not disappoint the sightseers who have come to Versailles for it. Let us go to luncheon."

Angélique made a deep bow, then started once more for the door of the King's conference room.

His Majesty addressed her again. "I understand you have sons. Are they of an age to be in service?"

"Sire, they are still very young—six and eight years old."

"The same age as the Dauphin. He will soon be out from under female domination and will be put under the charge of a tutor. I should like him to have some playmates then to share his games and give him some competition."

Angélique bowed for the third time under the envious gaze of the assembled courtiers.

chapter 5

A VERITABLE army of servants under the command of their superior officers had laid the table and arranged the seating according to protocol. After he had inspected everything, the Grand Chamberlain opened the banquet hall to those members of the Court who wished to be present at the dining of His Majesty. They took their places in line in an order that had been previously determined, while in the antechambers and the corridors there gathered the ordinary mortals who were to be admitted for the mere sake of passing before the King's table.

The King himself appeared in the doorway, stopped a moment to incline his head by way of acknowledging the deep reverences of those already present, then entered the room with a smile and took his place at the table.

Presently Monsieur, his brother, dashed up and, bowing very low, gave the King his napkin.

In the antechamber the guards were urging the crowd to keep a passageway clear for a strange parade that moved forward like an ecclesiastical procession. An extremely tall guardsman led on servants carrying on their shoulders a huge reliquary draped with cloth of gold embroidered in silver. Behind them marched the High Steward, carrying his staff of office, the Gentleman Usher, the Gentleman Butler, and the other officers of the household staff, followed by their subordinates.

In the reliquary was the King's dish.

Slowly the crowd filed past the royal table—tradesmen and their wives from Paris, clerks, artisans, laborers, working girls—each extracting from the experience everything his memory could possibly retain. They seemed less impressed by the gorgeous display of crystal and the gold service than by the sight of the King of France dining in all his glory.

The King said little, but he missed nothing. Several different times Angélique saw him rise slightly to nod to a lady of the Court as she entered and waited for the Chamberlain to rush up to her with a footstool. But for other Court ladies, there was neither a nod nor a footstool. These were the more numerous—the "unseatable" of whom Angélique herself was one. Her legs were growing numb with fatigue.

Madame de Choisy, next to her, whispered: "I heard the King was talking to you about your boys just a while ago. How lucky you are, my dear! Don't hesitate for one moment. Your sons will go far if you train them like this to associate only with people of quality. They will get used early to being agreeable, and that manner of being completely at home anywhere, which only life at Court can give, will stay with them the rest of their lives. Look at my son, the Abbé. I brought him up that way ever since he was a tiny tot. He is not quite twenty, yet he has learned how to make his way so subtly that now he is on the verge of getting a bishopric."

Angélique, however, was for the moment less concerned about the future of Florimond and Cantor than she was about getting something to eat and, if possible, sitting down. She left the banquet hall as discreetly as she could, and fell in with a few ladies who had gathered around one of the card tables. Footmen were passing them platters of dainties in which the elegant ladies were foraging with their fingers without once taking their eyes off the cards.

A tall, heavy woman rose and kissed Angélique on both cheeks. It was the Grande Mademoiselle. "I am always delighted to see you, dear. It seems to me you have been rather snubbing the Court lately. Many times these last few months I have wondered where you were, but I did not dare ask the King. Between us, you know, every session begins badly and ends worse. Still, he is my cousin and we do understand each other. But you're here at last anyway. You look as if you were trying to find someone."

"If Your Highness will excuse me, I'm trying to find a place to sit down."

The generous princess looked around her in dismay. "You really can't sit here. Madame is with us."

"My rank does not allow me to sit in your presence either, Your Highness."

"There you are mistaken. You are a lady of the nobility and I am only a kind of granddaughter of France, through Henri IV, my grandfather. So you do have the right to sit in my presence either on a hassock or a footstool, and I would gladly let you. But with Madame here, who is a daughter of France through her marriage to Monsieur, it is absolutely impossible."

"I understand." Angélique let a little sigh escape her.

"But," continued the Grande Mademoiselle, "come and join our game. We're looking for another player. Madame d'Arignys has just left after losing every *sou* she had."

"How can I play without sitting down?"

"But you can sit down," said the Princess. "Come on now."

She led Angélique up to curtsy before Madame, who was encumbered with her cards in one hand, and a chicken wing in the other. She smiled absently at Angélique.

But Angélique had no sooner sat than Madame de Montespan sailed up and grabbed her arm. "Hurry, this is the time for me to present you to the Queen."

Angélique stammered out some excuse or other and dashed after her friend.

"Athenais," she said, trying to catch up with her, "you'll have to put me straight about all this footstool business. I don't know what they're talking about. When and why and under what conditions and with what rank can a Court lady set her behind down on a seat?"

"Almost never. Certainly not before the King, or before the Queen either, unless she belongs to the royal family. Still, there are all kinds of rules and all kinds of exceptions to the rules. Why, to have the right to sit on a footstool is everyone's dream, and has been ever since the time of the Druids. Then it was a privilege granted only to men, but it still survives and it has been extended to women also. The footstool is a symbol of the highest rank or of the highest favor. You get it only when you become a member of the King's or the Queen's household. But then, of course, there are special conditions."

"Such as?"

"Playing cards, for instance. If you are playing, you can sit even in the presence of the sovereigns. And also if you are doing needlework. You have to have your fingers busy about something that looks like work. Some get by with just holding a ribbon. You see, you can get around it by all sorts of means."

The Queen was in the hands of her women, who were arraying her and doing her hair for the evening's entertainments. On one table lay open the cases in which were some of the Crown jewels which she was trying on one by one—diamond chokers, earrings of pear-shaped oriental diamonds said to be the largest in the world, bracelets, tiaras.

Angélique made innumerable curtsies and kissed the Queen's hand. Then she withdrew a little. Her mind went back to the Infanta whom she had seen at St. Jean de Luz the evening of her marriage to the King. Where now were those silky ash-blonde locks combed over wire frames, the heavy Spanish skirts stretched, as befitted her ancient lineage, over huge farthingales? Now the Queen was gowned in the French style, which was less becoming to her full figure. Her porcelain skin with its delicate coloring, which the gloomy Spanish palaces had kept intact, was heavily rouged. Her nose could now be red from weeping and no one would notice it. Angélique was astonished at the way this poor homesick little woman had managed to retain so much of her natural majesty. In spite of her piety and her lack of wit, she had a certain light touch, and her Spanish temperament was clearly visible in her jealous rages and passion toward the King. She loved Court entertainments and the artificiality of life there, and the smallest sign of attention from the King completely delighted her simple soul.

Noticing that Angélique was staring at her, she said: "One should look that way, not this way." The diamond collar flashed from her throat.

Barcarole, who was playing in a corner with the Queen's lap dogs, winked at Angélique conspiratorially.

The weather was pleasant, and so everyone went for a stroll through the gardens. Then as soon as the lamps were lit everyone ran to his room to change his clothes.

Angélique dressed in the antechamber of the Queen's Maids of Honor. Madame de Montespan called her attention to the fact that the jewels she had brought were too simple for the Court. There was no time for her to send back to the Hôtel de Beautreillis in Paris for other ones; but two jewelers from Lombardy, who were attached to the Court, came to her rescue. For a modest rental they loaned their quite handsome wares for a few hours, but not until after their clients had signed a pile of papers guaranteeing that they would not disappear with the ornaments they had borrowed.

Angélique signed, and handed over the "modest" rental, which came to two hundred *livres.* For that amount she could have bought at least two fine bracelets. Then she went down to the great hall on the ground floor where the theatre had been set up.

The King had already taken his seat. The strict etiquette had not left a single bench available, and Angélique in the rear of the hall had to be content with sensing the action of the play from the bursts of laughter that came from the front rows.

"What do you think of Molière's message?" said a voice in her ear. "Very instructive, isn't it?"

The voice was so pleasant that Angélique thought she was dreaming when she turned to see Philippe standing near her. He was a vision in a suit of pink satin trimmed with silver braid. Only his high color and his blond mustache kept him from appearing ridiculous in it. He was smiling.

Angélique forced herself to reply casually. "It's one of Molière's quaintest, but from where I am I can't see a thing."

"What a pity. Let me help you to a better position."

He slipped an arm around her waist and led her along. People cheerfully moved out of their way. The high favor in which Philippe basked made others deferential to them. In addition his rank of Marshal granted him many prerogatives, such as being able to drive his coach into the courtyard of the Louvre or to sit in the King's presence. Nevertheless his wife did not enjoy these.

They easily found a place at the right of the stage. They still had to stand, but they could see perfectly.

"This is a good spot," Philippe said. "We can see the play, and the King can see us. What could be better?"

He had not taken his arm from Angélique's waist. Now he was leaning his face so close to hers that his silky locks tickled her cheek.

"Do you have to stand so close?" she whispered. After reflection she had decided that this new attitude of her husband was rather suspicious.

"Yes, I do. Your shocking behavior has put the King on guard. I do not want him to have any doubt whatever of my loyalty to him. His slightest wish is my command."

"Ah, so that's what it is!"

"That's what it is. Just keep on staring at me straight in the eye. Then no one can doubt that Monsieur and Madame du Plessis-Bellière are reconciled."

"Is that important too?"

"The King wishes it."

"Oh, you are . . ."

"Be still."

His arm was like a band of steel although his voice was level.

"You're squeezing me. Don't be such a brute!"

"How I would like to be. Be patient, perhaps I yet may be. But this is not the time or the place . . . Look, Arnulphe is making Agnès read the eleven rules of conduct for marriage. Listen closely, Madame."

Angélique found it impossible to pay as full attention to the play as she wished. It bothered her to have Philippe so close to her. "If I could only believe," she thought, "that he was holding me tight without any grudges, without even remembering our quarrels."

She half wanted to turn to him and say: "Philippe, let's stop acting like surly, spoiled children. We have lots of things in common that could hold us together. I truly believe it. You are still the big cousin I worshiped and dreamed about when I was a girl."

She stole a glance at him, surprised to find that his concern for her had not affected his magnificent body, so virile in spite of his effeminate costume. Let the scandal-mongers spread all the hideous tales they wanted about the Marquis du Plessis-Bellière, he was no petty noble, no Chevalier de Lorraine. He was the god of war himself—Mars, hard, implacable, and cold as marble.

He wore his vices as he did his clothes, with assurance and style and even perhaps with a secret boredom. But behind this front was all the passionate warmth of a man who seemed devoid of the most basic feelings. Angélique could not help feeling that she was no more than a wooden statue to him. It was a depressing thought.

In *The School for Wives* Molière was writing of all men, whether businessmen or gentlemen, who storm when they are deceived, yet make themselves ridiculous for the sake of a pair of sparkling eyes and change color whenever a pretty girl leans against them flirtatiously. But on a man like Philippe du Plessis-Bellière all the great playwright's knowledge of human nature seemed lost. How could she reach him?

"Molière is very facile," Philippe said a little later when, the play being over, they were returning to the ballroom by way of the gardens. "He never forgets that he is writing for the King and the Court, so he puts everything in terms of the common people. But he knows human nature so well that everyone can recognize himself in these characters without giving himself away."

"Philippe is not so stupid after all," Angélique thought.

He had taken her arm. She grew apprehensive.

"Don't act as if I were going to burn you," Philippe

said. "I agree not to embarrass you in public. In hunting the idea is to box one's game into an inescapable position and then face it. Well, let's get to the point. You won the first round in forcing me to marry you. I won the second by punishing you slightly, less than you deserved. You won again by coming to Versailles in spite of my forbidding it, and being received there. I acknowledge that. Now we go into the next match. I won the first round in kidnaping you. You won the second by escaping, I should really like to know how. In short, we're even. Who is going to win the next match?"

"That's up to fate."

"And the strength of one's weapons. Perhaps you will win again. Your chances are good. But I want to warn you of one thing, I will win in the end. I have a wide reputation for being persistent and sticking to my guns. How much will you bet that some day you will end up, thanks to me, spinning thread in a convent, with no hope of ever getting out?"

"How much will you bet that some day you are going to be madly in love with me?"

Philippe froze. His breathing was heavy, as if this suggestion had overwhelmed him with anger.

"All right, let's make a bet," said Angélique, "since you proposed it. If you win, I shall give you all my money, my business and my ships. What good will they do me if I am to be shut up in a convent, starved, and reduced to babbling idiocy by your torments?"

"You're laughing," he said, staring at her. "Well, go ahead and laugh!" he added menacingly.

"What am I supposed to do? I can't weep all the time."

Still tears sprang to her eyes. As she raised her head to return his stare, he saw at the base of her slender throat, under the necklace she had rented, the bruises he had given her.

"If I win, Philippe," she murmured, "I shall demand that you give me the gold chain which has been in your family since the days of the first kings, and which the eldest son in each generation is supposed to hang about the neck of his fiancée. I don't exactly recall the legend that is attached to it, but I know they say in the country it has magic powers and gives the Plessis-Bellière women courage and virtue. You had no use for this tradition."

"You had no need for it," Philippe answered quickly. And leaving her there, he strode away toward the palace.

So many thoughts raced through Angélique's brain on her return trip that the journey in the hack from Versailles to Paris seemed short. She could hardly believe that three whole days had gone by. All her new experiences at Versailles had raised her to a fever pitch of excitement, had fascinated her and worried her, but had clearly delighted her as well. It would take her a long time to sort out all her many different impressions. The pomp and the merry-making this time had overruled the hubbub of that highly conventionalized society which was usually as formally organized as a ballet and as likely to erupt as a smoking volcano.

The comparative calm of her hôtel on the Rue Beautreillis was a comfort. Her joints were stiff from all the thousands of curtsies she had had to make; a courtier's life, she concluded, must do a great deal for keeping one's muscles supple even into advanced age. She was out of training.

Angélique had a light supper of soup, a ragout of carp roe and blanched barley, and a salad of cabbage shoots that were then called broccoli. She went to bed and slept soundly.

In the morning the first thing she did was to write her father in Poitou, entreating him to come to Paris at once with all her servants and her two sons, Florimond and Cantor, who had been in his charge for several months. But when she rang for her private letter carrier, Roger reminded her that he had disappeared several days ago with the horses, as had all the stable help. Madame le Marquise had forgotten that her stables were empty of carriages, horses and men except for two sedan chairs.

It was hard for Angélique to restrain herself before her servant. She told Roger to discharge every one of those traitors when they came back, and withhold their last wages. Roger remarked that there was little chance

of ever seeing them again, for they had already been
hired by Monsieur le Marquis du Plessis-Bellière. Besides, he explained, most of them had seen nothing
wrong in taking the horses and carriages of the Marquise
to the Marquis' stables.

"I am the one who gives orders here!" said Angélique.

She told Roger to get to the Place de Grève as quickly
as possible and hire some new footmen, then to the fair
at Saint-Denis for some horses—four, plus two saddle-
horses for spares. Then he was to go to the carriage-
maker at the sign of the Gilded Wheel who had made
her former coaches. It was like throwing money out
the window. Philippe had committed a theft, no more
no less. Why couldn't she turn him over to the sergeants
of the night-watch or to a court of justice? No, there
was nothing for her but to submit, and that was the
hardest thing for her to do.

"What about the letter that Madame le Marquise
wishes sent to Poitou?" asked Roger.

"Get it there by the fastest public post possible."

"The public post does not leave till Wednesday."

"That doesn't matter. The letter can wait."

To calm her nerves Angélique had herself carried
in a sedan chair to the Quai de la Mégisserie, where
her tropical bird shop was. She selected a gaudily plum-
aged parrot that swore like a pirate, reflecting that this
would not offend the ears of Athenais. Quite the contrary, as a matter of fact.

She also added to her gift a little Negro dressed as
gaudily as the bird in an orange turban, a green waistcoat, red breeches, and red stockings with gold cloches.
What with patent-leather shoes as shiny as his face, he
looked like one of those wooden Venetian torchères
that had just come into vogue.

Angélique knew Madame de Montespan would appreciate her generosity. It was well worth while. So long as
those fools were determined to see her as the next favorite, however faulty their information, Athenais was
almost the only one who could steer her on the right
course. How stupid people are, she thought!

The following day Angélique decided that she could not do without the atmosphere of the Court, and set out for Saint-Germain-en-Laye, which for three years now Louis XIV had made his favorite residence.

chapter 6

*A*FTER the first snowfall, which came early that year, the Court moved to Fontainebleau, where the peasants had besought the aid of their feudal lord, the King of France, to help them rid the countryside of ravaging wolves.

The gray clouds hung low as the long line of coaches, vans, men on foot and on horseback, filed past fields that slept under an unspotted blanket of white. An entire city was on the march, transporting everything from the "King's Mouth" to the King's chapel to the King's apartments adjoining those of the Queen, the tennis court, the guardhouse, the hunting equipment, even sumptuous tapestries to deaden the clammy chill of the walls. They would be there for a week's wolf-hunt, and there would be balls, plays and delightful late suppers in the Spanish fashion, called "midnights."

As night came on, the pitch torches were lighted, and the procession arrived at the gates in a kind of shower of dripping flame.

Angélique was looking everywhere for Philippe—whether because she wanted to see him or was afraid to, she could not decide. She had no reason to suppose that any good would come from their meeting; he would have nothing for her but harsh words and sour looks. Probably it was better that he did ignore her and was far less chivalrous to her than to any other woman in the Court. He seemed to have forgotten her existence, but perhaps that was simply a truce inspired by the King's suggestion. She kept herself continually on the alert, for she knew that when she did see Philippe she would not be able to suppress her complex feelings toward him of humble admiration and secret hope that her dreams of long ago might come true. Then she was just a gawky little girl enraptured by her glamorous blond cousin.

"How long," she thought, "the dreams of childhood take to die!"

The first day she was at Fontainebleau there was no sign of Philippe. He was too busy preparing the hunt. The courtiers were trying to outdo one another in telling how terrorized the peasants were by the savage wolves. Sheep had been carried off right from the fold. A ten-year-old child had been attacked and devoured. An especially dangerous pack seemed to be led by a huge male—"as big as a cow," said the locals, who had seen him prowling on the very edges of the hamlets. Nothing daunted him. At night you could hear him snarling and slavering at the cottage doors, while inside the children clung to their mothers and sobbed with terror. No one went out after dark.

The hunt suddenly took on the impassioned dimensions of a crusade as everyone prepared to attack this monster. Hundreds of peasants showed up armed with spears and pitchforks to help the whippers-in keep the hounds on the scent. No one stayed behind.

Tales of such animals were the common experience of everyone. Hardly a one of the courtiers and ladies had not frozen with fear in their childhood at stories of their depredations under the very walls of their castles. They inherited a hatred of these bold raiders, the scourge of the countrysides, who spared neither noble nor serf if he foolhardily wandered from the highways.

The horns of the hunt woke the echoes of the great rocks and cliffs of the forest of Fontainebleau, and even the marble domes of the summer-houses and the icicle-fringed balconies.

Angélique had just emerged into a snow-carpeted clearing enclosed by such a rocky palisade that it was like being at the bottom of a mossy well. The brave music of the horns was wafted here in so harmonious a blend of notes that its melody awoke in her the sweet melancholy of the memory of old, forgotten, far-off things. She reined in her horse and listened.

Ah, the forest! How long it had been since she had thrilled to its magic! The raw wind, laden with the

sweet scents of death—rotted wood and mouldering
leaves—swept away in an instant all her years amid the
clamorous stench of Paris and took her back to her
joyous early days in the forest of Nieul. Still clinging to
the black boughs were scattered clutches of russet and
crimson leaves, and the snow that rustled down from
the higher branches with the soft murmur of a woodland spring set off these bright tones and made them
sparkle in the glimmers of the wintry sun as if they
were strewn with diamond dust. The bright red beads
of a holly bush peeped out from the underbrush. How,
she recalled, she used to gather great armfuls of holly
back at Monteloup around Christmas time! So long
ago! Could just one little sprig bridge the chasm that lay
between Angélique de Sancé and Angélique du Plessis-
Bellière?

"Life never robs us of ourselves," she murmured to
herself. A shiver of emotion ran through her, as if she
had heard tidings of great joy.

Immature, perhaps, but then she had never put away
those childish thrills no woman can do without. To relish them once more was a luxury she could now easily
afford.

Slipping down from her mare and tossing Ceres' reins
over a hazel branch, she ran to the holly bush. From
among the jeweled gewgaws that hung from her belt she
selected a little pearl-handled penknife that she used
for paring fruit. It would be just the thing.

She did not notice that the sound of the horns and
the shouting of the hunters had drifted farther and farther away, nor observe how skittish Ceres had become,
until with a whinny of fright the mare yanked the reins
from the hazel bush and galloped off in a frenzy.

"Ceres!" Angélique called. "Ceres!"

Then she perceived what had caused the mare to
dash away. Across the clearing, half-hidden in the
thickets, prowled a sinister form.

"The wolf!"

The instant she had stepped out of the shelter of the
bushes on to the untrodden snow she realized that there
crouched the terror of the countryside, his back arched

and his shaggy pelt bristling. Without making the slightest movement he fixed on Angélique eyes that glowed with the evil fire of a demon's. Huge was he indeed, and as gray and russet as the forest tones themselves.

Angélique let out a piercing scream.

The beast leaped up, backed off a bit, then slowly crept toward her, his slavering jaws baring fearful fangs. At any moment he would spring upon her.

Angélique glanced over her shoulder at the high wall of rock that towered above her. "I must get up it. Just as high as I can."

Gathering all her courage, she managed to scale its lowest ridge. Then she could go no further. Her nails slipped on the sheer surface. She could find no handhold.

The wolf had sprung, but had reached only the hem of her dress. Crouched again, he lay in wait for her to fall, never taking his baleful, bloodshot eyes from her.

She screamed again at the top of her lungs. Her heart was pounding so violently that she could hear nothing but its deafening drumbeat. With frantic haste she tried to piece together the words of a prayer: "Lord! Lord God, don't let me die like this . . . Do something, oh God, do something . . . !"

Suddenly a horse dashed up and skidded to a stop in a cloud of flying snow. Its rider jumped to the ground. As if she were dreaming Angélique saw the great wolf-hunter, her husband Philippe du Plessis-Bellière. He seemed to take in the extraordinary situation in one second. A silver-trimmed white buckskin jacket girdled his body, and the fur at its neck and cuffs was the color of his own blond hair. Steadily his silver-spurred white leather boots moved forward. His hands were bare, for he had stripped off his gauntlets before dismounting. In his grip was the silver haft of a long slim hunting knife.

The wolf turned upon this new adversary. Slowly, relentlessly, Philippe moved toward it. When he was two yards away the beast sprang, its scarlet gullet yawning beyond its knife-sharp fangs.

With a lightning movement Philippe thrust forward

his left arm, wrapping it like a tentacle around the wolf's throat. With his knife he slit its belly from haunch to breast. The beast writhed with blood-curdling guttural snarls as its lifeblood spurted like a geyser. At length its death-struggles grew weaker. Philippe heaved the panting carcase aside, trailing its guts over the snow as it fell.

From every quarter now the whippers-in and the horsemen were dashing into the clearing. The lackeys kept the howling pack from the carcase.

"Good work!" said the King to Philippe.

In the confusion the plight of Angélique had escaped notice. She took advantage of this distraction to slide down from the cliff, clean her skinned hands and pick up her hat. One of the whippers-in led her horse back to her. He was an old man who had grown gray in his service as King's huntsman and had a blunt manner of speaking. Having followed close upon Philippe's heels, he had arrived in time to see the end of the struggle.

"You had a good fright, didn't you, Madame?" he said. "We knew the wolf was over here somewhere, and when we saw your horse come back with empty stirrups and heard you scream . . . ! On my honor, Madame, it was the first time I ever saw our Master of the Hunt turn pale—deathly white."

It was not until the feast that followed the hunt that Angélique met Philippe. It had been impossible for her to join him ever since the moment when in his bloody hunting jacket he had thrown her a furious look before remounting his horse. Doubtless he had wanted to give her a couple of good slaps. Nonetheless she admitted that a wife who has had her life saved by her husband owes him a thank-you at least.

"Philippe," she said as soon as she could get his attention between two courses at the banquet, "I am much obliged to you. If it hadn't been for you, it would have been all up with me."

He waited to set his empty wineglass on a tray that a footman was passing before he grasped her wrist so tightly she thought he would snap it.

"If you don't know how to follow a hunt any better than that," he whispered crossly, "you had better stay home with your needlework. You are always putting me into embarrassing situations. You're nothing but a crude peasant, an uneducated shopkeeper. Someday I'll find a way of having you expelled from the Court, and getting quit of you."

"Then why didn't you let the wolf tend to business, as he was so eager to do?"

"I had to kill the wolf. What happened to you was no concern of mine. Don't laugh, you are exasperating. You are just like all women, thinking you are irresistible and that everyone is willing to die for you gladly. I'm not that kind of man. Someday you'll learn, if you haven't done so already, that I am a wolf too."

"I don't doubt it, Philippe."

"I can prove it to you," he said with a frigid smile that foretold bad things to come. Then he took her hand with a tenderness she suspected and raised it to his lips. "The barrier you raised between us on our wedding day, Madame—hatred, rancor, revenge—can never be removed. Take that as a fact."

Her delicate hand was against his mouth. Suddenly he bit it savagely.

Angélique had to summon all her self-control to keep from screaming with pain. In pulling away from him she kicked Madame, who was rising from the table. She cried out.

Angélique turned from scarlet to white as she stammered: "Pray forgive me, Your Highness."

"How clumsy you are, my dear."

To which Philippe added snidely: "You must be a little more careful how you move, Madame. The wine has been too much for you."

His eyes were gleaming wickedly. He bowed very low before the princess, then left the women to join the King, who was moving toward the salons.

Angélique tied her lace handkerchief over the marks his teeth had left on her hand. The pain had made her faint. Dizzily she groped her way through the throng and reached a vestibule where the air was cooler. There she sank on to the first sofa she came to in a bay window. Cautiously she removed the bandage and rolled it into a ball. Her hand was turning blue, and pinheads of dark blood were oozing from the wound. How fiendish he had been to bite her like that, and how scandalous his insinuation! "Be careful how you move, the wine has been too much for you." Now the gossip would start that Madame du Plessis had been so drunk she had jostled Madame. She would be put down as too inexperienced to be in society.

The Marquis de Lauzun passed by and recognized her. "Now I am really going to scold you," he said. "Alone again! Always alone! And at Court, and as beauteous as the day, too! Taking sanctuary in this corner that is so hidden away they call it Venus' laboratory. Alone this way, you defy the most basic rules of pleasant company, not to mention the laws of nature."

He sat down beside her, as if he were a father scolding his little daughter. "What is troubling you, my darling? What melancholy demon has so possessed you that you are determined to spurn all our compliments and isolate yourself from the devotion we would so gallantly offer you? Have you forgotten that Heaven has given you incomparable charm? Do you want to repudiate that gift of God? Ah, what's this I see? Angélique, my darling, don't take it so seriously." Putting his finger under her chin, he turned her face up to him. "You're weeping. Is it because of a man?"

Spasmodic sobs so choked her she could only nod her head.

"Why, why," said Lauzun, "that's a crime. You should be making others weep. My lamb, there isn't a man here worth the salt in your tears. Even I, though I still hope . . ."

Angélique tried hard to smile. Presently she found her voice again. "Oh, it really isn't so bad. I'm just nervous. I don't feel well."

"Where?"

She showed him her hand.

"What monster did that?" Péguilin exclaimed in outrage. "Tell me his name, Madame, and I shall demand satisfaction."

"Don't bother, Péguilin. He has, I'm sorry to say, complete authority over me."

"Do you mean your husband, the handsome Marquis?" Angélique only burst into tears again.

"Ah, what more can you expect from a husband," said Péguilin in disgust. "That's just the thing about him that made you choose him. But why are you so determined to keep on seeing him?"

Angélique sobbed all the harder.

"Come, come, now," Péguilin said tenderly, "don't go on like this. For a man, and just for a husband? You're out of style, my jewel, or out of your head. For a long time now you've been carrying on in this unnatural way, and I want to take this chance to talk to you about it. But first dry your eyes."

He took out a spotless square of lawn and gently wiped her cheeks and eyes. She looked up at the cheerful wisdom of his expression which the entire Court including the King himself had learned to watch for signs of coming mischief. His worldly life, his excesses, had already scarred the corners of his mouth with lines of irony, yet his face as a whole radiated his love of life and his inner happiness. He was from the South, a Gascon, sunny as the livelong day and as lively as a trout in a mountain stream.

She sighed once more, then looked at him sweetly. He smiled.

"Feeling better?"

"A little."

"We'll fix everything up," he said.

A moment went by in which he studied her in silence. They were screened from the eternal passing-by of the courtiers and servants in the corridor. The alcove was a little off the beaten track, and its space was entirely filled by the sofa whose high armrests hid them from the gaze of the curious. The crimson rays of the setting sun streamed on them through the window as the early

winter twilight deepened. Beyond, the marble urns on
the terrace and the frozen pools of the fountains glimmered faintly in the evening mist.

"So this is known as Venus' laboratory?" said Angélique, her voice still unsteady from her emotion.

"Yes, here we are sheltered, as much as anyone can
be at Court, from inquisitive eyes. It's common knowledge that too impatient lovers often come here to offer
their sacrifice to the goddess. Angélique, don't you
think you are wrong to ignore her?"

"Ignore the goddess of love? Péguilin, I am more inclined to blame her for neglecting me."

"I'm not so sure," he said dreamily.

"What do you mean?"

He shook his head, then leaned his chin on his finger
as if thinking deeply. "Damn Philippe," he sighed, "who
will ever know what's hidden beneath that rascal's hide?
Haven't you ever tried to slip some medicinal powder
into his wineglass some evening to keep him away from
you? They say La Vienne, who runs the public baths
on the Rue du Faubourg Saint-Honoré, has potions to
restore vigor to lovers exhausted by too frequent sacrifices, as well as for old lechers and those whose temperament is too cold for worship at Venus' altar. I have
heard marvelous things about one of those substances
called *polleville*."

"I don't doubt it, but I don't care for such methods.
You see, I should need a chance to get near enough to
Philippe to touch his—wineglass. That does not often
happen."

Péguilin's eyes popped. "You can't mean that your
husband is so utterly indifferent to your charms that he
never comes to visit you?"

"Yes," Angélique sighed, "it's true."

"But . . . what is your so-called husband thinking of?"

"I don't know."

"What! Well, then . . . what about your—er—lovers?"

Angélique did not answer.

"Do you mean to tell me you have none?"

"I do indeed, Péguilin. It is the truth."

"Impos—si—ble!" Péguilin looked as if he had just got news of a mighty catastrophe. "Angélique, you ought to be spanked."

"Why?" she protested. "It is not my fault."

"It is entirely your fault. With your complexion, your eyes, your figure, you have only yourself to blame for this mess. You are an unnatural creature, exasperating and formidable." He put his finger to his forehead. "What goes on in your naughty little head? Nothing but schemes and politics and business deals daring enough to stagger Colbert and even Tellier? A conservative businessman would box your ears, and a young one would be so dazzled he would not know how to keep you from getting your hands on his last penny. And on top of all that, the face of an angel, eyes that drown a man in their radiant depths, lips that one only has to look at to want to devour with kisses! Your cruelty is an exquisite torture. You are like a goddess revealed in a vision. And for whom? Tell me!"

Angélique was baffled by his vehemence. "I have enough to do," she said.

"And what the devil more can a woman have to do than make love? Really, you are just an egoist imprisoned in a tower of your own making to protect yourself."

His perspicacity astonished her. "That's only partly true, Lauzun. How could anyone know what I am really like? You have never been in hell."

Suddenly she felt very tired. She leaned her head back and closed her eyes. A few moments ago she had been boiling hot, now the blood in her veins ran cold. It was like the onslaught of old age. She wanted to cry out to Péguilin for help, yet her better judgment told her he would rescue her only to lead her into greater dangers. She decided to move to safer ground.

Straightening up, she asked playfully: "By the way, Péguilin, you haven't told me whether you finally got your appointment as Grand Master."

"No," Péguilin said tonelessly.

"Why not?"

"You have tried to put me off before, but this time I'm not going to get caught. You aren't through with me yet. Right now, my appointment as Grand Master doesn't interest me in the least—only how you can rule your life from your calculating head, and not from here." He laid his hand on her breast.

"Péguilin!" she protested, standing up.

He caught her to him, and tipping her against his right arm, slipped his left hand under her knees so that she lost her balance and fell back upon the sofa with him leaning upon her bosom.

"Be still," he ordered her, "and relax. Let the doctor diagnose your trouble. It's serious, but not hopeless. Come now, tell me the names of all those noble lords who swarm about you and lie tossing the night through at the very thought of you."

"My word, do you think there are that many?"

"I forbid you to act so surprised!"

"But Péguilin, I swear I don't know what you're referring to."

"Do you mean you did not even notice the Marquis de la Vallière fluttering like a mad butterfly when you appeared? Or Vivonne, Athenais' brother, faltering like a schoolboy? Or Brienne's compliments? Or Saint-Aignan or Roquelaure, or even the bold Louvois turning pale when talking to you?"

She giggled with pleasure.

"I forbid you to laugh," interrupted Péguilin. "If you haven't noticed all that, you are further gone than I thought. Haven't you felt the heat of the flames you have kindled? By Beelzebub, I think you must have the hide of a salamander." He tickled her neck with his finger.

"You did not mention yourself as one of those on fire, Monsieur de Lauzun."

"Not I," he said quickly. "I would never dare. I am too scared."

"Of me?"

His eyelids drooped. "Yes, of you . . . and of everything about you. Your past, your future, your mystery."

Angélique stared at him for a moment, then with a tremor buried her face against his blue coat. "Péguilin!"

He was such an old friend, Péguilin the gay, bound

up with all the drama of her former life. In every one
of her crises he had popped up like a puppet in a
Punch and Judy show—appearing, disappearing, reap-
pearing. And now here he was again, just as always.

"No, no, no," he replied. "I don't like such risks. The
pangs of heartache terrify me. Don't expect me to make
love to you."

"What are you doing now?"

"Comforting you. It's not the same thing at all." His
finger traced little curlicues down the length of her
silken throat, then followed the line of her necklace of
rosy pearls gleaming lustrously against her milk-white
skin. "You've been so badly treated, and tonight you
have such grief to bear. My God, what do they want to
do, abuse you till you're tough as a swordblade? Anyone
would think no man's hand had ever touched you. Oh,
how I would like to give you a little lesson . . ."

He leaned toward her. She tried again to escape, but
he held her too tightly. His eyes glittered like a man's
who has lost all hope of salvation.

"We have teased you enough, my pet. The hour for
revenge has struck. Besides I am dying to comfort you,
and I know you need consolation badly." He began to
kiss her eyelids lightly, then her temples. Then his hot
lips pressed against the corner of her mouth.

A tremor ran through her as the sudden lash of an
animal passion struck her. A perverse curiosity tempted
her to test the talents of this Don Juan of the Court.

Péguilin was right. Philippe meant nothing to her.
The empty charade of the Court was all that mattered
to her now. She knew she could never live again on the
edge of things, alone, for all her beautiful gowns and
costly jewels. She would gradually become like the rest,
exist as they did, caught in the same whirlpool of intrigues and adultery. It was a heady draught, poisoned
perhaps, but sweet to the taste. She would have to drink
deep of it or die.

A sigh welled up from within her. The curing touch
of his caresses was overcoming her inhibitions. When
Lauzun's mouth touched hers she little by little opened
her lips until she had wholly yielded to their passion.

A flash of light from the torches that two troops of servants were bringing to fix in brackets along the walls of the corridor separated them for a moment. Angélique had forgotten that darkness had enclosed them. A servant set a six-branched candelabra on a table near their alcove.

"Hey, boy," whispered Péguilin, leaning over the arm of the sofa, "take your lantern further off."

"I cannot, sir. My boss would bawl me out."

"Then blow out three of your candles," said Lauzun, tossing him a gold piece.

He took Angélique into his arms again. "How lovely you are! How sweet to all the senses!"

Anticipation had driven them crazy. Angélique groaned and bit the silken epaulette of his blue coat. Péguilin laughed softly.

"Easy, my little vixen. You'll get what you want."

She yielded to him. The golden veil of voluptuous oblivion descended gently over them. She was merely an ardent body, greedy with desire, unconscious of where she was or even of the partner whose practiced touch made her whole being quiver.

"My child, you have grievously sinned, but in consideration of the repentance you have made and the zeal with which you have tried to mend your ways, I believe it is my duty to grant you the blessing of little god Eros, and his absolution. For penance you shall recite . . ."

"You are terrible," she giggled, still languishing in his arms.

Péguilin separated a lock of her blond hair and pressed it to his lips. Privately he was amazed at his own delight in her. He felt none of the melancholy that follows satiation. Why? he wondered. What kind of woman was this?

"Angélique, angel, I fear I have forgotten all my good resolutions. I am burning to know more. Will you come to me tonight after the King retires? I beg you to."

"What about Madame de Roquelaure?"

"To hell with her!"

Angélique raised herself from his shoulder on which

she had been leaning, and drew the lace of her bodice over her bosom—a gesture designed to keep him in suspense.

A few steps away from them, silhouetted in black against the glow of the lighted corridor, was the motionless figure of a man. There was no need for them to see his features to identify him. It was Philippe.

Péguilin de Lauzun was fully experienced in situations like this. Quickly he adjusted his garments, rose and bowed deeply. "Sir, your seconds? I am at your service."

"And my wife is at everyone's service," Philippe replied slowly. "Please, my dear Marquis, don't disturb anyone." He bowed as deeply as Péguilin had, and strode away.

The Marquis de Lauzun seemed changed into a pillar of salt. "The devil," he swore, "I've never met a husband like that before." Drawing his sword, he took the three steps of the platform in one bound and dashed after the Master of the Hunt.

Still running, he burst into the Salon of Diana at the very moment at which the King, followed by the ladies of his family, was coming from his audience chamber.

"Sir," shouted Péguilin in ringing tones, "your contempt is insulting. I demand satisfaction. Your sword must answer for you."

Philippe lowered his icy gaze on his gesticulating rival. "My sword is at the service of the King, sir. I never fight over a whore."

In his rage Lauzun had relapsed into his native dialect. "I have cuckolded you, sir," he shouted, "and I demand satisfaction from you!"

chapter 7

*I*N THE ashy gray dawn Angélique sat on the edge of her bed. Her head throbbed and her mouth tasted sour. She ran her fingers through her tangled hair. Her scalp hurt her. She started to get a looking-glass from her dressing table but winced with pain. Her hand was badly swollen. She looked dully at the wound and suddenly remembered Philippe.

She leaped from the bed and stumbled about in her high-heeled slippers. She must get the latest news about Philippe and Lauzun at once. Had the King talked them out of a duel? If they had fought, what fate awaited the survivor? Arrest, prison, disgrace?

No matter how she looked at it, she was trapped in a dreadful situation. A scandal, a frightful scandal. She was burning with shame at the very thought of what had transpired at Fontainebleau.

Back to her mind came the vision of Lauzun and Philippe drawing their swords and calling *en garde* right before the King's eyes. De Gesvres, de Crequi and de Montausier had separated them, and Montausier had pinioned the arms of the fuming Gascon who was screaming, "I have cuckolded you, sir!" while all the eyes of the Court turned toward her as she stood crimson with embarrassment in her magnificent apricot-colored gown.

She could not now recall what miracle had prompted her to approach the King as if to speak to him and the Queen, make her deepest curtsy and then withdraw, holding herself erect, between two banks of jeering and scandalized faces, whispers, stifled laughter and finally a silence so complete and terrifying that she was tempted to gather up her skirts and flee on the run. But she had kept her dignity to the very end, and had made her exit without haste. Then, more dead than alive, she had sunk upon a bench on an empty, poorly lit stair-landing.

There Madame de Choisy joined her a few moments later. Swallowing hard like a shocked pigeon, this noble lady informed the Marquise du Plessis-Bellière that His Majesty was in the process of lecturing Monsieur de Lauzun in private, and that the Prince had taken charge of the deceived husband, and that everyone hoped this unseemly quarrel would end there. Of course, Madame du Plessis would understand that her presence at Court was no longer desired. Madame de Choisy had been instructed by the King to advise her of the necessity of leaving Fontainebleau at once.

Angélique received the verdict with a kind of relief. She had rushed into her coach and had driven all night long in spite of the grumbling of her coachman and lackeys, who were afraid to drive through the forest lest they be attacked by bandits.

"It's just my luck," she said to herself as she gazed bitterly at the dark circles under her eyes. "Every day and every night innumerable women at Court deceive their husbands with all the ease in the world, and the one time I try it, lightning strikes. No luck whatever!"

On the verge of tears, she yanked the bell cord. Javotte and Thérèse appeared, yawning and rubbing their eyes. She ordered them to help her dress, then sent for Flipot and told him to run to the hôtel of the Marquis du Plessis, in the Rue Faubourg Saint-Antoine, and hurry back with all the news he could glean.

She was finishing dressing when the noise of a coach turning slowly into the courtyard of her hôtel froze her. Her heart was pounding. Why should anyone come to see her at six in the morning? Who could it be? She rushed into the hall, went down a few stairs cautiously, and leaned over the bannister.

It was Philippe, followed by La Violette holding two swords and leading the Marquis' confessor. Philippe raised his head.

"I have just killed Monsieur de Lauzun," he said.

Angélique gripped the bannister to keep from falling. Her heart started pounding again. Philippe was alive!

She ran down the stairs. As she drew near her husband she could see his shirt-front and waistcoat spotted with blood. For once he could not swish his cloak, for he was cradling his right arm in his other hand.

"You are wounded," she said faintly. "Is it serious? Oh, Philippe, come, let me bandage you, please!"

Almost supporting him, she led him to her own room. He must have been quite exhausted, for he made no comment, merely dropped heavily into an armchair and closed his eyes. His face was as white as her collar.

Angélique's hands shook as she picked up her sewing kit, extracted her scissors and began to cut away the blood-stiffened cloth. Meanwhile she was shouting at the servants to fetch hot water, lint, powders, salves and the Queen of Hungary's elixir.

"Drink this," she said as soon as Philippe revived a little.

The wound did not seem deep. It was a long rip from the right shoulder to the left breast, but it had not penetrated much beyond the surface of the skin. Angélique washed it and applied a mustard plaster, powdered lobster shell, and a poultice.

Philippe endured these administrations without moving a muscle, even when the mustard plaster was applied. He seemed to be deep in thought.

"I wonder how this matter of etiquette will be decided," he said at last.

"What etiquette?"

"My arrest. In principle, the Captain of the King's Bodyguards is supposed to arrest duellists. But the Captain is none other than the Marquis de Lauzun. He cannot arrest himself, can he?"

"Hardly, since he is dead," said Angélique with a nervous laugh.

"He hasn't a scratch."

"But didn't you just tell me . . . ?"

"I wanted to see whether you would faint."

"I was not going to swoon over Péguilin de Lauzun. I was shocked to be sure, but it is you, Philippe, who were wounded."

"I had to do my best to stop that foolishness. I was not

going to destroy a twenty-year friendship with Péguilin over such a trifle."

She turned white and her eyes grew dim as she felt faintness overcoming her.

"That's what the King called you, isn't it? A toy?"

Her eyes filled with tears again. She put her hand on his forehead. How weak he seemed for one so hard.

"Oh, Philippe," she whispered, "what a mess! And to think you had just saved my life. Why couldn't things have turned out differently? I would so much have liked to love you . . . to be able to love you."

The Marquis raised his hand in an imperious gesture for her to be silent. "I think they are here," he said.

The marble staircase resounded with the clank of spurs and sabres. Then the door slowly opened and the Comte de Cavois entered, his face haggard.

"Cavois," said Philippe, "have you come to arrest me?"

The Comte nodded feebly.

"It is a good choice. You are Colonel of the Musketeers, and next to the Captain of the King's Bodyguard the duty should be yours. What has happened to Péguilin?"

"He is already in the Bastille."

Philippe stood up painfully. "I am at your service. Madame, be so good as to put my doublet over my shoulders."

The mere mention of the word Bastille made Angélique's senses reel. Everything was starting all over again. Once more a husband was being torn from her to be shut away in the Bastille. Her lips white, she clasped her hands in prayer.

"Monsieur de Cavois, not the Bastille, I beg you!"

"I am sorry, Madame, but those are the King's orders. Are you unaware that Monsieur du Plessis has greatly offended him in fighting this duel in spite of the severe edicts against it? However, don't worry. He will be well treated and well cared for, and his valet may accompany him."

He offered Philippe his arm to lean upon.

Angélique moaned like a wounded animal. "Not to

the Bastille! Lock him up wherever you want, but not in the Bastille!"

The two nobles were at the door. They turned to her with a look of total bewilderment.

"And where would you like to have me locked up?" Philippe asked in annoyance. "In the Châtelet, perhaps, with the rabble?"

Yes, everything was starting all over again. The endless waiting, the lack of information, the paralysis of action, the inevitable tragic ending. Once more she saw herself going over the same ground, stumbling, and already she was choking with anguish as if she were having one of those nightmares in which one tries in vain to escape but is rooted to the ground. For a while she thought she was going to lose her mind.

Her servants, distressed to see their mistress, whom they had known in a more vigorous state, so overwhelmed, finally thought of something that might calm her.

"You should go to see Mademoiselle de Lenclos, Madame. Mademoiselle de Lenclos." They almost forced her into her sedan chair.

It was good advice. Ninon was the only one, with all her worldly wisdom, her great human understanding, her generous heart, who could listen to Angélique's tale of woe without taking her for a fool or being scandalized. She rocked her in her arms, called her "dear heart," and when Angélique's panic subsided a little, undertook to show her how petty the whole incident was. There were many precedents. Every day husbands fought duels to avenge their honor.

"But the *Bastille!*" The name was blazoned in letters of fire before Angélique's eyes.

"But people do get out of it, my dear."

"Only to go to the stake."

Ninon stroked her forehead. "I don't know what you are referring to. There must have been some terrible event in your past to make you lose courage like this. As soon as you're yourself again, you'll see just as I do

that the rumors about the Bastille which have made
such an impression upon you are nothing to be afraid
of. It's just the King's dark closet. Is there any of our
fine lords who hasn't spent a few days there to pay for
some rudeness or disobedience that their high spirits
have embroiled them in? This is the third time for
Lauzun himself. Possibly the fourth. His example alone
proves that one can get out of the Bastille and achieve
an even greater position of honor than before. Let the
King birch his naughty schoolboys. He will be the first
to long for the return of that naughty rogue Lauzun or
for his Master of the Hunt."

Her words of wisdom comforted Angélique and
calmed her. Now she could see that her panic had been
groundless and foolish.

Ninon advised her to do nothing until the gossip died
down. "One scandal covers up another, and the Court
has plenty of them. Patience! I bet that within a week
another will have replaced yours on the lips of the
scandalmongers."

On her advice Angélique resolved to make a retreat
in the Convent of the Carmelites, where her young
sister Marie-Agnès was a novice. This would be the
best solution for getting away from the eyes of the world,
and still remaining in it.

In her nun's coif young Marie-Agnès de Sancé, green-
eyed and endowed with a mysterious smile, was like an
archaic angel on the portal of a cathedral. Angélique
was surprised to find her still determined to take the
veil. She was barely twenty-one years old. A life of self-
denial and prayer seemed hardly suited to her younger
sister's temperament. At twelve she had a reputation for
being devilish, and her brief experience as Maid of
Honor to the Queen had been one long sequence of
rash and suddenly terminated affairs. Angélique suspected that Marie-Agnès had learned more from the
book of love than she herself had. And after the young
nun had heard her confession, Angélique was surprised
to hear her sigh indulgently: "How young you are still!
Why get into such a fuss over a commonplace thing?"

"Commonplace, Marie-Agnès! I have just told you I deceived my husband. That's a sin, isn't it?"

"Nothing is more commonplace than sin. Only virtue is unusual. So unusual these days that it is almost unique."

"How can that be? I don't understand. I did not want . . ."

"Listen," said Marie-Agnès in the cutting voice that was a family trait, "either you wanted something like this, or you did not. And if you did not want it, then why did you go to live at Court?"

Perhaps that was the explanation of why she had divorced herself so completely from the world.

Angélique thought of doing penance there in the blanketing silence of that holy house, where the din of the world grew faint. A visit from Madame de Montespan, however, shattered her heavenly aspirations and brought her back to earth and all its complex problems.

"I don't know if my procedure is wise," the beautiful Athenais said to her, "but when all is said and done, it's to my advantage to put you on guard. But do what you want, and don't consider me. Solignac has turned to his own account this duel scandal. By which I mean that your husband's affairs are going badly."

"What has the Marquis de Solignac got to do with it?"

"The same old story—protecting God and His holy cause. I warned you he was a waspish, contradictory creature. He's got it into his head that duels are signs of heresy and atheism. He has seized on this one of Lauzun and your husband and is urging the King to be severe and to 'Make an example.' It may be necessary to prepare an auto-da-fé."

Seeing Angélique turn dead white, the astonished Marquise gave her a playful tap with her fan. "I was joking. But be careful! That fanatic is quite capable of getting them a long imprisonment and a thumping disgrace, and don't I know it! The King will listen to him because he remembers that Lauzun has irritated him too often. And he does not like it that these two nobles have gone beyond his limits of propriety. He doesn't care anything about the duel itself, but it is a question of law, and so the general opinion is that the pyre may be kindled. If I were you, I would try to intervene while there is still time and before the King has made up his mind."

Angélique threw down her prayerbook and left the pious convent at once.

When she went back to see Ninon de Lenclos, she was urged once again not to take the matter of a deceived husband so seriously. "Who," said Ninon, "would be so foolish as to make an issue about it? In a general epidemic doctors do not take pains with individual cases."

Louis XIV, when he heard this, smiled. This was taken as a good sign.

Nevertheless the great hetaera wrinkled her brows when Angélique told her of Solignac's meddling. She recalled the time that Richelieu had hacked off the heads of foolish nobles to "make an example," and forced the young lords to abandon their detestable habit of fighting duels and decimating their ranks.

"If Monsieur de Solignac has the notion that your husband's sword has interfered with God's will, we can be sure he will be just as importunate with the King as anyone wanting a favor.'"

"Do you think the King will let himself be influenced by him?"

"It is not a question of weakness on his part. Even if the King thinks Solignac a nuisance, his arguments carry a certain weight. He has both church and civil law on his side. If the King is forced into a position of invoking one or the other, he will have to do so. Only discretion can make the thing come out right now, and discretion is extremely indiscreet."

Angélique lowered her head in reflection. Now that she had a battle on her hands, she had no time to waste.

"What if I went to see Solignac?"

"Try it."

Even though it was pouring rain, Angélique stopped for a moment or two outside the iron-barred gates of Saint-Germain. She had just been informed that the

Court had moved to Versailles. She almost abandoned her mission. Then her determination returned.

Climbing back into her coach she called to the coachman: "On to Versailles!" She could hear him grumbling as the heavy vehicle turned around.

Outside the streaming windows of the coach the bare trees of the forest loomed out of the fog. It was being a wretched winter, with nothing but rain and cold and the eternal mud. Everyone yearned for Christmas to bring a new, clean snowfall.

Angélique scarcely noticed how cold her feet were. From time to time she set her mouth grimly, and her eyes flamed with what Mademoiselle de Parajonc called her "battle expression." She was running over in her mind her interview with the Marquis de Solignac, which he had granted at her insistence—not at his home, or at hers, but in an icy little parlor at the Convent of the Celestines. He had wanted it a secret meeting.

Once away from the Court, where his height and his towering wig gave him a certain noble bearing, the Queen's High Chamberlain seemed to her a rather pitiful figure, suspicious of everything. He never missed a chance to imply that her attitude made this rendezvous with her, which should have been ultra-dignified, somewhat lacking in propriety.

"Do you think, Madame, that you are still one of the flames of the Court, and that I am one of those fops who flutter around you like moths? I have no idea why you wished this meeting, but since I am quite aware of the regrettable situation in which your carelessness has placed you, I must ask that out of shame you put aside this pretense at melancholy with which you attempt to charm me as if to make me think you crushed with woe."

She grew more and more astonished at him. With his eyes half shut so that they seemed to peer into her soul, he asked her whether she fasted on Fridays, if she gave to charity, if she had seen *Tartuffe*, and if so, how many times.

Tartuffe was Molière's comedy that had offended many sanctimonious persons. Angélique had not been at Court when it was given there, and so had not seen it.

Angélique had underestimated the strength of the Brotherhood of the Holy Sacrament. Her temper rose, and the argument grew bitter.

"Woe to him—or her—who causes scandal!" concluded the unyielding Marquis.

Angélique had been routed. She was less brave now than angry. She made up her mind to go to the King.

She passed the night at an inn near Versailles. As soon as the salon for the petitioners was opened she appeared, and after making obeisance to the golden ship on the mantelpiece, which symbolized the person of the King, she waited while the room filled up with the usual army of old soldiers seeking pensions, impoverished widows, ruined noblemen, waifs and strays. Weary of petitioning the Goddess of Chance in vain, they now were directing their prayers to the monarch omnipotent. Near her stood Madame Scarron in her old worn cloak, the archetype of them all, for who was more experienced a seeker than she?

Angélique did not wish to be recognized by her, and pulled the hood of her cloak over her face.

When the King passed her, she fell to her knees and bowed her head low, merely stretching forth her petition in which she humbly begged His Majesty to grant an interview to Madame du Plessis-Bellière. Her hopes soared as she noticed that the King did glance at her and kept the petition in his hand instead of turning it over, as he did with the others, to Monsieur de Gesvres.

When the throng dispersed, however, it was de Gesvres who came over to her and asked her softly to follow him. Presently she found the door of the King's audience chamber opening before her.

Angélique had not expected her prayers to be answered so quickly. Her heart was pounding as she advanced a few steps and again fell to her knees while the door was closed behind her.

"Rise, Madame," she heard the King's indulgent voice say, "and draw near."

She waited until she reached the table before she lifted her hood.

The room was gloomy. Torrents of rain were splashing

on the gravel of the terrace outside. Still she could discern the trace of a smile on Louis XIV's lips.

"It grieves me," he said winningly, "that one of my ladies should feel obliged to be so secretive about seeing me. You could have come and been announced quite openly. After all, you are the wife of a Marshal."

"Sire, my embarrassment is so . . ."

"We shall come to that. I recognize your embarrassment. You are forgiven. It might have been wiser for you not to have left Fontainebleau so precipitately the other evening. Your flight was not in keeping with the great dignity you displayed during that painful incident."

Angélique was just about to remind the sovereign that it was on his orders, relayed to her by Madame de Choisy, that she had departed.

But the King forestalled her. "We will pass over that. What is the purpose of your visit?"

"Sire, the Bastille . . ." The very sound of the dreadful word she had let escape silenced her. What a bad beginning! She wrung her hands in anxiety.

"Well," said the King gently, "for whom have you come to intercede—Monsieur de Lauzun or Monsieur du Plessis?"

"Sire," Angélique's spirit revived, "the fate of my husband is my only concern."

"Would that it had always been so, Madame. From what I have been given to understand, I cannot help thinking that for one tiny instant the fate of your husband and his honor were perhaps not foremost in your thoughts."

"That is true, Sire."

"You are sorry?"

"To the very depths of my soul."

His penetrating eyes revealed to her the monarch's intense curiosity about the private lives of his subjects. She had heard that he was very inquisitive, but that he was also a paragon of discretion. The King *knew,* he never spoke—or rather, he silenced. In this respect, more than any other, he manifested his profound interest in human beings and his desire to know their darkest secrets so that by this sure means he might guide them and possibly make them his slaves.

Angélique's eyes wandered from his serious, transparently pale face to his hands that rested on the table in such tranquil immobility that they seemed to typify all the power of the King himself.

"What weather!" he said, pushing back his chair to rise. "Here it is only noon, and we need candles already. I can hardly make out your face. Come over here to the window so that I can truly see you."

She followed him obediently to the bay window down which the rain was streaming.

"I could not really believe that Monsieur du Plessis was as indifferent to his wife's charms as to the use to which she put them. It must be your fault, Madame. Why do you not live at your husband's hôtel?"

"Monsieur du Plessis has never invited me there."

"How funny! Come, my little toy, tell me what happened at Fontainebleau."

"My conduct, I know, was inexcusable, but my husband had just hurt me deeply . . . and in public, too."

She glanced involuntarily at her hand which still bore the marks of Philippe's insult. The King took her wrist and looked at it, but said nothing.

"I was so hurt that I wished to be by myself. Monsieur de Lauzun happened . . ." She described how Lauzun had undertaken to console her, first with words, then in a more concrete manner. "It is hard to resist Monsieur de Lauzun's undertakings, Sire. He is so accomplished that it is impossible for one to think of propriety or self-protection before the situation reaches a point where one would have to make an embarrassing scene to get out of it."

"Aha, so that is what happened!"

"Monsieur de Lauzun is very sophisticated and perhaps a little irresponsible, but at heart he is the kindest and most generous man in the world. I am sure Your Majesty knows that as well as I."

"Hmm," said the King slyly. "That depends on one's interpretation. How charming you are, Madame, when you blush as you are doing now! You are full of tantalizing contrasts—bashful, yet brave; gay and serious. The other day when I was visiting the greenhouses I noticed among the tuberoses a flower of quite a clashing color. The gardeners wanted to pull it out by the roots, they said it was a wild one. But actually it was as breathtaking as the others, different though it was. You make me think of that wildflower whenever I see you among the other ladies of the Court. Now I am willing to believe that it is Monsieur du Plessis who is wrong."

The King's pleasant expression darkened into a frown. "His reputation for brutality has always displeased me. I do not like to have in my Court anyone who might lead foreigners to think that the manners and customs of the French are still coarse, even barbarous. I preach courtesy toward women as a necessary discipline for the good name of our land. Is it true that your husband struck you in public?"

"No!" Angélique said stubbornly.

"Indeed? Well, I think our handsome Philippe might get a great deal of good out of a protracted period of meditation within the walls of the Bastille."

"Sire, I came to ask you to set him free. Release him from the Bastille, Sire, I entreat you."

"So you love him? I would have said that the milestones along your married life marked more bitter memories than happy reconciliations. I have heard that neither of you really knows himself, or the other."

"Perhaps. But we have known each other a very long time. He used to be the big cousin I adored . . . when we were children."

Once again she could picture Philippe with his blond curls dangling on the lace collar of the sky-blue jacket he wore the first time he came to the castle of Sancé.

She was gazing out the window, smiling. The rain had stopped, and a thin ray of sunlight squeezed between the clouds to glaze the marble pavement, over which was approaching an orange-striped coach drawn by four black horses.

"Even then he would not kiss me," she sighed. "Whenever my sisters and I came near him, he would wave us away in horror with his lace handkerchief."

She began to laugh.

The King was staring at her. He had long known she was beautiful, but now for the first time he was close to her. His eyes feasted on her porcelain skin, her peach-like cheeks, the ripe, pulsing fullness of her lips. As she brushed a stray blond curl from her temple, he sensed the fragrance of her flesh. She exhaled life, warm life, from every pore. Impulsively he stretched his hands toward her, grasped her to him. How yielding she was! He bent to her lips parted in a smile. Sweet, sweet and warm, so warm. Penetrating her mouth, he found her pearl-smooth teeth hard against his own . . .

Robbed of her will, Angélique could barely feel her head forced back by his warm hypnotic kiss. Then, emerging from her trance, she shuddered. Her hands grasped the shoulders of the King.

He stepped back, smiling. "Do not fear. I wished only to judge where the responsibility truly lay and determine for myself whether the fault was yours through such coldness or reticence as might paralyze the normal desires of a husband."

Angélique was not so naive as to be deceived by this excuse for what she recognized as a surrender to an overpowering passion.

"Your Majesty is devoting more attention to assessing this matter than it deserves," she said with a smile.

"Indeed?"

"Indeed."

The King returned to his chair behind the table, but he did not seem annoyed. "What difference does it make? I do not regret my efforts. From henceforth my opinion is that Monsieur du Plessis is a fool, pure and simple. He has more than deserved his punishment, and I shall take pains to tell him so. I hope that this time he will heed my advice. I intend to send him to the army in Picardy for a while to teach him a lesson. Don't cry, little toy, you'll get your big cousin back."

In the marble courtyard Monsieur de Solignac, High Chamberlain of the Queen, was just alighting from his orange-striped coach.

chapter 8

W HEN Madame du Plessis-Bellière returned home with her head in the clouds, she found the courtyard of her hôtel obstructed by a mailcoach that had been already unhitched and from which a quantity of baggage was beging unloaded. On the steps of the house stood two little apple-cheeked boys stretching out their hands toward her.

Angélique came back to earth with a thud. "Florimond! Cantor!"

She had completely forgotten the letter she had so hastily sent to Poitou demanding that they come to her. Now she could not tell whether their arrival was opportune or not. The joy of seeing them, however, overcame her doubts. She hugged them to her ecstatically.

They looked as ill at ease, as uncommunicative and stupid as any rustics in a big city for the first time. Their boots were hobnailed, their thick woolen stockings were twisted, their clothes smelled of peat-smoke.

Angélique gasped to see how Cantor had grown. At seven he was as tall as his older brother who was tall for his age himself. The two had nothing in common except their mops of tousled hair, Florimond's black, and Cantor's light chesnut. Florimond was a child of the South, with a sunny alert face. Cantor's green eyes were like the marsh weeds that glow in the dark reaches of the Poitou swamps; their liquid depth was unfathomable, betraying nothing.

Barbe, the servant who had brought them up, broke the spell of this uncomfortable greeting. She was wild with joy at being back in Paris. She had no use for eking out the winter, she said, in the depths of a country castle with only dull peasants for company and two naughty little boys running wild in the fields. And their grandfather, the Baron, letting them do whatever they wanted, no matter what she said. It was high time they had a good strict schoolteacher to teach them their alphabet and not spare the rod.

"They are going to Court," Angélique whispered to her, "to be playmates for the Dauphin."

Barbe's eyes expanded with joy. She clasped her hands and looked at her two "bandits" with new respect.

"We'll have to see they learn some manners!"

"And how to wear a sword and a plume."

"And how to make a bow."

"And to wipe their noses, and not to spit, and not to pee wherever they want."

"And to speak to ladies, and answer them with something better than a grunt."

How to complete the education of these two young future courtiers was going to be a problem. Speed was of the essence.

Madame de Choisy took it upon herself to handle it. The next day she arrived at the Hôtel de Beautreillis with a young abbé in tow, as slender as a girl with doe eyes peering out from under his powdered wig. She introduced him as one of the junior branch of the Lesdiguières, from around Chartres, a good but poor family. She had been entrusted with young Maurice by his parents, to whom she was distantly related, to help him into society. What better could she do than recommend him to Madame du Plessis-Bellière as supervisor of her two boys' education? After all he had completed his own education and had been a page to the Archbishop of Sens.

Madame de Choisy added that there must also be a tutor on the staff, and a dancing master, and a riding master, and a fencing master. She knew three young men who would be just right for these jobs. One was named Racan, who was a Bueil. He had studied law, but was too poor to buy himself a practice and so was willing to go into service. The dancing master was a grandson of the Marquis de Lesbourg, an old nobleman of Flanders, whose family, as everyone knew, had all been members of the Order of the Golden Fleece. The third was different in that he came from an exceedingly rich family, whose only heir he was, but was so determined to be a professional swordsman that he had forfeited his inheritance. He could handle any weapon known to man, including a crossbow, and he could teach a child anything.

Madame de Choisy also highly recommended two maidens of the house of Gilandon in the Chambord country. Their grandmother was one of the Joyeuses, and their sister had married the Comte des Roches. They were not unintelligent, but they had no beauty, and they would be content to work for small wages because their father had deserted them after discovering his wife had got pregnant while he was away in Spain.

"But what am I supposed to do with these maidens?" Angélique asked.

"Put them in your suite. You shouldn't be seen without chaperones. It doesn't look well for a woman of your position who is on the way up at Court."

She explained to Angélique that among the retainers of a well-appointed house there were persons from every stratum of society: the clergy, as almoners and confessors; the nobility, as squires or pages; the middle class as stewards, majordomos, valets, chefs; and lastly the plebs as lackeys and ladysmaids, kitchen help, postillions and stableboys.

Madame du Plessis did not have a retinue in keeping with her reputation and her rank, was the opinion of Madame de Choisy, who wanted only to be of help to her. She also hoped the Marquise was devout enough to see to it that her staff attended both morning and evening prayers, and went to Mass regularly.

Angélique had not yet succeeded in figuring out what role Madame de Choisy had played at Fontainebleau. Had she deliberately misrepresented the King's orders? Then she had seemed scandalized, but now she was brimming over with kindness.

She was well past forty, but there was still a twinkle in her eyes and charm in her smile. Still, there was something forbidding about her that made friendship difficult. The backstairs gossip was that her house was like a prison. If a girl went into service with her, she could never go out, and she would be worked to death and punished severely to boot. Her porter did not dare open her gates without her express orders, and the one time he had disobeyed he was whipped. Once she had almost beaten a servant-girl to death. They said she had even taken a whip to her husband, but was so repentant afterward she buried herself up to her neck in a swamp by way of penance.

Angélique was sure that these tales were exaggerated, but Madame de Choisy's propensity for projecting herself into the lives of others was sometimes vexing. Rather than see her find some other protégé, however, Angélique engaged the whole tribe of Racans, Lesdiguières and Gilandons, including the maidens.

Furthermore Florimond and Cantor definitely had to be put under some regime or other. They had reached the age of being wild about horses, and would ride anything from their grandfather's mules to the bannisters of the great staircase of the Hôtel de Beautreillis, which rang with the shouts of their mock battles and charges.

Angélique was so busy with her new domestic arrangements that it was only through street gossip she got the news that Philippe had been set free. He did not come to see her. She was unsure of what was best for her to do. Madame de Montespan insisted that she return to the Court as if nothing had happened.

"The King has pardoned you. Everyone knows you were with him alone for a long, long time. He scolded Monsieur du Plessis in private, but that very night your husband had the honor of handing the King his nightshirt at Saint-Germain. Everyone knows how much His Majesty likes both of you."

Madame de Choisy offered her opinion also. Since the King had expressed a wish that Madame du Plessis present her sons to him, she should not delay. The royal whim was fickle, and later he might not be so well disposed to them. She had seen Madame de Montausier, the wife of the Dauphin's tutor and governess of the royal children. They set a day for Florimond and Cantor to be presented at court.

The boys made their appearance at Versailles dressed

in teal-blue satin with the proper number of ribbons
and rosettes, white stockings with gold cloches, high
heels, and at their sides little swords chased with silver.
On their curly mops of hair they wore round felt hats
with red feathers which were not quite plumes but
which stuck out beyond the brim in the latest style. Because of the cold weather they wore cloaks of black velvet trimmed with gold braid. The Abbé de Lesdiguières observed that Florimond knew instinctively
how to flourish a cape, something that common persons
never could learn.

Canton was more awkward. No one worried about
how Florimond would behave, for he had quickly learned
how to bow and walk elegantly, but they could only
hope and pray that Cantor would be inspired to want
to do well, for he could if he put his mind to it.

The royal children's apartments had a coziness that
was utterly different from the atmosphere of the rest of
the palace of Versailles. In one corner was a huge bird-
cage and beside it the cradles of the two little princesses,
swathed in priceless white lace in which was woven the
coats-of-arms of their estates. Together with the rustling
coif of Madame Hamelin, the King's old nurse who often
came there to spin, these made a continual fluttering of
white wings that rendered the rooms cheerful and bright.
Madame de Montausier had not brought up her royal
charges too strictly. Good soul that she was, she knew
well enough how soon they would be enslaved by the
harsh discipline of their tutors and the rigid etiquette
that would govern every one of their steps.

The Dauphin was a fat little boy whose mouth always
hung open because of his stuffed-up nose, or so his governess said. Of no more than average intelligence, he
already seemed ill at ease in his difficult role as the son
of Louis XIV, an impression he would give for the rest
of his life. He had grown up as an only child, for his
two little sisters had died at birth. One had been as
dark as a Moor, it was said, because the Queen had
drunk too much chocolate while pregnant.

Angélique could see that in spite of being overgrown
for their age, her boys were more graceful, more self-

confident and more real persons than the heir to the
crown. She looked fondly at them as they made their
bows in perfect style, and then advanced one behind the
other to kiss the hand that the Dauphin shyly extended
to them after Madame de Montausier had nodded that
it was all right for him to do so. And she almost burst
with pride when Florimond's sweet natural voice said
respectfully: "Say, Your Grace, that's a damn fine shell
you've got there."

It happened that the "shell" was a priceless jewel
the Dauphin had found that very morning lying on the
gravel of the terrace and had insisted on pinning to his
coat between the Order of Saint-Louis and the star of a
Grand Admiral of the Fleet. It was, he insisted, to be
his very own decoration, and the Maids of Honor had
ended by giving it to him.

Florimond's remark reminded the Dauphin of his
treasure, which he proceeded to display in all its details
to his new friends. His shyness vanished, and he dragged
them to see his collection of china monkeys, his toy
cannon, his drum with cloth-of-silver heads.

Florimond's intuitive sense of what to do and say
completely dispelled any anxiety on the part of his tutors.
The young abbé and Racan glanced knowingly at Angélique, who was herself so gratified that she resolved
to slip them thirty *écus* that evening.

Apparently spontaneously, but actually by prear-
ranged protocol, the Queen with ten of her Ladies and a
few of her retinue of noblemen put in an appearance.
After making his bows Cantor was asked to sing for
the Queen. This produced the first false note in the
otherwise perfect performance, for the boy knelt on one
knee and after strumming a few introductory bars,
launched into his favorite song:

> Let the drums roll, said the King,
> All my ladies fair to bring.

The abbé descended on him and snatched up his
lute, which he said loudly was quite out of tune. While
he was tuning it, he whispered to his pupil, who will-

ingly began another song.

Hardly anyone noticed the incident, and least of all the Queen, whose Spanish background had left her totally unacquainted with French folksongs.

Angélique vaguely recalled that Cantor's interrupted song dated from a century ago and referred to the sub rosa love affairs of Henri IV, but she was quite grateful to the abbé for covering up the blunder in time. Yes, she was very thankful to Madame de Choisy for all her recruits.

Cantor had the voice of an angel, ineffably pure and unwavering, and he could hold a note without a tremolo. It had none of the monotonous insipidity of most children's voices.

The Ladies had been prepared merely to listen politely, but were overcome with delight at this infant prodigy. Florimond, at first the center of attention, now had to take second place. Everyone commented on the radiance of the little singer's face, and how his eyes shone and sparkled when he sang.

Monsieur de Vivonne was the most enthusiastic of all, and his previous attempts to flatter Angélique were nothing compared to his eloquent compliments now. Like many other gay blades of the Court, he had several talents that he practiced in private for his own amusement. Brother of Madame de Montespan, Captain of the Galleys and a Lieutenant-General in the Navy, he yet composed poetry and songs, and could play several musical instruments. On several occasions he had been entrusted with the production of the Court ballets, and had had many triumphs. He now asked Cantor to sing some of his ballads, naming the least indecorous of them. One was a Christmas carol, full of gentle grace, which quite transported the company. The Queen demanded that Lully be fetched at once.

The King's music master was rehearsing his choirboys, and came quite unwillingly, but his face lit up as soon as he heard Cantor. A voice of such quality was rare indeed, he said. He could not believe the child was only eight, for he had the soundbox of an eleven-year-old.

Then the music master grew gloomy again and pouted.

The career of the prodigy was destined to be short. His voice would certainly be ruined when it changed unless he were castrated when he was ten or eleven. Such emasculated voices were in great demand. Young eunuchs with their superb tones were the finest ornaments of the princely chapels of Europe. They were recruited generally from the children of poor musicians or mountebanks who wanted to assure their sons a splendid career rather than subject them to a normal life in which they might never rise above mediocrity.

Angélique let out a cry of protest. Castrate her manly little Cantor! How horrible! Thank God, he was of noble birth and his future would not suffer from the loss of his gift. No, he would learn to wield his sword in his King's service and grow up to have a long line of descendants.

Lully's opinions gave rise to several jokes around the Court where lords and ladies had a knack for coining phrases. Cantor passed from hand to hand and was petted, complimented, encouraged. He accepted all these tributes with his customary air of a purring tomcat, but he gave them scant attention.

Everyone agreed that when men took over the Dauphin's education, Florimond and Cantor would be among the suite that would accompany him to the riding academy, the tennis courts and soon enough to the hunt.

chapter 9

*I*T WAS that season of the year when Paris began gradually to awake to the sound of violins and the ring of happy laughter. In spite of the fact that the treaties had brought peace, a wartime atmosphere still obtained, and most of the nobles were away.

Angélique noticed wryly that it was becoming hard for her to keep up with things. Her pregnancy was beginning to slow her down. Here again Philippe was the cause of a handicap that would soon put her in the shadows. She was already so big that she could no longer get into her favorite gowns. It was just her luck that this child would have to be the biggest of all she had carried.

Except for the royal festivities, she still continued to go to Saint-Germain, where anyone could appear without an invitation. The conduct of the kingdom's business filled the corridors with a motley crowd.

Government clerks with goose-quills stuck behind their ears jostled ambassadors. Learned aldermen discussed markets among great ladies and fluttering fans.

There she encountered an old alchemist named Savary who had come to her house as a petitioner.

A young woman stopped as she was about to pass them and let out a little shriek, as she seized Savary by his lapels and stared at him intently. Angélique recognized her as Mademoiselle de Brienne.

"I know you," she whispered. "You are a soothsayer, perhaps even a sorcerer. Can we come to terms?"

"You are mistaken, Madame. I have a little fame, and it is true that they speak well of me here, but I am only a modest scholar."

"I know," she insisted, her lovely eyes shining like jewels, "I know how much you can do. You have potions you have brought back from the East. Listen, you must get me the privilege of the footstool. Name your own price."

"Things like that are not got with money."

"Then I will give myself to you, body and soul."

"Oh, my poor child, you are out of your head."

"Think it over, Monsieur Savary. It can't be hard for you. I can see no other way of getting the King to give me the footstool. And I must have it, I must. I will do anything to get it."

"Well, well, all right, I'll think it over."

But he refused the purse Mademoiselle de Brienne tried hard to slip into his hand.

Later Angélique encountered Mademoiselle de Brienne again at a card table. Mademoiselle de Brienne was a pretty brunette, rather tantalizing, but also stuck-up and extremely ill-mannered. She had been at Court since she was a child. She had a one-track mind, if mind indeed it could be called. Cards, drinking and lovemaking were as harmless pastimes for her as embroidery and lace-making were for middle-class girls her age.

Soon she had lost 10,000 *livres* at cards to Angélique. She admitted she could not raise that much to pay the debt at once.

"I might have known that old devil of an alchemist would bring you luck," she said, pouting like a child on the verge of tears. "What I would give to get his help! I've lost almost thirty thousand *livres* this one week. My brother is going to raise hell with me and say I am ruining him." Then, realizing that Angélique was apparently not going to extend her credit very long, she added: "Would you like to buy my office of Consul of Candia? I have been thinking of selling it. It's worth forty thousand *livres*."

At the word "office" Angélique pricked up her ears. "Consul?"

"Yes."

"Of Candia?"

"That's some city or other in Crete, I think," Mademoiselle de Brienne informed her.

"But a woman can't be a consul . . ."

"Yes she can. I have had it three years now. It doesn't

require actual residence and, as a matter of fact, gives
one a certain rank at Court where any consul at all,
even one in a petticoat, has permission to reside, and
can even be obliged to do so. If you were to buy it I
hope you would buy the perquisites also. Oh dear, that's
not the way it ought to be either. The two managers I
sent there are pirates and all the business they do goes
into their pockets, but I still have to pay their wages. I
shouldn't be telling you this when I'm suggesting you
buy it, but I'm an awful fool anyway. Perhaps you could
do better than I. Forty thousand *livres* isn't much. I
could get out of debt and have something left over."

"I will think about it," Angélique said noncommit-
tally.

The thought went to her head like strong drink. Consul of France! She had dreamed of many titles, but never
of that.

The interior of Colbert's home and particularly his
office was a model of simple bourgeois comfort. So cold
by temperament that Madame de Sévigné nicknamed
him "Monsieur North Pole," he had no taste for luxury.
Frugality was so inherent in him that he allowed no
gratification of his vanity other than the impeccable and
overdetailed way in which he kept his accounts, and the
establishment of his family tree. No expense was too
great for the latter, and he paid a whole army of clerks
to do research in the illegible scrawls of family records
in order to prove some relationship that might entitle
him to a claim to nobility. This maggot, however, did
not keep him from seeing quite clearly all the faults of
the aristocracy and how the middle class was destined to
grow in importance, for it was then the only vital and
intelligent class in the kingdom.

Madame du Plessis apologized for disturbing him. She
told him she was about to acquire the Consulate of
Candia, and because she knew he superintended the distribution of such posts, she wished his advice.

Colbert scowled at her at first, then softened. It was not
often, he admitted, that beautiful dimwits stopped to
think of the consequences before accepting a post. Most

of the time he had to play the unsympathetic role of
censor of petitions, being often obliged to refuse demands that were too foolish or unsuitable, or too liable
to interfere with the progress of government, or too burdensome financially—a role that hardly endeared him to
those who had thought their petitions granted.

Angélique perceived that for a woman to hold the
post of Consul did not disturb him, that it was a common enough thing.

To him Candia, the capital of Crete, was the best
slave market in the Mediterranean. It was also the only
place where one could buy strong, sober Russians for
only 100 or 150 *livres* apiece from the Turks who captured them during their continual battles in Armenia,
the Ukraine, Hungary and Poland.

"This consideration is not unimportant for us now
that we are striving to expand our maritime trade and
increase the number of our galleys in the Mediterranean. The Moors, Tunisians and Algerians we capture
in our battles with the pirates are poor workers. They
are useful only to fill out a retinue when one can't afford
better, and to exchange for Christian captives. They are
no good as galley slaves either, for they get seasick and
die like flies. The best galley slaves are the Turks and
Russians sold in the markets of Candia, for they are excellent sailors. I am tired of saying that the basis for the
fine crews of the English ships consists of these Russian
slaves. The English hold them in high esteem and pay
their agents well to get them. For all these reasons Candia
is not lacking in interest to me."

"What is the situation of the French there?" Angélique asked him. She had not quite pictured herself as
a slave dealer.

"Our representatives are respected, I believe. Crete is a
Venetian colony. For years the Turks have tried to conquer it, and the island has had to repulse many attacks."

"But is it safe to invest money there?"

"That depends. Sometimes a nation's commerce does
well in time of war—that is, if the nation is neutral.

France has firm alliances with Venice as well as with Turkey."

"Mademoiselle de Brienne told me frankly she got no revenue from her post. She blamed her managers who, she said, work only for their own profit."

"That is quite possible. Get me their names and I will investigate."

"Well—will you support my candidacy for this post, sir?"

Colbert did not answer her at once. Finally he said, frowning again: "Yes. In every way it would be better off in your hands, Madame Morens, than in those of Mademoiselle de Brienne or of some idiotic nobleman or other. Besides, it fits in perfectly with the projects I had in mind for you."

"For me?"

"Yes. Did you think we would let abilities like yours go unused for the good of the nation? One of His Majesty's greatest talents is his knack for making arrows out of any kind of wood. So far as you are concerned the only obstacle is his doubt that a woman of your beauty and charm can have other qualities such as good business sense. I convinced him that he should not appoint you too quickly to just any position at Court, which any fool could fill. You have more important things to do than solicit a place in the Queen's suite or some other silly post. Leave that to the daughters of impoverished aristocrats who have only their virginity to pay for it. Your fortune is immense and well invested. In that lies your power."

The blunt approach of the Comptroller awoke in Angélique a certain bitterness. So it was he who had opposed all her requests! He had no tact, and the King proved himself a man of integrity in supporting him.

"Of course I have money," she said drily, "but surely not enough to save the kingdom."

"Who said anything about money? It's a question of *work*. It's *work* that will save the country and bring back its squandered wealth little by little. Look here, once I was a simple linen draper, now I am Comptroller, but is that to my credit? On the other hand I am proud of being director of the royal manufactories.

"We not only can but should invest more in France than in foreign countries. But our loyalties are too divided. For instance, I could have continued in business for myself and increased my own fortune, but I preferred to learn statecraft from Cardinal Mazarin and lend my business acumen and organizational abilities to the State. As a result the nation has grown stronger, and I along with it. The King himself, young as he is, began early to follow the same principle. He too was one of the Cardinal's pupils, but he was wiser than his teacher, for he knew the goods he was selling. The late Cardinal knew nothing about the French, even though he had great powers of intuition, both as to politics and human nature. Our sovereign works harder than four other kings, and he does not think it beneath him to assemble around him plenty of persons to whom he can delegate responsibility."

The longer he spoke, the more angry Colbert seemed to grow. When he finally stopped, his expression was so furious that Angélique could not keep from asking him why.

"Because I don't know what's got into me to tell you all this. If my wife ever heard me gossiping this way, there would be the devil to pay."

Angélique reassured him that many other men with a reputation for being close-mouthed had also blamed her for drawing them out of their reticence.

"Believe me, sir, I won't betray your confidence. Everything you have said interests me deeply, so deeply that it should encourage you to continue this discourse with which you have been so kind as to honor me."

Colbert looked like a bird that has swallowed a worm too big for it. He hated flattery because he always suspected an ulterior motive behind it. But when he glanced dourly at Angélique, he saw she was sincere.

"After all," he growled, "the capacity to be interested in what someone else is saying is rare." His smile returned. "Always show it to old fools like me. Your own charms are enough for the young fools. And your whole manner can easily persuade women to follow you. In fact, you have a formidable battery of assault."

"But how should I deploy this arsenal?"

The Comptroller reflected a moment. "First of all, you should never leave the Court. Attach yourself to it, follow it wherever it goes, and make an effort to know as many people as possible and as intimately as possible."

Angélique had a hard time concealing the extreme satisfaction his advice gave her. "This . . . this kind of work does not seem very hard."

"We shall use you for various missions, especially those dealing with maritime trade, or, in short, all kinds of trade and its adjuncts, such as fashion."

"Fashion?"

"I mentioned fashion to convince His Majesty that he could entrust important assignments to you, a woman. Let me explain. For example, I want to steal the secret of making *point de Venise* lace which is all the rage now and which no one can imitate. I have tried to prevent the importation of it, but these lords and ladies smuggle in collars and cuffs made of it under their cloaks, and so three million *livres* a year find their way into Italy. Whether legal or illegal, it is a sad thing for French industry. Otherwise there would be no reason for stealing the secret of that lace which our dandies have to have. I want to establish the manufacture of it here."

"I should have to go to Venice."

"I do not think so. In Venice you would be under suspicion. I have good reason to believe that these agents operate at Court. They are courtiers themselves. Through them you can trace the thread back to the spider and learn at lest the source of supply. I suspect the two members of the Marseilles Board of Trade. It must bring them a huge fortune."

Angélique was deep in thought. "This work you want me to do looks very much like spying."

Colbert agreed. The word did not shock him. Spies? Everyone used them everywhere.

"Business goes the same way. For instance, some new shares in the East India Company are soon going to be released. Your market for them is the Court. It will be up to you to make the Indies fashionable, get the conservatives to invest, and so on. There is money at Court. Why let it all go up in smoke or be frittered away? Don't you see already how many opportunities you will find to exercise your talents? The only thing that worries us is what official title to give you. Wait, your Cretan Consulate will do as a façade and as an alibi."

"But its perquisites are very small."

"Don't be silly! It's understood that your official duties will bring you enormous stipends. They will be fixed according to each job. You will be able to have an interest in all that goes well."

Out of habit, she began figuring. "Forty thousand *livres* is a lot of money."

"It's a pinch of salt to you. Think a moment that a post as procurator would cost you 175,000. Mine cost my predecessor 1,400,000. The King paid it for me because he wanted me in the position. But I feel indebted to the King. That's why I won't rest until I have earned him many times that amount through making his country prosperous."

"So this is the Court," Angélique said to herself, "or so the guileless think—dancing the night away at the Palais-Royal, flooded with light, a stage for one everlasting festivity."

Her face concealed by a black velvet mask, she was watching the dancing couples. The King had opened the ball with Madame in his costume of Jupiter from the ballet of "A Feast on Olympus." All eyes were on him. His golden mask could not preserve his incognito. He wore a gold helmet encrusted with rubies and rose diamonds and topped with a flame-colored crest of feathers. His entire costume was of cloth of gold, sparkling with the thousands of diamonds sewn into its embroidered patterns.

The next day the poet Loret himself could only say in praise of that costume:

> The trappings of the prince
> Would buy a whole province

"So much wealth," thought Angélique. "That's the Court!"

Yes, that was the Court—folly, extravagance. Yet if one looked closely, what a surprise! A young, discreet king pulling the strings of marionettes. And an even closer look revealed that behind their masks the marionettes themselves were alive, burning with passion, mean ambitions, strange consecrations . . .

Her recent conversation with Colbert had opened new and unimagined vistas to Angélique. As she thought of the role he had assigned her, she wondered whether every mask here did not conceal some secret mission. "It is not the King's custom to let abilities go unused . . ."

Once in this same Palais-Royal, which then was called the Palais-Cardinal, Richelieu had walked in his purple robe as he hatched his schemes to dominate the realm. No one ever entered here then who was not in his service. His net of spies was like a mammoth spiderweb. He employed many women. "Those creatures," he would say, "have an instinctive gift for deception and dissimulation." Was the young king adopting the same principle for himself?

As Angélique left the ball, a page handed her a note. She turned away to read it. It was from Colbert.

"You may consider the post at Court you solicited granted permanently under the stipulated conditions. Your title of Consul of France will be in your hands tomorrow."

She folded the note and slipped it into her purse. A smile played around the corners of her mouth. She had won at last.

And, taking everything into consideration, what was so strange about a marquise being a Consul of France, when baronesses were fishmongers, and duchesses sold theatre seats, and the Minister of War wanted the mail-coach franchise, and where the most licentious people in the whole Court were endowed with the benefices of the Church?

Part Two

Philippe

🌱 🌱 🌱

*A*NGÉLIQUE dismissed her servants and the Gilandon girls, and undressed herself slowly. Her mind was too busy running over the last episodes of her victory to put up with their fussing around her. Earlier this same day her business manager had delivered 40,000 *livres* in cash to Mademoiselle de Brienne's, and she had received her commission from the King through the agency of Colbert. She had affixed her signature to a great quantity of documents, blotted with sand innumerable pages of writing, and paid out 10,000 more *livres* in taxes, registration fees, and other supplementary impositions.

She could not have been more satisfied, except for a worrisome thought in the back of her mind about Philippe.

What would he say when he found out? Previously, he had defied her to remain at the Court and had given her to understand that he would do everything in his power to keep her away from it. But his imprisonment in the Bastille and his army duty had given Angélique plenty of leisure in which to conduct her own affairs.

And so she was victorious—but not without apprehension. Philippe had come back from Picardy a week before. The King himself informed Madame du Plessis-Bellière of this fact, implying how much his wish to please her had led him to wipe off the slate Philippe's serious offense in disobeying his express orders by fighting a duel.

Angélique thanked His Majesty, and then asked him how she should behave. What should a wife's attitude be toward a husband who had been thrown into prison because she had deceived him? She was in doubt, but everything led her to believe that her husband's attitude would be much more clearly defined. Laughed at, blamed by the King, blocked at every turn, Philippe would hardly be in a kindly frame of mind toward her.

She considered all the actual grievances Philippe might hold against her, realizing that she could expect the worst. Hence her haste in concluding a bargain which would be a defense for her against her husband's being ostracized. That was a *fait accompli* now.

Nothing had been heard from Philippe. She learned that he had gone to pay his respects to the King, and that the King had received him with affection. Then he had been seen at Ninon's in Paris. He had also gone hunting twice with the King. This very day, while she was signing documents at Colbert's, Philippe was in the forest of Marly.

Had he decided to leave her in peace? She wished she could believe he had. But Philippe nursed grudges. His silence was more likely that of a tiger crouching to spring. Angélique sighed.

Deep in these thoughts, she unfastened the bows that held her bodice, dropping the pins one by one into an onyx tray. Once she had it off she undid the shoulder knots of her three petticoats, letting them drop around her feet. Stepping out of this pool of ruffles, she took from the back of an armchair the nightgown of fine lawn that Javotte had laid out for her. Then she bent down to unfasten her satin garters studded with precious stones. All her movements were slow and thoughtful. In these latter weeks she had lost much of her usual quickness.

As she took off her bracelets she moved toward her dressing table to replace them in their cases. The big oval mirror reflected her image in a golden haze from the candlelight. A little sadly she contemplated the perfection of her face and the fresh pink coloring of her cheeks and lips. The lace of her nightgown set off the youthful fullness of her shoulders and the round supple neck which rose swanlike above them.

"This *point de Venise* is certainly beautiful. Colbert is right in wanting it domesticated in France."

She fluffed up the flounces of lace with her fingertip.

Her pearly skin seemed to glimmer through the almost transparent flowers of the exquisite handiwork. A panel of lace stretched low over her breasts, which peeped through it like violets from among their leaves.

Angélique raised her bare arms to unfasten the strand of pearls she had wound in her hair like a diadem. It fell in lustrous coils on to the table. Even with her distended abdomen, yes, she was still lovely. The insidious question Lauzun had asked her haunted her: "For whom?" How could her body be so desirable to one and so unalluring to another?

With another sigh she took up her dressing gown of crimson taffeta and wrapped herself in it with due consideration for effect. Yet what was she going to do tonight? She was not sleepy.

Should she write to Ninon de Lenclos? Or to Madame de Sévigné, whom she had rather neglected lately? Or go over her accounts as she used to at times like this when she was in business?

She heard a man's footsteps moving along the entrance hall, and the jingle of spurs as they began to mount the staircase. No doubt it was Malbrant, Florimond's and Cantor's riding master whom they had nicknamed "Swordthrust." He was probably coming back from one of the fencing matches he loved.

But the steps came nearer and nearer her door.

Suddenly Angélique realized whose they were. She sprang up to slip the bolt, but she was too late. The Marquis du Plessis-Bellière stood before her in the doorway.

He was still wearing his silver gray hunting coat trimmed with black fur, a black hat with a single white plume, and black boots covered with mud and slush. In his black-gloved hands was his long dog-whip. For a moment he stood there motionless, his legs spread, while his eyes took in the whole picture of her before her dressing table surrounded by all the disorder of her clothes and jewels. A smile spread slowly over his lips.

Then stepping inside the room, he shut the door behind him, and shot the bolt into its socket.

"Good evening, Philippe."

Her heart leaped with an emotion compounded of fear and pleasure at seeing him.

How handsome he was! She had almost forgotten how handsome, how distinguished, how glitteringly perfect in every detail. He was the handsomest man in the Court, and he was hers, as once she had dreamed he might be.

"Weren't you expecting a visit from me, Madame?"

"Yes indeed I was . . . that is, I was hoping . . ."

"My word, you are brave! Didn't you have good reason to fear my wrath?"

"Yes. That is why I thought the sooner our meeting took place, the better. Nothing is gained by postponing a dose of bitter medicine."

Philippe's face plunged into an expression of insane anger. "Hypocrite! Traitor! You will be hard put to persuade me you wanted to see me when all the time you have been trying your best to outmaneuver me. Haven't I just found out that you have got two permanent posts at Court?"

"You are well up on things."

"I certainly am," he snarled.

"You . . . you don't seem to like that."

"Did you think I would after you got me in prison so that you could set your snares in peace? And now . . . now you think you have escaped me. But the last card has not been played. I'll make you pay dearly for your trading. You couldn't possibly conceive the price of the punishment I have prepared for you."

His whip cracked on the floor with a noise like thunder. Angélique shrieked. Her resistance crumpled.

She ran to the bed alcove for refuge and began to weep. No, no, she could not go through another scene like her wedding night at Plessis.

"Don't hurt me, Philippe," she pleaded. "Oh, please, don't hurt me. Think of our child."

Philippe stopped cold. His eyes opened wide. "Child? What child?"

"The one I am carrying. Your child!"

A heavy silence descended over both of them, broken only by Angélique's muffled sobs. Finally the Marquis began to peel off his gauntlets, laying them along with his whip on the dressing table. He moved toward his wife, suspicion written on his face.

"Show me," he said.

He ripped open her dressing gown, then flinging back his head, he roared with laughter.

"My God, it's true! You're as big as a cow!"

He sat beside her on the edge of the bed and drew her toward him by her shoulders. "Why didn't you tell me sooner, you wild little beast? I would not have frightened you so."

She was weeping in short nervous starts, her willpower quite gone.

"Come now," he said, "don't cry. Don't cry."

It was a strange thing for her to find her head leaning against her brutal husband's shoulder, her face buried in his blond curls perfumed with jasmine, and to feel his hand softly stroking her belly where a new life quivered.

"When will it be born?"

"Soon. In January."

"It must have been at Plessis," he said after a moment's thought. "I am overjoyed to think that my son was conceived under my ancestral roof. Hmm! All our violent quarrels will do him no harm. They're a good omen. He will be a warrior. Haven't you something here for us to toast him with?"

He went to a cabinet and fetched two goblets and a bottle of Beaune which were put there daily in case guests should come.

"Come, let's drink to him, even if you don't wish to clink glasses with me. It's only fitting that we salute our common enterprise. Why do you look at me with such stupid astonishment? Because at last you've spied out a way to disarm me? Be patient, my dear, I am too pleased at the thought of having an heir not to treat you well. I will honor our truce. We can resume the battle later. Just be sure you don't take advantage of my good humor to play me one of your dirty tricks. In January, did you say? Good. From now on I am going to keep my eye on you."

He drained his glass and sent it crashing on the flagstones, shouting: "Long live the heir of Miremont du Plessis de Bellière!"

"Philippe," murmured Angélique, "you are a puzzling person, the most so I have ever met. For a man to receive such an announcement from me at such a moment and not tell me to my face that I was saddling him with a paternity for which he was not responsible! I was sure you were going to accuse me of marrying you when I was already pregnant by someone else."

Philippe was drawing on his gauntlets again. He looked at her darkly, almost angrily. "In spite of the gaps in my education," he said, "I can still count up to nine. If this child is not mine, nature by now would have compelled you to show it to the world. Just the same I will say I think you capable of any trick in the world, but not of quite such a despicable one."

"It's not unusual with women. From someone like you who hates them so, I expected a less trusting reaction."

"You are not a woman like other women," he said. "You are *my wife!*"

Then he strode out, leaving her dreaming and stirred by an emotion something like hope.

On a bleak morning in January when the pale sun on the snow crust cast ghostly reflections on the dark tapestries of her walls, Angélique felt that her time was come. She had Madame Cordet, the midwife whose services she had engaged, summoned from the Marais quarter. Several great ladies of her acquaintance had recommended her, for she had the strong character and also the good humor necessary to satisfy a demanding clientele. She brought with her two apprentices to lend importance to her mission, and had a big trestle table set up by the hearth on which she could work, as she put it "more comfortably."

A brazier of coals was fetched to raise the temperature of the room. Servants were put to rolling balls of lint, and boiling water in copper kettles. Madame Cordet began by steeping medicinal herbs, and the room soon smelled like a country meadow under the summer sun.

Angélique was terribly nervous and short-tempered. She did not look forward to her accouchement, and wished someone else could have her baby for her. Unable to stay in bed, she kept pacing the room, stopping every time she passed the window to look out at the snow-padded street. Through the tiny leaded panes she could just make out the smoky outlines of the passers-by. A lurching, rocking coach pitched along, drawn by four horses emitting clouds of steam from their nostrils. Its occupant was shouting at the driver, and the coachman was swearing while the neighbors laughed.

It was the day after Epiphany and all Paris had sore throats from yelling "The King drinks," or was sick from overeating the huge Twelfth-night cakes and drinking goblet after goblet of wine. There had been much feasting at the Hôtel de Beautreillis. Florimond was the "King," wearing a gold paper crown and lifting his glass to all the cheers. Today everyone was sleepy and yawning. A fine day to bring a child into the world!

In her impatience Angélique kept asking about housekeeping details. Had the left-overs been given to the poor? Yes, four baskets had been taken to the cripples' pole that very morning. Two buckets had been taken to the Blue Children, the orphans of the Temple district, and to the Red Children, the orphans of the Hôtel-Dieu. Had the tablecloths been set to soak? The plates been put away? The knives cleaned with pumice?

Madame Cordet tried to calm her. Why did she need to worry about such things, when she had plenty of servants, and could leave all those matters to her major-domo? There were more important things for her to think about. But Angélique did not wish to think about them.

"No one would ever believe this was your third baby," scolded the midwife. "You're putting on a big enough act for a first."

Indeed she had made less fuss the other times. She remembered how quiet she had been when Florimond arrived, even though she was frightened. She had been more courageous then, had all the reserve strength of a young animal that has not lived long enough to doubt its capacities. Now too many misfortunes had sapped her energy. Her nerves were tenser.

"The baby's too big," she groaned. "The others weren't so big."

"Bah, don't tell me. I saw your youngest outside there. Built the way he is now, he couldn't have tickled much when he came through."

The birth of Cantor! She did not want to remember that nightmare, that dark, icy whirlpool of pain and sorrow. In thinking of the horrible charity hospital where so many innocent babes uttered their first wails, Angélique grew ashamed of her complaints and tried to appear less irritable.

She consented at last to sit in a big armchair with a cushion at the small of her back, and a footstool under her feet. One of the Gilandon girls offered to read her some prayers, but Angélique told her to go for a walk. What business did such a silly girl have in a delivery room? She said for her to find the Abbé de Lesdiguières and if they could find nothing to say to each other, then they could pray for her or go light a candle at Saint-Paul's.

Eventually her pains became more frequent and more severe, and Madame Cordet made her stretch out on the table before the fire. Angélique did not restrain her screams as the moment approached when the fruit ready to fall seemed to tear up with it the roots of the tree on which it had been ripening. Her own ears rang with her groans. She thought she heard a disturbance outside, and a door slam.

"Oh, Monsieur le Marquis!" said Thérèse.

She did not understand until she saw Philippe standing by her pillow, more noticeable than ever among these women busy about women's things. He was in Court dress, wearing his sword, his lace cuffs, his wig, his white-plumed hat.

"Philippe, what are you doing here? What do you want? Why did you come?"

His expression was ironic and haughty. "Today my

son will be born. Don't you think I have any interest in that?"

Her indignation brought Angélique back to life. She raised up on one elbow. "You just came to see me suffer," she said. "You are a monster. The most cruel, the most cowardly, the most . . ."

A new spasm cut her off. She fell back gasping for breath.

"Come, come," said Philippe, "don't waste your strength."

He laid his hand on her moist forehead and began stroking her brow and murmuring words she scarcely understood but which soothed her with their sound.

"Easy, easy, now, my dear. Everything is going fine. Courage, my sweet . . ."

"That is the first time he has ever caressed me," Angélique thought. "They are the same words he uses for his bitches or his mares when they are in labor. Why not? What else am I now but a poor animal? They say he will stay patiently with them for hours, comforting them until they give birth, and that the most ferocious of them will lick his hands . . ."

He was indeed the last man in the world to whom she would have gone for help at such a time, but, as she herself had said, Philippe du Plessis-Bellière would never cease to astonish her. Under his hand she relaxed and felt stronger.

"Does he think I can't bring his child into the world? I'll show him what I can do. I won't utter a single yell."

"Everything is going fine," said Philippe's voice. "Don't be afraid. You other hothouse plants, help her a little. What the hell do you think . . ."

He was addressing the women as if they were kennel-keepers.

In the semi-consciousness of the last moments Angélique looked up at Philippe. In her dark-circled eyes, veiled with a pathetic tenderness, he caught a glimpse of what would be her downfall. This woman he had thought made wholly of stony ambition and underhanded plotting was capable of weakness. Her look

brought back the past. It was the look of a little girl in
a gray dress whom he was holding by the hand and presenting to the mocking laughter of his friends as the
"Baroness of the Doleful Garb." Philippe ground his
teeth. He put his hand before his eyes to blot out that
look.

"Don't be afraid," he repeated. "There's nothing to
fear now."

"It's a boy," said the midwife.

Angélique saw Philippe holding at arm's length a little red bundle wrapped in linen, and shouting: "My
son! My son!"

They carried her back to the perfumed sheets of her
bed that had been heated with a warming pan. Sleep
overcame her, but before she yielded to it she looked
for Philippe. He was leaning over his son's cradle.

"Now I am no longer of interest to him," she said to
herself. But a feeling of happiness remained with her as
she slept.

It was not until she held the new baby in her arms
for the first time that Angélique realized what this new
existence meant.

He was a lovely infant. His swaddling clothes of fine
linen bordered with satin so completely enswathed him,
even to a hood over his head, that only a little pink
porcelain circle peeped out dotted with two tiny circles
of pale blue that soon would become the same dark
sapphire color as his father's. The nurses and the servant girls kept saying his fuzz was as yellow as a baby
chick's and he was as plump as a cherub.

"It is the child of my bosom," thought Angélique,
"and yet it is not Joffrey de Peyrac's child. I have mixed
my blood, which belonged to him, with a stranger's."
She saw in the child the fruit of a betrayal she had not
hitherto realized. "I am no longer your wife, Joffrey,"
she whispered.

Would he have wished it thus? She began to cry.

"I want to see Florimond and Cantor," she called between sobs. "Bring my children to me."

When they came toward her she shuddered at the

sight of them dressed, by chance, in black velvet. How
different they were from each other, yet so alike in
their equal height, their pale coloring, their thick hair
falling over their lace collars. They placed their hands in
hers in the old familiar gesture of babyhood, as if they
seemed thus to draw strength from her to follow the
course of their perilous future. Then they bowed to her
and sat down on two footstools. The unusual sight of
their mother stretched out in bed made them quiet.

Angélique tried hard to swallow the lump that rose
in her throat. She did not wish to upset them.

She asked them if they had seen their new brother.
Yes, they had. What did they think of him? Apparently
they had no thoughts at all about him, but after ex-
changing looks with Cantor, Florimond admitted that he
was a "nice little cherub."

The result of the combined efforts of their various
tutors was truly remarkable. A system of rules admin-
istered by a birch rod had done part of the work, but
most of it had been due to the intelligence of the boys
themselves in coping with their difficult new disciplines.
Because they had endured hunger and cold and fear,
they could adjust themselves to anything. Give them the
freedom of the countryside, they became wild savages;
dress them in fancy clothes and oblige them to bow
and make polite conversation, they became perfect little
noblemen. Angélique was aware now for the first time
of their amazing flexibility. "Adaptable as only poverty
could teach them to be!"

"Cantor, my troubadour, won't you sing something for
me?"

The boy went for his guitar, and after strumming a
few chords, began:

> Let the drums roll, said the King,
> All my ladies fair to bring.
> And the first one he did see
> Roused his curiosity . . .

"You loved me, Joffrey, and I adored you. Why did
you love me? Because I was beautiful? You loved beauty

so—a beautiful object in your Palace of Gay Learning . . .
But you loved me more than that. I knew it when your
strong arms held me so tight I gasped for breath . . . I
was still a child then . . . But honest . . . Was that perhaps the reason you loved me so . . ."

> Marquis, tell me if you know
> Who's that girl as white as snow?
> Sire, the Marquis quick replied,
> That girl is my blushing bride.

My bride!
The other night when he called her his wife, her
blond Marquis had worn such an impenetrable look. I am
no longer your wife, Joffrey. He claims me now. Your
love is slipping from me like a barge drifting down a
swift river. Forever, forever! How hard it is to say forever . . . to allow that you are becoming but a ghost even
for me.

> More luck than I, have you, Marquis,
> With a bride as fair as she.
> If you wish your love to show,
> You will let me have her now.

Philippe had not come back to see her. He showed no
more interest in her. Now that she had done her job, he
had no further use for her. Why hope? She would never
understand him. What did Ninon de Lenclos say about
him? "He is the nobleman par excellence. He is in
agony over questions of etiquette. He is afraid of having a mudstain on his silk stockings. But he is not
afraid of death. And when he dies, he'll be as lonely as a
wolf, and won't ask help from anybody." He belonged
only to the King and to himself.

> Since you are my monarch, Sire,
> I must grant your least desire;
> Were you but another man,
> I'd revenge your wicked plan.

The King . . . the omnipotent King, strolling in his
festive gardens. The elms glittering with frost like fairy

trees. The plumed courtiers following him from grove to grove. The marble statues cloaked with snow. At the end of one walk the golden figures of Ceres and Flora and Pomona mirrored in the clear ice of a fountain. The King with his walking stick in his gloved hand, the hand of a young man, yet capable of directing destiny, controlling life and death.

> Farewell, my life; farewell, my love;
> Farewell, my hopes of things above.
> Serve we must our lord, the King,
> Even to our long parting.

Good heavens, weren't those the verses Cantor had almost sung before the Queen the other day at Versailles? If it had not been for the Abbé de Lesdiguières, what damage might he not have done! The abbé is surely a help. I must give him another token of gratitude.

> The Queen has had a nosegay made
> Of the fairest lilies in the glade.
> The Marquise sniffed their fragrance sweet,
> And fell down dead at the Queen's feet.

Poor Queen Marie-Thérèse! She would be quite incapable of sending her rivals bouquets of poisoned flowers as Marie de Médicis once did to one of Henri's favorites. She could only weep and dab at her red nose. Poor Queen!

chapter 11

MADAME DE SÉVIGNÉ wrote Madame du
Plessis-Bellière some news of the Court:

> Today at Versailles the King opened the ball with Mad-
> ame de Montespan. Mademoiselle de la Vallière was there,
> but did not dance. The Queen, who remained at Saint-
> Germain, was forgotten . . .

The traditional visits to the new mother, which were
delayed until after the service of the Churching of
Women, invested the Hôtel de Beautreillis with unaccustomed splendor. The favor with which the King
and Queen welcomed their new subject into this world
encouraged all Paris to come to pay court to the lovely
young Marquise.

Proudly Angélique displayed the casket of blue satin
embroidered with fleurs-de-lis, which was the Queen's
gift. It contained a length of cloth of silver and two of
scarlet, a cape of blue taffeta and an exquisite layette of
tiny Cambrai shirts, embroidered baby caps and flowered
bibs. The King had sent two candy-dishes of silver-gilt
and precious stones, filled with Jordan almonds.

Monsieur de Gesvres, the High Chamberlain himself,
delivered the presents of their Majesties to the young
mother, as well as their good wishes. These attentions
from the royal family, flattering as they were, were quite
according to protocol; the wife of a Marshal of France
was entitled to them.

But it was all that was needed to spread, like a flame
in a hayrick, the rumor that Madame du Plessis-Bellière
held the King's heart in her hands. Wicked tongues even
went so far as to whisper that in the veins of the plump

little doll enthroned on his crimson velvet cushion ran the blood of Henri IV.

Angélique disregarded these allusions, and shrugged her shoulders. Foolish people, but bothersome nonetheless! Her bedroom was never free of them, and she received from her bedside like a blue-stocking. Many faces she had almost forgotten turned up there. Her sister Hortense, the wife of a procurator, for instance, turned up with her whole brood. She was rising daily in the ranks of the upper middle class, and she could not have missed the opportunity to acknowledge a relative so much in the limelight as her sister the Marquise du Plessis-Bellière.

Madame Scarron came too. By chance Angélique was alone, and so they chatted freely. The young widow was pleasant company. Always even-tempered, she seemed above complaining or sulking. She was neither resentful of others nor hard on them. But Angélique was surprised not to find in her the warm trusting friendship that she got from Ninon de Lenclos.

Françoise, she thought, is at the bottom of the heap because she will not give up either her virtue or her dignity in her struggle for existence. Frugal to a fault, she never spent a penny she did not have to. Cautious, she never got into a situation she could not get out of. In spite of her poverty and her good looks, she had no debts, no lovers. She relentlessly persisted in presenting petition after petition to the King, for to ask of the King is not to beg, but merely to demand from the government not only one's livelihood but also one's due place in life. Yet none of her petitions had ever been granted, largely because she was so poor. If one has a little money, one can usually get more.

"I don't like to set myself up as an example," Françoise said to Angélique, "but just keep in mind that I have presented either myself or through the agency of some well-situated friend over eighteen hundred petitions to the King."

"You don't mean it!"

"And except for a few meager benefices which were

given me just a short while ago, I have got nothing for my pains. But I'm not giving up. The day will come when I can do something honest and useful for His Majesty or for some noble family, and it will be worthy of its price—possibly only because such a thing is so unusual."

"Are you sure that is the right way to go about it? I have heard His Majesty complain 'that the memorandums of Madame Scarron litter his offices like leaves in autumn,' and that you are well on your way to becoming as permanent a fixture as the tapestries on the walls of Saint-Germain or Versailles."

Her remark did not alter Françoise's composure. "That's not bad news. Although the King might be the last one to admit it, nothing pleases him more than persistence. If you want to succeed you must attract the sovereign's attention, that's certain. So I am certain I will get what I want."

"Which is?"

"Success!"

There was a fine light in her eyes, but she continued in her well-modulated voice: "You remember the ridiculous prophecies that old sorceress Monvoisin made us? What all three of us were going to be someday—Athenais de Montespan, you and I? Well, I don't put any stock whatever in what Monvoisin said. Any inspiration she gets comes out of a jug of wine. The prediction I do keep thinking of was made me at Versailles three years ago by a young workman. You know, simple people who work with their hands, whose minds are uncluttered with all the claptrap of sophisticated living, sometimes have second sight. This fellow was an apprentice mason. He stammered and he had a club foot. One day when I was walking past the sheds around the palace, where His Majesty was having some new additions made, as usual, this boy left his work and came over to me, with all kinds of bows and flourishes. His fellow workers did not laugh, because they knew he could see into the future. His face lit up and he hailed me as 'the first lady of the kingdom.' Then he went on to say that the very spot on which we were standing would be covered by a palace far larger and grander than anything we have now, and he could see all the courtiers doffing their hats and bowing to me as I moved through it. Whenever I get discouraged I think of that, and then I go back again to Versailles, where after all my destiny is supposed to lie."

She was smiling, but her dark eyes were lit with an inner fire. Coming from another the story would have made Angélique smile, but being Madame Scarron's it made a deep impression on her. She saw her now in her true light—grandly ambitious and commandingly conceited. Her simple, obsequious exterior concealed a towering pride and determination.

Far from increasing her dislike of Madame Scarron, this conversation with her made it seem quite advantageous for Angélique to cultivate her friendship.

"Tell me," Angélique said, "since you can shed so much light on so many matters, I have no idea how many obstacles I will encounter at Court, but I have long had a suspicion that my husband is intriguing against me . . ."

"Your husband is a babe in the woods. He knows what is going on, for he has been at Court so long, but he has no intention of interfering. For one thing, you are too beautiful."

"But how can that do me any harm? Whom would it antagonize? There are more beautiful women there than I, Françoise. Don't flatter me so foolishly."

"It is because you are too . . . too different."

"As a matter of fact," said Angélique almost to herself, "that's what the King himself told me."

"You see! Not only are you one of the most beautiful women at Court, but you have a way of setting yourself off. From the moment you open your mouth you can have anyone eating out of your hand because you are charming and amusing. And besides, you have that one thing that so many other beauties would die for but never get."

"What is that?"

"A soul," said Madame Scarron resignedly.

The light had gone out of her eyes. She stared at her pretty hands that hard work had coarsened in spite of all the pains she took with them. "And so," she said with a hopeless sigh, "how can you help . . . making enemies as soon as you put in an appearance?" She burst into tears.

"Françoise," Angélique entreated, "don't tell me you are crying just on account of me and my 'soul.'"

"No, I'm not, really. Only because I was thinking of my own fate. When a woman is beautiful and has a soul, how can she ever fail to get what she wants? That's the trouble. I have missed so much because I haven't that."

The remark served to convince Angélique that Madame Scarron would never be one of her enemies and that she was vulnerable too, even at the end of her rope. Perhaps the King's remark about her had struck home more than she cared to show. Angélique was sorry she had repeated it, for the widow had obviously gone hungry a long time. She would have rung for a snack, but she was afraid she might hurt Françoise's feelings.

"Françoise," she said, "dry your tears. Think of your apprentice's prediction. It's not a liability, as you seem to think, but a trump card that will win you more than anyone else. You are able, and you have already got important and devoted advocates. Isn't Madame d'Aumont one of your patronesses?"

"And so are Madame de Richelieu and Madame Lamoignan." Madame Scarron had by now recovered her composure. "I have been going to their salons regularly for three years now."

"Rather numbing affairs, aren't they?" said Angélique. "They bore me to death."

"Maybe so, but you can get ahead there in due time. That's your one mistake, Angélique, and it will get you into trouble. Mademoiselle de la Vallière made the same one and now she's on the way out. So long as you frequent the Court you cannot be neutral. You must decide for one camp or the other. You don't belong to the Queen's party or Madame's or the Princess'. You have made no choice between the important people and the lightweights, or between the butterflies and the single-minded."

"The single-minded? How much do you think they matter?"

"I mean the truly religious. They matter a great deal, not perhaps in the sight of God, whose true nature we seek to find in our prayer-books, but in the eyes of Justice which hands down the verdicts."

"I don't know what you mean."

"Doesn't Evil wear its most sinister mask at Court? The Lord God of Hosts must put it to rout."

"So, you are advising me to choose between God and the Devil."

"Just about," said Madame Scarron gently.

She rose and took up her cloak and the black fan she never opened because it was full of holes. She kissed Angélique on the forehead and stole silently away.

"What a time to talk about God and the Devil, Madame! Oh, such a terrible thing has happened!"

Barbe's old red face peered through the bed-curtains. She had been there a while before, then had escorted Madame Scarron to the door, and returned. Her eyes were haggard. When her sighs and sobs had failed to attract her mistress' attention, because Angélique was so lost in thought. Barbe decided to speak up.

"Madame, what a frightful calamity!"

"Now what?"

"Our little Charles-Henri has disappeared."

"What Charles-Henri?"

Angélique had not yet got used to the name of her last-born: Charles-Henri-Armand-Marie-Camille de Miremont du Plessis-Bellière.

"You mean the baby? Doesn't the nurse know where she put him?"

"The nurse is gone too. And the cradle rocker as well. And the diaper-girl. In fact, all of little Charles-Henri's staff."

Angélique threw back her covers and commenced to dress without speaking a word.

"Madame," Barbe moaned, "are you out of your mind? A fine lady can't get out of bed just six days after giving birth."

"Then why did you come after me? I supposed it was because you wanted me to do something. There's just one chance in a thousand that there's some truth in what you say, but I suspect you've acquired a certain fondness for the bottle. Ever since the abbé took over the boys, you have had less and less to do, and that hasn't done you any good."

Nevertheless the evidence was conclusive. The baby's rooms were deserted. His cradle was gone, and so was his chest of baby clothes and his first toys and even the flask of absinthe oil and musk which was used to massage his navel.

Barbe had alerted the other servants. They were crowding outside the door in alarm.

Angélique started her investigations. What was the last time anyone had seen the nurse and her assistants? That morning, when the diaper-girl had come to the kitchen for a kettle of hot water. The three had had a good dinner as usual, then there was no sign of them. It turned out, though, that while the servants were having a post-prandial siesta, the porter had gone off to play a game of skittles with the stableboys in the courtyard behind the house. The entrance court had therefore been deserted for a good hour or so—more than enough time for three women to sneak out, one carrying the baby, another his cradle, another his layette.

The porter swore the game of skittles had not lasted more than fifteen minutes.

"So you were part of the plot too!" Angélique accused him.

She vowed she would have him whipped, something she had never done before to any of her servants.

As the minutes ticked by, she recalled frightful stories of children who had been kidnaped and burned.

The nurse had been recommended to her by Madame de Sévigné, who said she was reliable and co-operative. But how could anyone trust that accursed

breed of servants who keep one eye on the households
they work in and the other on their own nefarious interests?

In the meantime Flipot dashed in saying that he knew
all about it. With the knack he had acquired as a
former minion in the Court of Miracles, he had been
quick in sniffing out the trail. Charles-Henri du Plessis-
Bellière had quite obviously been moved bag and baggage to his father's house in the Rue Faubourg Saint-
Antoine.

"The Marquis ordered all the coaches and horses
moved there, didn't he? And kidnaped you one dark
night and locked you up in a convent?"

"Damn Philippe!"

She could not dissemble in front of her servants who
five minutes before had seen her frantic anxiety. So
she let her rage boil. To win them over, she told them
that this was the chance they had been waiting for to
give a sound thrashing to the whole insolent staff of
the Marquis du Plessis who treated them as if they were
delivery boys instead of having just as much right to
the Plessis blue and buff livery which the King himself
deferred to.

She told each one of them, from the meanest scullion
right up to the young abbé, to arm himself with a club
or pike or even a sword, and march to the Faubourg
Saint-Antoine. She herself would go along in a sedan
chair.

The squadron thundered on the oaken door of the
Hôtel du Plessis. The porter leaned out of the barred
window of his lodge and tried to parley. He had strict
orders from the Marquis not to open the gate for anyone
—anyone at all, the whole day.

"Open up to your mistress," roared "Swordthrust" Malbrant, brandishing two cannon fuses which by some
miracle he had in his coat pockets, "or, by my reputation as a swordsman, I'll light these fuses right under
your nose and blow your whole gate and your lodge too
straight to hell."

Racan had already lit a long piece of tow.

The terrified porter said that he would open the gate

to Madame la Marquise on condition that all the rest stay outside. Angélique promised that there would be no immediate attack or battle, and he opened the gate just wide enough to let her and the Gilandon girls slip through.

As soon as she was inside the house she had no difficulty locating the deserters. She struck the nurse, snatched up the infant, and was on her way out when La Violette loomed before her. The Marquis' son, he swore, would leave the house only over his dead body.

Angélique railed at him in her Poitou dialect which he, being a native of the same region, understood perfectly.

The valet finally backed down, throwing himself on his knees at her feet and begging her with tears in his eyes to have pity on him. The Marquis had threatened him with the direst of punishments if he let the child go. One of the threats was that he would be discharged, and that he could not bear, for he had been with the Marquis for years and years. They had hunted their first squirrel together in the forest of Nieul, and he had followed him in all his campaigns.

Nevertheless a lackey in blue and buff livery was already galloping along the road to Saint-Germain, hoping to reach the Marquis before his servants and his wife's cut one another's throats in Paris.

The Marquis' confessor came to try to make the bereft mother listen to reason. Unsuccessful, he had the family's business manager, Molines, sent for. When Angélique saw his authoritative figure, straight as an arrow in spite of his white hairs, her vindictiveness subsided.

Molines suggested they sit down together before the fireplace. He congratulated her on her beautiful child which he was overjoyed to see would carry on his father's line.

"But he wants to take him away from me."

"It is his son, Madame, and—you must believe me—I have never seen a man of his station so ridiculously happy over having an heir."

"You are always on his side," Angélique said, not unhumorously. "I can well imagine how happy he is, probably because of all the suffering he has caused me. His meanness has gone beyond even what you told me."

Still, she agreed to send home her servants and possess her soul in patience until her husband got back —on one condition, that Molines act as an impartial judge.

At nightfall Philippe returned, his spurs jangling as always. He found Angélique and the manager still in a friendly conversation by the hearth.

Little Charles-Henri was clasped tightly to her jealous breast, like the precious thing he was to her, suckling away greedily. The firelight shone on her round white neck. Philippe was so entranced with the sight that Molines had time to rise and take his leave saying how terribly upset Madame du Plessis had been at discovering her child gone. Didn't Monsieur du Plessis know that an infant had to be nursed by its mother? The baby's health was not so robust yet as its appearance implied, and to deprive it of its mother's milk would seriously endanger its very life. And Madame du Plessis was risking a quartain fever, which might cause her milk to dry up.

No, Philippe knew none of these things—they were too far removed from his experience. His face showed his struggle between worry and disbelief. But Molines knew what he was talking about. He was a pater-familias himself and also a grandfather.

The Marquis made one last attempt. "He is my son, Molines. I want him under my own roof."

"In that case, Monsieur le Marquis, Madame du Plessis will have to live here with him."

Angélique and Philippe both shuddered at the thought. Neither said a word. Then they looked at each other like sullen playmates about to make up after a quarrel.

"I cannot leave my two other children," Angélique said.

"They could stay here too," said Molines. "The hôtel is big enough."

Philippe did not deny it.

Molines left, his mission accomplished. Philippe con-

tinued to pace the room, throwing a dark look at Angélique from time to time. She gave all her attention to
Charles-Henri. Finally Philippe drew up a footstool and
sat down next to her. Angélique looked at him suspiciously.

"So," said Philippe, "you can be afraid in spite of all
your bold airs. Perhaps you wanted things to turn out
this way. Well, here you are, right in the wolf's den.
So why are you looking at me so suspiciously when I
sit down next to you. Even a brute of a peasant likes
to sit by the hearth and watch his wife suckle their
first-born child."

"That's just it, Philippe. You may not be a peasant,
but you are a brute."

"I'm glad to see you haven't lost all your zest for
battle."

She turned her head toward him sweetly. His eyes
followed the line of her swanlike throat to her snow-
white breast to the sleeping infant.

"How could I ever dream you would play me such
a dirty trick so soon, Philippe? You were so sweet to me
the other day."

Philippe reacted as if she had insulted him. "You
are wrong. I am never sweet. I just don't like to see a
thoroughbred mare miscarry, that's all. It was my duty to
help you. But my opinions about people and especially
about women and their wiles have not changed a whit.
Besides, I wonder how creatures so little above animals
can still have so much pride. You were not so haughty
the other day. And just like any other stubborn bitch
you wanted your master's hand to reassure you."

"I don't deny it. But your knowledge of feminine
psychology is a little limited, Philippe. Just because you
understand animals better than human beings, you can't
judge one by the other. To you a woman is some strange
hybrid, somewhere between a bitch, a she-wolf and a
cow."

"With a touch of serpent thrown in."

"The dragon of the Apocalypse, in short."

They looked at each other and laughed. Philippe bit
his lip to stop.

"The dragon of the Apocalypse," he repeated, never taking his eyes off Angélique's flesh glowing in the firelight. "My point of view is as good as anyone else's," he said after a moment. "It keeps me free of illusions. The other day at your bedside I remembered a bitch, the most ferocious of the whole pack, on the night I helped her drop a litter of seven pups. There was an almost human look in her eyes, and she yielded to me with a touching devotion. Two days later she chewed a kennel-boy to death just for coming near her puppies."

Suddenly he asked: "Is it true what I heard, that you had fuses set under the gatekeeper's lodge?"

"Yes."

"If he hadn't given in, you would have blown him sky high?"

"Indeed I would!"

Philippe burst into laughter. "By the devil that made you, you do amuse me. You have every fault known to man, but no one could accuse you of being boring." He circled her throat with his hands. "Sometimes I wonder if there's any other way out but to strangle you or . . ."

"Or what?"

"I'll think about it," he said, releasing her. "You haven't won yet. For the moment, I have you in my power."

Angélique took plenty of time to settle herself in her husband's house with her children and their staff and the several servants of her own she wished to keep with her. Philippe's hôtel was gloomy and had none of the modern charm that hers did. But she arranged rooms for herself that turned out handsome and in the best of taste. La Violette told her the apartment she had chosen had formerly been the dowager Marquise's, but that Philippe had had it entirely redecorated only a few months before.

Angélique was astonished to hear this, but she did not dare ask, "For whom?"

A short time later an invitation from the King to a ball at Versailles caused her to leave her new home. For a great lady of the Court, endowed now with two

offices, she had devoted enough time to family affairs.
It was time for her to take up again her duties to the
world. That was what Philippe was doing. She saw him
now less than when she was staying at Court. Realizing
there would be no more evenings at the hearthside, she
set out once more for Versailles.

On the evening of the ball she had a terrible time
finding a place where she could change her clothes. This
was the perpetual affliction of the Court ladies when
they stayed at Versailles, at least for those who were
willing to sacrifice to modesty. For others who did not
object to prurient peeps it was easy.

Angélique took refuge in a little antechamber be-
longing to the Queen's apartments. She and Madame du
Roure helped each other dress, for their maids were
housed the Lord knew where. There were innumerable
intruders—courtiers who paid them compliments as they
passed through, and some who offered to help them.

"Let us alone," Madame du Roure kept squeaking like
a guinea-hen, "or you'll make us late, and you know how
the King hates that." Then she had to run off to find
some pins.

Angélique was taking advantage of her absence to
pull on her silk stockings when a muscular arm seized
her around her waist and tumbled her, her skirts flying,
on a little sofa. A greedy mouth explored her throat.
She let out a scream, and fought desperately to free herself, and as soon as she did gave her assailant two re-
sounding slaps.

She was winding up for a third blow when she found
herself staring at the King. Her arm froze in its outstretched position.

"I never . . . I . . . did not think it was you," she
stammered.

"I did not think it was you either," he said good-
humoredly, but still rubbing his smarting cheek. "Nor
that you had such lovely legs. Why did you show them
if it embarrasses you for people to see them?"

"I can't put on my stockings without exposing my
legs."

"Then why do you choose to put on your stockings in

the Queen's antechamber if not to expose your legs?"

"Because I couldn't find another spot to do it in."

"Are you implying that Versailles is not big enough to accommodate your precious person?"

"Perhaps I am. It's just like a great big theatre without any wings. Precious or not, my person has to stay in center stage all the time."

"So that's your excuse for your unpardonable behavior?"

"And so that's your excuse for your no less unpardonable behavior?"

Angélique tried to rearrange her skirts. She was angry, but a glance at the troubled face of the King restored her sense of humor. She smiled broadly, and the King's features relaxed.

"Little toy, I am a fool."

"Well, I am too quick."

"Yes, you are a wildflower. Believe me, if I had recognized you, I would never have behaved in such a way. But when I came in and saw your blond curls and—my word!—such handsome legs . . ."

Angélique gave him a sidelong look, pursing her lips as if to show that she was not too displeased by his attentions, provided he did not renew them. Even a King might have felt foolish under such a look.

"Will you forgive me?"

She held out her hand, less to be coquettish than to indicate that their tiff was over and forgotten. The King kissed it. He said she was a wonderful woman.

A little later, as she was crossing the marble courtyard, she encountered a guard who seemed to be looking for someone. He accosted her: "I have been instructed by the High Chamberlain to tell you that an apartment has been reserved for you in the wing of the royal princes. May I escort you there, Madame?"

"I? You must be wrong, my good man."

He consulted a notebook. "Madame du Plessis-Bellière? That is your name? I thought I recognized you."

"That is correct."

In a daze she followed the guardsman through the

royal apartments, and those of the highest princes of
the blood royal. At the end of the right wing one of
the quartermasters had just finished writing in chalk
on a little door: "Reserved for Madame du Plessis-
Bellière."

Angélique was so dazzled with joy she could have
fallen on the neck of the quartermaster and the guard.
She gave them several gold pieces. "Drink my health
with that."

"We'll wish you the best of luck and lots of fun," they
said, winking at her knowingly.

She asked them to tell her footmen and maids to bring
her wardrobe and bedclothes. Then with childish glee she
took possession of her apartment, which consisted of
two rooms and a retreat.

As she sat waiting, Angélique meditated with sheer
delight on what befuddled sensations can inspire the
favor of a monarch. Then she stepped out into the
hallway once more to see the inscription: "Reserved for
Madame du Plessis-Bellière."

"So you got it at last, the wonderful 'Reserved for'!"

"I hear the gentlemen in blue have chalked up your
'Reserved.'"

Everyone had heard about it. No sooner did she appear in the ballroom than all eyes were fastened on her
in admiration and envy. She was radiant until the arrival of the Queen's procession somewhat dampened her
enthusiasm.

As she passed, the Queen bowed graciously to those
she recognized, but she pretended not to see the Marquise
du Plessis-Bellière, and stared at her frigidly. Angélique's neighbors did not fail to notice this.

"Her Majesty gave you a sour look," sneered the Marquis de Roquelaure. "Her hopes were reviving when she
saw Mademoiselle de la Vallière slipping from grace, but
now she has a new rival, and a more dazzling one."

"Who?"

"You, my dear."

"I? How silly!"

She had seen in the King's gesture only a wish to be

forgiven and a desire to remedy the situation she had complained about. The courtiers saw in it a new proof of his love for her.

Angélique entered the ballroom.

Brilliantly colored tapestries masked all its walls, and it blazed with the light of the thirty-six chandeliers that hung from its vaulted ceiling. The dancers were forming into rows facing each other, the ladies on the right, the lords on the left. The King and Queen sat in a box apart. At the far end of the room on a stage hung with garlands of gold leaves the musicians were turning up under Lully's direction.

"The Queen is weeping now because of Madame du Plessis-Bellière," croaked a voice. "They say the King is already having apartments readied for his new mistress. Beware, Marquise!"

Angélique had no need to turn around to recognize the source of the voice which seemed to issue from the floor.

"Don't put any faith in that gossip, little Sir Barcarole. The King is not lusting after me—no more than after any other woman of his Court."

"Well, still beware, Marquise. Bad luck is in store for you."

"What do you know about it?"

"Nothing really. Just that Madame de Montespan and Madame du Roure went to see Monvoisin to find some way of poisoning La Vallière. She told them to use magic to turn the King's affections, and already Mariette, her Black Mass priest, has dropped some powders in the royal chalice."

"Be still!" she said in horror.

"Beware of those girls. The day they get to the top of the ladder is the day you'll fall to the bottom."

The violins sang out the first bars of the gay dance rhythms. The King rose and after bowing to the Queen, opened the ball with Madame de Montespan.

Angélique moved forward to take her place in the line.

Behind a tapestry the little cockscombed gnome cackled with laughter.

chapter 12

*T*HE KING was so intrigued with the idea of
going to war that he had a camp set up in the game-
preserve of Saint-Germain. The pavilions were quite
handsome. Lauzun's—he had been restored to favor—
had three rooms hung in crimson silk, in which he gave
a reception for the King followed by a great banquet.

At Fontainebleau, where the Court went next, the
troops were garrisoned, and the ladies could enjoy the
spectacle of military reviews at which the King liked to
show off the fine appearance and splendid discipline of
his troops.

La Violette was polishing his master's steel corselet,
more of a decoration than a necessity, which the Marshal wore under his lace collar. His tent had cost 2,000
livres, and he required five mules to carry all his baggage.
Saddle horses had been provided. The musketeers of his
personal regiment were equipped with chamois coats
as thick as a silver coin with gilded belts and trousers
of buckskin trimmed with gold braid.

There was a warlike spirit everywhere. The rabble
shouted as they passed along the banks of the Seine:
"Hey, King, when are you going to give us a real war?"
They reached the ears of the young sovereign who in-
haled the call to glory in every wind. For war alone
brings true glory. A triumph of arms is always necessary to complete a monarch's grandeur.

The war came as an aftermath to seven years of
peace. Its resplendent spirit evoked in everyone, from
King to princes to nobility to vagabonds, the eternal
thirst of the human race for the epic game of conquest. Their spirits yearned for adventure. (The middle classes, the artisans and the peasants were not consulted, lest they show some disinclination.) For the

nation that undertakes it, war promises victory, riches,
vain dreams of freeing itself from unbearable servitude.
They had confidence in their King. They had no love
for the Spanish or the English or the Dutch or the
Swedes or the princes of the Empire.

It seemed the psychological time to prove to Europe
that France was the greatest nation in the world and was
no longer going to take but give orders.

There was no good excuse for the war, but Louis
XIV charged his apologists with finding one in either
present or past politics. After considerable research they
discovered that Queen Marie-Thérèse, daughter of
Philip of Spain by his first marriage, had a right of inheritance to Flanders to the exclusion of Charles II,
Philip's son by his second marriage.

Spain countered that this right was founded only
upon a purely local law of the Netherlands which ex-
cluded children of a second marriage from an inheritance in favor of children of a first one. As the laws of
Spain were superior to those of any of its provinces,
this local regulation could not obtain. Spain also
pointed out that by her marriage to the King of France,
Marie-Thérèse had forfeited all right of inheritance to the
lands of Spain.

France answered that since Spain had not yet paid
the 500,000 *écus* which it owed the King of France
under the Treaty of the Pyrenees as a dowry for Marie-
Thérèse, this default annulled all preceding promises.

Spain replied that the dowry had not been paid because the dowry stipulated for the daughter of Henri IV
when she became Queen of Spain in 1621 had not been
fully paid by France.

France put a stop to the researches of the his-
torians right then and there on the principle that the
best memory in politics is a short one.

The army departed to conquer Flanders, and the
Court set out behind it on a pleasure jaunt.

It was spring, a rainy spring to be sure, but still the
right season for hatching all projects including bellicose
ones. As many coaches and carriages followed the army
as the troops had cannons and baggage wagons.

Louis XIV wanted the Queen, as heiress to the cities of Picardy, to be acclaimed as sovereign in each conquered town. He also wanted thus to dazzle the population which had been accustomed for more than a century to the autocratic and colorless Spanish rule. Furthermore he wanted to thrust at the Dutch industries whose merchant marine was roaming the seas as far as Sumatra and Java, whereas the French merchant fleet, reduced to practically nothing, was being far outclassed. In order to give the French ship-chandlers time to outfit vessels, Holland had to be crushed. But Louis XIV did not make public this ulterior purpose. It was a secret between him and Colbert.

Under torrential rains the coaches, the carriages and the spare horses advanced over roads that the infantry, the artillery and the cavalry had previously churned into veritable seas of mud.

Angélique was sharing a choach with Mademoiselle de Montpensier, whose friendship she had enjoyed ever since Lauzun was released from the Bastille. At a crossroad they were stopped by a coach that had just turned over. They were told it belonged to one of the Queen's ladies. The princess caught sight of Madame de Montespan on the road-bank and waved to her.

"Come along with us. There's room."

Athenais lifted her skirts and jumped from puddle to puddle to reach their coach into which she tumbled in gales of laughter.

"I have never seen anything so funny," she said, "as Lauzun carrying his hair in his hat. The King kept him riding outside for two hours, and Lauzun's wig got so sopping wet he finally had to take it off."

"But that's terrible," exclaimed the Grande Mademoiselle. "He'll catch cold."

She ordered the coachman to whip up the horses. Around the next bend they caught up with the King's coach. There indeed was Lauzun on horseback, dripping wet, and looking as bedraggled as a moulting sparrow. The Grande Mademoiselle came to his aid in a pathetic voice.

"Cousin, haven't you any feelings at all? You are letting this unhappy gentleman risk an ague. If you aren't
touched by pity, then at least take into consideration
how much you would lose in the person of this loyal
servant of yours."

The King did not even turn his head, but kept staring
before him through his gold and ebony spyglass.

Angélique looked about them. They were on a slight
rise that permitted a view of the black, steaming plain
of Picardy. Under the low-hanging clouds rose the battle-
ments of a little town that seemed as drowned by the
rain as if it lay on the bed of a brook.

French earthworks surrounded it. A second trench outside the first was just being finished. In the rear the
cannon fire intermittently cast a rosy glow over the
landscape. The noise was deafening. The Grande Mademoiselle covered her ears with her hands as she resumed her pleas.

Finally the King put down his spyglass. "Cousin," he
said deliberately, "you are very eloquent, but you always
choose the wrong moment for your harangues. I think
the garrison is about to surrender."

He transmitted to Lauzun the order to cease fire. The
Marquis galloped off.

In fact, they could already make out some activity
at the gate of the citadel.

"I see the white flag," shouted the Grande Mademoiselle, clapping her hands. "In only three days, Sire!
You've captured the town in only three days! Oh, how
magnificent war is!"

When they halted that evening in the conquered
town, and while the shouts of the townspeople still rang
out around the hôtel where the Queen was lodged,
Lauzun searched out Mademoiselle to acknowledge her
intervention on his behalf. The Grande Mademoiselle
smiled. A blush suffused her pale complexion. She excused herself from the card table where she was playing
with the Queen, and asking Angélique to take her
place, drew Lauzun into the recess of a window.

Her face shone as she drank in his words. Seen by

the light of a single candelabrum on a table near them, she seemed almost young and pretty.

"My word, but she's lovesick," thought Angélique.

Lauzun had on his Don Juan expression, but he was careful to keep his distance. Damn Péguilin, that Gascon! Into what romantic boobytrap was he misdirecting the trusting heart of this granddaughter of Henri IV?

The room was full but it was hushed. There were four tables of cards. The monotonous bets of the gamesters and the clink of the *écus* were the only sounds that disturbed the quiet tryst that was going on and on and on.

The Queen for once looked happy. She was pleased to be able to add one city more to the jewels of her crown, but there were more personal gratifications involved. Mademoiselle de la Vallière was not on the expedition. Before setting out on his campaign Louis XIV, in a public law enacted by his Parlement, had made a gift to his mistress of the duchy of Vaujoux in Touraine and also of the barony of Saint-Christophe, two estates of equal value both for their revenues and for the number of their tenants. He had also acknowledged his child by her, little Marie-Anne, who henceforth would be known as Mademoiselle de Blois.

These gestures of the King's neither deceived nor interested anyone. It was the usual parting gift, but the Queen saw in it a return to propriety, a sort of liquidation of all his past errors. The King heaped attention upon her. Whenever they entered a city, she rode by his side, sharing with him the responsibilities as well as the hopes of the campaign. But whenever her eye lit on the Marquise du Plessis-Bellière, her heart began to ache with a new anxiety, for she had been told that the King was infatuated with her and that he had insisted she join his entourage.

She was indeed a very beautiful woman with something serious about her, and attitudes that were at once spontaneous and calculated. Marie-Thérèse deplored the lurking suspicion she had of her, for she liked the Marquise and would have liked to make her her confidante.

But Solignac said she was an immoral woman, lacking in piety. And Madame de Montespan accused her of having a skin disease caught in the slums she liked to frequent. How could one trust appearances? She seemed so healthy and fresh, and her children were so handsome. How trying it would be if the King made her his mistress! And what grief it would cause her! Could the heavy heart of a Queen find no balm?

Angélique knew how painful her presence was to the Queen and took advantage of her first opportunity to withdraw.

The house which had been put at the disposition of the sovereigns by the burgomaster was small and crowded. The nobles of the first rank and the King's suite were literally jammed into it, while the rest of the Court took quarters among the townspeople. The welcome the populace gave the French had forestalled violence and pillage. There was nothing to steal because everything was freely given. The muffled sound of songs and laughter penetrated even into the dimly lit hôtel which still smelled of the *tourte picarde,* a mammoth confection of pears covered with custard, that three of the town women had brought on a silver platter.

Threading her way through the stacks of trunks and other baggage, Angélique found the staircase. The room she had chosen to share with Madame de Montespan was on her right, the King and Queen's on the left.

A little shadow appeared in the dim flicker of the nightlight and took the shape of a black mask in which two white eyes presently gleamed at her.

"No, Ma'am, don't go in."

Angélique recognized the little Negro she had given Madame de Montespan.

"Hello, Naaman. Let me by."

"No, Ma'am."

"What's the matter?"

"Som'un's dere."

She could just barely hear a tender murmuring. She guessed that some romance was afoot.

"All right, I'll go away."

The page's white teeth glistened in a grin framed in ebony. "The Kink, Madame. The Kink. Shhh!"

Angélique went down the staircase ruminatively. The King! And Madame de Montespan!

The next day everyone left for Amiens.

Angélique dressed early and went to the Queen's apartments, as was her duty. At the entrance Mademoiselle de Montpensier was clucking nervously.

"Oh, what a state Her Majesty is in! It's a great pity, a great pity!"

The Queen was indeed in tears, at the end of her tether, as she said. Madame de Montausier was comforting her as she sobbed and groaned, and Madame de Montespan kept repeating in a voice that got louder and louder how completely understandable Her Majesty's sorrow was. The news was that Mademoiselle de la Vallière had just rejoined the army; after driving all night, she had arrived at daybreak and had come to pay her respects to the Queen.

"What effrontery!" Madame de Montespan kept exclaiming. "May God keep me from ever being the King's mistress! If such a thing ever happened to me, I would never be so inconsiderate as to appear before the Queen!"

What was the meaning of this return? Had the King demanded the presence of his favorite?

Then everyone went to church where the Court was to hear Mass before proceeding.

Marie-Thérèse ascended the stand reserved for the royal party. The Duchesse de la Vallière was already there. The Queen did not look at her. The favorite left the platform. Then she presented herself before the Queen once more as Marie-Thérèse was entering her coach. The Queen did not speak to her, so bitter was her disillusionment. She could no longer ignore the situation as, for better or worse, she had done while the relationship between her husband and this woman was still official. In her rage she forbade anyone even to bring her food, and she ordered the officers of her guard of

escort to allow no one to get ahead of her coach for fear
that Mademoiselle de la Vallière might rejoin the King
before she herself did.

Toward evening the long line of jolting coaches
caught up with the army on a little rise. Mademoiselle
de la Vallière was aware that the King was below. With
a courage born of despair she ordered her coach to dash
across the open fields at top speed.

When the Queen saw this, her anger was uncontrollable. She wanted to order her guardsmen to follow the
coach and stop it, but everyone kept begging her not
to, and to calm herself. The arrival of the King himself,
who had got there before the Queen by following a
different road, resolved this half pathetic, half farcical
crisis.

He was on horseback and spattered with mud from
top to toe, but in an excellent humor. As he dismounted
he apologized for not entering the Queen's coach because of his dirty clothes, but after he had talked to
her a while through the door he stopped smiling.

The rumor was passed along that the King had not
desired and had certainly not commanded the arrival
of Mademoiselle de la Vallière. What had she heard to
cause such unusual impetuousness? She had always been
such a patient, shy sort. What suspicions had inspired
her? Or what facts?

Alone at Versailles, covered by her new dignities and
surrounded by her new wealth, she had suddenly realized she had been abandoned. At her wits' end she had
ordered her coach and set off at a gallop toward the
north in direct disobedience to the King. Anything
rather than be tortured with thoughts that his heart
had changed and that the man she loved might be already in the arms of another.

She did not put in an appearance at the dinner that
followed at the halt. It was a wretched cantonment,
a town containing no more than four stone houses, the
rest being mud hovels.

Accompanied by the Gilandon girls and her three
maids, Angélique was searching for a lodging when she

ran into Mademoiselle de Montpensier, who was in the
same shelterless condition.

"Well, we are certainly off to the wars, aren't we?"
she said. "Madame de Montausier couldn't find anything but a pile of straw in an outhouse for a bed, and
the Queen's ladies are stowed away in a pile of wheat
in a loft. As for me, I'll be lucky if I can find an ash-
heap."

Angélique finally found a hay barn. She hoisted herself up a ladder to the loft, where she could sleep comfortably, while her companions stayed below in the bin.
A big lantern hanging from the joists shed a dull red
glow over the scene—just enough light for Angélique
to perceive taking shape like a black ghost the jet
features, the white eyeballs and the crimson and apple-
green turban of the little Negro Naaman.

"What are you doing there, you imp of Satan?"

"I waiting Ma'am Montespan. Watch her bed for she.
She sleep here too."

At that moment the lovely face of the Marquise came
into view over the top rung of the ladder.

"What a good idea, Angélique, to share my 'green
room,' as our brave soldiers call a billet like this! We
can play piquet if we can't get to sleep." She fell into the
hay, stretched and yawned with all the sensuous relaxation of a cat. "Oh, how soft it is! What a marvelous
bed! It's like when I was a child back in Poitou."

"That's just what I was thinking," said Angélique.

"There was a haybarn right near our dovecote. My
little lover used to meet me there. He was a shepherd
boy, only ten years old. We loved to listen to the pigeons
cooing as we held hands."

She stripped off her tight bodice. Angélique followed
her example. Then they peeled off their outer skirts,
rolled off their stockings, and burrowed into the hay,
ecstastically rediscovering sensations they had long since
forgotten.

"From shepherd boy to King," whispered Athenais.
"What do you think of my future now, darling?" She
propped herself up on one elbow. The ruddy light of

the lantern deepened the glow of her cheeks and warmed
the alabaster of her neck and shoulders. She giggled as if
she were tipsy. "To be loved by a King! How intoxicating!"

"Suddenly you seem very sure of that love. A while
ago, you weren't so sure."

"Ah, but now I have proof! I need never doubt
again. . . . Last night he came to me . . . I knew he
would come sometime on this trip. The way he left La
Vallière at Versailles showed the way he was feeling,
didn't it? He gave her a few trinkets as a parting gift."

"Trinkets? A duchy and a peerage? A barony?"

"Pooh! They might seem tremendous to her, and she
probably thinks she's at the peak of her power. That's
why she thought she had the right to rejoin the Court.
Ha-ha, she's a bad loser. . . . I'll never settle for baubles like those. He can't treat me like some opera dancer.
I am a Mortemart!"

"Athenais, you frighten me talking this confidently.
Have you really become the King's mistress?"

"Yes, I have. His mistress! Oh, Angélique, what fun
it is to know the power you have over a man like him!
To see him tremble and grow pale . . . to hear his
entreaties . . . And he so self-controlled, so solemn, so
majestic, even terrifying sometimes . . . It's true what
they say about him, when he makes love he is a wild
man. There's nothing subtle about him then. He's
greedy with lust, but I can satisfy him."

She laughed with mad delight, rolling her blond head
back and forth in the hay and writhing her arms with
sensual abandon, as if she were reliving an all too recent
moment of passion, that Angélique could hardly bear
it.

"That's just fine," she said sarcastically. "Everyone will
want to know who the King's new mistress is, and now
I won't have to be bothered listening to all their silly
suspicions."

Madame de Montespan sat up abruptly. "Oh no, darling, not that. You must not breathe a word of it. We
are depending on your discretion. The time hasn't come
yet to acknowledge my position openly. That would

just complicate everything. Please oblige us by doing what we expect of you."

"And what is that? And who is 'we'?"

"Why . . . the King and I."

"Do you mean to say that you—the King and you— hope the rumor will spread that he is in love with me in order to throw everyone off your trail?"

Under their long lashes Athenais' dark blue eyes surveyed Angélique with an evil glint. "Why, of course. You see, that would help us out. I am in a delicate situation. On the one hand I am Lady-in-Waiting to the Queen, and on the other an intimate friend of Mademoiselle de la Vallière. The King's attentions would ruin my reputation. There has to be some sort of red herring. I don't know why they've begun talking about you, but the King has certainly helped the gossip by giving you so many posts. And the Queen has been very cool to you. Poor Louise can burst into tears just at the mere mention of your name. No one thinks about me any more. They've lost the scent. I know you have enough good sense to have seen this right from the beginning. The King is much obliged to you. So don't say anything, will you? Do you mind?"

Angélique did not answer. She picked up a wisp of hay and began chewing on it nervously. Inwardly she felt hurt, and as if she had been more gullible than she liked to let herself be. And here she was supposed to know how to outwit the trickiest businessmen and traders in the kingdom! Yet when it came to worldly intrigues like this she was still basically a naive, countrified peasant girl.

"Why should you mind?" Madame de Montespan continued, all sweetness. "It's quite flattering for you, and you have already got rewards and a certain glory. Do you think you've been misled? Hardly. I can't imagine you ever took that little farce seriously. In the first place, you love your husband, or so it seems. How funny! He is not very ardent, but he is handsome, and they say he's very susceptible to flattery . . ."

"Would you like to play cards?" Angélique asked tonelessly.

"I'd be glad to. I have a pack in my bag. Naaman!"
The little Negro handed her her traveling kit. They
played several hands without taking much interest in the
game. Angélique lost out of absent-mindedness, and
this did not improve her humor. Madame de Montespan
dropped off to sleep at last, with a smile on her lips.

Angélique was not in a smiling mood. She kept biting
at a hangnail as her vexation increased, and as the night
wore on she conceived more and more plans for revenge. By morning the name of Madame de Montespan
would be on everyone's lips. She had been very unwise
to think Angélique would fall for her insincerity.

Athenais had found an exquisite pleasure in revealing her triumph and the part she had unwittingly assigned her. Sure of the King's support and of her control over him, she had allowed herself the enjoyment
of tearing to pieces a woman of whom she had long
been jealous but whom she treated well for opportunistic
reasons. Now she had no further need of her or of her
money. She could humiliate her and make her pay
through the nose for the success her beauty and wealth
had won for her.

"Idiot!" thought Angélique, more exasperated than
ever at herself. She wrapped herself in her cloak and
stole down the ladder, leaving Madame de Montespan
sound asleep and resting as lightly on the hay—and as
unclothed—as a goddess on a cloud.

Outside, the east was brightening, and a few drops of
rain were falling. From the direction of the reddening
horizon drifted the sound of fifes and drums as the regi-
ments broke camp.

Angélique trudged through the sticky mud to the
house where the Queen was lodged and where she knew
she would find Mademoiselle de Montpensier. In the
entryway she spied Mademoiselle de la Valliére shivering
on a bench and looking abjectly wretched. Her young
sister-in-law and two or three maids were with her,
all dreary and red-eyed from sleeplessness. They all
looked so forlorn that they touched her heart and she
stopped in spite of herself.

"What are you doing there, Madame? You'll catch your death of cold."

Louise de la Vallière raised her blue eyes, too big for her waxen face, and shuddered as if she had been roused from a trance.

"Where is the King?" she said. "I want to see him. I can't leave here without seeing him. Where is he? Please tell me."

"I do not know, Madame."

"You do know. I am certain of it. *You* know . . ."

Out of pity Angélique took into her own the two thin, cold hands the Duchess held out to her. "I swear I do not know. I have not seen the King since . . . I don't know when. And I can assure you he hardly cares a rap about me. It's sheer madness for you to stay out here on such a cold night."

"That's what I keep telling her," groaned the sister-in-law. "She's exhausted, and so am I, but she will not give in."

"Haven't you a room in the village?"

"Yes, but she wants to wait for the King."

"Stop being so foolish." Angélique seized the Duchess under the arms and yanked her up. "You are going to get some warmth into you and then you are going to lie down. The King won't like it if you show up before him looking like a ghost."

In the house where some shelter had been reserved for the favorite, she commanded the lackeys to build up the fire. Then she passed the warming pan between the damp sheets, prepared a tisane, and put Mademoiselle de la Vallière to bed with such unrelenting authority that the Duchess did not dare protest. Under the coverlets which Angélique heaped over her, she seemed terribly frail. The epithet "gaunt" which a vindictive pamphleteer had bestowed upon her seemed hardly exaggerated. Her bones stuck out through her skin. She was in the seventh month of pregnancy, her fifth in six years. She was only twenty-three years old. Behind her already was the greatest love affair any woman could hope for; before her a long long life of tears. Just the

previous autumn she had shone with what had proved to
be a sunset glory. Only a few months later the change
was overpowering.

"That's what loving a man can do to a woman,"
Angélique thought. Her anger flared again. She remembered Barcarole's story of how La Vallière's rivals wanted
to poison her, and shuddered.

"How good you are," murmured Louise de la Vallière. "But they said . . ."

"Why do you pay any heed to what 'they' say? You
just injure yourself needlessly. I can't do anything about
wicked tongues any more than you can. I'm just like you
in that respect."

She was about to add: "And just as stupid. I've been
an unwitting screen." Then she thought, "What good
would that do?" Why turn Louise's jealousy in another
direction? Soon enough she would find a revenge so
sweet it would make her best friend's betrayal look
feeble.

"Go to sleep now," she whispered. "The King still
loves you." It was the only thing she could think of to
soothe the ache of poor Louise's wounded heart.

Louise gave her a pathetic little smile. "He has not
been good to me."

"How can you say that? Hasn't he just shown his
devotion by giving you all those titles and other presents
which leave no doubt of how he feels about you? You
are Duchesse de Vaujoux, and your daughter will
not be condemned to obscurity."

The favorite shook her head. Tears seeped out of her
closed eyes and dribbled down her temples. She who
had always concealed her pregnancies at the cost of
unspeakable torment, who had seen her babes torn
from her as soon as they were born, who had never permitted herself to grieve for the three sons she had lost,
even to the point of appearing at a ball smiling in order
to deceive anyone as to her true grief, who had always
done her utmost to give the lie to her scandalous position, had suddenly seen herself publicly declared the
mother of a daughter by the King without having even
been consulted about the announcement. And wasn't

there a rumor that the Marquis de Vardes was being re-called from exile by the King in order to marry her?

All Angélique's words of comfort and encouragement were empty. They had come too late. Angélique said no more, just sat holding her hand until finally she fell asleep.

As she was going back to the Queen's house, Angé-lique glimpsed a coach lamp. It made her think of the Queen, also waiting for the King, tortured by a thousand suspicions, imagining him in the arms of La Val-lière, who all the time was waiting in the cold one floor below her. What good would it do to tell her the name of her true rival? It would add only one more drop of venom to her already over-poisoned cup. Madame de Montespan was justified in sleeping soundly in her nest of hay. She knew—she had always known—that Madame du Plessis would hold her tongue.

Charleroi, Armentières, Saint-Vinoux, Douai, Ouden-arde, the fortress of La Scarpe, Courtrai—all fell like houses of cards.

In each the King and Queen of France were received with pomp and harangued by aldermen, and after pa-rading through carpeted streets, went to hear a *Te Deum* in some old lacy-gothic church of the North whose slender flèche seemed to pierce the sullen sky.

In between *Te Deums* the war would break out in a kind of convulsion, and the fire of cannon and musket sound in the distance. The garrison risked sorties that sometimes resulted in casualties, but the Spanish were few in number and Spain was far away. Cut off from reinforcements and under the pressure of inhabitants who had no wish to suffer the pangs of starvation for the sake of glory, the towns surrendered.

Beneath the walls of Douai the horse of one of the King's guards was killed under him. Louis XIV was very much in the field. The smell of powder intoxi-cated him, and he took delight in leading a squadron to the attack. Once the siege of Lille had begun, he would climb down into the trenches every day like a common soldier, much to the concern of the courtiers.

After Turenne saw him covered with dirt from a cannon ball that had just landed near him, he threatened to raise the siege if the King continued to be so rash. But the King had led the charge right up to the breast-works in full view of the army, and refused to retreat. The Marshal du Plessis-Bellière said to him: "Take my hat and give me yours. Then if the Spaniards aim at the plume they will get the wrong man."

The next day the King was more prudent. Philippe was awarded the blue ribbon of the Order of Saint-Louis.

Summer arrived, and the weather grew hot. The smoke of the mortars rose in little clouds into a sky of peri-winkle blue.

Mademoiselle de la Vallière had remained at Com-piègne, but the Queen rejoined the army, taking with her in her carriage Mademoiselle de Montpensier, the Princesse de Bade, Madame de Montausier and Madame de Montespan. Behind them, in another coach, came Mesdames d'Armagnac, de Bouillon, de Créqui, de Béthune and du Plessis-Bellière. They were all tired to death and terribly thirsty.

As they alighted they were surprised to encounter a caravan consisting of a wagon laden with cakes of ice. It refreshed them merely to look upon it glistening in the sunlight. Escorting it were some ungainly fellows, with jet-black mustaches and dour looks, in patched uniforms. The officer who rode with them left no doubt whatever of their origin. His full plaited ruff and his lofty manner revealed him as a true hidalgo of His Most Catholic Majesty. He explained to the ladies that Monsieur de Brouay, the Spanish governor of Lille, sent ice every day to the King of France out of chivalry—or perhaps sheer bravado.

"Ask him," said the King, "to send me a little more."

"Sire," answered the Castilian, "my general saves it because he hopes it will be a long siege and he is afraid he may run out of ice for Your Majesty."

The old Duc de Charost shouted to him from the King's side, "Good for him! Tell Brouay not to follow the

Governor of Douai's example. He surrendered like a craven rogue."

"Are you insane, sir?" the King said sharply. "Do you want to encourage our enemies to resist?"

"Sire, it's a matter of family pride. You see, Brouay is my cousin."

The life of the Court continued in the camps. The fields were strewn with many-colored pavilions symmetrically disposed. The King's, which was the largest, consisted of three rooms—one sleeping room and two conference rooms. It was hung with Chinese silk and furnished with gilded chairs and tables. His arising and retiring went on with exactly the same ceremony as at Versailles.

Everyone enjoyed the sumptuous meals all the more by thinking of the Spaniards behind the somber ramparts of Lille, reduced to gnawing horseradishes.

Louis XIV entertained the ladies of the Court at his table. One evening at dinner his glance fell on Angélique sitting not far from him. His recent victories, not to mention the more personal one over Madame de Montespan, and the exhilaration of triumph, had somewhat dimmed his usually keen powers of observation. He thought he was seeing her for the first time during the campaign and asked her pleasantly:

"So you have left the capital? What were they saying in Paris when you set out?"

Angélique looked at him coolly. "Sire, they were saying evening prayers."

"I meant, what was new?"

"Green peas, Sire."

Her answers might have seemed funny if they had not been uttered in a tone as icy as the look in her eyes. The King fell silent in astonishment, and since he was not quick-witted, his cheeks grew red.

Madame de Montespan came to the rescue by laughing infectiously. She explained that the latest game was to answer direct questions as absurdly as possible. Everyone was playing it in Paris in the salons and at the receptions of the intellectuals, trying to get the best of one another, and Madame du Plessis was very clever at it. Soon everyone at the table was trying it, and the meal ended in fun.

On the following morning Angélique was applying her make-up under the eyes of an inquisitive cow when the Marshal du Plessis-Bellière had himself announced. Like all the other great ladies who had taken the field, she suffered few of the inconveniences of travel. As soon as she could find a place to set up her dressing table, she carried on as at home. The scent of her face powder and perfumes mingled with the stink of manure, but neither the great lady in her filmy negligee nor the black and white cows that kept her company bothered one another. Javotte was helping her into her first skirt, which was pink silk with pale green stripes, while Thérèse tied its laces.

When she saw her husband Angélique sent the maids away, but she continued to concentrate on her reflection in the mirror, in which Philippe's stormy face appeared over her shoulder.

"I hear foul rumors about you, Madame. I thought it my duty to leave my post to lecture you, perhaps punish you."

"What are these rumors?"

"You made fun of the King when he did you the honor of speaking directly to you."

"Is that all?" said Angélique, selecting a beauty patch from a little box of chased gold. "There are plenty of other rumors about me making the rounds which might have disturbed you long ago. The only time you seem to remember your marital duties is when you think you should apply the matrimonial lash."

"Did you answer the King impertinently? Answer yes or no."

"I had my reasons."

"But . . . you were speaking to the King!"

"King or not, he is still nothing but a naughty boy who needs to be put in his place from time to time."

If she had uttered blasphemy, Philippe could not have been more overwhelmed. He seemed to be choking.

"Have you lost your mind?"

He paced up and down, then leaned against the wooden manger and began to stare at Angélique as he chewed on a piece of straw.

"Aha, now I see which way the wind blows. I gave you a bit of freedom in honor of my son whom you bore and nursed, and you are trying to take advantage of it. It's high time I started cracking the whip again."

Angélique shrugged her shoulders, restraining herself from answering him too smartly, and gave her entire attention to her mirror as she performed the delicate operation of affixing a patch to her right temple.

"What would be a fitting punishment to teach you how to behave at a King's table?" Philippe said. "Exile? Hum! You would find some way of showing up again behind me just as soon as I turned my back. You need another taste of my dog whip. Yes, I remember that made you hang your head. Or . . . I can think of a few other even more exquisite measures, such as the end of a rope, that I am tempted to try on you."

"Don't tire your imagination, Philippe. You are too strict a schoolmaster. It was only three words that just happened to pop out . . ."

". . . in answer to the King!"

"The King is only a man after all."

"That is where you are mistaken. The King is the King. You owe him obedience and respect and loyalty."

"And what else? Am I to give him the right to dictate my life, to sully my reputation, to betray my confidence?"

"The King is our master. He has all rights over you."

Angélique swung around and squinted at Philippe defiantly. "Oh yes? And if it strikes his fancy to make me his mistress, what am I to do then, pray?"

"Agree. Doesn't it occur to you that all his ladies, the gems of the Court of France, are there only for the prince's pleasure?"

"Well, you certainly are a generous husband! If your affection for me doesn't, then your proprietary instincts certainly should absolutely refuse."

"Everything I own belongs to the King. I would never refuse him anything, from the smallest trifle right up to my life itself."

Angélique screamed with vexation. Her husband had a way of wounding her to the quick. But what had she expected? Some indication that he was jealous? That was too much. He cared nothing for her, and did not disguise the fact. His passing interest in her by the hearthside was only for the person who had happened to have the honor of delivering his infant heir. She turned back to her dressing table, snapped shut the box of patches, and, her hands shaking with rage, picked up first one comb and then another.

Philippe watched her with grim satisfaction.

Angélique's anger burst forth in a flood of harsh words. "I forgot. It is true, a woman to you is nothing more than a thing, a piece of furniture, good only for bringing children into the world. Less than a broodmare, less than a stableboy. Something to be bought and sold, or put out to pasture when she has ceased to be of use to you. That's what women are to men of your kind. At best, they're a piece of cake or a bowl of stew you leap on when you're hungry."

"A pretty picture!" said Philippe. "I don't deny it's true. I must confess that with your rosy cheeks and your plump figure, you are appetizing. As a matter of fact, I feel hungry all of a sudden."

He tiptoed up to her and laid his hands possessively on her shoulders. Angélique jerked away and laced up her bodice tightly.

"Don't count on anything like that, my boy," she said icily.

In a frenzy Philippe ripped open her bodice, tearing off three of its diamond-studded hooks. "Do I have to say 'Please,' you simpering fool?" he growled. "Can't you ever understand that you belong to me? Ha-ha, that's where the stick really hurts, isn't it? The proud Marquise still would like to think she's entitled to pretty little attentions!"

He sripped off her bodice, tore away her chemise, and seized her breasts with the brutality of a mercenary soldier on a night of rapine.

"Have you forgotten your origins, Madame la Marquise? Once you were nothing but a little peasant girl with a runny nose and dirty feet. I can see you now in your tattered short skirt, your hair hanging down in your eyes, and proud as Satan."

He grasped her head to bring her face close to his, squeezing her temples so hard she thought her skull would split.

"And this is what crawls out of a crumbling old castle and thinks she can answer the King impertinently! The stable is where you belong, Madame de Monteloup, and it would suit you better even now. I am going to revive some of your peasant memories."

"Let me go!" screamed Angélique, trying to strike him.

But she bruised her knuckles on his metal breastplate and had to shake her aching fingers, groaning with pain. Philippe laughed, and twisted her while she struggled.

"Now, little brat of a shepherd-girl, we'll truss you up without any further ado."

He lifted her up in his arms and tossed her onto a pile of hay in a dark corner of the barn.

"Let me go! Let me go!" Angélique kept screaming.

"Shut up! Do you want to rouse the whole garrison?"

"Yes. So much the better. Then everyone could see the way you treat me."

"What a fine scandal! Madame du Plessis raped by her own husband!"

"I hate you!"

She was half smothering in the hay where they struggled, but she succeeded in biting his hand until it bled.

"Bitch!"

He struck her several times across the mouth, then pinioned her arms behind her back, paralyzing her movements.

"Good Lord," he panted, half jokingly, "I never had to deal before with such a madwoman. I need a whole regiment."

Angélique felt her strength ebbing. This would be just like the other times. She would have to submit to his humiliating ownership in the bestial subservience he de-

manded. Her pride reared up against it, and her love too
—the bashful love she had borne Philippe, which would
never die, which she would never confess.

"Philippe!"

He was achieving his ends. This was not the first time
he had had a struggle like this in the hay in some dark
corner of a lonely barn. He knew how to subdue his
prey and tear it to pieces as it palpitated pantingly under him.

Tiny pinpoints of gold danced in the thin shaft of sunlight that shot into the deep shadows from between the
boards of the wall.

"Philippe!"

He heard her call his name, but her voice sounded
strange to him.

Out of fatigue or perhaps the soporific odor of the hay
Angélique succumbed. She had had enough of anger,
and accepted the attentions and the mastery of the man
who had treated her so cruelly. It was the same Philippe
she had loved ever since the days at Monteloup. What
difference did it make that she was hurt so long as it
was by him?

She surrendered to the elation of her instincts and became only a female yielding to the demands of a male.
She was his victim, his thing. He had a right to use her
as he pleased.

In spite of the raging passion that possessed him,
Philippe perceived the moment of capitulation which
suddenly relaxed her. Fearing he had wounded her, he
controlled his blind desire a little and tried to guess
what the darkness concealed in the sudden silence. Then
he felt the gentle touch of her hand on his cheek, sending
a thrill through him and so unnerving him that he sank
feebly against her body.

He resolved to restrain himself, and withdrew not
knowing that he had almost brought her to the point of
ecstasy.

Glancing at her out of the corner of his eye, he guessed
that she was arranging her clothing. Each of her movements brought him the warm perfume of her flesh. He
began to suspect her compliance.

"My compliments seem to have displeased you less than I thought. Don't forget they were intended as a punishment."

She let a second slip by before she answered in a sweet, shy voice: "Perhaps they were a reward."

Philippe leaped to his feet as if he sensed a present danger. He felt unnaturally weak. He would have liked again to lie in the warm hay near Angélique and talk intimately, but such an unfamiliar temptation disgusted him.

He left the barn with the uncomfortable feeling that this time he had not had the last word.

chapter 13

VERSAILLES sweltered under the broiling sun of a July afternoon. To find a little coolness Angélique and Madame de Ludre and Madame de Choisy were stro ing by the Water Arch, a pleasant walk shaded by trees and cooled by fountains that shot upward on both sides behind a grassy bank to join above in a vault so lofty that one could walk beneath it without getting sprinkled. Here they encountered Vivonne.

"I have a proposition to discuss with you, Madame," he said to Angélique. "I address you now not as the most ravishing nymph of these groves, but as a wise mother such as the ancients would have revered. In a word, I ask your consent to add your boy Cantor to my suite."

"Cantor? But how could such a child be of use to you?"

"You might as well ask how one could wish to have a songbird. The boy has completely captivated me. He sings so sweetly and plays so many different instruments so well, I should like to have him along on my expedition so that I may continue composing verses and listen to them sung by his angelic voice."

"Your expedition?"

"Don't you know that I have just been appointed Admiral of the Fleet? The King is sending me to fight the Turks besieging Candia in the Mediterranean."

"So far away!" Angélique exclaimed. "I don't want to let my boy go. He is much too young, only eight years old . . ."

"He looks eleven. He would not be lonely. My pages are all boys of good family. My steward is a mature man who has several children of his own, and he can be trusted to take good care of your sweet little boy. In addition, Madame, don't you have interests in Candia?

Shouldn't you be sending one of your sons to look after your fief?"

Angélique refused to take the proposal seriously, but she did say she would think it over.

"It would be to your advantage to grant Vivonne's request," Madame de Choisy remarked after the Admiral had left them. "He has a very high position now. His new promotion has made him one of the most important persons in France."

Madame de Ludre smiled acidly. "And don't let's forget that His Majesty is more and more disposed every day to honor him, if for no other reason than to get in the good graces of his sister."

"You talk as if Madame de Montespan were already the favorite," said Madame de Choisy. "She is being very discreet about it."

"What she shows and what she does are not necessarily the same, as you should have learned from experience by this time. Perhaps Madame de Montespan would rather not disclose her romance, but her jealous husband hasn't given her a chance. He is making as much of a scandal out of it as if his rival were some Paris fop or other."

"Don't mention that man's name! He's a fool and one of the most dissolute men in the kingdom to boot."

"I hear that recently he came to a little dinner party of Monsieur's without a wig, and when he was asked why, said he had two horns on his forehead that kept him from wearing one. He really is funny!"

"What he dared say to the King yesterday at Saint-Germain isn't so funny. We were coming back from a walk on the terrace when we saw Montespan's coach all shrouded in black with silver tassels. He was in black too. The King seemed to be very concerned and asked him who he was in mourning for. He answered very sorrowfully, 'For my wife, Sire.'"

Madame de Ludre laughed loudly, and so did Angélique.

"Go on and laugh," Madame de Choisy said in a tone of injured dignity. "That kind of behavior is all very

well for a street carnival, but not for the Court. The King
won't stand for it. Montespan is risking the Bastille."

"That's where everyone winds up."

"How can you be so cynical, Madame?"

"The King won't go to such lengths. It would amount
to a public confession on his part."

"As far as I'm concerned," Angélique said, "I had just
as soon have Madame de Montespan's conduct made public. I have had to endure the ridiculous gossip that's
been spread about the King and insignificant little me.
Then they could see there was absolutely no basis for it."

"Well, I must say I thought for a long time it was you
who would succeed Mademoiselle de la Vallière," said
Madame de Choisy almost wistfully. "But I do admit you
have kept your reputation." She sounded as if she were
annoyed that her predictions had proved false.

"You didn't have to cope with as uncooperative a
husband as Monsieur de Montespan," said Madame de
Ludre, "always throwing poisoned darts. He isn't even
at Court now you are here . . ."

"He has had to be at the front, first in Flanders and
now in Franche-Comté."

"Now don't get cross, dear. I was only joking, and after
all he is only a husband."

As they chatted they came to the broad walk that led
to the palace, where they had to keep dodging workmen
and servants carrying or climbing ladders to hang lanterns on the bushes and the long rows of elms. Axes
were ringing deep in the thickets. The park was getting ready for a fête.

"I hope we'll have time to change our clothes," said
Madame de Choisy. "The King seems to be preparing
some wonderful surprise for us, but ever since we arrived everyone has been twiddling his thumbs while
His Majesty has held conference after conference."

"The fête is supposed to begin at twilight. I think
our patience will be rewarded."

The King wanted to celebrate his triumph of arms
with a series of great fêtes. The glorious conquest of
Flanders and the lightning winter campaign in Franche-

Comté had borne fruit. An astonished Europe was keeping its eye on the young king, who previously had been regarded as the victim of treacherous advisers. His pomp and pageantry had already become the talk of the world; now his audacity in warfare and his subtle diplomacy were drawing equal attention. Louis XIV wanted the brilliance of his fêtes to be noised abroad, like clashing cymbals to accompany the trumpets of his fame.

He had charged the Duc de Créqui, the first gentleman of the bedchamber; Marshal de Bellefonde, the chief steward; and Colbert, as well as his master of the works, to oversee the organization of pageants, banquets, triumphal displays, illuminations and fireworks. The plans were quickly drawn and executed.

Just as Angélique appeared in a gown of turquoise blue frosted with so many diamonds that she seemed clad in a rainbow, the King entered the great hall from his apartments. He was no more splendidly attired than usual, but he had never seemed more charming. Everyone realized that now the hour for pleasure had struck.

The gates of the palace had been opened to the populace, who were now invading the courtyards, the salons and the gardens, their eyes popping as they ran from point to point throughout the grounds to see the royal procession pass. The King kept hold of the Queen's hand. She was like a child for delight, even though her narrow shoulders could hardly bear the weight of the gold-embroidered dress that encased her like a gothic shrine. She adored such an array of gorgeous finery, and the fact that the King was by her side made her seem beside herself with happiness. It was as if her aching heart knew a little respite from its pain, for the tattling tongues of the Court had not yet agreed on who the new favorite was to be.

Of course, Mademoiselle de la Vallière and Madame de Montespan were there, the former rather crushed, but the latter as merry as usual. And Madame du Plessis-Bellière was there, too, more beautiful and distinguished than ever. And Madame de Ludre and Madame du Roure. But they were merely part of the crowd, and no one paid them any particular attention.

The King and Queen, with the Court following them at a slight distance, walked across the lawns that led down to the Fountain of the Dragon on the right of the palace. It had just been completed, and the King wanted to show off its beauty and the intricate mechanisms of its operation.

In the center of a huge pool a dragon wounded by an arrow spurted like its lifeblood a tremendous jet of water that broke into spray and fell like rain into the pool. Water spouted and sprayed from the mouths of dolphins swimming around the central figure. Two putti, mounted on swans whose beaks shot streams of water before them, attacked the hideous monster from the front, while two more harassed it from the rear. The statues were patinated with green gold, the swans with silver, and the network of spraying water lent the ensemble the mystery of some subaqueous drama.

After everyone had had a chance to gasp in admiration, the King resumed his progress, and slowly the procession wound along the walks that led past the Fountain of Latona toward the Great Terrace. The late sky had crimsoned and the trees grown bluish, but there was still enough light for the bronze statues to reflect it and glow in the radiance of the setting sun. At that period the entire park of Versailles was alive with color, for the sculptures that were not glided were painted in natural hues.

At the entrance to the maze Aesop in a red hood, his misshapen body wrapped in a blue cloak, greeted the princes with a sly glint in his eyes and a cynical smile on his lips. Before him stood the God of Love to signify that love often involves one in tangled webs, while worldly experience and a sense of humor provide a thread to guide one out of love's labyrinths and triumph over them.

The King explained the allegory to the Queen, who seemed greatly entertained by the charade.

The maze itself, which was an indispensable ornament of royal gardens then, was one of the wonders of Versailles. It consisted of an enclosure of closely planted bushy trees hedging narrow paths which crossed and

blocked one another until it was wellnigh impossible
not to get lost. At every turn the courtiers gasped with
amazement as they discovered one or another of the
thirty-nine groups of statuary surrounded by rock gardens or shell-like reflecting pools, placed there to divert
the wanderers and cause them to lose their way even
more. They represented the animals in Aesop's Fables,
and had been scrupulously copied from living models in
the zoo. Thirty-seven quatrains of Benserade, carved in
golden letters on the bronze pedestals, recited the story
connected with each.

Up until then the progress had been no more than the
usual one that the Court indulged in every day as it followed its master who never tired of admiring the beauty
and the development of his gardens. But suddenly, at
the intersection of five walks, the company came upon a
spectacular summer-house in the shape of a pentagon,
shaded by lofty elms. Each of the five sides was decorated with a carved tracery of foliage framed with garlands, and the central area contained three marble urns
decorated with red, pink, blue and white flowers. In the
middle a jet of water spurted upward in a snowy shaft,
and surrounding the pool into which it fell were five
marble tables facing each of the intersecting paths.
These were separated by majolica jars in which grew
orange trees bearing candied fruits.

On each of the tables was a mouth-watering confection. One represented a mountain in whose caves were
all sorts of cold dishes. Another was topped with a miniature palace of marzipan and *petits fours*. The third
bore a pyramid of candied fruit. On the next was a vast
number of crystal goblets and silver pitchers filled
with all kinds of liqueurs. The last offered an assort-
ment of bonbons—brown for the chocolate-flavored ones,
golden for the honey, red for the cinnamon. They
paused to admire the charm of this cool, refreshing
room, then fell to with greedy hands on the palace of
marzipan until it lay in ruins, or gobbled up the bonbons, or drained the glasses of liqueurs. Reclining on the
grassy banks, the noble lords and ladies threw themselves
wholeheartedly into the informal spirit of a picnic.

From this central point they could gaze down the five paths bordered with arches of cypress trees under each of which was a potted fruit tree laden with magnificent fruits. Presently they roamed along them picking pears, apples, peaches, lemons and cherries.

At the end of one vista a statue of Pan reflected one last crimson ray while behind it two satyrs and two bacchantes danced in dim silhouette against the pale green sky.

"What good spirit has transported us to Arcady?" exclaimed Mademoiselle de Scudèry.

"Any minute now we'll catch sight of Corydon and Phyllis and their beribboned sheep!"

Just as they spoke, a fuse began to sputter, lighting first one and then another of the thousand lanterns hung amid the bushes and in the trees. The shepherds and shepherdesses they had imagined came into reality, singing and dancing, while forty satyrs and bacchantes scaled a high rock on which they whirled their thyrses and clashed their cymbals before descending to surround the company and lead it toward the theatre.

An open carriage and sedan chairs were awaiting the King, the Queen and the Princess to bear them along the linden-bordered avenues.

The theatre where the evening's comedy was to be acted had been constructed in a large open space where the Royal Avenue converged with several other paths. Hideous confusion broke out as the guests of honor and the courtiers fought for seats that had not been systematically distributed. The whirling satyrs and bacchantes added a wild, saturnalian note to the scene. The door of the King's carriage was opened then quickly shut again. The Queen's sedan chair could not get through the mob. Its bearers shouted in vain: "Make way for Her Majesty the Queen!" No one budged. For half an hour Marie-Thérèse tried to get through, but was forced to wait seething with rage. Finally the King himself came after her.

From the very beginning of the melee Angélique had withdrawn. Her good sense told her not to endanger her delicate costume in that hurlyburly, and she extricated

herself from the swarming anthill along with a few
others who had also resolved to wait. The play would
go on for a long time. The night was mild and the park
of Versailles with its lanterns and the plashing of its
fountains was like a fairyland. She relished being alone.
Glimpsing a marble tempietta half-hidden by the shrub-
bery that twinkled with tiny lanterns like a story sky, she
directed her steps toward it. The scent of honeysuckle
and rambler roses enveloped her as the tumult of the
crowd faded from her ears.

As she looked up, she thought she must be dreaming.
There on the steps of the tempietta a snow-white phantom was bowing to her, and as it straightened she recognized Philippe.

She had not seen him since their love-struggle in the
barn which Philippe had so wickedly engineered and
which had left her, in spite of herself, with an unpleasant
memory. While the Court returned to the capital, Philippe had remained in the North and then had led the
army to Franche-Comté. Angélique had heard of his
movements only by public report, for naturally Philippe
had not taken the trouble to write her.

She sometimes wrote to him, however—little notes in
which she told him about Charles-Henri and the Court
—but she had hoped in vain for any reply from him. Now
suddenly there he was before her very eyes, a shadow of
a smile on his lips.

"I greet the Baroness of the Doleful Garb," he said.

"Philippe," she exclaimed, spreading her heavily
brocaded skirt, "there are ten thousand *livres* worth of
diamonds on this dress."

"The one you used to wear was gray with light blue
bows at its bodice and a white collar."

"Do you really remember that?"

"Why shouldn't I?"

He went up the steps and leaned against one of the
marble pillars. She held out her hand to him. After a moment he kissed it.

"I thought you were with the army," Angélique
said.

"I received a message from the King urging me to re-

turn to the Court to appear at the fête he wished to
give this evening. I was to be one of its ornaments."

There was nothing fatuous about his last remark, only
a recognition of the part he accepted with punctilious
obedience. The King wanted in his suite the most beautiful women and the most splendid lords. On this day of
days he could not have dispensed with the handsomest
noble of his Court. "By all means the handsomest,"
thought Angélique as she surveyed his lean, dashing
form in its white, gold-embroidered costume. His sword
had a gold pommel, and his soft white leather shoes had
gold heels. It had been many months since she had seen
him.

"Has the King relieved you of your command?" she
asked.

"No, I asked him not to."

"Why?"

"I like war."

"Did you get my letters?"

"Your letters . . . oh . . . yes, I think so."

Angélique snapped her fan shut. "Perhaps you never
learned to read."

"When I'm with the army I have other things to do
than read *billets doux* and nonsense like that."

"Just as gracious as ever, aren't you?"

"And just as mettlesome. I'm pleased to see you in
such a good humor. As a matter of fact, I must say I've
rather missed your belligerent spirit. A military campaign is tedious. Two or three sieges, a few skirmishes
. . . You would have certainly found some way to liven
things up."

"When are you going back?"

"The King has told me he wants me at Court from now
on. We shall have plenty of time to squabble."

"And time enough for other things too," said Angélique, looking him straight in the eye.

The night was so soft and their isolation in the little
temple of love so complete that she did not care how
bold she was. He had come back to her, had searched
her out among the crowds of courtiers, had not been able
to resist his desire to be with her. Under all his sarcasm

lurked the confession that he had missed her. Wasn't this an indication that they were on their way to some understanding?

Philippe grasped her wrists. His lips pushed her bracelets up her arms as he kissed her silken skin. Then his finger stole beneath the heavy jeweled collar that encased her neck and spread over her shoulders.

"A well-defended town," he said. "I have always admired the strategy with which beautiful women arrange to be both half-exposed and yet unassailable."

"That's the strategy of jewels, Philippe—a woman's armor. It's what lends charm to our fêtes. Do you find me beautiful?"

"Too beautiful," he said enigmatically. "Dangerously beautiful."

"For you?"

"And for others too. What difference does it make, though? It suits you. You jump with joy at the very thought of playing with fire. It would be easier to make a plowhorse out of a thoroughbred than to change the nature of a whore."

"Philippe! Oh, dear, and you were talking like a real gallant!"

Philippe laughed. "Ninon de Lenclos always advised me to keep my mouth shut. 'Don't talk, don't smile, just be handsome and appear and disappear, that's for you,' she used to say. And whenever I have disregarded her advice, I have got into lots of trouble."

"Ninon isn't always right. I like to hear you talk that way."

"Every woman likes a parrot."

He took her hand and led her down the marble steps. "The violins are louder. The play must be over and the doors must be open. It is time for us to join the King and his suite again."

The walked back along a path bordered by fruit trees growing in silver jars. Philippe picked a rosy apple. "Do you want it?" he said.

She took it almost shyly, smiling as their eyes met.

Then they were separated in the bustling crowd. The audience were discussing the merits of the play and how

Molière could make them laugh at the same time he was clarifying their knowledge of human nature.

The dark tent of the night sky and the trees formed a perfect setting for the brightly lighted building to which they came next. It was another dream palace, guarded by gilded fauns piping on mossy pedestals, and urns of translucent alabaster from which trickled little waterfalls, the whole encased in a crystal dome of light.

The King stopped for a moment to admire the sight, then entered the dainty edifice. Its ceiling was of green boughs bound to a delicate lattice-work studded with gold. Around the cornice were porcelain vases filled with flowers interspersed with crystal prisms that flashed rainbows on the ceiling. Garlands of flowers hung from it on silver cords, and hundreds of dangling lamps illuminated it like a palace in the Arabian Nights. Between each of the doors two torches flanked a jar that spilled a satiny sheet of water over stair-stepped scallop shells as it flowed to one of the fountains. Opposite the entrance an étagère held magnificent examples of the goldsmith's art—bowls, vases, covered dishes, platters and ewers for serving the King.

In the center was Pegasus with outspread wings striking with its hoof the crest of a high rock and causing the fountain of Hippocrene to spurt forth. Below this symbol of inspiration were ranged on a lawn of green spun-sugar, trees that bore candied fruits, a flowery meadow of cakes and bonbons, and lakes of jellies, in the midst of which Apollo consorted with the Muses. They seemed to be presiding over the royal table which, festooned with flowers and laden with silver vessels, encircled the rock of Pegasus.

This was the moment for the grand supper. The King took his place, and the ladies whom he wished as companions formed a dazzling chaplet about him, each one's costume rivaling the others.

With a certain relief Angélique saw that she had not been designated to sit at the royal table. She could hardly have expected such an honor. Ever since the Flemish campaign the King's attitude toward her had been ambiguous; he had shown no displeasure with her, nor had

he been any less affable, but there had risen a barrier
between them to a degree that she sometimes wondered
if she were not being merely tolerated at Court.

With an ironic glance she identified the elect who en-
framed the Sun King and thought that but for a few exceptions it was wholly an assemblage of downright har-
ridans exhausted by the debauches of their past. Everyone knew that Madame de Bounelle-Bullion, the wife of a
Secretary of State, ran a disorderly house; that the Court
Almanac had assigned Madame de Brissac forever to what
was euphemistically termed "Pleasure Island." Marshal
de la Ferte and the Comtesse de Fiesque were carrying
on mincingly as if to cover up the fact that the shameless Bussy-Rabutin's scandalous *History of the Loves of
the French* had pilloried them. At a little distance from
them the Duchess of Mecklenburg, that old warrior of
the Fronde, whose love affairs and intrigues had caused a
fearful scandal, was ostentatiously stuffing her fat jowls.

Among the exceptions were the serious Madame de La-
fayette and, to a certain extent, the subdued Duchesse
de la Vallière, who had been relegated to the end of the
table, where she nibbled gloomily at the dishes the
King's footmen passed her. No one paid the slightest attention to the fallen favorite. Louis XIV did not even
glance in her direction.

What female face was in his thoughts as with his usual
good appetite he gobbled the delicacies of the five
courses that the nimble waiters of Le Duc, the head chef,
passed to the fifty-six guests at the royal table?

Madame de Montespan was not among them.

Angélique was told that she was to sit at Madame de
Montausier's table, which was one of those set up under
tents and presided over by the Queen and her Ladies-
in-Waiting. There were forty places set. Angélique sat
between Mademoiselle de Scudèry, whom she knew
slightly from having attended her salon, and a woman
whom she had to look at twice before she could believe
her eyes.

"Françoise, you here?"

Madame Scarron beamed at her. "Yes, my dear Angélique, but I must confess I am as incredulous as you. I

can hardly believe my good luck when I think what a
wretched state I was in just a few months ago. Did you
know I was about to leave for Portugal?"

"No, but I did hear that Monsieur de Cormeil wanted
to marry you."

"Oh, don't talk to me about that. Because I refused
him I lost all my patrons and friends."

"Isn't he quite rich? He could have made life easy for
you and relieved you of your eternal worries."

"But he is old and terribly worn out with debauchery.
That's what I told everyone else who urged me to accept
him. They were displeased with me because they thought
I had no right to pick and choose in my situation and
that I had not had such an opportunity since I married
Scarron. I told Madame la Maréchale all this just as
emphatically as I could, and as reasonably, but she just
blamed me for all my misfortunes. Ninon was the only
one who said I was right, and her approval almost made
up for my other friends' cruelty. They dared to compare
that old man with Scarron, what do you think of that!
Oh, my Lord, what a difference! He didn't have money
or leisure, but he surrounded me with all the wittiest,
most brilliant people. Cormeil he would have loathed.
Scarron had a love of life and a generous spirit that all
the world envies. No one had so much of it as he. As
for Cormeil, he's neither intelligent, nor lively nor even
steadfast. Whenever he opens his mouth he puts his foot
in it. My husband was no lightweight. I corrected his
licentiousness, but he was neither stupid nor vicious.
He was noted for his honesty and sincerity . . ."

She spoke in a subdued voice but with an intensity
she permitted herself only when talking in confidence.
Angélique, who acknowledged the charm of her personality, thought once more how truly pretty and attractive she was. The simplicity of her attire was perhaps in-
appropriate, but her brown velvet dress was in excellent
taste and her double choker of jet and small rubies
suited her brown hair and her warm coloring.

She went on to say how she had been reduced to such
an extremity that she had finally agreed to accompany as
a third lady-in-waiting—practically a chambermaid—the

Princesse de Nemours, who was going to marry the King
of Portugal. As she was making her farewell round of
visits she had met Madame de Montespan, to whom she
had described her plight, and who was horrified by it.

"Without disparaging me you can believe it. Athenaïs
listened to me attentively even though she was getting
dressed. You know we were boarding school friends and
come from the same province as you, Angélique. Since
she came to Paris I have had opportunities to do her a
few small favors. Finally she assured me that she would
take it upon herself to speak to the King about the dis-
continuance of my pension and my unavailing petitions.
I wrote about it once more on her advice, and ended
by saying: 'Two thousand *livres* is more than enough for
my lonely welfare.' The King received it graciously and,
miracle of miracles, my pension was restored. When I
went to Saint-Germain to thank Athenaïs, I had the hon-
or of seeing His Majesty, who said to me: 'Madame, I
made you wait a long time, but I have been jealous of
your friends. I myself wanted to be the one to assist you.'
Those words wiped out all my long hard years. I began
to breathe easily again, to live. I was free from all those
gnawing mean worries. I found my place again in society
which had looked at me so coldly, went out in the world
again, and . . . well, here I am at Versailles."

Angélique assured her sincerely that she was delighted.

Madame de Montespan laid her hand on her protégée's
shoulder as she passed behind her. "Happy?"

"Ah, my dear Athenaïs, I shall be grateful to you as
long as I live."

The tables were emptying. The King had just risen
with his suite and started down a long garden path, and
the crowd was flowing into the banquet hall from all
sides to plunder the dishes and the baskets of cakes and
fruit that were left over.

The walk seemed to come to a dead end in a wall of
light, but this opened up as the parade approached to
reveal another orchestration of cascading water, intricate
patterns of light, silvered tritons and rocky grottoes.
They passed through a grassy corridor arbored with flow-

ers and bordered by laughing satyrs or jets of water, and
came to fountains in which golden dolphins sported under lights that changed from hue to hue or shone in all
colors at once.

This magical promenade led to the ballroom of
porphyry and marble. Silver candelabra hung from the
beams of the ceiling which were decorated with golden
suns on a deep blue background. Garlands of flowers
draped the cornice, and between the columns which supported it were platforms for the musicians, and two
grottoes in which were statues of Orpheus and Arion
smiting their lyres.

The King opened the ball with Madame and the princesses. Then the noble lords and ladies joined in, displaying their gorgeous costumes in complicated dance
figures. The old-fashioned dances were fast, but the
new-style ones were extremely slow, almost like religious
processions, and much more difficult to follow, consisting
as they did of artful steps and studied gestures of hand
and arm. A relentless movement, as precisely detailed
and almost as mechanical as a clock's, involved the
dancers like automatons in an interminable round. It
seemed completely calm at first, but little by little the
music imbued it with undisciplined excitement, filling
the slow approaches with hot desire, electrifying the
brief handclasps, inspiring passion in the lingering looks
cast on fleeting partners, personalizing the symbolic gestures of love and its refusal until the corranto became
demonic. The Court was wild about these superficially
innocuous rhythms, recognizing under their deceptive
mask the approach of Love which is less the child of
flame than of night and silence.

Angélique danced well, and took pleasure in the intricate figures. Sometimes a hand would clasp hers mean-
ingfully, but she was too involved in the dance to notice.
Nevertheless she was aware of the two royal hands in
which hers rested during the course of a rondeau. Her
eyes met the King's, then dropped quickly.

"Still angry?" whispered the King.

Angélique pretended to be baffled. "Angry? At such a
fête? What can Your Majesty mean?"

"Can such a fête sweeten the attitude you have taken toward me, lo these many months?"

"Sire, you confuse me. If Your Majesty had such feelings about me lo these many months, why did he not show them?"

"I was afraid you might throw green peas in my face."

The dance separated them. When he passed her again she saw his imperious brown eyes searching for an answer.

"The word 'afraid' does not suit Your Majesty."

"The war was less terrifying than the grim expression on your lovely mouth."

As soon as she could Angélique left the dance and hid herself in the back row of seats among the dowagers beating time to the music with their fans. A page came looking for her there and told her to follow him at the King's request.

Outside the ballroom the King was waiting for her in a secluded part of the garden path where the light was dim.

"You are right," he said jokingly. "Your beauty tonight rekindles my bravery. The moment has come for us to make up."

"But is it the right moment? Everyone tonight is eager for your company and in a minute or two their eyes will start searching for you and they will wonder why you are absent."

"No, they will go right on dancing. They will just think I am at the other end of the ballroom. This is the moment I have longed for to exchange a few words with you without attracting their attention."

Angélique felt herself growing stiff as a steel rod. His technique was perfectly plain. Madame de Montespan and the King had put their heads together again in order to involve her in the game she had provided for them at her own expense.

"How stubborn you are," he said, taking her arm gently. "Haven't I the right to thank you?"

"For what?"

"Colbert has told me several times what a magnificent job you have done in the duties he assigned you in regard to certain persons at Court. You have been able to gain their confidence about matters of credit, to explain them, to put their minds at ease, and all in such a casual way they do not suspect you. We have no doubt that certain financial successes of ours are entirely due to you."

"That's nothing," she said, breaking away from him. "Your Majesty does not have to acknowledge that. It's all to my own good, and that is quite enough thanks."

The King gave a start. The shadows into which he had drawn her were not so deep that she could not perceive his features. The silence between them became embarrassingly tense.

"You do have a grudge against me. Please tell me why."

"How can Your Majesty be ignorant of the cause. This is not like your usual perspicacity."

"My perspicacity often fails me when women are concerned. I can never be sure what they are thinking or feeling. What man, King or not, could ever be?"

In spite of his light tone, he seemed uncomfortable. His nervousness increased.

"Let us return to your guests, Sire, if you please . . ."

"There's no hurry. I want to get to the bottom of this matter."

"I have decided to be a shield for you and Madame de Montespan no longer," she burst out. "Colbert is not paying me for that. I treasure my reputation enough to want to squander it as I please, not make a gift of it to someone else . . . even to the King."

"Ah, so that's it. Madame de Montespan wanted to work you like a marionette and turn the suspicions of her impossible husband in your direction. Not a bad idea."

"As if Your Majesty did not know that."

"Do you think I am gullible or a hypocrite?"

"Do I have to lie to the King or displease him?"

"So that's the opinion you have of your sovereign?"

"My sovereign does not have to act that way toward me. What do you take me for? Do you think I am some toy you can throw away when you are tired of me? I do not belong to you."

He grasped her wrists violently. "You are mistaken. All my ladies belong to to me by right."

Both of them were trembling with anger. They stared at each other for a moment with flashing eyes.

The King was the first to recover himself. "Come now, let's not quarrel over nothing. Would you believe me if I told you I tried to persuade Madame de Montespan not to choose you as a victim? Why her, I kept saying to her. 'Because,' she would answer, 'only Madame du Plessis-Bellière can surpass me. I won't have it said Your Majesty turned from me to someone less glamorous than I.' You see, that's proof of the high regard she has for you. She thought you were naive enough to play the game without seeing your stake in it. Or perhaps artful enough to do it anyway. She was wrong on both counts. But it is not right for me to have to bear your ill will. Why has this little scheme hurt your feelings so, little toy? Is it such a great dishonor to be thought the mistress of the King? Don't you get a certain fame out of it? Flattery? Opportunities?"

His arm gently drew her close to him and held her there, while he whispered to her, leaning over her and trying to discern her features in the dim light.

"Did you say your reputation had been sullied? Not at the Court, it hasn't. On the contrary, it has acquired a new lustre, I assure you. So, am I to think that you ended up by letting yourself get caught in a trap? That you believe this farce? Is that what it is? Were you deceived?"

Angélique did not answer. She buried her head in the velvet of his doublet, inhaling its scent of orris root and relishing the soft embrace of his arms that held her to him ever more tightly. It had been a long time since she had been so tenderly treated. Ah, how sweet it felt to be rocked like this, petted like a child, even scolded a little.

"How could such a practical little person as you be so taken in by an illusion?"

She shook her head without answering.

"No, I didn't think so," the King laughed. "Still, it is funny, isn't it? If I were to tell you that I have never looked at you without desiring you and that often the thought has come to me . . ."

Angélique wrenched herself away. "I would not believe you, Sire. I know Your Majesty's heart lies elsewhere. Your choice is a good one . . . except for the nuisance of a jealous husband."

"Rather a sizable nuisance," said the King wincing.

He took Angélique's arm again and led her down a walk of topiary yews. "You can't imagine what that Montespan has done to annoy me. He will end by hailing me before my own Parlement. I'm sure Philippe du Plessis would be a more cooperative husband than that swaggering de Pardaillan. But we haven't come to that yet," he ended with a sigh.

He released her so as to look her square in the face. "Let's make up, my little Marquise. Your King humbly asks your pardon. Won't you melt a little?"

It was easy for her to imagine the charm of his smile and the light in his eyes. She shivered. His face bending near hers, his smooth smiling lips, the warmth of his glance, attracted her irresistibly. Suddenly she took to flight, lifting up her heavy rustling skirt for speed. But she ran head on into the thick hedge.

Panting, she leaned against the pedestal of a statue and looked around her. She was in the little glade of the Girondelle. In the velvet blackness she discerned a silvery jet of water surrounded by ten smaller jets that fell in snowy arches into the pool of the fountain. Above, in the blue-black sky, the moon shed its calming light on this earthly fairyland. Far in the distance she could hear the music of the fête, but here reigned a silence that was disturbed only by the plashing of the fountain and the steps of the approaching King grinding the damp gravel of the path under his heels.

"Little girl," he murmured, "why did you run away?"

He seized her in his arms again, forcing her to nestle into the warm hollow of his shoulder, and leaned his cheek against her hair.

"They tried to hurt you and you did not deserve it, but I knew how cruel women can be to one another. It's up to me, your sovereign, to protect you. Forgive me, little girl."

Angélique felt her strength ebbing and her senses reeling in a sweet swoon. The King's features were invisible under the shadow of his great Court hat, a shadow that enveloped both of them, but she could hear his low, winning voice.

"The creatures who live together here are frightful, my child. Believe me, I rule them with an iron rod, for I know what insurrections and what bloody madness they would be capable of if I did not. There isn't one of them who wouldn't incite a city or a whole province against me and cause my people woe. That's why I keep them under my eye here in my Court at Versailles, where they are harmless. I shall let not one of them escape. Some of them sail so close to shore that they do themselves great damage in their greedy savagery. You have to have strong, sharp teeth and claws to survive. But you are not like them, my pretty little toy."

In a voice so low that he had to lean his ear to her lips to hear her she asked: "Are you trying to make me understand that I do not belong at Court?"

"By no means. I want you there. You are one of its greatest and loveliest ornaments. Your taste, your charm, your grace captivate me. I have told you all this for your own good, so that you can escape these birds of prey."

"I haven't come off very well so far," said Angélique.

The King leaned his hand gently on her brow to tilt back her head and bring her rose-petal face into the light of the moon. Under the dark fringe of her lashes Angélique's green eyes were like a woodland spring guarding the mystery of its divinity. Almost fearfully the King pressed his lips to hers. He had not intended to frighten her, but soon he was only a man greedy with desire, and at his touch her youthful mouth, at first stubbornly shut, quavered, then opened knowingly.

"Ah . . . she is experienced," he thought. Intrigued, he looked at her with new eyes. "I love your lips," he said. "They are like no others—a woman's and yet a young girl's, cool yet burning."

He went no further, and when she slowly drew away, he did not hold her. They remained tentatively a few feet apart. Suddenly a series of explosions rustled the branches of the trees.

"The fireworks are beginning. We must not miss them. Let's go back," said the King reluctantly.

Silently they walked to the edge of the ballroom. The rumble of the crowd punctuated by the explosions of the fireworks rolled toward them with a noise like the sea. Rounding a clump of jasmine they were suddenly drenched in brilliant light.

The King took Angélique's hand to push her gently away and look at her. "I haven't congratulated you yet on your gown. It is beautiful. Only your own beauty surpasses it."

"Thank you, Your Majesty."

Angélique made a deep curtsy. The King bowed, and clicking his heels, kissed her hand.

"Now, are we friends again?"

"Perhaps."

"I shall dare hope so."

Angélique drew away, blinded by the strange lights and stunned to see how the palace loomed out of the darkness in the distance as if surrounded by a ring of fire.

Cries of startled admiration burst from the spectators. The door framed a fiery image of the two-faced Janus. The windows of the ground floor blazed with trophies of war, and images of the Virtues glowed in the second-story ones. At the top of the roof flamed a huge sun; on the ground level, a balustrade of fire surrounded the pile.

The King's coach passed by, drawn by six curvetting horses ridden by torchbearing postillions. The Queen, Madame, Monsieur, Mademoiselle de Montpensier and the Prince de Condé were in it. They stopped by the Fountain of Latona which reflected the palace like a lake of fire in which supernatural beings moved beneath its vault of interlacing waterspouts. Phosphorescent vases helped the ancient candelabra to outline the sweeping horseshoe curve. The King had his carriage stop so that he might contemplate the wondrous pattern of light. Behind the vehicles the hastening crowd filled the night with shrieks of wonder.

The carriages turned and took the wide road bordered

with a double row of hermae which some strange mechanical process seemed to have rendered transparent. Suddenly streamers of light flashed between the statues. In the depths of the park thousands of rockets burst with a noise like thunder. The fountains flared like craters of volcanoes. As the din increased the crowd grew panicky. Terrified women ran for refuge into the trees and the grottoes. The whole park of Versailles seemed aflame. The canals and the lakes crimsoned with the reflection of the flames.

Mighty rockets pierced the night sky like bolts of lightning or striped it with ribbons of fire. Others streaked across it like the tails of comets or wriggled like giant caterpillars. Finally at the moment when from all points on the horizon the paths of the rockets made a grand arch, there appeared floating in the air like dazzling butterflies an "L" and an "M," the initials of the King and Queen, until the night breezes wafted them slowly away in the ruby smoke of the vanishing fairyland.

The last rosy lights of the fête mingled with the dawn tints of the eastern sky. Louis XIV gave the order to return to Saint-Germain. The weary courtiers followed him on horseback or in coaches. Everyone vied to see who could best describe this fête as the grandest since the world began.

chapter 14

*I*T WAS a fête Angélique would long remember. She had had two romantic strolls along the dark garden paths, had seen an illumination that still dazzled her, and might yet be floating on a garden cloud if it were not for an aftertaste of anxiety that gave a bitter flavor to her otherwise pleasant memories. Such was her state of mind the morning after that night at Versailles.

And in her wandering thoughts there gnawed one minor worry which curiously came to the foreground—the round face of little Cantor, whom Vivonne wanted as a page.

"That's the first thing to settle," Angélique said to herself, rousing herself from her daydreaming.

She got up from the sofa on which she was recovering from the fatigue of the night before. As she crossed the hall of the Hôtel du Plessis, Cantor's voice drifted down to her from the upper floor:

> More luck than I, have you, Marquis,
> With a bride as fair as she . . .

She hesitated a moment before the black oaken door. She had never yet ventured this far. It led to Philippe's apartments. She withdrew thinking her procedure not too sensible.

The voice of the eight-year-old singing above of the extramarital affairs of Henri IV made her laugh. She changed her mind.

La Violette answered her knock. Philippe was standing before his looking glass adjusting his blue tunic in preparation for his departure for Saint-Germain, whither Angélique was to follow him later. She had been invited to one of the Queen's parties, and supper afterward. The courtiers spent little time tending to family problems.

Philippe showed no surprise at finding his wife in his rooms. He courteously invited her to sit while he finished dressing, and waited until she volunteered the purpose of her visit.

Angélique watched him slip on his rings. He was choosing them deliberately, trying them on and surveying his hands critically. No woman could have taken greater pains. She thought as she watched him concentrate on so trivial a matter of how his coldness was really the result of vanity. What could she hope to get from him? Advice? It seemed laughable.

Finally, to break the embarrassing silence, she said: "Monsieur de Vivonne has asked me to lend him Cantor."

Philippe merely sighed, and took off all the rings from his right hand as the array did not suit him. He went on poring over the open jewel boxes. Then as if suddenly remembering she was there, he said in a bored voice: "Oh? Well, my congratulations on such good news. Vivonne is rising in favor, and his sister Madame de Montespan can be counted on to keep him up there a long time."

"But Vivonne is to lead an expedition to the Mediterranean."

"More proof of the King's confidence in him."

"The boy is still quite young."

"What boy? Oh, Cantor . . . why, he seems to want to go with Vivonne. What's so remarkable about that? Vivonne spoils him, gives him candy whenever they meet. Still no eight-year-old should decide for himself. I wonder . . ." Philippe raised his eyebrows in an expression of mock surprise. "Do you want him to have a career?"

"Yes, but . . ."

"But what?"

She spoke rapidly, her cheeks on fire. "Vivonne has a bad reputation. He was one of Monsieur's gang, and everyone knows what that means. I should not like to entrust my son to a man who might corrupt him."

The Marquis du Plessis had put on a huge solitaire diamond ring and two smaller ones. He stepped to the window to see if they sparkled in the sunlight.

"To whom would you like to entrust him then?" he said slowly. "To that rare bird, a person of pure morals, not an intriguer or a hypocrite, someone who has influence with the King and has received many honors from him, who . . . who just does not exist? Apprenticeship to life is not easy, nor is skill in pleasing the great."

"He is so young," Angélique repeated, "I am afraid he will see things that will spoil his innocence."

Philippe snickered. "For an ambitious mother, you have a great many scruples. I was barely ten when Coulmers got me into bed with him. Four years later, when my voice had hardly changed, Madame du Crécy wanted to sample a little springtime vigor and offered me —or rather forced me into—the shelter of her bed. She must have been forty. How do you think this emerald goes with this turquoise?"

Angélique said nothing. She was terribly frightened. "Philippe! Oh, Philippe!"

"Yes, I guess you're right. The brilliant green of the emerald dims the blue of the turquoise. I think another diamond would go better next to the emerald." He glanced at her and snickered again. "Stop looking so worried. If you don't like what I said, why did you come to me for advice? Either you don't know or you are pretending not to know what a young nobleman's education consists of. Let your children get started on their course of honor."

"I am their mother. Honors are nothing. I cannot neglect their morals. Didn't your mother ever think of yours?"

Philippe pouted scornfully. "That's right, I forget we weren't brought up the same way. If I remember correctly, you grew up barefoot in an atmosphere of cabbage soup and ghost stories. In such an environment there probably was such a thing as a mother. But in Paris and at Court, it wasn't the same for a child."

Returning to his dressing table, he opened some more

jewel cases. She could not see his face, only a blond head
which seemed bowed beneath an ancient yoke.

"Naked and shivering with cold," he murmured, "sometimes starving . . . cared for by footmen or maids who
perverted me . . . That was my life here in this very
hôtel I was to inherit some day. But when I was to be
showed off, then nothing was too good for me—the
richest clothes, the softest velvets, the most delicate laces.
For hours on end the barber would work over my hair.
Then when my part in the pageant was over, back I'd
go to the darkness of my little room and the loneliness
of long empty halls. I was bored. No one took the trouble
to teach me to read or write. I thought it was a gift
from heaven to be able to enter Coulmers' service. He
liked pretty boys like me."

"Sometimes you came to Plessis . . ."

"Just for short stays. I had to appear at Court and re-
volve about the throne. The only way to get ahead is to
be in evidence. My father, whose only son I was, wouldn't
think of leaving me off in the provinces. He liked to see
how quickly I was getting on. I was very ignorant and had
hardly any personality, but I was good looking."

"That's why you have never understood what it is to
love," Angélique said as if to herself.

"Oh, but I have. It seems to me I have had many varied
experiences in that field."

"That's not love, Philippe."

She felt a chill go through her, saddening her, and filling her with pity, as if she had seen some poor unfortunate deprived of the very necessities of life. "The death
of the heart is worst of all misfortunes!" Who was it had
said that to her with the cynical melancholy of one who
had everything? The Prince de Condé, one of the greatest lords by virtue of rank, fortune and renown.

"Have you never never loved . . . even once . . . or had
any special, private feelings for . . . any woman?"

"Yes . . . My old nurse, probably. But that was a long
time ago."

Angélique did not even smile. She stared at him seriously, her hands clasped in her lap.

"That feeling," she murmured, "that can give one a

sense of all the grandeur of creation, the sweetness of all
fleeting dreams, the elation and power of living . . ."

"You are very eloquent. No, I swear I don't think I
have ever known such a transport of feeling. . . . But I
can see what you mean. Once I held her hand . . but
then the dream fled."

His eyes were half shut. His sleek face, the suspicion
of a smile on his lips, his enigmatic expression, made
him seem like a stone effigy on the tomb of a king. Never
had he seemed so far away from her as now, when perhaps he had never before been so close to her.

"It was at Plessis. I was sixteen and my father had just
bought me a regiment. We were in the country to recruit
it. At a party I met a girl the same age as I, but in my
jaundiced eyes only a child. She was wearing a gray dress
with blue bows on its bodice. I was ashamed when they
told me she was my cousin. But when I took her hand to
dance I felt it tremble in mine, and then I experienced a
new and wonderful sensation. Up until then it was I
who had trembled before the imperious desire of mature
women or the teasing flirtatiousness of the young minxes
at Court. This girl baffled me. The look of admiration
in her eyes was balm to my soul, an intoxicating draught.
Suddenly I realized I was a man, not some plaything; a
master, not a servant. Then I introduced her jokingly
to my friends: 'This is,' I said, 'the Baroness of the Doleful Garb.' She ran away. I looked at my empty hand, and
was desolate. The same feeling as when I had caught a
bird I wanted to make a pet of, and it flew out of my
grasp. The sun went out of the sky. I wanted to find her
again and calm her anger and see her radiant face once
more. But I didn't know how, because none of the
women who had initiated me into the art of love had
ever taught me how to woo a sullen lass. As I searched
for her I picked a fruit to give her. . . . It was an apple,
I think, as pink and golden as her cheeks. I looked for
her all through the gardens, but I never found her that
evening . . ."

"What would have happened if we had found each
other that evening?" Angélique thought. "We would
have looked at each other shyly . . . he would have offered

me the apple, and we would have walked in the moonlight, holding hands . . ."

Just a blond boy and a blond girl in the rustling paths of the park where the does of the forest of Nieul came to feed . . . just a boy and a girl ecstatically happy, happy as only sixteen-year-olds can be, wanting to swoon to death as they kissed in a long embrace in the dark . . . Her life might have taken a far different course.

"And did you never find that girl again?" she asked aloud with a sigh.

"Yes. Much later. Just to show how strange the illusions, the first passions, of youth are, she had become mean and hard and grasping, more dangerous than all the others . . ."

He stretched out his hands, the fingers spread. "What do you think of my rings now? Perfect, eh?"

"Yes, I guess so. But a single ring on the little finger is more subtle, Philippe."

"You are right."

He took off the superfluous rings and put them back into their boxes, then rang for a footman to go for Cantor.

When the boy appeared Angélique and Philippe were facing each other silently. Cantor had a way of walking all his own. He was trying to make his spurs click, for he had just returned from his riding lesson. That was the only reason he did not have his guitar with him.

"Well, sir," Philippe said humorously, "you look as if you were setting out for war."

The boy's sober face lit up. "Has Monsieur de Vivonne told you our plans?"

"I see you like the idea."

"Oh, sir, to fight the Turks! That would be wonderful!"

"Take it easy. The Turks aren't lambs you can charm with your songs."

"I don't want to go with Monsieur de Vivonne just to sing. I want to travel. I've been thinking about it a long time. I want to go to sea."

A shiver passed through Angélique, and her hands fidgeted. She saw again her brother Josselin with his eyes aflame, heard him whisper intensely: "I'm going to sea, I am."

So at last the time had come for them to be separated! . . . How one struggles for one's children, protects and shelters them, works so hard for them in the hope of enjoying their company, learning to know them . . . And then when that day arrives, whisk, they're already grown up and gone.

Cantor's eyes were steady. He knew where he wanted to go.

"Cantor no longer needs me," she said to herself. "I know him, he's just like me. Did I ever need my mother? I used to run free all over the countryside, living life to the full. When I was only twelve I set sail for the Americas without once looking back . . ."

Philippe laid his hands on Cantor's head. "Your mother and I are going to decide whether to let you have this baptism of fire. Few boys your age have the honor of hearing the cannons roar. You have to be brave."

"I am brave. And I am not afraid."

"We shall see, and we will let you know our decision."

The boy bowed before his stepfather and went out with great dignity, full of his own importance.

The Marquis took from La Violette's hands a gray velvet hat and flicked a speck of dust from it.

"I shall see Vivonne," he said, "and ascertain whether his intentions are pure in regard to the boy. If they are not . . ."

"I would rather see him dead," Angélique said fiercely.

"Don't talk like a classical mother. That's not the way of the world we live in. I rather think Vivonne is an aesthete, as infatuated with our little artist as with a gallant gesture. Cantor's commission won't cost you a penny. So, figure it out and have a good time." He kissed her hand. "I must leave you, Madame. The King requires me, and my horses will have to gallop like wildfire to make up for my tardiness."

Just as she had done the night of the fête, when he offered her the apple he had picked in the King's garden, she searched his pale, impenetrable face.

"Philippe, the little girl from long ago is always there, you know."

Later, as she rode in her coach across the sunset-crimsoned countryside on her way to Saint-Germain, she thought of him again.

She knew now that what had lowered her in Philippe's eyes was precisely the vast knowledge she had of men. She knew all their vulnerable points and how to attack them with sure weapons. She and he could never meet except in the purity of heart they had known when they were young. They had been destined to meet at sixteen, still full of insatiable curiosity, the wonder of their innocence still unsullied, when their young bodies overpowered by strange desires could not touch without frightening them and shaming them, when so little was enough for them, such as the touch of a hand, a smile, the bliss of a kiss. Was it too late for them to rediscover this lost happiness? Philippe had wandered down evil ways. Angélique had become a woman. But the basic things of life were still strong enough in her to put forth new leaves, she thought, like the trees in the spring after their long cold winter's sleep.

And the spark glows. At the least expected moment the dead fire springs into flame.

Angélique was in the salon of the Hôtel du Plessis, inspecting it before the great reception she was to give for the leaders of Parisian society. It would have to be magnificent, for it was not beyond all possibility that the King himself would be present.

Pouting and sighing, she toured the great room, dark as a well and furnished with the stiff pieces of Henri IV's time. The two huge dark-surfaced mirrors did little to enliven it, and no matter what the season it was chilly —so dank, in fact, that the first thing Angélique had done after moving there from her Hôtel de Beautreillis was to have her heavy Persian rugs spread over the flagstones. Their soft rose and white colors only accentuated the austerity of the oaken furniture.

She was still inspecting it when Philippe entered to

look for his decorations, which he kept in one of the many drawers of the writing desk.

"I'm worried, Philippe," she said. "It depresses me to have to receive my guests here. I have nothing against your ancestors, but it would be hard to find a more old-fashioned house than yours."

"Are you complaining about your rooms?"

"No, they are delightful."

"It cost me plenty to have them redecorated," he said jokingly. "I had to sell my horses to pay for it."

"Did you do it for me?"

"Whom did you want me to do it for?" he mumbled, slamming a drawer shut. "I married you, against my will, it is true, but I did marry you. They said you were fussy and difficult. I didn't want to have to suffer the scorn of a rich businesswoman."

"Did you think of having me live here right after we were married?"

"It's the usual thing, isn't it?"

"Then why did you never invite me here?"

Philippe came over to her, his face a mixture of emotions, but Angélique thought she saw him blush.

"I thought things had begun so badly between us that an invitation from me would only bring a refusal from you."

"What do you mean?"

"You must have thought of me with loathing after what happened at Plessis. . . . I have never been afraid of any foe, the King is my witness, but I would rather have faced the fire of a hundred Spanish cannon than you when I woke up that morning after . . . Ah, it was all your fault. . . . I had drunk too much, and you ought to have known better than to irritate a drunken man the way you did. . . . You have to handle them carefully . . . You drove me wild. You were *eating*," he shouted, shaking her, "eating like a glutton that night, when you knew I was ready to strangle you!"

"But Philippe," she said astonished, "I swear I was scared to death. I can't help it if I get hungry when I'm upset. . . . So you were attracted by me then?"

"How could any man not be?" he shouted furiously.

"There's no length to which you wouldn't go to attract attention to yourself. You show up before the King without being invited . . . you get yourself attacked by wolves . . . you have children . . . love them . . . what else? You're not short on imagination. Good lord, when I saw your horse come back with empty stirrups that day at Fontainebleau . . . !"

He moved swiftly behind her and forced her shoulders back till she thought he would break them. He questioned her close to her face: "Were you in love with Lauzun?"

"No. Why?" She blushed as she remembered the incident. "Are you still brooding about that, Philippe? I swear I was not, and I can't imagine Péguilin making anything of it. I was so angry at myself I wondered how such a silly thing could ever have occurred. It was just one of those things that happen at a party—too much to drink, too much irresponsible talk, a little resentment. You were so hardhearted, so indifferent. You acted as if the only use you had for me as a wife was to hurt me and threaten me. I had made myself beautiful for nothing. . . . I'm only a woman, Philippe!

"Being scorned is the only thing a woman cannot stand. It gnaws at her heart, destroys her whole being. She longs for tenderness. I was at the mercy of anyone who could be sweet like Péguilin. All he told me about how lovely my eyes were, or my skin, was like finding a spring of cool water in a desert. Besides, I wanted revenge."

"Revenge? Oh, but, Madame, you're reversing our roles. It was I who should have taken revenge on you. Didn't you begin by forcing me to marry you?"

"But I have asked your forgiveness."

"That's just like a woman! As soon as they ask to be forgiven they think everything has been forgotten. It didn't matter that I had for good and all become your husband under a threat. Do you think you could wipe out such an injury merely by asking my forgiveness?"

"What more could I do?"

"Pay for it!" he shouted, raising his hand as if to strike her.

But she caught the playful glint in his blue eyes, and smiled. "It would be a welcome penalty," she said, "a lot different from the rack or hot needles under my fingernails."

"Don't tease me. I did threaten you, I admit, but I was wrong. I already feel that with the inconceivable magic of your sex you are hypnotizing me the way a poacher does a silly rabbit."

She laughed and leaned her head back against Philippe's shoulder. He had only to move a trifle to press his lips against her forehead or on her eyelids, but he did not. Still his hands tightened on her waist and his breath came faster.

"My indifference is hard for you to bear, is it? I rather had the notion that our meetings were distasteful to you, if not downright hateful."

Angélique laughed again. "Oh, Philippe, with just one ounce of sweetness on your part, our meetings would have been enchanting for me. I had kept such a lovely dream in the bottom of my heart of the day when you took me by the hand and introduced me as 'The Baroness of the Doleful Garb.' I was in love with you already then."

"It is the duty of life . . . and of my whip . . . to shatter dreams."

"Life can build them again. And you can lay your whip aside. I have never renounced my dream. Even when we were separated, in my secret heart I . . ."

"Were you waiting for me?"

Angélique's closed eyelids were lavender shadows on her cheeks. "I was always waiting for you."

She felt Philippe's hands grow tense and febrile as they stroked her breast. He growled a low oath, and she began to laugh again. Suddenly he leaned down and kissed her pulsing throat.

"You are so beautiful, so completely a woman!" he murmured. "And I am nothing but a clumsy old soldier."

"Philippe!" She looked at him in surprise. "How absurd can you be? Wicked, cruel, brutal, yes, but never clumsy. No, I won't admit it because I never thought of

you that way. Unfortunately you have never given me the
chance to see how gentle a lover you can be."

"Other women have blamed me for that too. Perhaps
I fool them. For them to believe it, a man with the physical perfection of Apollo should be capable of . . . super-
human performance."

Angélique laughed louder, drunk with the madness
that was swooping down upon them like a hunting hawk
from the sky. A few seconds ago they had been arguing,
now Philippe's fingers were fumbling with the hooks of
her bodice.

"Gently, Philippe, for heaven's sake. You'll tear it,
and it cost me two thousand *écus* to have it embroidered with pearls. Anyone would think you had never
learned how to undress a woman."

"Foolish precaution, when all you have to do is lift her
skirt to . . ."

She laid her finger against his lips. "Don't be
vulgar, Philippe. You know nothing about love and you
know nothing about bliss."

"Then show me. Teach me what women like you do
when they are waiting for a lover as handsome as a god."

There was bitterness in his voice. She threw her arms
around his neck in sheer abandon, hung there with legs
too weak to support her. Gently he lowered her to the
deep pile of the warm rug.

"Philippe, Philippe," she murmured, "do you think
this is quite the time and place for such a lesson?"

"Why not?"

"On the rug?"

"Yes, on the rug. Soldier I am, soldier I stay. If I can't
take my own wife in my own house, then I have no interest whatever in love-making."

"But what if someone should come in?"

"What difference would it make? It's now that I want
you. I can feel how hot you are, how ready. Your eyes
are shining like stars, your lips are moist . . ." He stared
fixedly at her cheeks flushed with exhilaration. "Now,
my little cousin, we shall play together and have more
fun than when we were young . . ."

Angélique gave a moan of surrender and stretched

out her arms. She was in no condition to resist or escape the onslaught of passion. She welcomed it instead.

"Don't be in such a hurry, lover," she whispered. "Give me time to find my heaven."

He grasped her passionately, found her, penetrated her with a new curiosity that for the first time made him conscious that she was a woman. Her eyes slowly closed as she yielded to her dream of love. She forgot to stiffen and there no longer lurked in the corner of her mouth that defiance he had seen there so often. Her lips parted as her breathing grew rapid. No longer was she his enemy; he gained confidence from her cooperation. Tenderly he explored her, and with the thrill of discovery he realized she was leading him to even more ravishingly mysterious prospects. A hope was born and grew in him as her voluptuousness increased. The moment was approaching for their transcendent transfiguration, for him to pluck the taut string of her tantalizing womanhood and make it sound with the glorious music so long denied him. He must be patient, so delicately exquisite a thing it was to do. Every inch of his virile mastery was aroused as he advanced toward a goal which did not retreat from him. He thought of how she had humiliated him and that he had never hated anyone more, but when he looked at her his heart burst with a strange imprisoned emotion that fought for release. Where now was the proud young woman who had once defied him?

All at once he sensed her withdrawing from him like a frightened wounded thing, with helpless little gestures that seemed to ask his mercy.

First quivering and then steeped in languor, rolling their heads from side to side gently and rhythmically as they lolled on the pillow of her unbound hair, they separated slowly from each other, reaching that dim floating region where two beings mold into one.

As a long shudder shook her he knew that the moment was approaching when he would be her master. Each passing second exhilarated him more, instilling in him a sense of victory he had never known before, a conquering force that sprang forth sure of attaining its reward.

He was the victor in a well-matched tournament, whose prize had many times before eluded him but which he now had won by valor and vigilance. No longer would he have to rule her. She was bent within his grasp like a powerful bow.

As she yielded to him he felt the secret response of her flesh that he had awakened, and reveled in its delights. Then he succumbed to her. He knew it was this he had lacked all his life—his joy in her, the acknowledgment that the greed of his body could be satisfied, satiated at last, while she returned to life with great passionate sighs.

"Philippe!"

He leaned on her bosom, hiding his face from her. Reality returned with the severe furnishings of the Plessis salon as Angélique awoke from her trance. Her moment of abandon had been all to short. She did not dare believe her own transports or the intoxication which was leaving her trembling and on the verge of tears.

"Philippe!"

She did not dare tell him how much she appreciated the care he had taken with her. Had she deceived him?

"Philippe!"

He raised his head. His face was still a puzzle, but Angélique was not mistaken. A soft smile spread over his lips. She put a finger on his mustache where tiny pearls of sweat had broken out.

"My big cousin . . ."

Naturally what was bound to happen did happen. Someone came in—a lackey announcing two visitors—Louvois and his father, the terrible old Michel de Tellier.

The old man dropped his quizzing glass. Louvois turned crimson. Both reatreated in confusion.

The next day Louvois had to tell the whole Court. "In broad daylight! With her husband!"

How could the wooers and admirers of the beautiful Marquise endure such an insult? A husband! A rival right in her home! Love in one's own household!

In high indignation Madame de Choisy repeated the entire length of the Hall of Versailles: "In broad daylight . . . in broad daylight!"

They laughed about it at the rising of the King.

"The King did not laugh so hard as expected," remarked Péguilin.

He was not the only one to guess the sovereign's secret annoyance.

"He is quite touchy about anything connected with you," Madame de Sévigné told Angélique. "He would like you to make up with your difficult husband, but not necessarily exaggerated your devotion to him. Monsieur du Plessis is too eager to please his sovereign. Perhaps he will pay with a loss of favor for not having understood that certain orders do not require so complete an obedience."

"Be careful of the Brotherhood of the Holy Sacrament, my dear," said Athenais with a sly smile. "That's the sort of thing they don't like."

Angélique defended herself, her cheeks on fire. "I don't see what the Brotherhood of the Holy Sacrament can find to blame me for. If I can't receive my husband's attentions under his own roof . . ."

Athenais tittered behind her fan. "In broad daylight . . . and on the rug! That's the height of depravity, my dear. You could be forgiven only if it was with a lover."

Philippe was equally indifferent to the jokes and sarcasm, possibly ignoring both as he passed haughtily by. If the King was cool to him, he did not seem to notice it. In the excitement of the last great fêtes the King gave before the summer campaigns Angélique could not meet him herself.

One thing was strange. Philippe had become cold to her again, and when she spoke to him by chance during a dance figure he answered rudely. She concluded that sweet moment of bliss which she treasured in her memory like a full-blown rose had been only a dream. The fingers of the world were tearing off its petals, and Philippe was just like them, crude and destructive. She did not know he was the victim of complex and uncus-

tomary emotions composed of his own pride and the
panic Angélique inspired in him.

He did not know how to master her except through
hatred. If he lost this weapon, he would fall under her
spell. He had sworn never to let himself become a slave
to a woman, and yet here he was lovesick as a boy whenever he recalled her little ways of smiling or looking at
him. His former fears returned to haunt him. Confused
by a life in which he had known more disappointments
then rewards, he doubted he could have tasted so completely harmonious a physical union with one of those
accursed beings that all women were to him. How could
he admit that this was what they called love? Wasn't
it only a mirage? The fear of being deceived again tortured him. He would die of such vexation, he thought,
and of regret as well. Cynicism was better, and rape!

Angélique had never imagined such torments could
exist behind his impassive exterior. She suffered from his
cruel change of attitude. The magnificent fêtes could
not distract her. The King's attentions irritated her, and
when he feasted his eyes on her, she felt sick. Why did
Philippe so neglect her?

One afternoon when the whole Court was watching a
play of Molière's in the outdoor theatre, she was overcome by a tremendous melancholy. It seemed to her that
she was once again that poor, wild little girl who had
fled from the mocking pages into the night at the castle
of Plessis, her heart heavy with longing and spurned
affection. "I hate them all," she thought.

Quietly she left the palace and had her coach summoned. Later she was to recall this impulse that dragged
her away from Versailles and to regard it as a presenti-
ment. For when she arrived that evening at the hôtel in
the Faubourg Saint-Antoine, there was great excitement.
La Violette told her that her husband had been recalled
to the front and would have to leave at daybreak for
Franche-Comté.

Philippe was eating supper alone before two silver
candlesticks in the dark-paneled dining room. When he
saw Angélique in her pink taffeta cloak, he knit his
brows.

"What are you doing here?"

"Haven't I a right to come home when I want?"

"Your presence was requested at Versailles for several days."

"Suddenly I thought I was going to die of boredom there. I just slipped away from all those unbearable people."

"I hope you gave a good reason for leaving. Otherwise you will risk the King's displeasure. Who told you I was leaving?"

"No one, I assure you. I was greatly surprised to see all these preparations. So, you were going to leave without saying goodbye to me?"

"The King asked me not to talk about my departure, especially to you. He knows no woman can keep a secret."

"The King is jealous," Angélique almost shouted. Philippe would see nothing in it, and would not understand, or at least he would pretend he did not.

Angélique sat down at the opposite end of the table and slowly removed her pearl-embroidered gloves. "That's strange. The summer campaign has not begun yet. The troops are still in winter quarters. I don't recall at the moment anyone else the King is getting rid of under the pretext of sending him off to war. Your orders seem very much like banishment, Philippe."

He looked at her so long without speaking that she wondered whether he had heard her. "The King is our master," he said finally. He got up stiffly. "It is late, and I must get to bed. Take good care of yourself while I am away. I bid you adieu."

Angélique raised her startled eyes to him. "Is that all you are going to say?"

He did not seem to understand the imploring look she gave him. Bending he kissed her hand, and that was all.

Alone in her room his little cousin began to cry. All the tears she had restrained since her childhood poured forth in a torrent, tears of despair and discouragement.

"I shall never know him, never understand him."

He was going off to war. Would she ever see him again? Oh yes, he would come back, that was not what she feared, but the hour of grace would be gone.

The moon flooded the room through the windows that opened on the garden, and she could hear the song of a nightingale. Angélique bathed her tearful face. She reminded herself how she loved the old silent house because it was there she had lived with Philippe. It was a strange intimacy, theirs, resembling a game of hide and seek. But there had also been those fleeting moments, as if stolen from the greedy world, when Philippe had sat by her as she nursed little Charles-Henri . . . conversations when they had laughed together as they watched him . . . the morning Philippe kept trying on rings as he listened to Cantor . . . that day such a short time ago when they had yielded to the passion of their bodies and had been seized with an ardor that came close to love.

She could stand it no longer. Quickly she wrapped her filmy white negligée about her, and ran barefoot to Philippe's room.

She entered without knocking. He was sprawled naked across the bed, and through the heavy lace of the bed-curtains she beheld his powerful chest smooth and pale as marble in the moonlight. His face looked different in sleep. The short curly hair he hid under his wig, his long lashes, his relaxed mouth, bestowed on him the serene innocence of an archaic Greek statue. His head lolling on one shoulder, his outstretched arms, made him seem defenseless.

Standing at the foot of the bed, Angélique held her breath. His beauty touched her heart as she perceived details she had never seen before—a child's chain with a crucifix hanging around the neck of this gladiator, a mole on his left breast, scars that attested to battles and duels. She pressed her hand over her heart to still its beating. He made a slight movement. Slipping off her negligée, she crawled close to him. How warm his body was! The touch of his skin intoxicated her. She kissed his lips, moved his head until it lay heavy on her breast. He stirred, and half-waking, recognized her.

"So beautiful . . ." he murmured as his mouth searched her breast like a hungry infant's. Then he was wide awake, rage in his eye.

"You? You here! What insolence! What . . ."

"I came to say goodbye, Philippe, in *my* way."

"A woman waits for her husband's pleasure, not imposes her wishes on him. Stop it!"

He pulled back his hand to shove her off the bed, but she grabbed hold of it, beseeching him: "Philippe! Philippe, hold me close. Keep me near you tonight."

"No!"

He freed his arm, but she grabbed it again. She could sense that in spite of all his efforts he was not unmoved by her presence.

"Philippe, I love you. Hold me in your arms."

"What in the world do you want now?"

"You know."

"Have you no shame? Haven't you enough lovers to satisfy you?"

"No, Philippe, I have no lovers at all. Only you. And you will be away for months and months."

"So that's what you're after, you little whore? You have no more dignity than a bitch in heat."

He continued to rail at her, calling her all the foul names he could think of, but he did not repulse her. She crept even closer to him. His insults seemed to her the tenderest declarations of love. At last he sighed deeply and grasped her hair to lift back her face. She smiled as he gazed on her. She had lost all fear. She had never known fear, that was what had won him. Then with one last oath, he clasped her to him.

There was a tense silence which for Philippe concealed his fear of impotence. But Angélique's passion, the uninhibited joy she felt at being in his arms, her skillful lovemaking as she became the slave of the pleasure she partook of, overcame his doubts. The spark glowed, burst into flame. At the groan that betrayed the violence of his pleasure, Angélique knew she had overcome his reticence.

He would not admit it. The time of their quarrels was still too recent. He still would lie to her. He wanted her to feel no assurance.

"Go away," he said brutally as she lay beside him twisting his curls in her fingers.

This time she obeyed with such sweet docility that he did not know whether to strike her or embrace her passionately. He gritted his teeth, struggling between his regret at seeing her go and his desire to keep her even till dawn, snuggled in the hollow of his shoulders, in the warm darkness of his body like a little cuddly pet animal. A dangerous weakness! Pure madness! Happily the wind of battle and the whistling of the bullets would soon put an end to all this.

*   *   *

Shortly after the departure of the Marshal du Plessis-Bellière Cantor's turn to join the army came. At the last minute Angélique wanted to renege. She felt dreadfully sad and beset by all kinds of presentiments. She had begun to write often to Philippe in Franche-Comté, but he never answered her letters. Much as she fought against it, this silence on his part depressed her. When would Philippe ever admit he loved her? Perhaps never. Perhaps it was impossible for him to love, or to perceive that he was loved. He was no thinker, he was a warrior. Unconsciously believing he still hated her, he was trying to prove that he did. But he could not extinguish the spark that had been kindled between them, or obliterate his participation in the voluptuous pleasure that had drawn them together again. Nothing, not even the hypocritical fanatics, nor the scoffing libertines, nor the King nor Philippe himself could do anything about that.

Angélique tried to busy herself with getting Cantor ready to leave. She was seldom idle. And then Cantor went off too.

Angélique flung herself into all kinds of entertainments and scarcely had time to brood over her feelings that misty morning on which her little boy, in a veritable fever of anticipation, leaped into Vivonne's coach with his tutor Gaspard de Racan. He was dressed in a suit of green silk that matched his eyes, trimmed with plenty of lace and satin bows. A big black velvet hat trimmed with white plumes confined his curly locks. His

beribboned guitar kept getting in his way, for he
hugged it to him the way children do their favorite toy.
It was Angélique's parting gift to him, made of imported wood and inlaid with mother-of-pearl, and designed especially for him by the finest instrument-maker
in Paris.

Barbe kept weeping in the shadow of the porte-cochère,
but Angélique refused to betray her own emotions. Such
was life! Children go off on their own, as everyone knows,
but every step they take tears at the tender living bonds
that bind them to their mother's heart.

With increasing interest she kept up with the dis-
patches from the Mediterranean. In their objective of
aiding the Venetians against the Turks, who were trying to win this last bastion of Christianity in the Mediterranean, the French galleys were bent on a sacred
mission, and the Duc de Vivonne and his troops deserved the name of crusaders. Angélique smiled to herself at the thought of Cantor as a tiny cog in the mecha-
nism of this holy expedition. She imagined him sitting in
the prow of his ship, the ribbons of his guitar waving in
the breeze under a cloudless sky.

During her few moments of leisure in Paris she made
an effort to get closer to Florimond. She feared he might
miss Cantor, or be jealous of his younger brother's opportunity to rise so rapidly and savor the glory of battle.
But she quickly observed that although Florimond was
quite polite about staying with her alone, he had a terrible time sitting still for more than ten minutes at a
time. He had a thousand and one things on his mind—
exercise his horse, feed his falcon, tend to his dog, polish
his sword, get ready for a riding lesson or accompany the
Dauphin on a hunt. He was not restless only when his
Latin lesson with the Abbé de Lesdiguières was due.

"My mother and I are talking," he told his tutor then,
and the abbé did not dare press the matter.

Most of the time they talked principally about Master Florimond's skill as a swordsman. Sensitive and delicate as he appeared, the boy had all the love of violence
of children his age. He lived to wound and conquer and
kill in defense of his honor. He was never happier than

with a sword in his hand or at target practice. The
Dauphin was too much of a hothouse plant to interest
him.

"I try to liven him up," he sighed, "but it's no use.
Between us, Mother, and don't let it go any further, he
gives me a pain in the neck."

"I know, Florimond, I know," Angélique admitted
laughing. But his precocious knowledge of human nature disturbed her nonetheless.

She knew too that the Dauphin would have followed
Florimond to the ends of the earth, so captivated was he
by his fiery black eyes and his soldierly vitality. Florimond was indeed charming, attractive to everyone and
successful in everything he undertook. She suspected he
was very conceited, as doubtless all children are. But
she could see that he too was drifting away from her,
and this made her sad.

He pirouetted with his naked sword. "Look, Mother,
look at me. I parry, I feint, and then strike home. Right
in the heart. My enemy has fallen . . . dead!"

How handsome he was! Joy of living had kindled a
flame in him. Would he still come crying to her if he were
in trouble or hurt? How quickly a child's heart matures
and hardens in the bright sunlight of the Court!

The news of the battle off Cape Passaro arrived in the
middle of June during the last fête the King would give
before leaving to lead his campaign into Lorraine. Vivonne's galleys had been attacked off the coast of Sicily
by a Turkish fleet under the command of a renegade
Algerian, nicknamed Resquater, whose exploits in the
Mediterranean were celebrated. Vivonne had had to take
refuge in a bay protected by Cape Passaro. Here he had
given battle, but it was little more than a skirmish. Only
two of his twenty galleys had been sunk.

It was known, however, that there were a great many of
his household on one of these, and that Vivonne had
been forced to see go to the bottom his three secretaries,
ten of his kitchen help, four of his footmen, all twenty
of his choirboys, his confessor, his steward, his squire,
and along with them his little guitar-playing page.

chapter 15

HARDLY anyone offered condolences to Madame du Plessis-Belliére, for the son she had lost at Passaro was still only a child. What could one child matter?

The summer's lull put a temoprary end to the Court entertainments and allowed her to be alone in Paris with her grief. She could not believe the dreadful news was true, so unthinkable was it to her. Angélique absolutely refused to accept the horrible fact.

Barbe kept bewailing her loss night and day until Angélique, out of concern for the old nurse's health, ended by scolding her.

"Of course, Madame, of course," she murmured between sobs, "but Madame cannot understand. Madame never loved him as I did."

Dejectedly Angélique left her alone and returned to her own room, where she sat by the open window. It was getting on toward autumn, and it had drizzled all day long. The wet street reflected the evening sky. Angélique covered her face with her hands. Her heart was heavy, so heavy she knew nothing would ever lighten its burden again. How seldom had she taken the time to hold little Cantor on her knees and kiss his apple cheeks!

His looks were still a mystery to her. Because he looked like her, and like her young Sancé brothers whom she watched grow up, she never quite realized that Joffrey had been his father. But the lively, adventurous, irrepressible spirit of that great Count of Toulouse had been inherited by the lad. Once more she could see him going off to war in his big hat, serious and yet delirious with joy. Or she saw him singing for the Queen, heard his seraphic voice:

Farewell, my life; farewell, my love;
Farewell, my hope of things above . . .

The sluggish clopping of a horse's hooves below on
the cobblestones of the courtyard brought her out of
her memories. Unconsciously she looked out. For a moment she thought the horseman she saw mounting the
steps was Philippe. But Philippe was with the army at
the front in Franche-Comté, where the King had just
gone.

A second rider followed him across the courtyard and
under the portico of the hôtel. This time she made no
mistake. It was La Violette. She recognized his giant
figure, even though his head was bent against the rain.
So it was Philippe who had just arrived. She heard his
step in the hall, and before she had time to recover completely from her sorrowful thoughts he was with her,
covered with mud up to his waist and for once looking
bedraggled, with water draining off his hat and dripping from his coat.

"Philippe," she said, rising to greet him, "you're soak-
ing wet."

"It's been raining since morning and I've ridden
without stopping."

She tugged at a bell cord.

"I'm going to order you a hot supper. Perhaps we
should have a fire built. Why didn't you let me know
you were coming, Philippe? Your rooms are being done
over. I never thought you'd be back before fall, and I
thought . . . that this would be a good time for . . .
some redecorating."

He listened as if he did not hear her, his legs spread
apart as she had seen him stand so often.

"I heard your son was dead," he said at last. "I did not
get the news till last week."

In the silence that followed his remark, the daylight
suddenly failed altogether as clouds blotted out what
was left of the sun.

"He dreamed of going to sea," Philippe continued,
"and he seized the chance to make his dream come true.

I know the Mediterranean, blue and edged with gold like the King's own standard. It will be a fitting shroud for the little songster . . ."

Angélique began to weep, her tears blurring Philippe's image. He laid his hand on her hair.

"You hoped he would not be corrupted. Death has spared him the tears of shame that children taken unaware drop into their pillows. To each his fate. His was naught but joy and song. He had a mother who loved him."

"I never spent enough time with him," she said, wiping her eyes.

"But you did love him," he said. "You fought for him. You gave him what he needed to make him happy—the security of your love."

Angélique listened to him in a perplexity which gave way to total stupefaction.

"Philippe," she exclaimed at length, "you can't make me believe that you left the army and rode eighty leagues over rain-soaked roads just . . . to bring me these words of comfort!"

"It wouldn't have been the first foolish thing you've made me do," he said. "But I did not come for that alone. I wanted to bring you a present."

He drew from his pocket a kind of case made of old, shriveled leather, and opening it, extracted an unusual necklace consisting of a green gold chain from which hung three disks of red gold mounted with two cabochon rubies and a huge emerald. It was a magnificent ornament but so barbaric in workmanship that it seemed designed for some mighty Druid priestess.

"This is the great jewel of the Bellière women, made to be worn crosswise on their breasts. For centuries it has given them courage. It is worthy of a mother who has given her son for her country."

He stepped behind her to hang it about her neck.

"Philippe," Angélique gasped, "what does this mean? Do you remember the bet we made one day on the steps at Versailles?"

"I do remember, Madame. You have won."

He parted her blond curls and planted a long kiss on the nape of her neck. Angélique did not stir. He had to turn her around to see her face. She was weeping.

"Cry no more," he said, clasping her to him. "I have come to dry your tears, not to make you shed more. I could never bear to see you cry. Damn it, you are a great woman!"

"Mad with love, mad," Angélique kept repeating to herself. "That's what his giving me the necklace means."

So he did love her. He had even confessed it with a subtlety that soothed her troubled heart. She took his face in her hands and looked at him tenderly.

"How could I have known the behavior that terrified me so could ever conceal such beauty. You have the soul of a poet, Philippe."

"I am what I am, no more," he mumbled with humor. "One thing I know, though, and that is it disturbs me to see you in the necklace of the Plessis-Bellière women. None of my ancestors could wear it without soon planning battles and civil war. With those rubies on her breast, my mother raised the armies of Poitou on the side of the Prince de Condé. You remember that as well as I. What will you conjure up, now it's your turn? As if you needed any pluck!"

He pressed her to him again, rubbing his cheek against hers.

"There are your green eyes staring at me as always," he murmured. "I can torment you, beat you, threaten you, but you'll still carry your head high again like a flower after a storm. I can leave you crushed and humbled only to see you rise more beautiful and proud than ever. It has driven me crazy, but in the long run it has made me . . . trust you. I can't get over my astonishment at finding such constancy in a woman. I used to weigh the odds. Will she be true to me, I wondered. The day of the royal hunt, when I saw you meet the King's anger with a smile, I knew I could never win. At heart I was proud then that you were my wife."

He pecked at her with his lips as if he were bashful. Unaccustomed as he was to shows of tenderness, he had scorned such demonstrativeness until now when he felt the need of it. He hesitated to find her mouth. It was she who sought out his.

To her the lips of this man of war had the freshness of innocence about them. How strange that after the stormy life each of them had led, so spotted by the world, they could now at last exchange the pure, sweet kisses they had been cheated of that night in the gardens of Plessis when they were young.

"I must go back," he said suddenly with his usual brusqueness. "I've spent enough time on affairs of the heart. May I see my son?"

Angélique sent for the nurse. She came holding little Charles-Henri in her arms, swathed in white velvet like a falcon on a huntsman's wrist. With his yellow hair creeping out from under his pearled cap and his pink cheeks and big blue eyes, he was a gorgeous child.

Philippe took him in his arms and tossed him up in the air and dandled him, but he could not get the baby to smile.

"I've never seen such a serious child," Angélique said. "He almost frightens people. But it doesn't stop him from getting into all kinds of mischief now he's learning to walk. He has learned how to turn the spinning wheel and get the wool into a frightful tangle."

Philippe held out the child to her. "I leave him with you, entrust him to you. Take good care of him."

"He is the child *you* gave me, Philippe. He is very dear to me."

Still holding her baby in her arms, she leaned out the window to watch Philippe mount his horse and gallop out of the dark courtyard. By coming home to her, Philippe had turned her bitter brief into living joy, even though he was the last from whom she expected solace. But life is full of surprises. How would she ever have imagined that this ungovernable soldier who could put whole cities to fire and sword would ride four days through the rain because he heard in his heart the echo of her sobs!

A few days later Angélique returned to her hôtel to find Monsieur de Saint-Aignan just arrived from

Franche-Comté with a letter for her from the King.

"From the King?"

"Yes, Madame."

Angélique withdrew to read it in private.

"Madame," the King wrote, "our sympathy with you on the loss of your son who, however young, died in our service. This sad event leads us to take an even greater interest in the future of your older boy, Florimond de Morens-Bellière. Consequently we have decided to raise him to a more significant level and attach him to our household as cup-bearer under the supervision of Monsieur Duchesne, the First Gentleman of the Wine Service. We hope to see him assume without delay his new duties while we are with the army, and we especially wish to have you accompany him on his trip to join us. —Louis."

Angélique bit her lip as she stared at the imperious handwriting of the royal signature, wondering what to do. Florimond as cupbearer to the King! The heirs of the greatest families of France fought for such a post, which cost them plenty. It was an unprecedented honor for insignificant little Florimond. There was no question of her refusing it, but Angélique did hesitate about going with him. She hesitated for two days. Then she realized it would be absurd for her to refuse such an invitation, which would give her a chance to see Philippe again and distract her from her melancholy.

She went to Saint-Germain to get Florimond. Madame de Montespan did not receive her, being still in bed as a result of the shock to her nerves which the Marquis de Montespan's jealous rage had caused her. The whole Court was laughing about that incident. The few witnesses to it were not stingy with the details, and much as they might have wished to forget it all, they were prevented by the Marquise's parrot, which kept screaming at the top of its lungs, "Cuckold! Cuckhold!"—as Pardaillan had termed himself.

No one could fail to distinguish these words, even though they sounded very much like the bird's natural squawks. And they could also clearly distinguish,

"Syphilis, you wh—!" The Marquis de Montespan had threatened to infect his wife with the disease.

Even the servants couldn't restrain their laughter in public.

Madame de Montespan bravely carried her head high and pretended to laugh at the parrot to cover up her embarrassment. But when she saw Angélique, she burst into tears as she asked what had become of her husband.

Angélique told her that the Grande Mademoiselle had undertaken to calm him down and that for the time being he had promised not to make any more scenes.

Athenais dried her tears. "If you only knew how I suffer when I see him and that parrot catering to these guttersnipes! I have written the King. I certainly hope he will be stern this time."

Angélique implied that she doubted he would be. She did not think it good timing to tell her she had been invited by His Majesty to visit the army.

Her coach reached Tabaux at nightfall, and she went to the inn. She could have gone to the encampment, whose bivouac fires she could see across the fields, but she was tired after traveling for two days over the broken roads. Florimond was asleep, his chin resting on his rumpled lace jabot and his wig askew. He was not presentable. The Gilandon girls were asleep with their heads tipped back and their mouths open. "Swordthrust" Malbrant was snoring like an organ. Only the Abbé des Lesdiguières looked the least bit dignified in spite of the fact that his face was covered with dust. The heat had been terrible and they were all frightfully dirty.

The inn, they discovered, was full, for the proximity of the royal army had brought many camp followers to the village, but for the great lady who arrived in a coach drawn by six horses and with all her household, the innkeepers put themselves out. They found two rooms, and an attic which suited the fencing-master. Florimond went in with the abbé, and the bed in the other room was big enough for Angélique and her two companions. They washed up and sat down to a hearty meal of

Quiche Lorraine and meatballs, brussels sprouts with
butter, and stewed plums, for they knew they had to eat
well to get up enough strength for the morrow to face
the King and the life of the Court when it was in the
field with the army.

The Gilandon girls had gone to bed, but had not
drawn the bed-curtains. Angélique had got into her
dressing gown and was just finishing brushing her hair
when there was a knock at the door.

"Come in," she said. Then she gasped at finding
Péguilin de Lauzun in the open doorway.

"Here I am, my pretty one."

He tiptoed in, his finger to his lips.

"The devil take me if I ever expected to see you!"
said Angélique. "Wherever did you come from?"

"From the army, of course. I had no sooner heard of
your arrival from the village sutlers than I leaped on my
fine horse . . ."

"Péguilin, you're not going to get me into trouble,
are you?"

"Trouble? Don't be so ungrateful. By the way, are you
alone here?"

"No," Angélique said, nodding toward the Gilandon
girls sleeping away innocently in their nightcaps. "What
difference would it make if I were?"

"Don't be so touchy. My intentions are of the best, at
least so far as I am concerned."

He raised his eyes toward the ceiling like a stricken
martyr. "I'm not here for myself, I regret to say. Don't
lose any time, but get your little virgins out of here."
He whispered into her ear. "The King is outside. He
wants to see you."

"The King?"

"In the hall."

"Péguilin, don't try to fool me. I'm in no mood for
your tricks."

"I swear . . ."

"Do you really think you can make me believe the
King . . ."

"Shh! Take it easy. His Majesty wants to see you privately. Can't you understand he doesn't dare be recognized?"

"I don't believe you."

"This is too much! Hurry up, I tell you, and get them out of here, and then you'll see."

"Where can I put them? In 'Swordthrust' Malbrant's bed?"

She got up and tied the cord of her negligée defiantly. "If the King is in the hall, as you say, then in the hall I'll meet him."

She went out into the corridor and froze to find a man standing near the door.

"Madame is right," said the King's voice from under his gray velvet mask. "After all, what's wrong with the hall? It's dimly lit and, what's more important, empty. Péguilin, old man, will you please go down to the foot of the stairs and keep any pests away."

He laid his hands on Angélique's shoulders. Then, remembering his mask, he took it off. It was the King indeed. He was smiling.

"No, Madame, no curtsies, please."

He folded back the cuffs of her dressing gown so as to feel her wrists, and drew her gently toward a vigil light burning before an image in a niche.

"I couldn't wait to see you again."

"Sire," said Angélique with determination, "I have already told you I would no longer act as a blind, as Madame de Montespan so subtly got me to do, and I should like Your Majesty to understand . . ."

"You always keep saying the same thing, little toy. Surely you're clever enough to think up another answer."

Angélique was speechless.

"Tonight there's no need for a blind or for any masquerading. Why do you think I went to all the trouble of disguising myself to come to see you?"

What he said made sense, but left her more at a loss than ever.

"Well?"

"Well, it's very simple, Madame. I am not in love with you, but you don't seem to realize you have cast a spell over me. I cannot forget your lips or your eyes, nor that you have the prettiest legs in Versailles."

"Madame de Montespan is quite as beautiful as I.

And she loves you, Sire. She is devoted to Your Majesty."

"While you . . . ?"

His greedy eyes which reflected the vigil light like two sparks of gold seemed to hypnotize her. When he laid his mouth on hers she wanted to draw back, but she could not. He pressed his lips against hers, forcing them open against her tightly shut teeth. When he succeeded in making her part them, she yielded unconsciously to the power of this master who had no conception of what it was to be disobeyed. They kissed with a burning passion that consumed each of them, for he would not let her go until she responded to his lust. Finally she broke away, her head whirling. Weakly she leaned against the partition. Her lips were trembling from the hot pressure of his mouth.

The King's throat was tight with desire. "I have dreamed of a kiss like that," he whispered. "And of seeing you again with your head leaning back and your lovely eyelids shut, and your wonderous throat pulsing. . . . Shall I go? No, I haven't the courage. This inn is secluded and . . ."

"Sire, I entreat you not to lead me on further into something that horrifies me."

"Horrifies you? I thought you willing. I can't have mistaken your acquiescence."

"What else could I do? You are the King."

"What if I were not?"

Angélique confronted him boldly, quite in possession of herself. "I would have slapped both your cheeks good and hard."

The King paced up and down in a rage. "My word, how angry you can make me! Am I so poor a lover as that?"

"Sire, has it never occurred to you that the Marquis du Plessis-Bellière is your friend?"

The monarch's head fell in embarrassment. "Indeed, he is my faithful friend, but I do not think I am causing him any grief. Everyone knows that this Mars of ours has only one mistress—war. If I give him armies to lead to battle, what more can he ask? He cares nothing for love, as he has many times proved."

"He has also proved he loves me."

The King remembered the Court gossip. He continued to pace like a caged animal.

"So Mars has yielded to Venus! No, I cannot believe it! But I must say you are quite capable of making such a miracle happen."

"Suppose I told you that I love him and that he loves me, would you destroy such a new-found simple love?"

The King was struggling between his consuming passion and his conscience.

"No, I would not destroy it," he said at length with a deep sigh. "If that is the case, then I must yield to it. Farewell, Madame. Sleep well. I shall see you tomorrow at the camp with your son."

In his uniform of blue velvet trimmed with gold braid Philippe was waiting for her at the entrance to the royal tent. Bowing, he took her hand to lead her, head high, across the crowded room to the lace-covered table where the King was about to take his place.

"Greetings, husband," Angélique whispered.

"Greetings, Madame."

"Will I see you this evening?"

"If I can get away from my duties to the King."

His face was cold, but his fingers intertwined with hers and squeezed them.

The King was watching their progress. "Is there any handsomer couple than the Marquis and Marquise du Plessis-Bellière?" he asked his High Chamberlain.

"You are correct, Sire."

"They are also charming and devoted servants—both of them," the King added with a sigh.

De Gesvres looked at them out of the corner of his eye.

Angélique curtsied deeply. The King took her hand to raise her. She met his eyes, which roved from the jewels in her hair to her white satin slippers, not omitting her gown embroidered with nosegays of forget-me-nots. She was the only woman invited to dine with the King, and many of the nobles in his company had not for a long time had the pleasure of seeing so beautiful a woman.

"You are fortunate indeed, Marquis, to possess such a treasure. There's not a man here tonight—including your sovereign—who does not envy your good luck. We hope you realize that. The smoke of battle, the reek of gunpowder and the intoxication of victory have sometimes made you blind, you must admit, to the charms of the fair sex."

"Sire, there are some sights that can give eyes to the blind, and let victors savor other triumphs."

"An excellent riposte!" said the King with a laugh. "Madame, gather up your laurels."

He was still holding Angélique's hand in his, and with one of the winning gestures he managed so well and used freely in the informal atmosphere of the field camp, he put his arm about Philippe's shoulders.

"Mars, old man," he whispered, "you have all the luck, but I am not jealous. Your loyalty means a great deal to me. Do you remember our first battle when we were fifteen, how a bullet knocked off my hat? You ran right up to the firing line to get it back for me."

"Yes, Sire, I remember."

"You were insane to do it. And you've done plenty of other mad things for me since."

The King was a little shorter than Philippe, and his hair was dark instead of fair, yet they were alike in the fine proportions of their muscular bodies which had been trained like those of all other young nobles of their time in gymnasiums, riding academies and their early apprenticeship to military life.

"The glory of arms may make us forget love, but love can never make us forget that we are brothers-in-arms, can it?"

"You are right, Sire."

"Exactly. Well, Marshal, that's enough philosophizing for us soldiers. Madame, will you sit?"

As the only woman in the company, Angélique looked like a queen as she took her place at the King's right hand. Philippe remained standing to assist the High Chamberlain. The King kept admiring her profile as she bent over her plate, and the way her diamond ear-drop cast prismatic hues over her velvety cheek.

"Have you put your conscience at ease, Madame?"

"Sire, Your Majesty's concern overwhelms me."

"It's not a question of concern, I'm sorry to say, my dear little toy. How can we fight love? There's no compromise with it. If I cannot act ignobly, then I must act nobly. Any ordinary man in my position would find himself under the same obligation. . . . Have you noticed how well your boy fills his post?"

He pointed to Florimond, who was helping the High Cup-bearer. When the King wished to drink, the High Cup-bearer was notified by the footman. Then from a sideboard he took a tray on which a carafe of water had been set along with a full pitcher of wine and a goblet. Then, preceded by Florimond, who carried the taster's cup, he advanced toward the High Chamberlain, who poured a little water and wine into this silver mug and gave it to the High Cup-bearer, who drank it off. Now the King's drink was proved free from poison, and the King's goblet which Florimond held as if it were a chalice, was filled. Florimond performed the ritual like an altar boy.

The King complimented him on his performance, and Florimond bobbed his curly head in acknowledgment.

"Your boy does not look like you with his black eyes and hair. He has a swarthy, southern beauty."

Angélique blushed, then turned pale. Her heart began to thump. The King laid his hand on hers.

"How sensitive you are! When are you going to stop being afraid of me? Can't you understand that I won't do you any harm?"

As she rose he gave her his hand to lead her past him. His touch disturbed her more than if it had been a calculated gesture.

She returned with Philippe through the camp, where the bivouac fires burned red against the tents that glowed yellow from the candlelight within.

Philippe's tent was of yellow satin embroidered with gold. It was a marvel of military splendor, furnished with two armchairs of rare wood and a low Turkish ta-

ble, around which were strewn cushions of gold brocade.
A rich rug covered the bare ground, and a kind of
couch, also covered with rugs, gave it an oriental atmosphere. The Marshal had been rebuked for such luxury
more than once. Even the King was not so sumptuously
lodged as he on this campaign.

Angélique's heart was touched at seeing it, for it revealed another aspect of her husband—the force of character he had to lead a charge against the enemy in his
lace collar. Tonight on the eve of battle, there were
rings on his fingers, his mustache was perfumed, his
boots polished till they shone. Tomorrow he would know
all the sweat and filth and vermin that are an indispensable part of soldiering.

Philippe took off his baldric. La Violette entered, followed by the Marshal's young squire. They set a supper
of cakes and fruit and wine on the table. La Violette
offered to help his master out of his uniform, but
Philippe waved him away impatiently.

"Should I have your maids sent for?" he asked Angélique.

"I don't think that's necessary."

She had left the Gilandon girls and Javotte in the
care of the innkeeper's wife, and had brought along
only Thérèse, who was rather a headstrong girl. After
helping her mistress dress, she had vanished, and it
seemed fruitless to go looking for her.

"You can help me, Philippe," Angélique said with a
smile. "I imagine you have a few things to learn about
such matters."

She laid her head against him wheedlingly.

"Glad to see me?"

"Yes, I'm sorry to say."

"Why sorry?"

"I can't put you out of my mind. I have known pangs
of jealousy I never dreamed existed."

"Why? I love only you."

He lowered his forehead to her shoulder without answering. In the dim light of the tent she seemed to
see again the King's lustful eyes.

Outside a soldier was piping a poignant folksong. Angélique shivered. She must get away, leave Versailles and all its fêtes. Never see the King again.

"Philippe," she said, "When are you coming home? When can we start learning to live together?"

He drew away to look at her suspiciously.

"Live together? Is that possible for a Marshal of the King's armies and a great Court lady?"

"I want to leave the Court and go back to Plessis."

"That's just like a woman! There was a time when I used to beg you to go back to Plessis and you would rather have been hacked to pieces than obey me. Now it's too late."

"What do you mean?"

"You have important obligations the King has graciously given you. It would greatly displease him if you did not fulfill them."

"It's because of the King that I want to go away, Philippe. The King . . ."

She looked at him glassily, as if he had suddenly vanished.

"The King," she repeated desperately.

Daring to go no further, she began to undress herself mechanically. Philippe seemed lost in a dream.

"After what the King said tonight, he will understand," she thought, "if he has not already understood . . . for a long time . . . even before I myself did."

He came over to the couch where she was kneeling while she unpinned her hair. She put her arms around his neck. His hands sought the yielding flesh of her naked body under her filmy shift, stroking the warm soft hollow of her back, then returning to her swelling breasts, heavier since her last baby but still firm and pointed.

"Fit for a King indeed," he said.

"Philippe!" She clasped him close. "Philippe!"

There was a long moment of silence between them as if they were in the grip of some indescribable fear.

Outside someone was calling: "Marshal! Marshal!"

Philippe stepped to the entrance to the tent.

"They've just caught a spy. His Majesty needs you."

"Don't go, Philippe," Angélique begged.

"That would be a fine thing, not to go when the King calls me," he chuckled. "War is war, my dear. My first duty is with the enemies of His Majesty."

He smoothed his mustache and buckled on his sword again.

"What was that song Cantor used to sing? Ah, yes . . .

> Farewell, my life; farewell, my love;
> Farewell, my hope of things above.
> Serve we must our lord, the King,
> Even to our long parting."

She waited for him in vain through the long night until finally she fell asleep on the couch. When she awoke daylight was filtering through the yellow silk walls of the tent, leading her to believe the sun was shining. But when she went outside it was a gray, foggy morning. It had rained, and the puddles reflected the dark clouds. The muddy camp was half deserted. From the distance came the drumroll of reveille, and the ceaseless firing of cannon.

At her request "Swordthrust" Malbrant brought her her saddle horse. A soldier showed her the road to a knoll.

"From up there, Madame, you can see all the maneuvers."

On the hill she found Salnove, who had disposed his troops on the edge of a cliff. At the right a windmill slowly revolved its sails. The sun was trying to pierce the heavy clouds.

Angélique recognized the picture now familiar to her of a besieged town with its girdle of ramparts like slate roofs, its peaked belltowers and gothic spires. A pretty little river wound around it like a white scarf.

The French batteries were ranged above the river valley. Three rows of cannon protected the infantry whose helmets and lance-tips sparkled in the sun. With his riding crop Salnove pointed out to Angélique a brightly uniformed troop parading before the lines.

"The King himself went to the outposts early this morning. He is convinced the garrison will soon sur-

render. Neither His Majesty nor his chief officers had a
moment of sleep all night long. A spy was caught, and
they found out from him that the garrison would try to
attack during the night. That may have been what they
intended, but we were on guard and they had to abandon the plan. It won't be long before they surrender."

"But the bombardment seems very heavy to me."

"These are their last rounds. The governor cannot
raise the white flag until he has exhausted all his am-
munition first."

"That is just what my husband said last night," Angélique said.

"I am glad he shares my opinion. The Marshal has a
fine sense of strategy. I do believe we can have a victory
banquet in the town tonight."

A courier they had seen a while ago galloped around
a bend in the road. As he passed them, he shouted:
"Marshal du Plessis-Bellière is . . ."

When he saw Angélique he stopped, yanked on his
reins and returned.

"What's the matter? What's happened?" she asked
fearfully. "Has something happened to my husband?"

"Yes."

"What is it," demanded Salnove. "What happened to
the Marshal? Speak up, man. Is the Marshal wounded?"

"Yes," panted the ensign, "but not seriously. The King
is with him. The Marshal took a great risk and . . ."

Angélique had already spurred her horse down the
path from the hilltop. Again and again she almost broke
her neck before she reached the bottom. Once there, she
let the reins hang loose on the horse's neck and whipped
him across the plain.

Philippe wounded! A voice kept repeating inside her:
"I knew it. I knew this would happen." She drew near
the walls, past the firing cannon and the pikes of the
squared-off infantry like a portcullis, but she saw only
the distant knot of lace-trimmed uniforms gathered near
the front row of cannon.

As she approached, Péguilin de Lauzun came to meet
her. She shouted to him: "Is Philippe wounded?"

"Yes."

When she reached him, he told her: "Your husband took a terrible risk. The King wanted to know whether a pretended assault would hasten the town's surrender, and Monsieur du Plessis said he would reconnoitre. He rode right up onto the escarpment which had been swept by continuous cannon fire ever since daybreak."

"Is it serious?"

"Yes."

Angélique noticed that Péguilin had stopped his horse directly across and in front of hers so as to prevent her from moving forward. Her shoulders sagged under a leaden weight, and a deathly chill crept over her.

"He's dead, isn't he?"

Péguilin bent his head forward.

"Let me by," she said tonelessly. "I want to see him."

Péguilin did not move.

"Let me by," Angélique screamed. "He is my husband. I have a right to see him."

Péguilin pressed her forehead to his chest, stroking her hair sympathetically. "Better not, my darling," he murmured. "Alas, our handsome Marquis . . . had his head blown off by a cannon ball."

She wept hopelessly, sprawled face down on the couch where she had waited in vain for Philippe the previous night. She refused all comfort, would not let anyone near her. Her entire suite stood outside the tent terrified by the sound of her sobbing. She kept telling herself it wasn't true, yet she already knew she would never see him again. Nevermore could she clasp him to her heart, never stroke his forehead like a mother, as she had dreamed she might, nevermore kiss his long-lashed eyelids, now closed forever, and whisper "I loved you . . . you were the first I ever loved in the fresh ardor of my youth."

Philippe! Philippe in pink. Philippe in blue. Philippe in snowy white and gold, with his blond wig and his red heels. Philippe with his hand on little Cantor's head . . . With the hunting knife in one hand and the other grasping the throat of the savage wolf. Philippe du Plessis-Belliére, so handsome even the King called him Mars, had him immortalized as such by the painter's art on a ceiling of Versailles in a chariot drawn by wolves.

Why was he no longer by her side? Why had he vanished in a "puff of wind," as Ninon said. In the flaming wind of war! Why had he been so foolhardy?

The words of the courier and of Lauzun came back to her. She raised herself a little. "Why did you do it, Philippe?"

The silken drapery at the entrance of the tent was drawn aside. De Gesvres, the High Chamberlain, was bowing before her.

"Madame, the King has come to express his sorrow."

"I can't see anyone."

"Madame, it is the King."

"I don't want the King," she shouted, "or any of that bunch of cowardly gossiping dandies he keeps around him who have come to stare at me all the while wondering who will be the next Marshal."

"Madame . . ." he choked.

"Go away," she cried. "Get out!"

She buried her face in the cushions again, drained of anger, robbed of any power that might enable her to take up her life again.

Two strong hands raising her stilled her frenzy. The one thing that could always comfort her was the support of a man's shoulder. She thought it was Lauzun, and sobbed all the harder against the lapels of a brown velvet coat that smelled of orris root.

Finally her passion of despair spent itself. She raised her swollen eyes and met the deep brown ones of the King. Never before had she seen so tender a light in them.

"I have left those . . . gentlemen outside," he said. "I beg you, Madame, do not let your sorrow overwhelm you so. You must rise above it. Your grief distresses me."

Slowly Angélique backed away a few steps and leaned against the silken walls of the golden tent. In her dark dress and with her pale and streaming face, she seemed like a mourner at the foot of the Cross in some primitive painting. But her eyes, which never left the King, flashed like emeralds, and with the same hard glaze. Yet when she spoke her voice was level.

"Sire, I ask Your Majesty's permission to retire to my estates . . . to Plessis."

The King barely hesitated.

"I grant your request, Madame. I understand your need to be alone and quiet. Go to Plessis. You may remain there till the end of autumn."

"Sire, I wish to resign my duties."

He shook his head gently. "It's the shock of your grief that makes you say that. Time heal all wounds. I shall not relieve you of your duties."

Angélique made a feeble gesture of protest, then shut her eyes. Tears stole from beneath her lashes, tracing glistening furrows down her cheeks.

"Promise me you will return," the King insisted.

She remained speechless, motionless. He was afraid he had lost her forever, and withdrew without extracting a promise from her.

"Versailles will be waiting for you," he said gently.

Part Three

The King

✿ ✿ ✿

A HORSEMAN galloped up the avenue under the ancient oak trees, turned to circle the pond that reflected the gold of autumn in its placid surface, and came into sight again at the miniature drawbridge, where he stopped to pull at the bell.

Through the little panes of her bedroom window, Angélique watched him alight and recognized the livery of Madame de Sévigné. This must be an envoy from her. Throwing a velvet cloak around her, she hurried down the staircase without waiting for the proper maid to bring her his letter on a silver tray. She sent the messenger to the kitchens for refreshment, then climbed the stairs again to her room and sat down by the fire, turning the letter over and over in delight. It was only a note from a friend, but to Angélique it was as diverting as anything she might have chosen for herself.

Autumn was drawing to a close, and soon winter would be upon her. Lord knows, the winters at Plessis were dreary! The pretty Renaissance castle which had been built as a setting for summer holidays looked grim and cold now that the leaves were gone from the forest of Nieul. At night wolves howled at the very edges of the park. She dreaded the return of those gloomy evenings which during the previous season when she was nursing her grief had driven her half out of her mind.

Spring had brought her some peace of soul. She had ridden over the fields on horseback, but gradually the condition of the countryside came to depress her. The war weighed heavily on the peasants, and the sullen Poitevins talked of drowning the tax-collectors. If their poverty did not arouse them, then the arrogance of the Protestant villages, which then had the upper hand, stirred up bloody fracases with the Catholic ones. There

seemed to be no end in sight to this explosive rivalry.
Angélique grew tired of it all, and refused to listen to
complaints. More and more she withdrew into herself.

Her nearest neighbor was the county agent Molines.
Further off was Monteloup, where her father was dozing
away what was left of his life with her old nurse and her
Aunt Martha. She could hope for no visitors except du
Croissac, a crude country squire who snorted like a wild
boar as he paid his own kind of court to her, and whom
she did not know how to get rid of.

Impatiently she broke the seals and began to read.

Dearest, [the Marquise wrote] If this letter contains a mixture of abuse and affection, then I leave it to your good
sense to sort them out and see that they represent the deep
concern I feel for you. I haven't heard a word from you
for months since you locked yourself away and never gave
your friends the relief of comforting you in the dreadful
trouble you have had. Ninon is as resentful of your absence
as I am. Ever since I decided to have done with love, I have
let friendship take its place in my heart, and now when I
see my overtures useless and even repulsed, I find my life
totally empty.

Well, so much for reproaches. I can't go on in that tone.
I do love you so. And so do hundreds of others, and not all
of the male sex either. For your charm and your frankness
have won you favor even with the very woman who might
think you her rival. We miss you. No one knows how even
to tie their bows without your advice, and fashion languishes
lest it go wrong for want of your approval. So everyone
looks to Madame de Montespan, who had as good taste as
you and who does not miss you. In a word, she reigns in
glory. Furthermore her husband has paid for his folly. The
King gave him five thousand *livres,* and ordered him off to
Roussillon for keeps. No one knows whether he will really
stay there, but for the moment there he is.

While I'm on the subject of fashion, I must tell you that
Madame de Montespan dictates all the new styles. You
probably will not be surprised to learn that all these have
been made to suit her own. She has designed a skirt to be
draped over hoops *in front* as well as in the rear, which is
very handy for concealing one's outlines at certain times and
permits a good deal of secrecy. I'll bet there will be a sub-

stantial rise in population now this is in vogue. Madame de
Montespan is the first to take advantage of it. She has no
shame at all, but she is more beautiful than ever and the
King has eyes for no one but her. Poor La Vallière is only a
ghost, condemned to remain among the living. The King is
through with sentimental affairs, and has taken a mistress
who, for better or worse, is more demanding but suits him
better. How hard-hearted she is! Everyone says so, and no
one can stand up to her or surpass her among the Court
ladies now. I say "now" because you are not there. She
knows it too. Every time she mentions you she says "that
ragamuffin" . . .

Angélique was so angry she had to stop reading, but
since she had no one on whom to vent her wrath, she
returned to the letter.

Under her impulse Versailles has become a Land of
Cockaigne. I was there Monday and never saw such wonders. At three o'clock the King, the Queen, Monsieur,
Madame, Mademoiselle, all the princes and princesses,
Madame de Montespan—in fact, the so-called Court of
France—gathered in the King's splendid apartments. The
décor is simply divine. Madame de Montespan so surpassed
everyone else with her beauty that all the ambassadors
marvelled at her. Yes, she took all honors—and her jewels
were like her beauty and her wit like her jewels. She is very
quick, has impeccable timing, never uses clichés, and everything she does is so unconsciously appropriate that it's as if
she were speaking a language all her own and yet sweet to
the ear. Everyone is trying to copy her admittedly.
    She never goes out without an escort of bodyguards. When
I was there the wife of Marshal de Noailles carried her
train, whereas the Queen had only an ordinary page-boy for
hers. Her apartment on the second floor has twenty rooms,
whereas the Queen has only twelve on the third floor . . .

Angélique laid the letter aside. Was there some ulterior motive behind the Marquise de Sévigné's detailed
description of Madame de Montespan in all her
glory? Charitable as she was to a fault, the charming
Marquise had always been hard on Athenais. She admired
her, but she did not like her. "Beware," she had often

told Angélique, "Athenais is a Mortemart—beautiful as the sea and just as ruthless. She too will swallow you up on your voyage if you're not chary of her."

There was a good deal of truth in her opinion, as Angélique had already learned to her cost. So why was Madame de Sévigné so interested in letting her know how the Montespan had triumphed? Did she hope Angélique would spur herself back to Versailles to fight for a position she had never had? Madame de Montespan was the favorite. The King had eyes for her alone. Well, everything had turned out for the best. . . .

There was a light rap at the door, and then Barbe came in leading Charles-Henri by the hand.

"Our little cherub wants to see his mamma."

"Yes, yes," said Angélique absently.

She rose and looked out the window. Nothing was stirring in the black and white, sullen landscape.

"Can he stay here to play for awhile?" Barbe asked. "It would make him so happy! But, wait, it's not very warm here. Madame has let the fire die down."

"Put on another log."

The baby stayed near the door playing with a pinwheel. He wore a long blue velvet dress, and there were white plumes stuck in his glossy yellow curls, which hung down to his shoulders. Angélique gave him a routine smile. She took delight in dressing him in rich garments, for he was indeed ravishingly beautiful. But why should she spend so much money on these clothes when there was no one here to see them? What a pity that was!

"May I leave him then?" Barbe said.

"No, I have no time for him. I must write a letter to Madame de Sévigné so that the courier can take it back with him tomorrow."

Barbe could tell from Angélique's attitude that her mistress' mind was on other things. Sighing, she took the hand of her charge, who followed her obediently. Once alone, Angélique sharpened a pen, but she did not immediately begin to write. She needed to think. A voice she did not wish to listen to kept repeating to her: "Versailles will be waiting for you."

Could it be true? Perhaps Versailles had forgotten

her, and things would be better off that way. That was what she had wanted, yet now she was sorry. Dejectedly she had come to Plessis to avoid some vague danger and out of her need for expiation in regard to Philippe. She had hardly paused at his hôtel, where everything about the dark, sinister colors of the place reminded her of Philippe and his sad childhood—so handsome, so rich, and so forlorn. At Plessis she had enjoyed the flaming autumn colors and had beguiled her loneliness with her long horseback rides over the fields; but now winter was approaching, her confinement there depressed her.

A footman came to ask her whether she preferred to dine in her own room or in the dining room. In her own room, of course! It was freezing cold downstairs, and she could not summon the courage to sit alone at one end of the long banquet table laden with silver. She was twice a widow now.

When she had settled herself by the fire before a table covered with little red casseroles from which fragrant odors rose as she lifted first one lid and then another to sample them, it dawned on her bitterly that she was turning into an old dowager in retirement.

There was no man to laugh at the way she stuffed herself . . . or to admire her hands which once she would have creamed and bleached for two solid hours . . . or to compliment her on her coiffure. She ran to her mirror and studied her face for a long time. She was still magnificently beautiful. She sighed several times.

The next day Monsieur and Madame de Roquelaure arrived on their way to their estates in Armagnac. They had made a detour to call upon Angélique and bring her a message from Colbert.

The Duchess kept sniffling from a cold she said she had caught on the journey, but it was only an excuse to hide the bitter tears she could not restrain. She took advantage of a moment alone with Angélique to confide in her that her husband had taken offense at her flirtatiousness and had decided to get her away from the temptations of the Court by shutting her up in their far-distant castle.

"A fine time for him to get jealous," she groaned, "now that my affair with Lauzun is long since ancient history. He hasn't come near me for months. I've had a hard time. What can he find so interesting in Mademoiselle de Montpensier?"

"She is Henri IV's granddaughter," Angélique said, "and that's something. But I can't believe Lauzun would risk toying with the affections of a princess of the blood royal. He can't be serious."

Madame de Roquelaure insisted that, on the contrary, he was very serious indeed. The Grande Mademoiselle had asked the King's permission to marry the Duc de Lauzun, whom she loved desperately.

"And what did His Majesty say?"

"What he always does—'We will see.' . . . He appears to be confused by Mademoiselle's passion for Lauzun and the affection he himself bears him. But the Queen and Monsieur and Madame were outraged at the idea of such a marriage. So was Madame de Montespan. She let her indignation be known very publicly."

"What business is it of hers? She is not of royal blood."

"She is a Mortemart. She knows what is fitting and proper for a high rank. Lauzun is only an insignificant Gascon noble."

"Poor Péguilin! I suppose you have no use for him now."

"Alas," sighed Madame de Roquelaure, and began to cry again.

Colbert's letter was another matter. Without mentioning the gossip of the Court, with which he had no concern, he begged Madame du Plessis to return at her earliest convenience and undertake some business that had to do with the silk industry which only she could successfully manage. Baktiari Bey, ambassador of the Shah of Persia, was at the gates of Paris. Colbert was anxious to negotiate a treaty through him that would improve the conditions on which Persian silk could be imported by France.

Once she had read this letter, Angélique decided she could not do otherwise than return to Paris.

From Paris Angélique went straight to Versailles.

She met the King in the park, whose lawns were now covered with snow. Even though it was bitter cold, the monarch had not given up his daily walk. If the weather did not permit him to enjoy his flowers and trees, still the fine proportions of the structures and the graceful layout of the paths were more apparent in winter. He and his companions stopped before each of the new statues executed in marble as white as the snow or in painted lead whose reds, golds and greens shone more brilliantly than ever against the background of grayish bushes.

Slowly the Court circled the Fountain of Apollo. The reflection in its ice-covered surface of the gilded group consisting of the god in his chariot drawn by six chargers sparkled in the sunlight, made it a true apotheosis of the daystar.

Madame du Plessis-Bellière had been waiting in the shelter of a hedge with Flipot, her page, who carried the train of her long cloak, her two ladies-in-waiting, and "Swordthrust" Malbrant, her bravo. Now she advanced toward the King and made him a deep Court bow.

"What a charming surprise," said the King, nodding his head slightly. "I am sure the Queen will be as pleased as I am."

"I have paid my respects to Her Majesty, and she was gracious enough to tell me she was pleased."

"I completely share her pleasure, Madame."

After another courteous little nod, the King turned to the Prince de Condé and resumed his conversation with him. Angélique joined the King's suite and graciously received the expressions of welcome she was offered. She carefully inspected every detail of the new styles, which even in these few months had made her own seem old-fashioned and provincial. Had Madame de Montespan influenced everything? Angélique had deliberately avoided greeting her, but Athenais gave her a dazzling smile and waved at her as if she were glad to see her. Angélique had to admit that Madame de Montespan had grown more and more lovely. Her radiant face, glowing from the frosty air, was framed in a sumptuous blue-gray fur as soft and glossy as if it were still on the animal. All the furs, Angélique noticed, were very handsome. The King carried a big muff of the same fur as Madame de Montespan's hood, hanging from a gold chain. Many of the lords and ladies had copied it. Angélique overheard Monsieur's falsetto voice discussing it with Madame de Thianges.

"It's an absolutely divine style. I'm ready to do anything for the Russians who invented it. Did you hear they sent by their ambassador three wagonfuls of the most beautiful skins you could ever dream of—fox, bear, skunk—absolutely superb!

"This means the end of those little muffs no bigger than a pumpkin," he said, squinting at Angélique's. "It makes them look mean and shabby. How did we ever get along with them? . . . Yes, mine is astrakhan. Aren't all these kinky curls extraordinary? They look like the fleece of an unborn lamb . . ."

The group moved along the Royal Avenue toward the palace, whose windows the sun was speckling with golden glints. All the fireplaces were blazing because of the cold, and clouds of white smoke rose straight from the chimneys toward the blue sky.

Thanks to these huge fires and to the braziers placed along the walls the temperature was bearable indoors. In fact, in the Salon of Venus, where the King's table had been laid, and into which everyone was crowding, the atmosphere was stifling. In embarrassment Angélique hid her little muff "no bigger than a pumpkin" in a corner. Her black dress looked out of place too.

She owed it to herself still to wear mourning for her husband, and resigned herself to it because black made her hair seem even brighter. But she had to admit that her costume suffered in comparison with others. Madame de Montespan had indeed begun to mold the Court according to her own lights. At last in a position from which she could have her own way entirely, she was taking the Court in hand and stamping everything with the seal of her imagination and her fastidious taste.

As she stood among the courtiers, Angélique observed her at the table of the royal princes, laughing and chatting, and giving everyone a chance to shine in turn. She was truly a great lady, with all the perfection associated with high rank. Her new prerogatives gave her a unique elegance and sprightliness, and added to them was the fact that another royal bastard was expected in the New Year. Beside her everyone else looked second rate.

The Court had become gayer and less regulated, and although the protocol remained strict, the general behavior had acquired the easy freedom of classic dancers about a smiling king.

This was the day of the public banquet. The people who had gained admittance to watch the King dine, and who were now filing slowly into the banquet hall, beamed with pleasure at beholding their sovereign. Their delight was partially due to the birth of a second prince, Philippe, Duc d'Anjou, who had arrived in September and who with "Little Madame," the Princess Marie-Thérèse, now ten months old, comprised the royal family. But they also took note of Madame de Montespan, so beautiful and so charming and such a bitch! The tradesmen, merchants, artisans, their noses red with the cold and bundled up in their thick coats, returned to Paris feeling greatly honored by this glimpse of their ruler and his beautiful mistress.

Toward the end of the meal Angélique caught sight of Florimond performing his ritual service to the King, his mouth set in concentration as he filled the cup Duchesne was holding from the heavy silvergilt ewer. After tasting it the First Gentleman of the Wine Service gave it to the page to taste, then handed the goblet to the High Cup-bearer, who poured a few drops of water into it before giving it to the King. While everyone else drifted toward the Salon of Peace after the meal, Florimond joined Angélique. He was excited and proud.

"Did you see me, Mother? Don't I do my job well? I used to just hold the tray, but now I carry the ewer and taste the wine. Isn't that wonderful! If anyone ever tried to posion the King, I would die for him."

Angélique congratulated him for having so quickly
risen to such an important post. Duchesne told her that
he was very pleased with Florimond, who was extremely
conscientious about his obligations even though he
seemed irresponsible. He was the youngest of the pages
but the cleverest, what with his nimble memory, his
tact, and his sense of propriety—a perfect little courtier,
in fact! Unfortunately the question had arisen of re-
moving him from the King's service, for the Dauphin
had never got over being deprived of his favorite play-
mate. Montausier had spoken to the King about it, and
now he and the High Cup-bearer were discussing
whether or not Florimond could carry on two assignments simultaneously.

"It's too much for him," Angélique protested. "He
must have time to learn to read."

"Oh, the hell with Latin. Let me, Mother, let me!"
Florimond begged.

She shook her head with a smile and said she would
think it over.

This was the first time she had seen him for six months.
Twice he had paid quick visits to Plessis. Now she
thought his air of self-confidence and sociability made
him even handsomer. Perhaps he was a little thin, for
like all other pages he caught his meals on the run, and
had little time for good sound sleep. She felt his thin
wiry shoulder under his tunic and thought with great
tenderness how wonderful it was that this lively, intelligent boy was hers. He too was in mourning for his stepfather and his brother. As she glanced at their black reflections in the great gold-framed mirrors, a sudden sadness enveloped Angélique at the thought of herself as a
widow and her son as an orphan.

"Versailles will be waiting for you," the King had said.
No, no one was waiting for her. In a few weeks an
entire chapter in the annals of the Court had come to an
end, and another was being enticed into being under the
signature of Madame de Montespan. Angélique looked
around her in discomfort. She was waiting for there to
appear and dominate the crowd the handsomest of all
the courtiers, so casual in his bearing as he jauntily

carried his white-plumed hat—the Marquis du Plessis-Bellière, the great hunter, the great Marshal of the armies of France.

But she would never see him again. The earth had closed over him, and the gap had long since been filled by the living.

Angélique remained on the edge of things. Florimond had run off to chase Madame's nasty little dog. The Queen had left her apartments and was sitting next to the King, and around them was forming the semi-circle of the princes and princesses of the blood, and all the lords and ladies who had the right of the footstool. Mademoiselle de la Vallière was at one end; Madame de Montespan at the other. Still radiant, she took her seat with a great rustling of her full blue taffeta skirt. In her triumph over having at last achieved the footstool, she who had formerly been a Maid of Honor was being almost vulgar in attracting attention to herself.

The footmen began to circulate with glasses of liqueurs, frangipani or celery tonic, rossoli, anisette, and steaming infusions of blue, green and golden herbs.

The King's voice rose. "Monsieur de Gesvres," he said to his High Chamberlain, "kindly be so good as to bring a footstool for Madame du Plessis-Bellière."

Every conversation came to an immediate stop, as all heads turned in a single movement toward Angélique. She advanced, curtsied low, and took her seat next to Mademoiselle de la Vallière. As she reached for a glass of cherry brandy, her hand shook a little.

"So at last you have that 'divine' footstool," Madame de Sévigné called out to her as soon as she saw her. "Ah, my dear, I know what a wonderful feeling it is. Everyone is talking about it. I knew all you had to do was appear. Plenty of people were fooled, though, for it looked as if the King had just said a word or two to you when he greeted you. And so then, what a surprise! Oh, if I could only have been there!"

She kissed Angélique ecstatically. She had returned to Paris to see Molière's new play. Like her, many other guests of the King were stepping out of their coaches.

"Tomorrow another play, then a ball. The day after ... I don't know what's on the program, but we're to stay at Versailles all week. Have you heard the rumor that the Court may settle here permanently? Madame de Montespan is urging it. She hates Saint-Germain. What did she say about your footstool?"

"My word, I don't know."

"She must have looked daggers at you."

"I completely forgot to glance at her then."

"I can understand your preoccupation, but it's too bad you didn't. You would have got twice the pleasure out of it."

"I never thought you were so naughty," Angélique laughed.

"I'm not, but I like to see it in others."

They wormed their way into the theatre and squeezed into one of the rows of gilded chairs.

"Let's not get separated," said Angélique. "After the play I would like to go back to Paris with you. We can chat and go over together all these hateful months of silence."

"You're mad! Versailles hasn't just got you back only to lose you again. You must dine there all the time Their Majesties are there."

There was considerable commotion around the door as Madame de Montespan made her entrance.

"Look at who's coming," whispered Madame de Sévigné. "Isn't she gorgeous? At last Versailles has a real royal mistress of the order of Gabrielle d'Estrées and Diane de Poitiers. They were concerned in politics, were patrons of the arts, spendthrifts, willful, their passions lay close to the surface and their zest for love had what it takes to dominate a man, even a king. We shall know dazzling days under her reign."

"Then why did you want to see me replace her?" Angélique said.

Madame de Sévigné hid her face with her fan. "Because I pity the King." Then she closed her fan and fetched a long sigh. "You have everything she has, plus something she can never have. Perhaps that one thing is what gives you your strength. At least, it does not weaken you."

The curtain had gone up while they were talking. Angélique paid scant attention to the opening lines of the play. She was brooding over Madame de Sévigné's words. Pity the King? Such was a feeling it did not seem right for him to inspire. He had no pity for anyone, not even for the poor La Vallière, who looked thinner, sadder and more haggard than ever. The way in which the King forced her to appear as formerly, to be present minute after minute at the triumph of her successor, bordered on cruelty. Athenais openly scoffed at her. Angélique had heard her call: "Louise, help me pin on this bow. The King is waiting for me, and I'm going to be late." It was an insensitive, cynical attitude.

But the poor girl had obediently helped her. What did she hope to get by such humility? Did she think she could rekindle the love of the man who was still her heart's desire? That was highly unlikely. She seemed to understand this since the gossip was that several times she had asked the King to let her retire to a convent. But the King would not grant her boon.

Angélique leaned over to Madame de Sévigné. "Why won't the King let La Vallière leave Court?" she whispered.

Madame de Sévigné was beginning to chuckle at *Tartuffe.* She seemed astonished, but she whispered back: "Because of the Marquis de Montespan. He could still turn up again and claim that his wife's child belongs to him by law. Louise serves as a blind. So long as she has not been openly repudiated, it is possible to pretend that the favor of Madame de Montespan is only an ugly rumor."

Angélique nodded her thanks and turned her attention to the stage. Molière was certainly witty, but all through the play Angélique could not help wondering why Solignac and the great lords who belonged to the Brotherhood of the Holy Sacrament had seen red when the play was produced. They must have had a good deal of meanness and hypocrisy on their conscience to think they were being satirized by such a low-class, ignorant fellow as Tartuffe, whose swindling of well-intentioned persons hardly resembled their mediaeval asceticism.

The King's worldly experience kept him from being taken in by it. He knew that the true spirit of the Church was not being attacked in this comedy of manners, which put fanatics, who are useless both to God and to man, in their place. The King, who was a good Christian but no more, was the first to laugh uproariously at it.

It was not hard to follow his example, but some laughed out of the wrong side of their mouths. The battle over *Tartuffe* was not over. But the King, Madame and Monsieur, and even the Queen were on its side. There was long applause after it was over.

Angélique found her two maids, Thérèse and Javotte, lighting the fire in her apartments. The "Reserved for" was still on the door.

"Should I go to the King to thank him for all his favors?" she wondered. "Or would pretending to ignore his attentions be rude? Or should I wait until he speaks to me?"

She let the maids take off her black dress and put on another of pale gray embroidered in silver which seemed more appropriate for a state dinner.

Mademoiselle de Brienne knocked at her door in a state of high excitement. "I knew that old alchemist would finally get you a footstool. Oh, please, please tell me what I must do, what I should promise him to get him to do something for me. How did he go about it? Does he put on an astrologer's robes to work his spells? Did you have to take any of his powders? Did it taste terrible? . . ."

She kept pacing in such nervous agitation that she bumped into things and even knocked a few down. Angélique just managed to rescue one of her perfume bottles. The girl seemed quite out of her head. Her brother Lomenie de Brienne was said to switch from extreme sanctity to debauchery so regularly that people thought him crazy too.

"Calm down," she said, shrugging her shoulders. "He

had nothing to do with it. I came here straight from my country house."

"Then, was it old Monvoisin who helped you? They say she is very powerful, the greatest sorceress of all time. But I don't dare go to her. I'm afraid of perdition. But if there were no other way of getting a footstool . . . Tell me, what did she make you do? Did you really have to kill a newborn child and drink its blood? Or swallow a host-wafer made of filth?"

"Don't be so silly, my dear, you're wearing me out. I have had nothing to do with that witch, at least so far as the footstool is concerned. The King awards that distinction to those he wishes to honor out of his own free will, and there's no magic connected with it."

Mademoiselle de Brienne bit her lips and clung to her theory. "It's not so simple as all that. The King is not weak. He can't be influenced to do what he doesn't want to. Only magic could force him to. Look at how Madame de Montespan has succeeded."

"Madame de Montespan could turn any man's head these days. There's nothing magical about that either."

"She can't manage the affair of the Persian ambassador," the girl replied. "It's beginning to look as if he would return to Persia without having been received by the King. That would be a dreadful blow."

Angélique thought of Colbert's letter. "Where is this Baktiari Bey?"

"At Suresnes, in his sister Dionis' country house."

Angélique resolved to go there. She could get the lay of the land if she left early in the morning and returned by noon. She did not want the King to notice her absence when it came time for his walk in the gardens.

The next morning she sent for Malbrant, her two footmen and her coachman, and added Flipot for good measure. Such a retinue would give her prestige in the Persian's eyes. Her four escorts, in her daffodil-yellow and blue livery, rode black horses. She herself rode her bay mare Ceres, whose coat had been curried till it shone.

"I heard he was bringing a necklace of a hundred and

six pearls for the Queen, and pieces of lapis lazuli as big as a pigeon's egg," Flipot said.

Angélique looked at him suspiciously. "Keep your itching fingers in your pocket," she said. "And try to sit properly in your saddle."

Flipot had not mastered the art of riding. He kept slipping from side to side and regaining his balance as best he could while his fellows made fun of him.

"Look, what's going on over there?" Flipot said suddenly.

They had been following the high road that skirts Paris and leads to the west, and had arrived at a crossroad. In the distance a mob surrounded the mounted police with their pikes.

"I think it's an execution," said Flipot, who was long-sighted. "They're going to stretch some poor wretch on the wheel."

Angélique grimaced as she caught sight of the huge erect wheel. A black-robed priest and the executioner and his assistants in red stood out against the bare branches that scratched the sullen sky. Executions frequently took place on the outskirts of Paris in order to avoid the rabble that would gather to see them in the Place de Grève. But this did not prevent the suburbanites and the villagers from crowding to them in great numbers.

The wheel as a means of torture had been imported from Germany during the preceding century. The condemned was first tied to it with his arms and legs stretched to the rims and his body resting on two crosspieces of wood like a St. Andrew's cross. On each of these deep grooves were cut where the knees and elbows of the victim were to lie. The executioner would crack them again and again with a heavy crowbar.

"We're not too late," Flipot cheered. "They're just breaking his legs now."

His mistress reprimanded him. She had decided to ride cross-country rather than see the revolting spectacle of a human being broken into pieces as the mob watched with morbid fascination. She spurred her horse out of

the road and across the snow-filled ditch, and her servants followed her. But a little further on they heard
the gray-uniformed officers of the mounted police yelling
at them: "Halt! No one can pass until the crowd scat-
ters!"

A young police officer approached and bowed. She
recognized him as de Miremont from having seen him
at Versailles, where he was stationed as a subaltern.

"Please let me pass, sir," Angélique said. "I must
proceed to an appointment with His Excellency the
Ambassador of the Shah of Persia."

"In that case, allow me to escort you personally," the
officer replied, bowing again as he rode off toward the
place of torture.

Angélique had to follow him. He led her up to the
front row near the platform where the victim was groaning horribly as the executioner pounded away at his
arms and his pelvis. She kept her eyes on the ground so
as not to see it.

Then she heard Miremont's respectful voice saying:
"Excellency, allow me to present Madame du Plessis-
Bellière, who wishes to meet you."

As she raised her eyes she froze at finding herself in
the very presence of the Persian ambassador, who sat
astride a roan horse.

Mohammed Baktiari Bey had enormous black eyes
framed in velvety lashes and eyebrows, and a glossy black
beard framed his pale-yellowish face with its curls. His
long-sleeved, belted gown of silver damask was lined
with ermine, and was open above the waist to show
off his corselet which was decorated with pieces of
silver filigree. From his shoulders hung a long cape of
pale pink brocade embroidered with seed pearls in
arabesques and floral designs. On his head perched a
turban of white silk in the middle of which a delicate
red aigret sprouted from a rose-diamond. Beside him
and also on horseback was a little page straight out of
the Arabian Nights, clad in bright colored silks, a little
golden dagger with an emerald in its hilt at his belt.
He was holding a kind of metal vase from which issued

a long tube ending in a pipe. Three or four mounted
Persians made up the Ambassador's retinue.

The ambassador did not even turn his head at the
subaltern's introduction, but kept his eyes fixed on the
platform, intent upon the climax of the torture, while
he puffed from time to time at his narghile. The smoke
oozed out of his thick, sensuous lips in fragrant bluish
clouds which kept their shape for a long time in the
cold air.

Miremont repeated his introduction cautiously, then
indicated to Angélique that His Excellency obviously
did not understand French. Just then a person Angélique had not noticed before came to their rescue. This
was a priest wearing the black soutane, the wide belt
and the crucifix of a Jesuit. He steered his horse up to
Mohammed Baktiari Bey's and spoke to him in Persian.

The ambassador turned on Angélique an empty stare
which gradually softened. He dismounted like a serpent
wriggling to earth.

Angélique hesitated as to whether she should offer
him her hand to kiss, but she presently noticed that he
was stroking Ceres' neck and wheedling her. Suddenly he
spoke a few words in an imperious tone.

The Jesuit translated. "Madame, His Excellency asks
your permission to examine your horse's teeth. He says
that is the way they tell a thoroughbred."

Somewhat annoyed in spite of herself, Angélique remarked that the animal was high strung and did not
like to be petted by strangers. The priest translated. The
Persian smiled. He stepped directly in front of the mare
and said something softly to her. Then he pressed his
hands on her jaws. The mare shuddered but let him
open her mouth and inspect her teeth without the least
objection. She even licked his bejeweled hand as he
stroked her afterward.

Angélique felt as if a friend had betrayed her. She
forgot the torture wheel and the poor wretch howling
on the platform. It was she who was high strung. She was
ashamed of her attitude as the Persian crossed his hands
on his golden dagger and bowed to her several times as
a mark of deep respect.

"His Excellency says this is the first horse worthy of the name he has seen since he landed at Marseilles. He wants to know if the King of France has such a fine one."

"Whole stables of them," Angélique said shamelessly.

The Bey knotted his brows and spoke angrily.

"His Excellency is surprised that, if such is the case, the King did not see fit to send him some as a present worthy of his rank. The Marquis de Tercy called on him looking very shabby and left again with his horses on the excuse that His Excellency the Ambassador of the Shah of Persia did not wish to follow him . . . then . . . to Paris . . . and he says that . . ."

The torrent of the Persian's words increased in volume. His interpreter was finding it hard to keep up with him.

". . . And he says that he has not yet seen a woman worthy of his rank . . . That no one has given him any presents . . . or sent anyone to call upon him during the whole month he has been in France . . . and that the women he has had brought to him weren't fit to be porters in a bazaar and were rotten with disease to boot . . . He wants to know if your coming at last is some indication that His Majesty the King of France . . . has decided to pay him the honor due him . . . ?"

Angélique's mouth hung open in amazement. "Father, these are very strange questions you're asking me!"

A slight smile cracked the priest's stony face. In spite of his severe expression he was still young. His yellowed skin indicated a long stay in the Middle East.

"Madame, I can understand how such language coming from me might shock you. But I have been an interpreter at the Court of the Shah of Persia for fifteen years, and I must ask you to believe me when I say that I am translating exactly what His Excellency said." He added, not without humor: "In those fifteen years I have often had to hear—and to speak—worse than that. But will you please give me some answer to pass on to the ambassador."

"Why, tell him . . . that I am embarrassed. I did not come as an ambassadress, or even at the request of the

King, who does not seem to care very much about this ambassador from Persia."

The Jesuit's face and his yellowish eyes hardened. "That is a great shame," he murmured.

He was obviously hesitant about translating her answer. Fortunately just then the howling of the torture victim grew more blood-curdling and Mohammed Baktiari's attention was again diverted from Angélique. While they were talking the executioner had succeeded in breaking the victim's arms and legs and pelvis. Now he had tied arms and legs together and had stuck a spit through him in order to attach him to the axle of a coach that had been detached for this purpose. There the pitiful creature was to suffer for hours in the icy cold attacked by the swarms of crows which were already gathering out of the neighboring woods.

The Persian made an exclamation of disgust and renewed his angry flood of words.

"His Excellency is complaining that he missed seeing the last part of the torture," the Jesuit said to Miremont.

"I am sorry, but His Excellency was talking to Madame here."

"You should have waited until His Excellency could devote his full attention to the execution."

"Offer him my excuses, Father. Tell him this is not the custom in France."

"Poor excuse!" sighed the priest.

Nevertheless he began to appease the anger of his noble employer as if it were his duty to do so. The ambassador calmed down and his face lightened as he proposed a solution which apparently seemed to resolve everything as far as he was concerned. The priest said nothing until urged to translate, and then he did so reluctantly.

"His Excellency asks you to please to be so kind as to begin again."

"Begin what?"

"The torture."

"But that's impossible, Father," said the police officer. "There is no other victim."

The priest translated. The Bey pointed to the Persians behind him.

"He says to take one of his guard. He insists you do. He says that if you don't oblige, he will report you to the King, your master, who will have you beheaded."

In spite of the cold, beads of sweat broke out on Miremont's forehead.

"What can I do, Father? I can't just condemn anyone at all to death."

"I can tell him for you that your country's laws absolutely forbid you to touch a hair of a foreigner's head, no matter who he is, so long as he is a guest of your nation. We can't destroy one of his Persian slaves even with his consent."

"That's right. Tell him so, for heaven's sake."

Baktiari Bey permitted himself a slight smile and seemed to appreciate the niceties of the French law, but he could not get the idea out of his head.

"Just what is the purpose of your visit, Madame?"

"Curiosity."

The Reverend Father smiled sarcastically.

"Father, I hope you are not suggesting that we torture and kill an innocent man just for the sake of pleasing some barbarous prince?"

"No, indeed, but I must speak out against the discourtesy, the ill will and the clumsiness with which Baktiari Bey has been treated since he arrived in France. He came as a friend, but it is quite likely he will leave a bitter enemy and make the Shah of Persia irreconcilably hostile to France and, what is worse, the Church. If that should happen, we priests who have twenty-odd missions in the East will never be able to spread the Faith. These stupid blunders will set the progress of Christianity back centuries in these countries that are yearning for it. Now do you see why I am so out of patience?"

"Such weighty problems have weight, I agree, Father," said Miremont in an utterly bored voice. "But why does he still insist on more torture?"

"The ambassador has never seen this form of torture before. When he went out walking this morning he just happened to come upon this place of execution, and decided he must take home to the Shah of Shahs an exact description of these new methods. That's why he is so annoyed at having missed a few details."

"His Excellency is rather careless, I think," said Angélique with a smile.

The Persian had remounted his horse. He looked at her in surprise.

"I must say I admire his courage," Angélique added. There was a heavy silence.

"His Excellency is astonished," the Jesuit said at last, "but he is aware that women sometimes can be much more subtle than men, and he is eager to know what you can teach him. So speak, Madame."

"Well, hasn't it occurred to His Excellency that the Shah of Shahs might be tempted to put this new machine to an improper use? For instance, he might decide that being so new and all, it should be used only for the torture of the great lords of his country. And he might take it into his head to experiment with one of the greatest among these great, his best subject, such as His Excellency here. Especially if his mission for the Shah of Shahs is not successful . . ."

As the Jesuit translated, the ambassador's face lit up. To everyone's great relief he began to smile.

"Fouzoul-Khanoum!" [1] he exclaimed.

Crossing his hands on his chest, he bowed several times to Angélique.

"He says your advice is worthy of Zoroaster himself. He will abandon his idea of reporting this method of torture . . . His country has good enough methods as it is. And he asks you to go with him to his lodging for some refreshment."

Mohammed Baktiari Bey led the procession. Suddenly he became all charm and full of polite attentions. As they rode along he paid Angélique compliments, and it amused her to see the thin lips of the Jesuit uttering them as if he were saying his rosary—"tender gazelle of

---

[1] "Little witch! She devil!"

Kashan," "rose of Isfahan," and as a final tribute, "lily of Versailles."

They arrived quickly at the temporary lodging where the ambassador was waiting to make his formal entry into Versailles and Paris. It was a rather unpretentious country house surrounded by a garden and lawns dotted with a few pieces of rusty statuary. Baktiari Bey apologized for his humble quarters on the grounds that the owner had installed a Turkish bath in it, and so he could perform his ritual ablutions. The news that houses in Paris did not have such accommodations astounded him.

At the sound of their arrival several other Persian servants appeared, armed with scimitars and daggers, and after them two Frenchmen, one of whom, whose towering wig somewhat compensated for his short stature, said acidly: "Another prostitute! I hope, Father Richard, that you are not going to keep this hussy here long. Monsieur Dionis does not want the sanctity of his home profaned."

"I did not say that," protested the other Frenchman. "I quite understand His Excellency's need for amusement."

"Tsk, tsk," tutted the little prude, "if His Excellency wants that kind of amusement, let him go to Versailles and present his credentials instead of continuing this shameless delay indefinitely."

The Jesuit finally was able to get in a word and introduce Angélique. The little man in the wig turned all the colors of the rainbow.

"Forgive me, Madame. I am Saint-Amen, the chief of protocol, and the King has assigned me the duty of accompanying His Excellency to Court. Forgive my ignorance."

"You are quite forgiven, Monsieur de Saint-Amen. I can understand how my arrival could have confused you."

"Ah, Madame, pity me rather. I can't get used to these barbarians and their haughty ways. I can't persuade them of the need for them to hurry. Even though Father

Richard is French and a priest as well, he does nothing to help. Just look at him smirking slyly there . . ."

"You're no help to me either," the Jesuit snapped back. "It's your business to be a diplomat, so why not be a little diplomatic? I'm only an interpreter, not a counselor. I am in His Excellency's suite by special appointment, and you can thank your lucky stars that you have me as an interpreter."

"Your services are mine too, Father. Both of us are subjects of the King of France."

"You are forgetting that I am first a servant of God."

"You mean of Rome. Everyone knows your Order thinks more of the Pope than of the King."

Angélique did not hear the rest of the argument, for Baktiari Bey seized her by the wrist and dragged her into the house. They passed through a vestibule decorated with mosaics, and into another room, followed by their respective pages. The ambassador's was still carrying his inseparable narghile which kept gurgling and belching smoke. Flipot's eyes were like saucers as he surveyed the rich hangings, rugs and tasseled cushions of dazzling opalescent hues. Furniture of precious woods, and vases and goblets of blue pottery completed the décor.

The ambassador sat down cross-legged and gestured to Angélique to do the same.

"Is it a custom of the French," he asked, "to quarrel in front of their servants?" His French was slow but excellent.

"How well Your Excellency speaks our language."

"I have been hearing it for two months now—plenty of time to learn it. I have learned especially how to be disagreeable in it . . . and insulting. I am sorry, for I have other things to talk to you about."

Angélique began to laugh. The Bey stared at her.

"Your laughter is like a spring in the desert."

Then they both fell silent, as if they were guilty of something, as the priest and Saint-Amen joined them, each suspicious in his own way.

His Excellency, however, did not notice their disap-

proving manner. He began to speak in Persian again,
and ordered a light refreshment. His servants appeared
with trays of chased silver and poured a steaming beverage into tiny crystal glasses. It was black and had a
strange odor.

"What is this?" Angélique asked a little anxiously
before raising it to her lips.

Saint-Amen swallowed the contents of his glass in one
gulp and made a horrible face before answering her:
"Coffee, at least that's what it's called. I've had to swallow
this stuff for more than ten days now in the hope that
Baktiari Bey will reward my courtesy by consenting to
get into a coach for Versailles. I'll be sick before I get
him to."

The fact that she now knew the ambassador understood French made Angélique feel embarrassed. But the
Bey showed no irritation. He called her attention by
means of gestures to the crystal cups and the curious
porcelain pitchers with their beautiful lapis-lazuli
crackled-glaze.

"These date from the time of King Darius," said
Father Richard. "The secret of their glaze is lost. Most
of the ancient palaces of Isfahan are tiled with it, and
are over a thousand years old, but the newer ones are
not so beautiful. The same is true of their gold and
silver work which is so widely known."

"If His Excellency is so interested in works of art,
how he would enjoy Versailles!" said Angélique. "Our
King has very sumptuous taste and has surrounded himself with marvelous objects."

The ambassador seemed impressed. He asked Angélique several questions in rapid succession. She answered as best she could, describing the enormous palace
glittering with gold and mirrors, the masterpieces of all
branches of art, the splendor of the silver unequaled
throughout the world. The ambassador grew more and
more astonished. Through Father Richard he reproached
Saint-Amen for not having told him a thing about all
this glory.

"What does it matter? The greatness of the King of

France is not measured by his luxuries but by his renown. The rest is just gewgaws which can be flattering only to very childish minds."

"For a diplomat you seem to be quite forgetting that you are dealing with Orientals," the Jesuit said drily. "At any rate, it is clear that Madame here has done more for France in a few words than you have done these whole ten days."

"I see, I see! If you, as a man of the cloth, are so familiar with the customs of harems, then I don't see how I as a mere man of high rank can possibly answer you. I withdraw."

On this acidulous note Saint-Amen left. The priest followed him immediately.

Mohammed Baktiari's lips opened into a wide smile that made his teeth seem like a white scar on his dark face.

"Father Richard sees I need no interpreter to converse with a lady."

He carried his pipe to his mouth and puffed away at it without taking his dark, smoldering eyes off Angélique.

"My astrologer told me . . . that today, Wednesday, is a 'favorable' day. And so you came. . . . You I will tell . . . I am uneasy in this country. Its customs are strange and difficult for me . . ."

He signaled to his drowsing page to bring them bowls of fruit sherbet and pieces of translucent Turkish paste. Angélique said cautiously that she did not understand why His Excellency should be uneasy. What was it he found so strange in French manners?

"All the . . . fellahs . . . the—how do you say?—the people of the earth . . ."

"The peasants?"

"That's it. They watch me go by without even bowing. So insolent! Not one has touched his forehead to the ground. . . . Your King wants me brought to him like a prisoner . . . in a coach . . . with guards at the doors. And that little man who keeps saying 'Hurry up, we've got to go to Versailles' as if I were a *sichak*—I mean, a beast of burden like a donkey—whereas I think out of deference to your great monarch I should not hurry . . .

Why are you laughing, oh lovely *Firousi* whose eyes are like the most precious of precious gems?"

She tried to explain that there had been a great misunderstanding about everything. In France no one prostrated himself. Women curtsied, though, as she proceeded to demonstrate to the great amusement of her host.

"I understand," he said. "It's a kind of dance . . . slow and religious . . . that women perform before their lord. I like that very much. I shall teach my wives to do it. The King at last must think well of me since he sent you to me. You are the first person who has entertained me. . . . Frenchmen are terribly boring!"

"Boring!" Angélique protested violently, "Your Excellency is mistaken. The French have a reputation for being extremely gay and amusing."

Angélique prepared to take her leave. The ambassador's disappointment was evident. She had to invent all kinds of explanations and metaphors to make him understand that in France women of a certain station are not considered as vulgar prostitutes, and that one could win their favors only by paying them court in a Platonic fashion.

"Our Persian poets knew how to sing their praises," said the ambassador. "In ages gone did not our great poet Saadi say:

He whom you love knows eternal happiness;
In his ne'er changing Paradise he shall not grow old.
Now I have beheld you I know whither to direct my prayers—
For thou art my East, and to thee rise my behests. . .

"Is that the way one should talk . . . to win the recalcitrant woman of France? . . . You I shall call Madame *Firousi-Khanoum* . . . Madame Turquoise . . . the loveliest of all precious stones, the emblem of the ancient Medes and the Persians. In our land blue is the most beloved of colors."

Before she could even make a gesture of refusal, he had drawn from his hand a massive ring and slipped it on her ring finger.

". . . Madame Turquoise . . . this is the expression of my delight when I look into your eyes. This gem has the power to change color when any man or woman who wears it proves deceitful."

He turned a gentle yet mocking smile upon her which fascinated her. She would have liked to refuse the gift, but she could only murmur her thanks as she gazed at it glistening on her hand.

With a great rustling of his silken robes Baktiari Bey arose. His movements were like a cat's—lissome yet revealing a hidden strength that came from his training in horsemanship and in fighting with heavy wooden clubs.

"You are learning Persian fast . . . very fast. . . . Are there many women at Court as beautiful and as charming as you?"

"As many as the ocean has waves."

She was in a hurry now to get away.

"I shall let you go, then," said the ambassador, "since such is the singular custom of your strange country where you send presents only to take them away with you again. Why does the King of France treat me so? The Shah of Persia is powerful. He could expel from his country all the French priests and their twenty missions. He could refuse to sell you silk. Where does your King think he could get silk like ours? The mulberries bear white berries only in Persia, and it is these trees that feed the worms that make the finest silk. Elsewhere the mulberry fruit is red. The treaty we wished to sign will cover that, won't it? Tell your King that. And now I want to consult my astrologer. Come along."

chapter 17

*T*HE Jesuit and the two Frenchmen were waiting in the vestibule. Baktiari left them, but soon returned with an old man with a dirty white beard and the signs of the zodiac on his turban, and a younger man, with an enormous nose and a jet black beard, who spoke fluent and excellent French.

"My name is Agobian. I am an Armenian Catholic and a merchant, the friend and confidential secretary of His Excellency. This is his religious instructor and astrologer Hadji Sefid."

Angélique took a step toward them intending to curtsy, but stopped with she saw the astrologer recoil, muttering some words in which "*nedjess*," meaning "unclean," kept recurring.

"Madame, you must not go too near our venerable chaplain. He is very strict about coming into contact with women. He came with us to examine your horse to see if it involved any aspects of an unlucky star."

The austere astrologer seemed to be nothing but skin and bones wrapped in a coarse linen caftan bound by a metal belt. His fingernails were long and painted scarlet, as were his toenails which peeped out of sandals apparently made of pasteboard. He did not seem to mind the cold or the snow as they walked across the garden to the stables.

"What is your secret for not getting cold?" Angélique asked respectfully.

The old man shut his eyes and said nothing for a moment. Then in a voice that was surprisingly young and musical, he answered her. The Armenian translated.

"Our priest says the secret is simple. One must fast and practice abstinence from all earthly pleasure. He also said he answered you, even though you are a woman,

299

because you bring no evil. Neither is your horse inauspicious for His Excellency. This is indeed rather curious, for the present month is an unfavorable time."

Shaking his head, the old man walked around the horse, while the others kept silent in deference to his meditations. Then he spoke again.

"He says," translated the Armenian, "that even a very unlucky month can be changed into a more favorable one by earnest prayers and the conjunction of different planets. The prayers of those who have suffered are more acceptable to the Omnipotent. He says that sorrow has not marked your face, but has scarred your soul like a scourge. Where did you get such wisdom as few women possess? But you are still not on the way to salvation for you are too attached to worldly follies. He pardons you for this because you are not of evil aspect and because the conjunction of your life with that of his master may even bring great benefits . . ."

He had hardly uttered these words than the face of the astrologer changed suddenly. His thick, hennaed eyebrows wobbled, and his pale eyes began to flash. All the Persians took on the same expression of anger and surprise.

"He says," the Armenian exclaimed, "a serpent is among us, using our hospitality to steal from us . . ."

His scrawny red-nailed finger pointed straight in front of him.

"Flipot!" shouted Angélique in horror.

Already two soldiers had seized the young lackey and hurled him to his knees. Out of his vest spilled three precious stones—an emerald and two rubies.

"Flipot!" Angélique repeated in consternation.

Uttering some words of violence the ambassador strode forward with his hand on the hilt of the weapon at his belt, and drew his scimitar.

Angélique hurled herself in front of him. "What are you going to do? Father, intervene, I beg you. His Excellency can't be going to cut off his head . . ."

"In Isfahan it would have already been done," the Jesuit said coldly. "And I would risk my own by trying to interfere. It is a deplorable incident, and a final insult. His Excellency would never understand why he should not punish this little thief in his usual way."

He tried his best to restrain his disciple, while Angélique struggled against the soldiers who were trying to carry her off and while three other guards were trying to restrain "Swordthrust" Malbrant, who had already drawn his sword.

"His Excellency will settle for merely cutting out his tongue and chopping off his hands," said the Armenian.

"His Excellency has no business punishing my servants. This boy belongs to me. It is up to me to decide what punishment he should have."

Baktiari Bey turned his flashing eyes on her and seemed to grow less excited.

"His Excellency wishes to know what punishment you will give him."

"I shall . . . shall have him given twenty-seven lashes."

The ambassador seemed lost in thought. He made a guttural exclamation, then turned on his heel and headed toward the house. Dragging Flipot, who was speechless with terror, the soldiers drove the French out of the garden and shoved them off the property without further ado, shutting the gates behind them.

"Where are the horses?" asked Angélique.

"Those dastardly Turks have kept them," said Malbrant, "and I don't think they have any intention of giving them back to us."

"We'll have to walk home," agreed one of the lackeys.

Angélique was so dead tired she slept till ten the following morning. Then there was a knock at her door.

"Madame, there's someone to see you."

"Let me alone," she called out.

When she opened her eyes, she found Javotte shaking her.

"Madame," Javotte was saying, her face deathly white, "These two officers insisted I call you. They demand to be received, 'no matter what you're doing,' as they said."

"Let them wait . . . till I'm ready to get up."

"Madame," Javotte said in a quavering voice, "I'm

afraid. Those fellows act as if they'd come to arrest you."

"Arrest me? Me?"

"They've posted guards at all the doors of the house, and they've ordered your coach hitched up to take you away in."

Angélique got up, trying to collect her wits. What did they want of her? The time had passed when Philippe might be playing a trick on her. Just night before last, the King had given her a footstool. . . . Nothing had happened to confound her. . . .

She dressed in haste and received the two officers, trying to hide her yawns. Javotte had not been mistaken in thinking them the King's police. They handed her a letter. Why did her hands shake as she broke the seals?

In formal language the writ directed the addressee to be so good as to follow the bearer. The King's seal had been affixed to the bottom of the page, and it read like an order for arrest for questioning. Angélique was dumbfounded until presently she realized she must be the dupe of some plot that was using the name of the King to do her harm.

"Who gave you this letter and these orders?" she asked.

"Our superiors."

"And what am I supposed to do?"

"Follow us, Madame."

Angélique turned to her servants who had circled around her mumbling with anxiety. She ordered Malbrant, Roger her steward, and three others to saddle their horses and accompany her so that if she were enticed into some ambuscade she would have an escort to protect her.

The older officer interrupted. "I am sorry, Madame, but the King's orders are to take you alone."

Angélique's heart began to beat a tattoo. "Am I under arrest?"

"I don't know, Madame. All I can tell you is that I am to take you to Saint-Mandé."

Angélique got into the coach, still racking her brains. Saint-Mandé? What in the world was at Saint-Mandé? A convent, where she might be shut up incommunicado?

Why? Would she ever find out? What would become of
Florimond? Saint-Mandé?

Then it dawned on her that this was where the
former Comptroller of France, Fouquet, had built one of
his villas. She heaved a sigh of relief. She recalled that
after Fouquet had been arrested and imprisoned, the
King had given all his possessions to Colbert, who had
succeeded him. Who could be behind all this but Colbert? It was certainly a strange way of inviting a lady
to his house, and she made up her mind to tell him so,
important as he was.

Then her anxiety returned. She had seen plenty of
sudden and unexplained arrests. Sometimes the victims
appeared again smiling after everything had been
straightened out, but meanwhile their property had been
confiscated and their papers gone through. Angélique
had done absolutely nothing about protecting her money.

"That's a lesson for me," she said to herself. "If I get
out of this, I will be much more careful about my business in the future."

The coach had wound its way through the mud
of the Paris streets and was now rolling along more
rapidly over the frozen highway. The bare, icicle-
hung oaks by the roadside told her they were approaching the forest of Vincennes. At last the former residence
of Fouquet appeared on their right. It was less elaborate
than the one at Vaux, yet its vulgar extravagance had
been one of the chief charges against the famous finan-
cier who was now rotting away in the dungeon of a fortress in Piedmont.

Even though it was winter and everything was covered
with rime, the courtyard of the castle was humming
with activity like a woodyard. Everything was being un-
dermined or torn down. Beams and laths were piled at
the base of the walls in which were gaping holes from
which lead pipes were being tossed. Angélique had to
lift her skirts to cross a stack of these pipes which
barred the entrance. A foreman gave her his hand to help
her.

"What the devil is Colbert tearing his house down
for?" she asked him.

"Monsieur Colbert expects to make several thousand *livres* out of these lead pipes," he said.

The officer interrupted. "Madame is not permitted to talk."

"There's nothing wrong in talking about plumbing," Angélique protested. She had resolved not to take this adventure seriously. Now that she saw she could get an explanation from Colbert, she had stopped worrying.

Inside the house the same demolition was going on. Workmen were stripping the ceilings of the white gesso mouldings that the great artist Le Brun had designed. Angélique hated to see such destruction, but she kept her opinions about vandalism to herself. She had other fish to fry. It was especially important that she keep calm and collected.

She continued on to the wing of the castle where the present owner conducted his business. It had already been stripped of its decorations. The "shameless extravagance" of which Fouquet had been accused, seemed to have been limited to these gilded plaster veneers. Now they were gone, there remained only rough brick walls which bore no resemblance to the "marbled halls" which had helped get the former Comptroller imprisoned for life.

At the end of a long corridor Angélique found herself in the center of a waiting-room originally intended for the poor. Here now the flower of France crowded the simple benches. Saint-Mandé was less a residence of the powerful minister than his antechamber, and everyone who had a request to make of him had to wait stoically in these draughty halls.

Angélique took note of Madame de Choisy, Madame de Gamaches, the beautiful Scotch Baroness Gordon-Huntley, who was attached to the suite of Duchesse Henriette, and the young La Vallière, who pretended not to see her. The Prince de Condé was sitting beside de Solignac. As he saw Angélique he started to greet her, but de Solignac kept him back by whispering something in his ear. The Prince debated the matter for a while, then shook his sleeve free from de Solignac's

grasp and limped over to her, for the damp cold was hard
on his bad leg.

But Angélique's jailors interfered again. "Madame is
not permitted to talk."

To avoid any conflict with the great prince they took
Angélique into a little antechamber in spite of the
mutterings of the courtiers who thought she was getting
in ahead of them.

In this other room there was no one but a petitioner
whom she had not previously seen at Court—a foreigner
whom she glanced at a second time wondering if he
were not a Persian, for his complexion was quite dark
and his slanting black eyes gave him an Asiatic appearance. Still he was dressed like a European so far as she
could determine from the big shabby cloak he was
wrapped in. On the other hand, his red leather boots
topped with golden tassels and his kind of felt fez
trimmed with scallops of white lamb's wool indicated a
foreign origin. He was wearing a sword.

He rose and bowed to the newcomer without showing
any surprise at her being escorted by her two warders.
He suggested that she precede him, and his French was
correct even though he rolled his "r's" rather noticeably.
He would not have it, he said, that such a "charming"
lady wait any longer than necessary in such a sordid
place. As he spoke he revealed a set of dazzlingly white
teeth under his thin black mustache the ends of which
dropped over the corners of his mouth. It had been
a long time since anyone in France had worn such a full
mustache as this except for old men of another generation like the Baron de Sancé. At any rate, Angélique
had never seen one so disconcerting as this stranger's.
When he was silent it gave him a ferocious and barbarous appearance. She was quite fascinated by it. Every
time she stole a look at it, the foreigner gave her another
smile and insisted she go in before him.

The older police officer finally told him: "Madame is
indeed much obliged to you, sir, but do not forget
that the King is expecting you at Versailles. If I were you,
I would ask Madame to be so kind as to wait a few
moments more."

The foreigner seemed not to have heard him. He continued to smile boldly and fixedly at Angélique until she began to feel embarrassed. She was less surprised at the officer's lack of tact than at the respect he seemed to show this foreign petitioner. Whoever he was, he was at least very courteous.

She strained her ears to try to tell whether the minister's present visitor had been there long. The door of the conference room did not shut tight owing to the construction work and remodeling going on at Colbert's orders. She could tell from the tone of the voices that the conference was coming to an end.

"Do not forget either, Monsieur de Gourville, that you will be the secret representative of the King of France in Portugal. *Noblesse oblige*," Colbert concluded.

"Gourville," thought Angélique. "Wasn't he one of the condemned Comptroller's henchmen? I thought he had fled and was under sentence of death by default."

A gentleman whose face was hidden behind a mask appeared in the doorway, cordially escorted by the minister. He passed her with a nod.

Colbert knit his eyebrows. He hesitated a moment between the foreigner and Angélique, but when the former stepped aside, the minister's forced smile grew even more dour. He beckoned to Angélique to come in and closed the door right in the face of her two escorts.

Motioning her to an armchair, he sat down and stared at her in silence with a cold expression. Angélique recalled Madame de Sévigné's nickname for him—"Monsieur North Pole"—and smiled.

Colbert leaped up as if he could no longer bear Angélique's nonchalance. "Madame, can you tell me why you paid a visit yesterday to His Excellency, the Ambassador of Persia, Baktiari Bey?"

"Who told you?"

"The King."

He took a letter from his desk and tapped it irritably against his fingers. "This morning I received this order from the King to bring you here as soon as possible and get an explanation from you."

"His Majesty's spies get down to work fast."

"That's what they are paid for," Colbert fumed. "Well, what answer can you give me? Who got you to visit the Shah of Persia's representative?"

"Just curiosity."

Colbert cleared his throat. "Let us understand each other, Madame. This is a serious matter. The relations between this difficult person and France have become such that anyone, male or female, who visits him can be considered a traitor."

"How absurd! Baktiari Bey seemed to me to be very eager to meet the greatest monarch in the world and admire the beauty of Versailles."

"I thought he was just about to leave without even presenting his credentials."

"He was the first to be concerned about that. He suffered from a want of tact on the part of all those clowns who were sent to him—Tercy, Saint-Amen, and the rest . . ."

"You are speaking rather flippantly about experienced diplomats. Do you mean to imply they do not know their business?"

"They know nothing about Persians, that's certain. Baktiari Bey gave me the impression of being a well-intentioned man so far as politics is concerned."

"Then why does he refuse to present his credentials?"

"Because he thinks he has been discourteously received, and that for him to appear in a coach with guards at the doors is beneath his dignity."

"But that is the usual way all ambassadors are received in this kingdom."

"He won't do it."

"What does he want, then?"

"To ride through Paris in a shower of rose petals while all the people prostrate themselves before him."

The minister said nothing.

"In the last analysis," Angélique continued, "this is up to you, Monsieur Colbert."

"Me?" he said in a panic. "I don't know the first thing about such matters of etiquette."

"Neither do I. But I do know enough to say that it is not very sensible to refuse a little compromise rather than lose an alliance that might be favorable to France."

Colbert wiped his face nervously. "Tell me the details," he said.

Angélique gave him a quick description of her comic-opera expedition. Colbert listened to her without a trace of a smile, even when she described how His Excellency had wanted the torture to be repeated for him.

"Did he say anything to you about the secret clauses of the treaty?"

"Not a word. He simply mentioned in passing that your factories could never get such fine silk as Persian . . . and, oh yes, he did say something about the Catholic missions."

"He didn't say anything about a counter-alliance with the Arabs or the Russians?"

Angélique shook her head. The minister was deep in thought. Angélique let him brood for a while before resuming her account.

"All in all," she concluded merrily, "I have done you and the King a service."

"Not so fast! You have been hasty and extremely inefficient."

"How, for heaven's sake? I'm no enlisted army man who can't visit anyone I want without getting permission from my superiors."

"That is where you are mistaken, Madame. Let me tell you bluntly that you think you can act independently, but the fact is that the higher you rise the more you have to beware of the slightest false step. The world of the great is full of snares. You have just barely escaped being arrested . . ."

"I thought I had been."

"No. I will take it upon myself to let you go free until I have settled this matter with His Majesty. However, please be sure to be at Versailles tomorrow. I think the King will want to hear your story after he has checked on it. I shall be there too to speak to His Majesty about an enterprise I have just thought of in which you can be of assistance to us in dealing with Baktiari Bey."

He led her to the door and said to the two officers: "You can let her go."

Angélique was so shaken by the unforeseen happy ending to this forced visit that she sank into a chair in the antechamber after the police officers had left and paid no attention to the petitioner who had taken the place of the foreigner. Eventually he came out from his conference and, rolling his "r's," asked her to go with him to look for a cab they could hire, for he had no other means of getting back to Paris. Angélique followed him in a daze, and it was not till she encountered her own postillion that she came back to her senses.

"I beg your pardon, sir. It is I who should have asked you to do me the pleasure of driving back to Paris with me in my coach."

The foreigner took in the silver-gray trappings trimmed with silver, and the livery of her servants, and gave her a pitying smile.

"Poor child," he said. "I am much richer than you, you know. I have no possessions, but I am free."

"Quite a character!" she thought as the coach got under way.

In comparison with her anxiety of the morning, the ride back was wondrously comfortable. Now she could admit she had been scared to death, for she was well aware that such misunderstandings are seldom so easily straightened out. Relieved now of the strain she had been under, she made an effort at conversation with this well-bred person who had been so nice to her when everyone else was shunning her like the plague.

"May I inquire your name, sir? I do not believe I have seen you at Court."

"Ah, but you did—the other day when His Majesty asked you to take a footstool, and you moved with such beauty and dignity, and your black gown seemed a reproach to all those gay-plumaged birds."

"A reproach?"

"Perhaps that is not the right word. You were so different from the rest, so distinguished, that I wanted to shout: 'Not her! Not her! Take her away from here!' "

"Thank heaven, you did not."

"I should have," he sighed. "Ever since I have been in France, I have not been myself. The French are not so

spontaneous as other nationalities. They put their head
before their heart."

"Where do you come from?"

"I am Prince Rakoczy, and my country is Hungary."

The Prince told her that from his childhood he had
given up all his possessions to devote himself to his
people whose wretched condition had moved him deeply.
He had incited a revolution to depose the King of
Hungary, who had taken refuge with the Holy Roman
Emperor.

"His country must be in Europe, then," Angélique
deduced to herself.

"Subsequently we had a republic in Hungary for a
while. Then came the counter-revolution, and horrible
repression. I was denounced by my partisans for a mouth-
ful of bread, but I managed to escape and hid in a
monastery. Then I got across the frontier in spite of
being hunted, and came to France, where I found a
warm welcome."

"I am glad for you. Where are you living in France?"

"Nowhere, Madame. I am a wanderer like my ancestors. I am waiting to return to Hungary."

"But you are risking certain death there."

"I shall return just the same as soon as I have got your
King's help in starting another revolution. I am a revolutionary at heart."

Angélique stared in wonder. This was the first real
flesh-and-blood revolutionary she had ever seen. His ded-
ication to revolt had made him woefully thin, but there
was a light in his eyes that would keep anyone from pitying him or making fun of him. He seemed to be quite
content with his lot as a hunted man.

"What makes you think our King will give you assistance or money to help you dethrone another king? He
has a horror of such things."

"In his own realm, yes. But in another country an in-
surgent can sometimes be a useful tool. I have high
hopes."

Angélique grew thoughtful. "As a matter of fact,
they say Richelieu helped Cromwell with French money
and was really responsible for the beheading of the

English king, Charles I, even though he was a cousin of the King of France."

The foreigner smiled absently. "I am not familiar with English history, but I do know that the English have fallen under the domination of a royal dynasty again. There is no new blood to renew their energy, and they are not yet ripe for another revolution. Neither is France ready. But we Hungarians are heirs of the freest of all peoples, and we are ready."

"But we are free too," Angélique protested.

The Hungarian burst into such uncontrollable laughter that the coachman slowed down and turned around. Then with a shake of his head he resumed his speed. The Marquise was a good sort, but she did take up with the damnedest people!

The foreigner finally stopped laughing enough to exclaim: "You call yourselves free when two policemen hale you before the minister of a police state?"

"It was a misunderstanding," said Angélique. "You saw for yourself the policemen did not take me back."

"All the worse. They are *behind* you now. They will never be off your trail unless you work with them and for them, which means you have sold your freedom and your soul. If you want to escape a fate like that, you will have to get away."

Angélique began to be bored with his impassioned language. "Get away? What an idea! I have achieved quite an enviable position and I am quite well off here, thank you very much."

"Not for long, believe me. Not with a head like yours!"

"What's so unusual about it?"

"You have the head of an avenging angel, who cannot be swayed or influenced, but wields the sword of Justice and slashes the slimy bonds of compromise. Your piercing look makes others feel naked before you. There is no dungeon deep enough to extinguish the light of your eyes. Take care!"

"There is something in what you say," said Angélique shaking her head with a sad little smile. "I am very arbitrary, I know, but you don't have to fear for me.

My youthful errors have cost me dear, and have taught me how to be wiser."

"How to be a slave, you mean."

"You go to extremes, sir. If you want my opinion, then no country on this earth is perfect. The state of the poor is deplorable everywhere. You talk like some kind of evangelist. All such end up on a cross. That's not for me."

"An evangelist has to be a bachelor, or at least abandon his family, but I want to sow the seeds of freedom. That's the first thing I thought of when I saw you. Marry me and we shall flee together."

Angélique resorted to the device all women use to get out of such a ticklish situation—she laughed and changed the subject.

"Oh, look at all those people gathering up there. What's going on?"

They had regained Paris and now in one of the narrow streets of the Saint-Paul quarter a gay parade was blocking their progress. It was a tattered troop of veterans, doubtless recruited for a few *sols* apiece, who were escorting a patrol which had just halted in a little square. In the middle they were erecting a sort of gibbet from which dangled a straw man with a big white placard pinned to its chest. The patrol sergeant, the chief of the local police, and a sergeant-at-arms represented the official side of the ceremony. When the dummy was hoisted to the top of the gibbet two snare drums sounded a long roll, and the crowd began to howl even louder: "To the stake with cheats! Death to swindlers of the people!"

"A fine revolutionary scene," murmured the Hungarian with shining eyes.

"That's where you are wrong, sir," Angélique said, glad of the chance to get the better of him. "These people are cheering an act of justice on the part of the King. It's a mock execution. That's what they do when a criminal has been condemned to death but has managed to flee the country."

She stuck her head out the window to find out who it was they were hanging in effigy. A burly, good-humored tradesman told her it was Comte Hérauld de Gourville, tax-collector of Guyenne, who had been convicted of speculating with the public money and had been an accomplice of Fouquet whose iniquities had just recently come to light. Not a moment too soon either! Let 'em know a little about how they had been swindled!

The coach managed to get through the mob and continued on its way. Angélique lapsed into thought, as did her companion, at the sight of this spectacle.

"Poor wretch," he sighed at length. "Poor victim of tyranny, forced to live forever away from his native land to which he can never return on pain of death. Alas, how these outlaws wander over the face of the earth, banned from their fatherland by the rod of despots!"

"Which they doubtless well deserve. Don't waste any sympathy on the fate of Gourville or criticize the King's severity. What if I told you that he was in excellent health, was still in France, and actually working in the secret service of the King—in short, that he was the man in the mask we saw come out of Colbert's office this very morning?"

Rakoczy seized her wrist, his eyes ablaze. "Are you sure of what you are saying?"

"Almost certain."

His smile spread. "That's why your King will pay me and my revolutionaries to fight another king," he shouted triumphantly. "He is two-faced. He throws the gullible mob an effigy of the guilty as a bone to shut them up, but he keeps them working for him in secret. He signs a treaty of peace with Holland, and then encourages the English to make war on the Dutch. He negotiates an alliance with Portugal to break the back of Spain, with which he is also allied. And he needs me to harass the Holy Roman Emperor. It won't keep him from supporting that same emperor at St. Gothard against the Turks, or from getting all he can out of the agreements he has signed with those very same Turks. He is a great king, very skillful and very subtle. No one really knows what he is up to. And he will turn you into another one of his puppets without any soul of your own."

Angélique drew her cloak more tightly about her shoulders. The words of this intense Hungarian made

her blood run hot and then cold. She was utterly en-
raged by him and yet strangely fascinated.

"To hear you talk, no one could tell whether you
hate him or admire him."

"I hate his power, but I admire him as a man. He is
the nearest thing to a true ruler I have ever encountered.
Thank God, he is not my king. The man who could
topple him off his throne has not yet been born."

"You have a strange way of thinking. You talk like
some booby at Saint-Germain Fair whose only ambition
is to play at skittles with the severed heads of kings."

Far from being shocked at her comparison, the prince
was actually amused by it. "I like the light touch you
French have. When I stroll through Paris I love the cheer-
fulness of everyone I meet. I have yet to find a workman
who isn't either whistling or singing as he works. I've
been told they do it to try to forget how wretched they
are. But the faces you see behind the glass windows of
the fine coaches aren't so happy. Why? Can't the great
ones of the kingdom sing too to forget their woes?"

The coach came to a stop before the Hôtel du
Beautreillis. Angélique wondered how to get rid of this
man without hurting his feelings. But he jumped out
before her and offered his hand to help her alight.

"Here is your house. I used to have a palace."

"Don't you miss it?"

"It's only when you're free of worldly possessions that
you really begin to enjoy life. Madame, don't forget what
I asked you."

"What was that?"

"To marry me."

"Is that a joke?"

"No indeed. You take me for a fool because you're
not used to sincerely dedicated persons. The passion of
a lifetime takes only one second to spring into life. So
why don't you admit it now? The French keep their
feelings as they do their women—in steel corsets. Come
with me. I will set you free."

"No, thank you," said Angélique, laughing. "I will
stick to my corset. And now goodbye, sir, before you
make me say something I might regret."

chapter 18

*W*HEN she got to Versailles that afternoon, Angélique went at once to the Queen's apartments to try to discover whether she could still consider hers the little post she once had as assistant to the Mistress of the Wardrobe. She was told that the Queen had gone with her Maids of Honor to the village of Versailles to visit the parish priest. The Queen was in a sedan chair and her ladies on foot, so no one thought they could be very far away yet. Angélique went to catch up with them.

As she was crossing the north terrace a hail of snowballs struck her. She turned to discover the practical joker, and a fresh snowball hit her full in the face. She stumbled and slipped and tumbled in a great flurry of skirts and a cloud of powdered snow.

Péguilin de Lauzun appeared from behind a clump of trees, laughing loudly. Angélique was furious.

"How long before you quit these puppyish tricks? The least you could do is help me up."

"Certainly not," Péguilin shouted, leaping upon her and rolling her over and over in the snow, then kissing her and tickling her nose with his muff until she had to laugh and plead for mercy.

"That's better," he said, helping her to her feet. "I saw you coming along as sad as could be, and that doesn't go at Versailles—or with your pretty face. Laugh, now, laugh!"

"Péguilin, have you forgotten all my trouble of just a little while ago?"

"Yes, I have," he said gaily. "We have to forget those things just as we do our turn to settle our account with our Maker. Besides, you would not have come back to Court if you did not intend to forget. So stop brooding, and help me, little one."

He took her arm and led her into the maze of clipped and trimmed holly bushes that the winter had transformed into rows of sugarplums.

"The King has just given his consent to our marriage," he whispered as if it were a great secret.

"What marriage?"

"Why, the marriage of Mademoiselle de Montpensier with that insignificant Gascon nobleman Péguilin de Lauzun. Don't tell me you haven't heard? She is mad about me. She has begged the King again and again to let her marry me. The Queen, Monsieur and Madame have raised a terrible fuss, claiming such a match is an affront to the dignity of the throne. Pfft . . . the King is just and good. He likes me. He thinks no one has a right to force a relative to remain single, especially when she is forty-three and can't hope for a brilliant match. So in spite of all the cackling in the barnyard, he said yes."

"Are you serious, Péguilin?"

"I couldn't be more so."

"I am sorry for it."

"You shouldn't be. I'm as good as that great ulcerous hog, the King of Portugal, who once was intriguing for her hand, or the Prince of Silesia, a babe in swaddling clothes, who was also one of her suitors."

"I'm not sorry for her, but for you."

She stopped to regard his familiar face in which youth still lingered and his eyes still sparkled in spite of the creases in their lids.

"What a pity!" she sighed.

"I shall be Duc de Montpensier," Péguilin went on, "and get all kinds of wonderful perquisites thereby. In the marriage contract Mademoiselle is turning over nearly twenty millions to me. His Majesty is writing all the courts of Europe to announce his cousin's marriage. Angélique, sometimes I think I'm dreaming. In all my wildest ambitions I never dared aim so high. The King will be my cousin! I can't even believe it yet. That's why I'm scared and why I need your help."

"I don't see what for. Everything seems to be going your way."

"Alas, fortune is fickle. Until I am wedded to the lovely princess, I shan't sleep soundly. I have plenty of enemies, beginning with the royal family and the princes of the blood. Condé and his son the Duc d'Enghien are furious with me. Couldn't you use some of your charm on the one hand to calm down the prince, who thinks very highly of you, and on the other reassure the King lest he yield to all their protests? Madame de Montespan has already promised me her support, but I can't be sure of her. In this kind of politics two mistresses are better than one."

"I am not the King's mistress, Péguilin."

He flipped his head from side to side like a mocking-bird getting ready for a flourish. "Maybe that's good and maybe that's bad," he sing-songed.

They had come out of the gardens and up to the gates of the great courtyard. From inside a coach a man's voice hailed them.

"From all I can see, you are very much in demand," said Péguilin. "I don't want to stand in your way. But can I count on your help?"

"Absolutely not. Anything I could do would only be to your disadvantage."

"Don't refuse me. You don't know what power you have. You don't want to admit, but you can't fool an old courtier like me. I mean it, you can get the King to do anything."

"Don't be silly."

"You just don't understand, I keep telling you. You are like a thorn in the King's heart, causing him exquisite pain, so disconcerting a feeling that he doesn't know what to make of it. No sooner does he think he has you, than you're gone. And he is surprised to find that when you're gone he suffers indescribable torments."

"Torments whose name is Madame de Montespan . . ."

"Madame de Montespan is a tidbit, a sure meal, a hearty supper of meat and wit, everything a monarch needs to gratify his senses and his vanity. He needs her, and he has her. But you . . . you are a spring in a desert . . . the dream of someone who has never dreamed . . . the mystery of mysteries . . . longing, surprise, yearn-

ing . . . the simplest woman in the whole world . . .
and the most unfathomable . . . the nearest and yet the
farthest . . . the unassailable . . . the *unforgettable*."
Péguilin thrust his hand sadly into the lace of his jabot.

"You talk almost as well as the Persian ambassador.
I'm beginning to see how you lured poor Mademoiselle
on."

"Won't you promise to speak to the King on my behalf?"

"If I get a chance I will help you. Now, let me go,
Péguilin. I must join the Queen."

"She needs you less than I do. Besides here is someone else who is determined to usurp you for His Majesty's service."

Out of the coach from which the voice had hailed
them a man was hastily descending and was striving to
join them.

"It's Colbert," said Péguilin. "He has nothing to say
to me. I can't juggle money."

"I am happy to have found you so soon," said the
minister. "I am going to talk with His Majesty right now,
and later we will call you into conference."

"What if His Majesty doesn't care to hear me . . ."

"It would be only a whim—perhaps justified—but
he will listen to me. Come, Madame."

Colbert's optimism turned out to be premature. His
interview with the King took longer than was necessary
for a simple explanation. He had asked Angélique to
wait for him on a bench in the Salon of Peace. There
she saw coming toward her her brother Raymond de
Sancé, his tall figure in its austere black soutane con-
trasting with the brightly costumed crowd of courtiers.
She had had no occasion to see him since she married
Philippe. Was he coming to offer her his condolences as
a brother? He did so, but she quickly perceived such
was not his sole purpose.

"My dear sister, you must be surprised to see me come
looking for you at Court, where my ministry seldom
brings me."

"But I thought you had been made almoner, or something like that, to the Queen."

"Father Joseph was appointed instead of me. My superiors preferred to make me head of our house in Melun."

"That means . . ."

"That I am Father Superior, or something like that," he smiled. "Of our Order's foreign missions, particularly in the Orient."

"Aha, Father Richard . . ."

"Exactly!"

"Baktiari Bey . . . his refusal to ride in a coach . . . the blunders of Saint-Amen . . . the King's failure to understand and the crises both spiritual and material that have resulted . . ."

"Angélique, I have always admired your quick thinking."

"Thank you, Raymond dear, but in this emergency I would have been at a loss if I had not got the point."

"Let's come to the point. Father Richard, with whom I have just been talking, thinks you are the only person who can possibly set matters straight."

"I am terribly sorry, Raymond, but this is a bad time. I'm on the verge of disgrace."

"But the King welcomed you back with many honors. I heard you got a footstool."

"That's true. But what do you expect? The whims of the great are very changeable."

"It's far less a question of the King's whims than of the ambassador's. Father Richard hasn't even known what saint to pray to ever since they came to France. First the mistake was made of sending Saint-Amen to the ambassador. He is a diplomat if you want to call him so, but he is a Protestant, and unfortunately the teachings of that persuasion are diametrically opposed to those of the Orientals. Hence all this conglomeration of misunderstandings that have ended in the present crisis from which neither the King nor the ambassador can withdraw without losing face. You see, your visit yesterday pulled the trigger. The ambassador now seems to want to see Versailles and to speak deferentially with the King, and he now appears to understand that French customs can be different from his and not wholly de-

signed to heap insults upon him. It is thanks to your
visit that Father Richard has noticed this change for the
better. 'Women,' he told me, 'sometimes are more subtle
and have more instinctive wisdom than we men can
achieve with all our logic.' He confessed it had never occurred to him to boast about the porcelains or the flowers at Versailles as a means of persuading the ambassador
to present his credentials. 'Orientals,' he said to me,
'are sensitive to an intelligent woman because in certain respects she can come closer to their way of thinking than we Western men with our coldly mathematical
minds.' In short, he asked me to entreat you to continue
your happy intervention. You might return to Suresnes
some day soon and perhaps bring with you a kindly message from the King . . . who knows, perhaps even an invitation. You see, you are neither afraid of His Excellency nor offensively inquisitive as so many other French
people who have met him have been."

"Why should I act so foolishly?" Angélique said, fond-
ling the turquoise on her finger. "The Persian is perfectly charming, except for his hobby of wanting to cut
off everyone's head. But don't you think, Raymond, that
I am putting my soul in danger more than my life?"

The Jesuit looked at his sister with amusement. "You
don't have to compromise your virtue, just use your influence."

"What a nice little distinction! So the twenty-six missions in Persia are well worth a few languorous looks
for the envoy of the Shah of Shahs?"

The face of the Reverend Father de Sancé did not
change expression. A smile still flickered around the
corners of his mouth.

"You have nothing to fear, I see," he said, "for there is
nothing in this world that can frighten you. You have
acquired a new weapon since last we met—you've become cynical."

"I live at Court, Raymond."

"Are you trying to blame me for that? Where else
could you live, Angélique? What world do you think you
were made for? The country? A convent?"

He was still smiling, but in the hard light of his eyes

she could see the might of a sword designed to pierce human beings to their very souls.

"You are right, Raymond. So the Persian stakes are worth this much?"

"If Baktiari Bey goes back empty-handed, we will be expelled at once from all the missions we established, not without hardship, during the last regime under the impetus of Richelieu. We have missions in the Caucasus, at Tiflis, Batum, Baku, and so on."

"Have you converted many?"

"It's not so much a matter of the number of converts we have made as it is of our just being there. Not to mention the Armenian Catholic minorities or the Syrian ones who need us."

Angélique had spread her fan open on her knees. The one she had chosen that morning was of silk painted with exotic landscapes in which, in an oval surrounded with pearls, stood a representative of each of the five continents—an Indian with ostrich feathers in his hair, a Negro riding a lion into the lair of a dragon . . .

Colbert interrupted them as they were studying it.

"Nothing can be done," he said defeatedly. "The King is so furious with you I'm surprised to see you still at Court. He does not even want to hear about your visit."

"Didn't I warn you?"

She introduced her brother, the Reverend Father Raymond de Sancé. Although he denied it, Colbert was not without distrust of the Company of Jesus and its members. His cunning took measure of their intelligence and how capable they were of blocking his plans. But his face lit up when he was given to understand that this Jesuit was bringing grist to his mill. When he was informed of the situation Raymond de Sancé did not take it as such a tragedy.

"I think I detect the real reason for the King's displeasure with you. You have refused to tell him the reason for your visit."

"I shall tell no one."

"I daresay. I know how stubborn you can be, my dear Angélique. But if you refuse the King, how can you expect him to be any more indulgent to us? Can't we find some plausible reason which will explain your un-compromising attitude? Let's see. Ah, I've got it! Why not give him the same reason you gave me just now? You went to Suresnes at my request to establish contact with Father Richard, whose delicate situation kept him from receiving me in person among those suspicious Mohammedans. What do you think of that, Monsieur Colbert?"

"I think it will work if it is well handled."

"Reverend Father Joseph, of our Order, is an almoner of the King's. I'll go and get him right away. What do you think, Angélique?"

"I think you Jesuits are just as extraordinary as my friend the police chief Desgrez says they are."

As they strode away from her down the long hall she was amused to see how their outlines were reflected in the highly polished wood of the floor—the thickset states-man and the slender priest.

Suddenly she realized that there were no more passers-by. She was aware that she was terribly hungry. Doubt-less it must be quite late. All the Court must be at the King's dinner. She decided to go there too, but she con-tinued to stare dreamily at her fan.

"I have been looking for you," a timid female voice said in her ear.

Angélique could not reconcile it with its owner, the Grande Mademoiselle, whom she looked up to see bend-ing over her. What had so transformed the authoritative tones of the granddaughter of Henri IV?

"It must be her marriage," she thought as she hastened to make her curtsy.

Mademoiselle made her sit down beside her and took her hand with emotion. "My dear, have you heard the news?"

"Who has not heard it or is not delighted with it? Will Your Highness allow me sincerely to wish you the greatest happiness?"

"Haven't I made a lucky choice? Tell me, is there any other nobleman as brave and brilliant? Don't you find him delightful? Aren't you a great friend of his?"

"I certainly am," said Angélique, remembering the incident at Fontainebleau.

But Mademoiselle's memory was apparently short and there seemed to be no veiled allusions in her words. "If you only knew what a trance I've been in ever since the King gave his approval! And how worried!"

"Why, indeed? You have his assurance, so enjoy your happiness. The King cannot go back on his word."

"I wish I could be as sure as you," sighed Mademoiselle de Montpensier.

Her haughty head drooped with uncustomary tenderness. Her bosom was still as handsome as when Van Ossel had painted her portrait to be sent to all the royal suitors of Europe. Her hands were graceful, and her pretty blue eyes shone with the childish wonder of a young girl in her first love affair.

Angélique smiled at her. "How pretty you look, Your Highness."

"Really? How sweet of you to say so! I am so happy my face must show it. But I tremble at the thought that the King may revoke his promise before the marriage contract is signed. That fool Marie-Thérèse and my cousin Orléans and his pest of a wife are in league to ruin my plans. They do nothing but howl about it all day long. If you love me, try to defeat their arguments to the King."

"Alas, Your Highness, I . . ."

"You have a great deal of influence over the King's mind."

"But what good does it do to boast of a great influence over the King's mind?" Angélique exclaimed irritably. "You know him. You should know that he never follows any judgment but his own. He listens to opinions but when he makes a decision it is not because he has been influenced, as you suggest. It is because that decision seems right to him. The King is never of your turn of mind, but rather you are of the King's."

"So you refuse to intervene for me? I did my best for you a long time ago when you were in such trouble when your first husband was accused of sorcery."

So Mademoiselle's memory was not so short after all!

Angélique snapped her fan shut so abruptly she almost broke it. Finally she promised that if the occasion arose she would try to find out how the King felt about the matter. Then she asked leave to withdraw to get some soup or a roll, for she had not eaten since the night before, had not even found time for a glass of wine after Mass.

"You cannot!" said the Grande Mademoiselle taking her arm to drag her along. "The King is going to receive the Doge of Genoa and his suite in the Throne Room. Then there's going to be a raffle and a great display of fireworks. The King wants all the ladies there to do him honor. And especially *you!* If you don't come, we'll run the risk of seeing him in another temper like yesterday when you went running off Lord knows where."

That night Angélique was deep in a dream that for some time now had frequently repeated itself. She was lying in the grass of a meadow, and was cold. As she tried to pull the grass over her she found she was naked. Then she waited for the sun to come out from behind white, white clouds that drifted lazily in a deep blue sky. At last its rays warmed her body and she relaxed in a complete sense of well-being and extreme happiness until she observed that it was not a sunbeam caressing her, but a hand on her shoulder. At once she was cold again, and she kept saying to herself: "Of course it's cold because it's winter. But then, why is the grass so green?" And she would be confused by the chill of the weather and the green of the grass until she woke up shivering and rubbing her shoulder where she could still feel the touch of a soft warm palm.

This particular night the dream awoke her again. Her teeth were chattering. She pulled back up over her the bedclothes she had kicked off as she tossed in her dream. She was so cold that she debated calling for one of the Gilandon girls, who were sleeping in the next room, to light her fire.

Her apartment at Versailles comprised two rooms and

a little bathroom whose mosaic-tiled floor sloped toward
the center permitting the water to drain away through a
hole in the middle. Angélique decided she would warm
herself up by taking a footbath in lavender water. The
water in the kettle on the chafing dish was warm from
the charcoal embers beneath it. She flung back the bed
curtains and groped with her feet for her blue satin
slippers lined with marabou.

Arius barked.

"Shh!"

The silvery chime of a clock tinkled in the distance
telling Angélique that she could not have been asleep
for long. Indeed, it was hardly midnight. For a brief
spell the great palace of Versailles was quiet, seeking
respite from the balls, the late suppers, the enchantment
of the nighttime entertainments.

Angélique had to get down on her hands and
knees to search for her slippers. In doing so she discovered at her left near the bed-alcove a little door betrayed by the thin line of light that outlined its shape.
She had never noticed it before; only the flickering
light of a candle behind it revealed it to her now. Someone must be on the other side groping for the bolt. Then
there was a tiny click, and the beam of light widened
to cast the shadow of a man on the opposite wall.

"Who's there? Who are you?"

"Bontemps, the King's valet. Don't be afraid, Madame."

"Oh yes, now I recognize you. What do you want of
me?"

"His Majesty wishes to see you."

"At this hour?"

"Yes, Madame."

Without another word Angélique threw on her dressing gown. The little apartment "Reserved" for Madame
du Plessis-Bellière was luxuriously furnished, but not
without its traps.

"May I ask you to wait a moment, Monsieur Bontemps? I should like to dress."

"Certainly, Madame. But please be so good as not to
wake your attendants. His Majesty wishes us to be as

discreet as possible and to let the existence of this private door be known only to a very few people we can trust."

"I shall be careful."

She lit a candle for herself from Bontemps', and went into the adjoining room.

"There's nothing in this world that can frighten you," Raymond had told her. He was right. Her hazardous life had taught her to face up to danger rather than run from it. If her teeth were chattering, it was from cold, not fright.

"Monsieur Bontemps, will you oblige me by helping me hook up my dress, please."

Louis XIV's valet bowed and set his candlestick on a table. Angélique was very considerate of this pleasant little man who performed his unenviable tasks without seeming in the least servile. He was responsible for the King's household and for the feeding and lodging of the entire Court. Louis could not have done without him and burdened him with a thousand and one petty duties. Rather than bother his master at awkward moments, Bontemps frequently paid for things out of his own pocket. The King already owed him seven thousand *pistoles* that he had advanced him at the gaming tables and the raffles.

Angélique brushed a little rouge on her cheeks. Her cloak was in the next room, where her chaperones were sleeping. She shrugged her shoulders. "So much the worse," she said. "I'm ready, Monsieur Bontemps."

She had a hard time squeezing her full heavy skirts through the secret doorway, which closed behind them noiselessly. She found herself in a narrow passageway hardly higher or wider than a man. Bontemps led her up a little winding staircase, then down three steps to a kind of tunnel that wound darkly ahead of them. As they twisted along it she noticed many doors which presumably led to secret rooms, and wondered what mysterious occupants they were designed for, or what trysts.

This was an aspect of Versailles she had never imagined—of spies and secret meetings, visits incognito, secret conferences, clandestine rendezvous—an arcane Versailles sealed in its own thick walls and entwining its invisible coils around the great golden rooms that gleamed and glittered with a light like day.

They crossed one last buried room in which a bench and a tapestried hassock seemed to await some subterranean guests, and came to a door that opened into a much larger room whose steeply vaulted ceiling indicated that it belonged to some extensive apartment. As she looked around her, Angélique recognized the King's conference chamber. Two six-branched candelabra on a black marble table that reflected their flames revealed the sovereign bent studiously over his papers. Two big greyhounds were asleep by the embers on the hearth. They stirred and growled lazily, then curled up again.

Bontemps poked up the fire and threw another log on it, then melted away into the wall like a shadow.

Louis XIV, still grasping his pen, looked up. Angélique saw him smile.

"Pray be seated, Madame."

She perched apprehensively on the edge of an armchair. There was a dead silence in the room, any noise from the outside being muffled by heavy blue draperies at the windows and the doors.

At length the King rose and stood before her, his arms crossed. "So, you have not yet given the signal for attack? Not a word? Not a protest? Even at being dragged out of bed? Aren't you even cross?"

"Sire, I am at Your Majesty's service."

"Why so humble all of a sudden? Where is your usual stinging reply? What caprice is this?"

"Your Majesty makes me out to be a harpy, and puts me to shame. Is that what you think of me, Sire?"

The King did not give her a direct answer. "Reverend Father Joseph has been extolling your abilities to me for over an hour. He is a man of good judgment and a liberal mind, and I appreciate his advice. It would be ungracious of me not to forgive you now that I know the best minds of the Church have put you under the protection of their indulgence. Now, what have I said that makes you smile so sardonically?"

"I didn't expect to be awakened at this hour of the night to hear your austere almoner praised."

The King laughed. "Little witch!"

"Soliman Baktiari Bey calls me *Fouzoul-Khanoum.*"

"What does that mean?"

"The same thing. Isn't that proof that the King of France and the ambassador of the Shah of Persia can think alike?"

"We shall see about that." He held out his hands to her, palms up. "Little toy, pay homage to your sovereign."

With a smile Angélique laid her hands in his. "I pledge my allegiance to the King of France, whose liegewoman and vassal I am."

"That's better. Now, come here."

He helped her rise, and led her around to his side of the table. It was spread with a big open map on which was a wide expanse of blue among the lines of latitude and longitude and puffing cherubs at each of the four principal points of the compass. On the blue were inscribed in letters of white and gold enscrolled with many a flourish, the mighty words *"Mare Nostrum— Mater Nostra,"* the old name still given by geographers to the Mediterranean, the cradle of civilization: "Our Sea—Our Mother."

The King pointed out several places with his finger. "Here is France. There, Malta; there, Candia, the last stronghold of Christianity. Then we encounter the power of the Turks. And, as you can see, Persia is over there—that lion against a rising sun between the crescent of Turkey and the tiger of Asia."

"Did Your Majesty summon me here at this late hour to talk about Persia?"

"Did you want us to talk about something else perhaps?"

Angélique shook her head, keeping her eyes on the map and refusing to look him in the eye.

"No, let's talk about Persia, then. What interest does France have in that far-off land?"

"An interest that cannot be without interest to you,

Madame. Silk. Did you know that three-quarters of our imports come from there?"

"I did not know. That's a lot. Why do we need so much silk in France? What will we do with it?"

The King burst out laughing. "Do with it? You, a woman, ask that? My dear, how do you think we could get along without our brocades, our satins, our stockings at twenty-five *livres* a pair, our ribbons, our chasubles? Do without bread, rather! That's the way the French are. Their great business is not in spices, or oil, or wheat, or hardware, or any other vulgar things like that, but in fashion.

"In my father's time Richelieu tried to make dress simpler. You know what happened. He succeeded only in raising the prices of materials because they had to be smuggled in and thus were harder to come by. Now, this is where the shoe pinches and why a new commercial treaty with the Shah of Persia is important: the French must have silk, but it is too costly. It's a ruinous enterprise." He ticked off the reasons. "Duty to the Persians. Toll to the Turks for bringing goods through their country. Toll to various other intermediary agents—Genoa, Metz, Provence. We need another arrangement."

"Doesn't Monsieur Colbert envision replacing these huge imports with a local manufacture? He told me he was planning to convert the factories of Lyons."

"That will take a long time. We have not yet learned the secret of the oriental methods of manufacturing brocade and lamé. The mulberry trees I ordered planted in the South will not mature for many years."

"And they will not produce a silk like Persian silk for us. They bear black berries, whereas in Persia the silkworms feed on the white-berried trees which grow on their high plateaus."

"How do you know so much about it?"

"His Excellency Baktiari Bey told me."

"So he talked to you about the silk business? Then he must suspect it is an important part of our negotiations. Did he seem to know much about our problem?"

"He is a very literate man, something of a poet, and

highly civilized—in his own way. He has the ear of the
Shah of Persia, thanks to his gifts as a courtier, but he
has other talents as well which may be less appreciated
in his own country but are more of a threat to us. He is
an excellent businessman, unusual though that is for a
man of his rank, for the Persian nobles have in general
let all their business go to the Armenians and Syrians."

The King sighed resignedly. "I guess I will have to
yield to the opinions of Colbert and Father Joseph after
all. You certainly seem to be the only one able to un-
tangle this unholy mess over silk."

They looked at each other and laughed like fellow-
conspirators bound by a tie there was no need to mention. The King's eyes began to gleam.

"Angélique . . ." he said in a hollow voice. Then, in
his natural tone: "Everyone I sent to him has reported
nothing but asininities. Both Tercy and Saint-Amen
have described him as a gross barbarian, unable to adapt
himself to our customs or treat the King, his host, with
due respect. Now my intuition tells me you have properly
depicted him as a shrewd and cunning man, refined
but ruthless."

"I am sure, Sire, that if you had been able to meet him
yourself, instead of your ambassadors, these difficulties
would not have arisen. You have a gift for detecting a
person's true character at a glance."

"Alas, there are certain things kings cannot do for
themselves, but they have to know how to choose the
right person for a job. This is the first and most important
element in making a ruler great. I made a mistake in not
selecting carefully enough the men I sent to the ambassador as my representatives. Saint-Amen, whom I appointed chief of protocol, seemed the proper person,
and I did not take his liabilities into account. He is a
Huguenot, and like all others of his persuasion he has
a mean, suspicious nature that is more inclined to think
of his principles than compromise them for the sake of
his country's interests. This isn't the first time I have
pondered the nature of these Protestants. The most
devout are uncontrollable because of the curious rigidity

of their creed. Hereafter I shall be cautious about having any more of them in important positions."

He made a gesture with his hand signifying an impassable barrier. Then his face softened. "You have been kind enough, Madame, to come to our rescue in time."

"That's not the way Your Majesty was talking this morning."

"I admit it. It was small of me not to want to confess I had been wrong. I know what I must have and what I must avoid. You have shown me the surest way of getting what I want. If we do not arrive at some understanding with the Shah of Persia's ambassador, it's extremely likely that he will expel our Jesuits and keep us from all the silk of his mulberry trees. The fate of both issues is in your hands."

Angélique's eyes fell on her turquoise. "What am I to do? What part shall I play?"

"Find out what the prince is thinking and then let me know how I should deal with him so as to avoid any further blunders. If you possibly can, find out in advance what traps he is setting for us."

"In a word, seduce him. Try to cut off his hair like Delilah?"

The King smiled. "I leave it to you to decide what may be necessary."

Angélique bit her lip. "This is not an easy assignment. It will take a lot of time."

"That's of small importance."

"I thought everyone was in a hurry to have the ambassador present his credentials."

"Everyone but me. To tell the truth, when they told me at the very beginning that Baktiari Bey was hesitant about doing so, I was annoyed. Since then I have let things drift, and now, on the contrary, I want the interview postponed. I want first to receive the Russian ambassador, who is on his way. I can speak more freely with the Persian afterward. If the Russians agree, we can establish a new overland route for the silk and thus protect ourselves from the depredations of the Turks and the Genoese and others like them."

"So the bales of merchandise will no longer come by sea?"

"No, they will follow the ancient route of the Tartars that the merchants of Samarkand take into Europe. Look, here is the new route I have been sketching—by way of the Caucasian steppes, the Ukraine, Bessarabia, Hungary. Thereafter by these lands that belong to my cousin the King of Bavaria. When all is said and done, it will cost less on the whole than the raids of the Barbary pirates and the ruinous tolls we have to pay when using the sea route."

As they both leaned over the map following this extraordinary route their heads touched. Angélique felt the King's curls brush against her cheek. She straightened up quickly in alarm. A tremor ran through her. She went around the table to sit down again opposite the King, noticing that during their conversation the fire had died down. She began to shiver and wished she had brought her cloak. Now she would have to wait until the King himself indicated she might leave. This he did not seem disposed to do. He kept on talking about the plans of Colbert for the factories of Lyons and Marseilles.

Finally he stopped. "You aren't listening. What's the matter with you?"

Angélique was hugging her arms to keep warm and did not answer at once. Being of an extremely rugged constitution, the King was oblivious to cold, heat and fatigue, and rarely noticed that those who had the honor of being in his company minded them. To complain about them put him in a bad humor and often resulted in disgrace. Old Madame de Chaulnes had once expressed herself on the subject during a military review in an icy wind, and had been told to "nurse her rheumatism in her own castle."

"What's the matter?" the King insisted. "You seem lost in some plot or other. I trust you are not going to insult me by refusing the mission I have just entrusted to you."

"By no means, Sire. If such had been my intention I would not have listened to you. Does Your Majesty think I could be capable of disloyalty?"

"I think you are capable of anything," the King said soberly. "Do you think you may fail me?"

"No indeed."

"Then what is the trouble? Why have you suddenly become so abstracted?"

"I'm freezing."

The King looked astonished. "Freezing?"

"The fire has gone out, Sire. It's the dead of winter, and it's two o'clock in the morning."

An amused surprise was discernible on the features of Louis XIV. "So there is a trace of weakness in you? I have never heard anyone complain so."

"No one dares to, Sire. They're all afraid of displeasing you."

"But you . . ."

"I am afraid too, but I'm more afraid of getting sick. Now then, how shall I execute Your Majesty's orders?"

The King smiled at her thoughtfully, and for the first time she sensed that within his proud heart there was a little tenderness.

"Good," he said decisively. "I want to talk with you some more, but I don't want to kill you."

He peeled off his thick brown velvet coat and draped it about her shoulders. She sniffed its male smell mingled with the orris root perfume he loved and which characterized his prestige and the awe he inspired. It gave her an almost sensuous pleasure to pull the gold-braided lapels of the coat over her breast. The hand the King laid on her shoulder warmed her like the hand in her dream. She closed her eyes for a moment, then opened them again.

The King was on his knees by the hearth, efficiently poking at the logs and fanning the embers till they sprang into blaze.

"Bontemps is catching a little sleep," he said by way of explanation for his incongruous occupation. "I don't want to let anyone else in on the secrecy of our conference."

He got to his feet and dusted off his hands. Angélique was looking at him as if he were a stranger who had suddenly appeared in the room. In his shirtsleeves, his long embroidered waistcoat emphasizing his manly chest, he looked like a friendly young tradesman who had experienced some hard times during his poverty-ridden life. The discomfort of camp life, retreats over mud-rutted roads, the wretched draughty castles in which the Court had taken refuge during its exodus in 1649, straw pallets to sleep on—was that when the young king in tattered breeches had learned how to build a fire to get warm?

Angélique would never be able to see him in the same light again. He too saw that, and smiled at her.

"At this hour of the night we can forget the rules of etiquette. Kings lead a hard life accounting for every one of their actions and gestures to the whole world, and, I might add, to future ages. It's an obligatory discipline for them, and for all who surround them and watch them, to submit to rules that never permit them to falter but always live up to what is expected of them. Night brings them the escape they must have. It's then I sometimes remember who and what I am." As he finished, he raised his hands to his face as if to rediscover his own features.

"Is this the face he shows his mistresses?" asked Angélique.

Suddenly the idea struck her that Madame de Montespan was not worthy of him.

"At night I become a man again," the King went on. "I rather like to withdraw to this office and work here in peace and quiet. Think, yawn, talk to my dogs without having to watch that everything I say may be recorded for history." He was stroking the head of his greyhound. "At night I can meet anyone I want without immediately arousing the courtiers' feelings which can lead to a palace revolution or even to international complications. Yes, night is a king's best friend."

He fell silent, standing before her and leaning on the table in a languid attitude with his feet crossed. His hands were relaxed, for he had no need to make eloquent gestures with them. Angélique felt her admiration growing for this man who slept so little and whose days were a continual round of work, yes, but also meeting people, dancing, walking, hunting, getting embroiled in weighty complications, giving his attention to the smallest details, never showing the least exhaustion.

"I love to see you look at me," the King said suddenly. "A woman who looks at a man that way inspires him with courage and pride, and when that man is a king, it makes him want to conquer the world."

Angélique laughed. "Your people do not require so much of you, Sire. For you to keep them at peace and their frontiers safe is enough for them, it seems to me. France does not demand that you be another Alexander the Great."

"That's where you are wrong. Empires endure only in proportion to their growth—by eternal vigilance and by hard work. Never believe that the obligations I have mentioned to you are burdensome to me. It is a fine thing to be a king, and pleasing to one who desires to quit himself well in all he undertakes. Naturally, it is not free of hardship, pain and anxiety. It's the uncertainty that what he does may not be right that makes him despair. He must be quick to follow the way he believes is best. Still, I must say that responsibility agrees with me . . .

"To keep one's eyes wide open over all the earth . . . to keep eternally posted on the latest happenings in every province and every nation . . . to discover the weaknesses in every court and every foreign prince and minister . . . to be aware of an infinite number of things that he is thought to know nothing of . . . to uncover among his own subjects what they think they have best concealed . . . to search out the secret opinions of all courtiers and their most insignificant concerns that are reported through opposing interests . . . to note some progress every day in glorious enterprises and the prosperity of the people for whom they have been undertaken . . . I don't know of any other pleasure I would exchange for it if I had the chance. But I must stop, Madame. I am abusing your patience and your attention. I can see the moment coming when you will look me straight in the eye and say 'I'm sleepy.' "

"But I have been listening to you most attentively."

"I know that. Forgive me for teasing you. That's why I like to have you near me—you know how to listen so well. You can say, 'Who doesn't listen to the King? Everyone is silent when he speaks.' It's true, but there are many ways of listening and often I see only a servile audience, saying yes in stupid acquiescence. But you listen with your heart, with all the faculties of your intelligence and with a desire to understand. That is very dear to me. It is often hard for me to find someone to talk to when I desperately need to talk. One's mind clarifies its thoughts by speaking them. Once one is talking, one's mind unconsciously goes from topic to topic far better than in solitary meditation, and that is exciting and gratifying. When there is someone to argue with, then the mind finds a thousand new expedients. But that's enough for now. I shan't keep you longer."

On a bench behind the secret door Bontemps was dozing in the light and fitful sleep of all servants. He was on his feet at once. Angélique retraced her way through the dark labyrinth, and once she had reached her rooms sent back the King's coat by his valet.

The candle she had left burning in her bedroom was guttering and casting weird shadows on the ceiling. By its light Angélique could discern a pale face against the wall and two hands holding a rosary on a lap. The older of the Gilandon girls was piously waiting for the return of her mistress.

"What are you doing there?" Angélique said in considerable annoyance. "I did not have you called."

"The dog was barking. I imagined you might need something, and when you did not answer I was afraid you were sick."

"I might just have been asleep. You have too much imagination, Marie-Anne. It's a nuisance. Do I have to tell you not to mention this?"

"Of course not, Madame. Do you need anything?"

"Well, since you're up, you might rekindle the fire and put some hot coals into the warming pan to heat up my bed. I'm frozen."

"At least she won't think I'm fresh out of someone else's bed," Angélique said to herself. "But still she has an imagination. What if she recognized Bontemps when he held the door for me . . ."

She crawled into bed, but the sleep she hoped for did not come. In barely three hours Madame Hamelin, the old nurse, would pass through the corridors of Versailles in her lace cap to draw back the curtains of the royal bed, and Louix XIV's day would begin.

His melodious voice still sounded in her ears as he revealed his thoughts, so private and yet so universal. She thought of how there was something heroic in him, like the princes of the Italian Renaissance, for like them he was young, self-confident, attractive, loved glory and beauty. The echoes of his voice haunted her. He had made her more a prisoner by his speeches that night than by all his kisses.

chapter 19

BAKTIARI BEY leaped briskly into the saddle. Ceres appeared quite at ease under her exotic harness with its wide stirrups, and did not throw a glance at Angélique, who had just arrived at Suresnes.

The Persian horsemen with daggers on their chests and scimitars at their sides advanced down the avenue under the gray trees. All held long sticks painted in bright colors as they formed a semi-circle about the prince. He took a stick from his page, and rising in his wide, gold-fringed stirrups, led the whole troop behind him in a trot. The riders disappeared behind the foliage of the little park.

Angélique felt humiliated at being left behind on the steps of the house without a word, although she had had her visit announced the same morning. Agobian, the Armenian, who had remained with her, said:

"They are going to come back. They will divide in front of you into two parallel columns and then you will see their stick drill. That is a contest which our warriors have been practicing since long ago. His Excellency ordered it as a ceremony in your honor."

Indeed the riders had not gone far away. They could be heard stopping outside the village, then breaking into a trot and then into a frenzied gallop. They reappeared in two lines, yelling and whirling their heavy sticks in the air. Some were so skillful they could throw themselves under their horses' bellies and immediately regain their saddles without falling to the ground.

"We call that trick *djiguits* and one of the best at it is His Excellency himself. But he is not showing off all he can do for fear of frightening his new horse. It must grieve him not to be able to demonstrate his skill to you, Madame," explained the Armenian.

When they came abreast of the steps, the two lines of *djiguits* stopped cold, making several of the horses skid on the snow. The lines ranged themselves on the grass on opposite sides of the avenue like two armies. At a signal from Baktiari Bey they descended on each other, furiously whirling their sticks; then as they crashed together each rider stuck his stick under his arm like a lance to unseat his opponent or make him drop his weapon. Then the two sides separated, rode off, and dashed together again to renew the contest. Riders who were unseated or lost their weapons retired to the sidelines.

In spite of the inexperience of his horse the ambassador was among the last to retire, not that his opponents showed him any favoritism, but because he was stronger and more agile than they. When the mock battle was over, he rode up to his guest with a smile on his brown face.

"His Excellency would like you to understand that this has been the favorite sport of our nation since the time of the Medes. It existed even in King Darius' reign. We probably got the custom from Samarkand, the capital of Turkestan, where a brilliant civilization once flourished."

In public Baktiari Bey pretended ignorance of French and relied on his interpreter. Angélique did not wish to be left behind in matters of erudition.

"The French knights of the Middle Ages used to engage in tournaments like that," she remarked.

"They brought the custom back from their crusades."

"Soon," thought Angélique, "they are going to make me believe we owe our civilization to them." Then on reflection she realized that, as a matter of fact, it was almost true. She knew little enough about it, but she had heard enough sermons to have learned quite a few things about ancient civilizations. Heir to the brilliant history of the Assyrians, Baktiari Bey had not yet realized he now belonged to a backward people.

Angélique now understood what were non-controversial topics of conversation. Horses was one of them. His Excellency praised Ceres once again.

"He says he has never seen a horse in his own country so tame and yet so spirited. The King of France has indeed honored him with such a gift. At home we might offer a royal princess in exchange for such a horse."

Angélique said it was a Spanish horse.

"That's a country I should greatly like to visit," said the ambassador.

But he had no regrets, for his embassy had allowed him to meet not only the most powerful sovereign of the West, but also the beautiful women who frequented the court of this great monarch, and that was fair enough. Angélique took advantage of his good humor to ask when he would appear before "this great monarch."

Baktiari Bey grew thoughtful. With a sigh he explained that that depended partly upon his astrologer and partly on the degree of dignity with which his embassy would be received.

While they were talking they had entered the house and gone into the salon, which had been redecorated in the oriental style. As soon as the curtains at the doorway had fallen behind them, he began to speak in French again.

"I cannot present myself before the King except in a ceremony that would be worthy of him and of the ruler who sent me."

"Isn't that what our . . . grand vizier, the Marquis de Tercy, proposed?"

"Not at all!" exploded the Persian. "He wanted to take me there like a prisoner in a coach surrounded by infidel guards, and then he pretended, that arrant liar of a vizier's lackey, that I ought to present myself before the King bareheaded. That is not only undignified but insolent. In such an instance one should remain covered as in a mosque before God Himself."

"Our customs are just the reverse. We take off our hats before God in our churches. I suppose if a Frenchman wore shoes in front of your king you would make him take them off."

"True. And if he had an insufficient escort we would furnish him with one . . . to do him honor . . . and preserve the dignity of our Shah. Your king is a great ruler. He *must* honor me by granting me a triumphal entry, worthy of his own prestige, or else I must return without having accomplished my mission."

Angélique dared ask: "Wouldn't you risk disgrace by failing to accomplish your mission?"

"I would risk my head. But I would prefer that to public dishonor before your people."

She understood that it was a more serious situation than anyone realized. "It will be arranged," she said.

"I don't know."

"It must be arranged. Or else I shall have brought bad luck to your house."

"Bravo!" shouted the Persian.

"Furthermore I will have committed the crime of making the holy man of your household lie, for he assured me I would not harm you, and if you should lose your head, that would be proof of his faulty prophecy. It would be a great humiliation for him. Am I wrong, Your Excellency? I am only a woman, and a foreign one at that."

"You are not wrong," said Baktiari Bey soberly, "and your intelligence surpasses even your beauty. If my mission is successful I know what gift I shall ask of your king . . ."

There was a stirring behind the curtain accompanied by the piercing sound of fifes.

"My servants are coming to prepare my bath. After such violent exercise, it is well to bathe."

Two black slaves carrying a huge copper basin filled with steaming water entered, followed by other servants carrying towels, bottles of perfumed water and scented ointments.

Baktiari Bey followed them into the adjacent room, which contained the Turkish bath that Dionis had built. Angélique would have greatly liked to get a glimpse of it, but such curiosity seemed improper to her. From time to time Baktiari Bey's looks made her uneasy, and the further she explored his oriental mentality, the more her role as ambassadress seemed compromising, requiring complaisances, if not actual obligations, which she had

not by any means decided to consent to. She thought
vaguely of going away. She could explain that French
customs did not permit her to talk alone with a man for
more than two hours. But then the Persian might fly
into a rage and think her departure another insult, and
that would obviously wreck all the improvements she
had made in the situation.

When she made a movement as if to rise, the little
page, who had been ordered to amuse her, came forward, bringing her a heavy platter of dainties. Then he
scurried off to get more cushions for her back and arms.
He threw a pinch of powder into a little jar filled with
glowing coals and got down on his knees to pass the in-
cense-burner toward her so that she might whiff the
pungent blue smoke.

It was definitely time she should go. This room, its
air heavy with exotic perfumes, this prince who would
soon return with his dark eyes, his easy grace, and his
dignity that concealed unsuspected rages, was much too
seductive.

The little page removed the lids of the silver-gilt cups
and poured the blue porcelain flagons into them. With
bird-like twitters he urged her to help herself. Despair-
ing of making her understand, he lifted to her lips a little silver cup containing a greenish-gold liqueur. She
tasted it and found that it was like the angelica of Poitou.

The variety of the sweetmeats intrigued her. They
were of all colors, including translucent pink and green
jellies and pistachio nougats. Angélique bit into one of
each kind and discarded the ones she found distasteful.
She asked for more of the fruit sherbet that was kept
cool in a kind of ice-house. She would have liked to
smoke the narghile, but when the page understood what
she wanted, he prevented her by rolling his eyes in terror. Then he doubled up in high-pitched laughter that
made Angélique laugh too. She was finding it delightful
to have nothing to do but affect to be dignified amid
all this opulence.

She was still weak from laughing and was licking pink
Turkish paste off her fingertips when Baktiari Bey re-

appeared in the doorway. He seemed enchanted with her.

"You are ravishing. . . . You remind me of one of my favorites. She was as greedy as a cat."

He took a fruit in a cup and tossed it to the page, shouting an order. The boy, still laughing, caught the tip in the air and in two leaps was out of the room.

"That little Wise Man from the East made me drink something devilishly strong," Angélique said to herself.

Yet the sensation she was experiencing was not like drunkenness, but rather a vague warmth akin to true happiness. It made her extremely sensitive. Baktiari's new costume did not escape her notice. He wore only white satin trousers fastened at his calves, and bound at his waist by a belt studded with precious stones. His smooth bare chest, anointed with sweet-smelling oils, and his muscular arms and shoulders, suggested the lithe strength of a panther. His black hair, glistening with oil, was combed straight back and fell to the nape of his neck. With a quick movement he kicked off his embroidered sandals and stretched out on the cushions. As he nonchalantly carried his pipe to his mouth, he fixed Angélique with a look.

It would have been naive of her not to realize that the time for discussing matters of protocol was past. What were they to talk about now? She was dying to stretch out like him on the cushions, but her rigid stays prevented her and kept her upright. Suddenly they seemed to her a symbol of caution designed to permit sinners on the brink a chance to reflect. On the other hand, it seemed impossible for her to rise and take her leave without some explanation. Furtheremore, she did not want to. But, thanks to her stays, she had to remain upright. What a wonderful invention they were! They must have been thought up by the Brotherhood of the Holy Sacrament. The thought of that made Angélique laugh aloud again, rocking back and forth with amusement.

The Persian was obviously delighted with her gaiety.

"I was thinking of your favorites," Angélique said. "Tell me how they dress. Do they wear gowns like these Western ones?"

"In their own apartments or in their master's they wear a thin, fluffy *saroush* and a short sleeveless coat. When they go out they add a thick black veil with a gauze opening just big enough for them to see through. But in private they wear only a shawl as light as a cobweb, made of the hair of the goats of Beluchistan."

Angélique was dipping her fingers again into the rose jelly. "What a strange life! What do all those cloistered women think about? What did the favorite—the one who's greedy as a cat—say when you left?"

"Our women say nothing—nothing whatever—about such things. And my favorite could say nothing for another reason. She is dead."

"Oh, I am sorry," said Angélique, humming as she nibbled at a piece of fig paste.

"She died under the lash," Baktiari Bey said slowly. "She had one of the palace guards as a lover."

"Oh!" said Angélique again. She laid down the piece of candy and looked at the prince, her eyes wide with fright. "So that's what happened! Tell me, what other punishments do you inflict on faithless women?"

"We tie them back to back with their lover and expose them on the topmost watchtower of the palace. The vultures begin by eating their eyes, and the rest goes on a long time. I happen to be more merciful. I kill them by slitting their throats with my dagger. That is for those who haven't actually been unfaithful but have refused me out of caprice."

"Aren't they lucky," said Angélique sententiously. "You get them out of your sight and you give them admission to paradise."

Baktiari Bey shook with laughter. "Little *Firousi* . . . Little Turquoise . . . every word that passes your lips is as fresh as the snowdrops that bloom in the desert at the foot of the Caucasus. Don't make my lesson too hard for me . . . to learn to love Western women. A man has to talk to them a great deal, so you say, and sing the praises of his beloved . . . but then what? When does the time for silence come, the time for long-drawn sighs?"

"When the lady pleases."

The Persian leaped up, his face flushed with anger.

"No! It can't be! How can a man suffer such a humiliation! The French are brave warriors . . ."

"They surrender in the wars of love."

"No, it can't be true," he repeated. "When a woman receives her lord she must immediately disrobe and perfume her body and offer herself to him."

With an agile bound he was next to her, and she found herself tumbled back among the soft cushions which melted around her body and enveloped it with their heady perfume. The predatory smile of Baktiari Bey came nearer and nearer as he held her. Angélique put her hands on his shoulders to push him away, but the feel of his golden-brown skin made her tremble.

"The time has not yet come," she said.

"Take care. For the least insolence a woman deserves death."

"You have no right to kill me. I belong to the King of France."

"The King sent you to me for my pleasure."

"No, to honor you and to get to know you better, for he trusts my judgment. But if you kill me, he will chase you out of his realm in disgrace."

"I will complain that you behaved like a shameless whore."

"The King will not believe you."

"He sent you for me to possess."

"No, I keep telling you. He could not do such a thing."

"Who can then?"

She fixed him with her emerald eyes. "Only I can."

The prince relaxed his grip on her and looked at her perplexedly.

Angélique could not sit up again, the cushions were too yielding. She began to laugh. She saw no trouble ahead, rather everything seemed clearly etched as if the room had been invaded with sunlight.

"There is a world of difference," she murmured, "between a woman saying yes and a woman saying no. When she says yes, it is a great victory and the men of my nation like to fight to win her."

"I understand," said the prince after a moment of thought.

"So, please help me up," she said, extending her hand to him unconsciously.

He obeyed like, she thought, a great wild beast suddenly tamed. His shining eyes never left her. His strength was triggered to pounce upon her if she showed the slightest sign of weakening.

"What does a man have to have to make a woman say yes?"

She almost answered: "He has to be as wild and handsome as you." His nearness was overpowering her. How many times would she be able to play this dangerous game? Shivers ran through her flesh, as if she had a fever, but what she felt was actually a frustration of desire that could be appeased by a mad embrace alone. She was aware of how desirable his smile was to her, his moist lips and his wandering eyes, and she would have loved to be seized by him again. Still she wondered how long she could balance on this tightrope and on what side she would fall—the yes side or the no.

Baktiari Bey filled a silver cup and held it out to her. Angélique felt the metal cool against her lips and recognized the greenish liquor.

"It's every woman's secret to know why one man pleases her because he's dark, and another because he's fair."

Holding the cup at arm's length she inverted it and poured the liquor in a thin green stream on the gorgeous oriental rug.

"Chaitsoum," [1] hissed the prince between his teeth.

". . . Or one because he is gentle and the other because he could kill her with a blow of his dagger in his rage."

She had finally managed to rise. She assured His Excellency that she was overjoyed with her visit and that she would try to make the King understand the essence of his grievances, for they seemed reasonable and justified to her. With a threatening look in his eyes Baktiari Bey said it was the custom of his country to seal a friend-

[1] "She-devil."

ship by housing a guest "as long as the friendship remained."

Angélique shook her head. A curl of her blonde hair
hung down over her forehead, and her eyes were sparkling like champagne. His Excellency was right, but she
had to obey the same precept. He should understand
that because she had deep obligations to her own king,
she had to return to him and remain there as long as
their friendship lasted.

"*Shac!*" [2] he said, as if cursing.

A sing-song voice rose outside, piercing the heavy
draperies of the room.

"Isn't it time for your evening prayers? I wouldn't
have a foreign woman make you miss your devotions
for anything in the world. What is he chanting?"

"*Chaitsoum!*" repeated the ambassador.

Angélique smoothed down her skirts. fixed her disordered hair, and picked up her fan.

"I shall defend your point of view at Versailles and
try to smooth over all the difficulties of protocol. But
may I take back with me your promise to protect the
twenty Catholic missions in Persia?"

"That was my intention for the treaty. Wouldn't your
religion and your priests feel disgraced at being saved
by a woman's intervention?"

"In spite of all your pride, Your Excellency, it was a
woman who brought you into the world."

The Persian was speechless, but he smiled in admiration. "You are fit to be a *sultana-bachi.*"

"What is that, for heaven's sake?"

"The title given to a woman born to dominate kings.
There is only one in each seraglio. She is never chosen.
She is there because she has ways of ensnaring the body
and soul of the ruler. He can do nothing without con-
sulting her. She is superior to all the other women, and
it is only her son who can succeed to the throne."

He led her up to the silken door curtain. "The first
trait of a *sultana-bachi* is that she knows no fear. The
second, that she knows the worth of what she gives."

[2] "Stubborn mule."

With a sudden gesture he stripped all the rings from his fingers and piled them into her hands. "These are for you. You are the most precious. You deserve to be decked as an idol."

Angélique blinked in rapture at the rubies, emeralds and diamonds set in fine gold, but as rapidly as he had given them to her, she returned them to him. "Impossible!"

"Are you adding one more insult to all those you have offered me?"

"In my country when a woman says no, she says no to gifts also."

Baktiari Bey heaved a long sigh, but he did not try to dissuade her. As Angélique smiled, he slipped the rings back on his fingers one by one.

"Look," she said, extending her hand, "I am keeping this one, for you gave it to me as a token of our alliance. Its color has not changed."

"Madame Turquoise, when will I see you again?"

"At Versailles, Excellency."

Once she was outside, everything seemed horribly dreary to her—the muddy road, the clouds hanging low over the shabby snow. It was cold. She had forgotten it was winter and that she was in France, and that she had to go back to Versailles to report on her mission, parade around, listen to endless gossip, be cold, have her feet and legs ache, and lose her money gambling. She twisted her handkerchief savagely. She was on the point of bursting into tears.

"I liked it there on the cushions. Yes, I would have liked . . . that. To forget, to yield to love without restraint and without thinking of the consequences. Oh, what did God give me a brain for? Why can't I just be an animal that doesn't ask questions?"

She was furious with the King. All during her visit she could not rid herself of the feeling that the King was using her as an adventuress whose body might be useful for diplomacy. During the previous reign Richelieu had excelled in using intelligent women as conspirators, when they were light-moraled and beautiful and possessed by a devil of intrigue, and adored to

be in the thick of things and to compromise and . . .
prostitute themselves for master strategies whose end
they never clearly saw. Madame de Chevreuse, the old
friend of Anne of Austria, whom Angélique had met
at Court, was one of the few survivors of that species.
Always on the alert for a role to play, her beautiful eyes
watching under their now wrinkled lids for the merest
hint of a conspiracy, affecting an air of mystery about
every least bit of news, she was an object of pity and
ridicule to the young members of the Court. Angélique
could see herself like that some day soon, no one listening to her, wearing one of those big plumed military
hats now so out of fashion.

    She was almost weeping with self-pity. So that's what
the King wanted to turn her into! Now that he had
"his" Montespan, what did he care where Angélique
was or whom she gave her favors to? All she had to do
was "serve" the royal interests!

chapter 20

"*T*HE King said *no*," someone flung at her as soon as she set foot on the first step of the staircase leading to the royal apartments.

"About what?"

"The marriage of Péguilin and Mademoiselle. Everything's over and done with. Yesterday the Prince and the Duc d'Enghien, his son, threw themselves at His Majesty's feet to prove to him what a dishonor such a base alliance would be to princes of the blood like them. They would be the joke of all the courts of Europe, and he himself, who had just begun to make the world tremble, would be thought a monarch with no sense of dynastic dignity. Actually the King was rather inclined to their point of view anyway, and so he said NO! This morning he told the Grande Mademoiselle. She burst into tears and fled in desperation to the Luxembourg Palace for refuge."

"Poor Mademoiselle!"

In the Queen's antechamber Angélique found Madame de Montespan completing her toilet with the help of all her suite. Her gown was of scarlet velvet embroidered with gold and silver and studded with precious stones, and she was preoccupied with arranging a long white silk stole so that it would hang as she wished. Louise de la Vallière was on her knees, helping pin her.

"No, not like that, like this! Help me, for heaven's sake, Louise. You're the only one who can fix this silk properly, it's so slippery. But it is lovely, isn't it?"

Angélique was amazed to see how docilely Louise de la Vallière took to being a follower, checking by a glance into the pier-glass whether a fold might not be more appropriate than a loop.

351

"There, that's it, I think. Good for you, Louise, you've got it exactly right. I could never do without you when it comes to getting dressed. The King is so demanding! But you have a magic touch, thanks to Madame de Lorraine and Madame d'Orléans. They taught you taste when you were in their suite. What do you think, Madame du Plessis?"

"I think it's perfect," Angélique muttered.

She was trying to kick aside one of the Queen's lapdogs that had been yapping at her ever since she came in.

"He doesn't like your black outfit," Athenais said as she turned this way and that in front of her looking glass. "What a pity you have to wear mourning. It doesn't become you, do you think, Louise?"

La Vallière, who had got on her knees again to help her rival, raised her pale, watery blue eyes toward Angélique. "I think Madame du Plessis looks even handsomer in black."

"Better than I do in red, perhaps?"

Louise de la Vallière did not reply.

"Answer me," Athenais screamed, her eyes darkening like the sea in a storm. "Admit it, this red doesn't suit me."

"Blue is more your color."

"Why didn't you say so sooner, you stupid idiot! Help me out of it! Desoeillet, Papy, get me out of this dress! Catherine, run get my satin gown, the one I wear with my diamonds!"

It was hard to tell who was making more noise, the dog or Madame de Montespan as she tried to step out of her skirts alone. Just then in came the King in his Court costume except for his great robe embroidered with fleur-de-lis, which he never put on till the last moment before his state appearance. He was coming from the Queen's apartments, and Bontemps was with him.

"Not ready yet, Madame?" he frowned. "Hurry up. The King of Poland will be here any moment, and you must be at my side."

Madame de Montespan stared at him indignantly. Her royal lover had not accustomed her to his strictness, and he was in a bad humor, for the pain he had inflicted on his cousin, the Grande Mademoiselle, troubled his conscience. Now to have his favorite complain so violently that he was putting her to a great deal of trouble to find a suitable gown did not soften his mood.

"You should have taken care of that long ago."

"How was I to know Your Majesty wouldn't like my red dress? Oh, this is unfair!"

The King tried to raise his voice above the cacophony she and the dog were making. "Don't get into a state. There isn't time. At any rate, while I think to tell you, we are leaving for Fontainebleau tomorrow, so please make your preparations in time."

"Should I also prepare to go to Fontainebleau, Sire?" asked Mademoiselle de la Vallière.

Louis XIV looked darkly at the emaciated figure of his former mistress. "No," he said rudely. "There's no point in your going."

"But what shall I do, then?" she groaned.

"Stay at Versailles. Or else, go to Saint-Germain."

Mademoiselle de la Vallière sank onto a bench and dissolved into tears. "Alone? Without anyone to keep me company?"

The King caught the little dog which was annoying him and threw it into her lap. "Here's company quite good enough for you."

He walked past Angélique without making any sign of recognition. Then, on second thought, he asked her brusquely: "Did you go to Suresnes yesterday?"

"No, Sire," she said in the same tone.

"Where did you go?"

"To Saint-Germain Fair."

"What for?"

"To get some waffles."

The King's face flushed up to the very edge of his wig. He sailed into the adjacent room, while Bontemps quietly held the other door open for the ladies-in-waiting who were going for the blue gown.

Angélique went over to Mademoiselle de la Vallière, who was sobbing softly.

"Why do you let him torment you so? Why do you take

these humiliations? Madame de Montespan is playing
with you like a cat with a mouse, and the more docile
you are, the more relentless you make her."

The poor girl raised her streaming eyes to her. "You
have betrayed me too," she choked.

"I never swore fealty to you," Angélique replied sadly, "and I never pretended to be your friend. You are
mistaken, I did not betray you, and my honest advice is
leave the Court. Retire with dignity. Why be the laugh-
ingstock of these heartless people?"

For a moment her tear-stained face took on the holy
light of a martyr's. "My sin was done in public, Madame, and so it must please God to punish me in public."

"Bossuet would find you a good penitent. But do you
really think God demands such suffering? You'll lose your
health, your sanity."

"The King won't let me enter a convent. I have often
asked him to." She glanced at the door he had just
slammed so violently. "Perhaps he still loves me," she
mumbled. "Perhaps he will come back to me some day."

Angélique restrained herself from shrugging her
shoulders. A page had just come in and was bowing before her.

"Please be so good as to follow me, Madame. The King
is asking for you."

Between the King's bedroom and the Council Chamber lay the room in which his wigs were kept. It was not
often that a woman saw it. Louis XIV was choosing a
wig under the guidance of his hairdresser Binet and his
assistants. All around were glass cases storing the various wigs the King wore when going to Mass, or hunting, or receiving an embassy or going for a walk in the
park. Rows on rows of dummy plaster heads kept them in
shape or held them while they were being dressed.

Binet was suggesting that his august client wear the
wig called "the royal," which was dressed very high and
was so majestic that it seemed more fitting for a statue
than a living being.

"No," said the King. "Let us keep that for extremely
important occasions—the reception for the Persian ambassador, for instance."

He looked up at Angélique. She made a deep curtsy. "Come here, Madame. You were at Suresnes yesterday, weren't you?"

He had recovered his customary suavity, and his unctuously threatrical gestures, but he needed more than that to soothe Angélique's temper.

Binet withdrew with his apprentices to the far end of the room to search for the proper wig. He had acquired the tact of a true courtier.

"Give me some explanation for your insolence," the King said in a low voice. "I fail to recognize one of the most agreeable ladies of the Court."

"And I fail to recognize the most courteous monarch in the world."

"I love to see your anger make your eyes shine and your little nose twitch. I guess I was a little rude."

"You were . . . despicable. All you needed was the Queen to make you look just like a cock on a dunghill."

"Madame . . . ! You are addressing the King!"

"No, merely a man who toys with a woman's heart."

"What woman's?"

"Mademoiselle de la Vallière . . . Madame de Montespan . . . I myself . . . all women, as a matter of fact."

"That's a very subtle game you're accusing me of. How does anyone know a woman's heart? La Vallière has too much . . . Madame de Montespan hasn't enough . . . As for you . . . If I could only be sure I were toying with your heart . . . But it hasn't been reached yet."

Angélique hung her head. He had hit the mark. She waited for the final blow which would drive her from him forever.

"It's a naughty head that will not bend," said the King.

She raised her eyes. The sadness of his voice disconcerted her.

"Nothing has gone right today," he said. "I was greatly upset by Mademoiselle's despair when I told her I had decided I had to take the matter of her marriage under consideration again. She is fond of you, I think. Go and comfort her."

"What about Monsieur de Lauzun?"

"I don't know poor Péguilin's reactions yet. I suspect he is in the depths of despair. He was cruelly disappointed. But I know how to make it up to him. Did you see Baktiari Bey?"

"Yes, Sire," said Angélique.

"How are things going?"

"Very well, I think."

The door burst open to reveal Lauzun, his eyes popping and his wig askew.

"Sire," he blurted without any excuse for his interruption, "I come to ask Your Majesty what I have done to deserve such dishonor at your hands."

"Come, come, old man, calm down," said the King gently. He apparently felt his favorite's wrath was justifiable.

"No, Sire, no, I cannot bear such humiliation." Melodramatically he drew his sword and handed it to the King. "You have robbed me of my honor, now take my life too. Take it! I'm sick of living. I hate life!"

"Control yourself, sir."

"No, no, this is the end. Take it, I say. Kill me. Sire, kill me!"

"Péguilin, I know how disappointing all this is for you, but I will make it up to you. I will raise you so high that you will have no more regrets over the match I have forbidden."

"I do not want your gifts, Sire. I can accept nothing from a prince who has gone back on his word."

"Monsieur de Lauzun!" roared the King in a voice that vibrated like a swordblade.

Angélique let out a little scream of fright. Lauzun noticed her for the first time and turned his rage on her.

"So you're here, you little fool! How could you be so stupid! Where did you run off to yesterday to peddle your body after I had begged you to keep an eye on the movements of the Prince and his son?"

"That will do, sir," said the King icily. "Leave at once. I can excuse your state of mind, but I do not wish you at Court if you cannot be resigned to your lot."

"Resigned! Ha! Resigned! How you love that word, Sire! You want nothing but slaves about you. If by some whim or other you let them raise their heads an inch, it's only on condition they lower them again and prostrate themselves in the dust as soon as your mood changes. . . . I beseech Your Majesty to let me go. I shall always be glad to serve you, but I will never cringe . . ."

Lauzun stalked out without taking leave in any fashion.

The King looked at Angélique coldly.

"Shall I go, Sire?" she asked, feeling very uncomfortable.

He nodded.

". . . And don't forget to go to console Mademoiselle as soon as you return to Paris."

"I will, Sire."

The King walked over to his looking glass. "If this were August, Monsieur Binet, I would say the weather was stormy."

"Indeed, Sire."

"Unfortunately it is not August," sighed the King. "Have you made your choice, Monsieur Binet?"

"Yes, Sire, a most attractive wig. The two rows of curls along the center line add neither to its height nor to its width. I am calling it 'the ambassador.'"

"Perfect. You always think of just the right thing, Monsieur Binet."

"Madame du Plessis-Billière often complimented me for that too. Pray bend your head a little, Sire, so that I may set the wig in place."

"Ah, I remember, it was through Madame du Plessis that you came to me. She recommended you to me. I gather she had known you a long time?"

"Yes, quite a long time, Sire."

The King looked into the mirror framed in gilded bronze. "What do you think?"

"Sire, she is the only one worthy of Your Majesty."

"You don't understand. I was speaking of the wig."

"So was I, Sire," replied Binet, lowering his eyes.

When she entered the great salon Angélique asked whom they were waiting for. All the courtiers were in their best, but no one knew in whose honor.

"I bet it's the Russians," Madame de Choisy said to her.

"Are you sure it isn't the King of Poland? The King mentioned him a few moments ago to Madame de Montespan," said Angélique, happy to have information straight from the best source.

"It's an embassy in any case. The King has lifted the ban on all foreign noblemen. Look at that fellow with his barbarous mustache, the one staring at you. He makes my blood run cold!"

Angélique unconsciously turned her head in the direction Madame de Choisy had indicated, and recognized the Hungarian Prince Rakoczy, whom she had met at Saint-Mandé. At once he crossed the room to bow to her. He was dressed for the occasion in a wig and red heels, but he had exchanged his sword for a dagger whose chased hilt was set with blue stones and bound in gold.

"Ah, the archangel!" he said. "Madame, will you grant me a few moments of conversation?"

Angélique wondered whether he was going to ask her to marry him again, but since, in such a crowd, she had no fear that he might abduct her, she followed him obligingly into a bay window nearby. The blue stones in the hilt of his dagger reminded her vaguely of something.

"They are Persian turquoises," he explained.

"In Persian they're called 'Firouze.' "

"Do you know Persian? *Chouma pharzi harf mizanit?*"

Angélique made an indefinite gesture. "It's a very handsome dagger."

"It's all I have left of my former wealth," he said in a half embarrassed, half proud voice. "This and my horse Hospadar. Hospadar has always been my faithful companion. Thanks to him, I got across the frontier, but ever since I've been in France I've had to leave him in a stable in Versailles. The Parisians make fun of him every time they see him."

"Why is that?"

"When you see Hospadar you will understand."

"What did you wish to say to me, Prince?"

"Nothing. I just wanted to look at you a while, get you away from the crowd so that I could have you all to myself."

"That's quite an undertaking, Prince. Versailles has seldom been more full."

"Your smile makes dimples in your cheeks. You smile easily, I notice, even when there is hardly any reason for smiling. What are you doing here now?"

Angélique looked at him puzzled. His words always seemed to take an unexpected turn which disturbed her. Perhaps it was because, well as he knew French, he did not understand all its nuances.

"Why . . . I am a Maid of Honor at the Court. I must be here."

"What a stupid occupation!"

"It has its good sides, Monsieur Evangelist. What do you expect? Women don't have the necessary qualities for fomenting revolutions. They like to see and be seen, and it suits them to adorn the Court of a great king. I don't know of anything more diverting. Life at Versailles is never dull. There is something new every day. For instance, do you know whom we are expecting now?"

"No, I do not. One of the Swiss guards brought me word to the stable where I live with Hospadar that I should come to Court today. I hoped to have an interview with the King."

"Has he received you yet?"

"Several times. Your King is no despot, but a good friend. He will give me aid to liberate my fatherland."

Angélique was fanning herself as she looked around. The press was increasing every minute. Little Aliman, a half-breed she had bought for a page, was dripping with sweat as he held the heavy train of her emerald green dress embroidered in silver. She told him to let it drop for a while. She had been wrong to get so young a boy; now she would have to get another, older one, or else another of the same age to help Aliman carry her train. A jet black Negro and a light brown one, dressed either in different colors or the same, would be terribly amusing. She would be a *succès fou*.

Then she noticed that Rakoczy was still talking.

She cut him off. "That's all very well, but you still haven't told me whom we have been asked to honor in such numbers. Some say it's the Russian ambassador."

The Hungarian's face turned livid with hatred and his eyes became two black slits. "Russians, did you say? I shall never be able to bear being so close to them. They invaded my country."

"I thought it was the Emperor and the Turks you had it in for."

"Don't you know the Ukrainians have seized Budapest, our capital?"

Angélique humbly confessed that she did not know it and that she had not the faintest idea what Ukrainians were.

"You must think I am very silly," she said, "but I'd bet a hundred *pistoles* most Frenchmen don't know any more about it than I."

Rakoczy shook his head sadly. "Alas, how far removed these great Westerners are from our troubles, and yet we look to them for aid! Just knowing a language is not enough to break down the barriers between peoples. I speak French well, don't I?"

"Excellently," she agreed.

"And yet no one understands me here."

"I am sure the King will understand you. He knows everything that goes on in all the nations of the world."

"But he weighs them in the scale of his ambitions. Let us hope I shall not prove too light."

A movement of the crowd indicated that the important visitor was arriving. They left their alcove and moved toward the rest.

Angélique searched Rakoczy's face for the answer to the question she had asked him. He looked as if he had turned to stone.

"The Russians!" he said. Then he seized her wrist so hard she thought he would snap it, and leaning down to her said: "That man in the center is Dorochenko, the Hetman of the Ukraine, the first man to enter Budapest."

She felt him begin to quiver like a horse afraid. "The insult is . . . unpardonable," he said, ashy white.

"Prince, I beg you, don't make a scene. Don't forget that you are at the Court of France."

He did not seem to hear her, but fixed his eyes on the new arrivals as if they were thundering over the steppes instead of in the full light of Versailles. Suddenly he backed away and was swallowed up in the dense crowd of the French nobles.

Angélique breathed a sigh of relief. She had begun to worry lest some disturbance of his might spoil the fascinating scene. She did not want him to implicate himself and draw the King's wrath. The King had been unwise to let a revolutionary into his Court. Anything could be expected of a person like that.

Every three steps the Russian delegation bowed low in oriental salutations. The subservience of their bows contrasted sharply with their imperious looks. Angélique could not fail to see the power concealed in the limber spines of these wild beasts, tamed now, but ready to spring. They gave her gooseflesh. Rakoczy had infected her with some of his strange hysteria. She was afraid of an unknown something which would flash out like a thunderbolt and reduce Versailles to rubble.

Glancing at the King, she was relieved to see him unmoved and majestic as only he knew how to be. The "ambassador" wig that Binet had contrived was quite the equal in height to the Russians' bonnets.

Monsieur de Pomponne stepped forward. He had been Ambassador to Poland and hence knew Russian and could serve as interpreter. After the customary exchange of compliments the delegation presented the gifts they had brought from Russia: three bearskins—black, yellow and brown—from the Urals; white and blue sable skins from Siberia; a vast number of beaver pelts; an enormous blanket of black astrakhan made of over five hundred skins of newborn lambs found only in the herds that grazed on the shores of the Caspian Sea; curious tinfoil-wrapped bricks of red and green tea, tribute paid by the Emperor of China from the time of Ivan the Terrible to that of Alexis.

The Queen, for once sufficiently stimulated to make an intelligent comment, said she had heard about the tea and that it would cure more than twenty different ailments. She went into ecstasies over the precious stones, especially an emerald as big as a sugarloaf, and a blue six-faceted beryl from the Urals that took four men to carry it, since it was as high as a mounting-block.

The short-pile rugs from Bokhara and the long-pile ones from Khiva were unrolled, and the bolts of vivid red and yellow silk unfurled. There was also gossamer silk from Turkestan as well as heavy coverlets made of many-colored patchwork. One of the members of the delegation himself knelt before the King to offer him a huge nugget of gold from Lake Baikal, resting on a white satin cushion.

Everyone kept exclaiming in wonder. The women even dared touch the rugs and the silks, but it was the gigantic blue beryl that aroused the most admiration.

Then the Russians explained that having heard of the King's love of rare animals, they had brought him a pair of Punjab goats from whose hair were made the cashmere shawls of India.

The King thanked them warmly.

An extremely rare white Siberian tiger, they said, was waiting in the marble courtyard to salute its new master after its uncomfortable trip from the snow-covered steppes where it too reigned as a monarch. This announcement raised the excitement to fever pitch. The servants had to hurry and clear the gifts away to allow passage for the King and the ambassador and the whole Court to move out to the stairway.

Then it happened. A little shaggy-coated horse, as black as if it had leapt from the jaws of hell, dashed up the stairs to the very top. The rider rose in his stirrups and shouted something in a strange tongue, which he subsequently repeated in Russian and then in French.

"Long live Liberty!"

He raised his arm. A dagger whizzed through the air and stuck quivering in the floor at the feet of the Hetman of the Ukraine. Then the horseman wheeled and dashed down the marble stairway.

"On a horse! He rode up on a horse, and then down again . . . It couldn't have been a horse . . . Yes, it was,

what they call a pony . . . Impossible! A horse couldn't
gallop up a flight of stairs! . . ."

The French could see in it only an extraordinary feat
of horsemanship. But the Russians were gazing impene-
trably at the dagger. The King was speaking through
Pomponne in a level voice. His palace, he said, was open
to his people, for the people have a right to see their
king. He also welcomed foreigners to France. In spite of
the precautions of his police an unseemly incident like
this one sometimes happened—madmen, cranks whose
designs could not be guessed in advance, could perpetrate such inexplicable things. Thanks be to God, this
was not serious. The man would be pursued, brought
back and imprisoned. If he turned out to be insane, he
would be confined at Bicetre, and if he was sane, he
would, in all likelihood, he hanged. It meant nothing at
all, really.

The Russians remarked haughtily that the man had
spoken in Hungarian. They wanted to know his name.

"Thank God, they did not recognize him," thought
Angélique. She was shaking so her teeth chattered.
Everyone else thought the whole thing rather a joke,
but the dagger still stuck in the floor, and no one budged.
At last a little creature, all iridescent pink and green like
a tropical bird, swooped down on the dagger and disappeared with it. It was Aliman, who on a signal from Angélique had spirited the weapon away.

The procession moved on and descended into the
courtyard, where the royal tiger was pacing in a huge
cage mounted on a wagon drawn by four horses. The
sight of the magnificent beast banished all hostile
thoughts. It was taken in great pomp to the menagerie
at the end of the Royal Avenue near the Grove of the
Dome, an octagonal pavilion that fanned out into seven
courtyards, each one devoted to a different kind of animal. The Siberian tiger from then on would have as
neighbors a Numidian lion sent by the Sultan of Moroc-
co, and two Indian elephants. Pomponne acted as interpreter between the zoo-keepers and the slant-eyed
Siberian guards. For everyone's benefit he translated their
instructions as to the care and feeding of the new inhab-

itant of the menagerie, who proceeded to enter his new home with considerable good will.

On his return the King paid a visit to his gardens.

Madame de Sévigné wrote to her cousin, Bussy-Rabutin:

> I want you to share our fun! Today we had a great scandal in the Court of France. I saw it and I now understand how wars can break out in the antechambers of kings. With my own eyes I saw the firebrand himself. I was thrilled, and almost proud. Can you imagine a mounted horseman at Versailles? "That's not strange," you say. But this one dashed right into the great hall you know so well where the King was receiving the Russian embassy. Now, try to tell me there's nothing unusual about that! And what's stranger yet is that he galloped his horse. What do you think of that? That I'm dreaming? No, five hundred persons saw it as well as I.
>
> He hurled a dagger. No, I am not dreaming, and you don't need to worry about my sanity.
>
> The dagger stuck right at the feet of the ambassador, and no one knew what to do. It was then that I began to see the brand burst into flame. The foot that stamped it out is a tiny one. It belongs to Madame du Plessis-Bellière, whom you met at my house and who aroused just a tiny bit of passion in you. So, you see, this story should give you a double pleasure.
>
> She had the brilliant idea of signaling to her page, a little Negro so quick that he whisked the dagger off like a sleight-of-hand artist on the Pont-Neuf. Then everyone breathed a little easier. Peace returned with an olive branch in her hand, and we all moved on to see the wild beasts.
>
> Now, what do you make of this little story?
>
> Madame du Plessis is one of those women kings need to have about them. I think the King has known that for a long time. So much the worse for our victor, Canto.[1]
>
> . . . Still we can be sure she won't be dethroned without putting up a fight. And we can expect plenty of diversion at Versailles.

Angélique was not invited to Fontainebleau. But she did not forget that the King had advised her to go to

---

[1] The name Madame de Sévigné in her letters gave Madame de Monetspan.

comfort the Grande Mademoiselle, and so she returned
to Paris.

In her coach she drew out of the folds of her gown the
Hungarian prince's dagger and studied it with mixed
feelings of concern and satisfaction. She was glad she
had spirited it away. The "revolutionary" did not deserve to have it fall into other hands, for she was perhaps his only friend in the kingdom.

Noticing that the Gilandon girls sitting on either
side of her were looking at the dagger with as much
interest as their vegetable-like minds permitted, she
asked them if they knew what had become of the man on
the pony. The two girls actually came to life a little. Like
everyone else at Versailles, from the lowest scullion to
the High Chamberlain, they had been thrilled at being
present at a "diplomatic incident." No, they said, the
revolutionary had not been arrested. He had been seen
galloping off toward the forest after he descended the
staircase. The guards who had gone after him returned
empty-handed and stammering excuses.

"So he escaped them," Angélique thought. "Good!"

But she reproached herself for such a thought. For one
thing, such behavior deserved to be punished. But it had
been a splendid gesture just the same. She was secretly
proud of it. Louis XIV had wanted to play cat-and-mouse
to test the submissiveness of his slaves. Now he had to
cope with Prince Rakoczy and with Lauzun. Would
Lauzun be arrested? Where could Rakoczy run for
refuge? He would be recognized everywhere because of
his little wild horse like those the Huns had once ridden
right up to the gates of Paris.

"Wasn't it Saint Geneviève who kept the Huns from
entering Paris?" Angélique asked the Gilandon girls.

"Yes, Madame," they answered politely.

Nothing ever astonished them. This was one of their
assets. Their completely banal appearance and personality sheltered Angélique from the disagreeable intrigues of companions who were too bold or ambitious.
Their society hardly amused her, but Angélique did
not mind that. She was unlike most great ladies in that
she did not have to have someone to talk to every minute

of the day. To be alone with themselves was one of the greatest tortures imaginable for them, and to protect themselves from ever having to face such an odious eventuality they kept a companion just to read to them till they fell asleep or to keep them company in case they had insomnia.

Angélique took advantage of the Gilandon girls' natural aversion to conversation to do a little meditating.

The coach rumbled along through the forests of Meudon and Saint-Cloud. The cold, thick winter's night closed in around the torches so that one could not see beyond their misty haloes anything but the fog-enshrouded branches.

Where could Rakoczy be? Angélique leaned her head back against the velvet covering of the seat. When she was alone with herself like this, her nerves would throb right down to her fingertips. She thought of the green liqueur the crafty Baktiari Bey had given her to drink in an all too obvious attempt to thaw her. Surely it was an aphrodisiac.

The thought made Angélique realize she needed a lover or she would get sick. She had been silly to resist the handsome Persian's advances. What had made her do it? What lord and master was she keeping herself for? Who worried about her life? She had not realized how free she was . . .

The thought came to her more and more often in Paris, where the loneliness of her hôtel and her empty bedroom depressed her. She preferred to stay in Versailles and rush from the end of a ball to early Mass in the heart of the vast drowsy palace. Night to her was full of passion and romance. There one could be part of a whole, never left to one's own fate.

"To one's sad fate?" thought Angélique as she paced her room like the Siberian tiger in its cage.

Why hadn't she been invited to Fontainebleau? Was the King afraid of displeasing Madame de Montespan? What did the King want of her? What destiny was he pushing her toward with his sly, implacable hand? What sort of life were you created for, sister Angélique?

She halted in the middle of her room.

". . . The King!" she said aloud.

Her steward Roger came to ask what she would like for dinner. She looked at him a little wildly. She was not hungry. Marie-Anne de Gilandon came to offer her some herb tea. Angélique suddenly wanted to slap her, as if the suggestion was the peak of her mortification. Just to be contrary, she asked for a bottle of plum brandy. She tossed off two glasses one right after the other. Alcohol is a wonderful cure for the blues.

Rakoczy's dagger lay on the table. Angélique went to her mother-of-pearl inlaid ebony desk with its dozens of drawers and took out a casket which she opened to put the weapon into it.

Any prying servant who had wanted to know what treasure Madame du Plessis-Bellière kept so carefully hidden in that casket would have been completely astonished and disappointed at finding such heterogeneous, valueless articles. But they had a meaning all their own for her. They were like seashells washed up on the beach of her past by waves of a stormy sea. Many times she had wanted to get rid of them, but she could never bring herself to throw them away.

Angélique drank another glass of brandy. The blue stone on her finger shone with a soft luster beside those adorning the hilt of Rakoczy's dagger.

"I am under the sign of the turquoise," she thought.

Two swarthy faces rose before her eyes—that of the rich Persian prince and that of the poverty-ridden Hungarian.

She wanted to see Rakoczy again. What he had done revealed him to her in his true colors. His rashness was not absurd but inspiring. How was it that she had not been able to discern the quality of a hero in his words? Had she grown so used to hearing nothing but twaddle that she had lost the power to recognize a real man when she saw one?

Poor Rakoczy! Where could he be? She almost sobbed as she thought of him. She had another brandy. Now, perhaps, she could go to bed and sleep. How dreary it was to be alone!

If she went back to Suresnes with a "Yes" on her lips,

would she see the end of her torments? She dreamed of
finding forgetfulness in a sensual delirium. "I'm only a
woman after all. Why struggle against my fate?"

She shouted at her mirror. "I am beautiful!"

Then she grew sad at her reflection. "Poor Angélique
. . . why so, so alone?"

She drank another brandy. "And now that I'm quite
drunk, I guess I can get to sleep."

Then it occurred to her that if Mademoiselle was suffering from a sorrow like hers, she would not be able
to sleep either. Perhaps she would like to have a visit
from Angélique, even if it was the middle of the night.
Nights are so long when you're alone.

Angélique woke up her people. She ordered the coach
and set out through the dark streets for the Luxembourg
Palace.

She had guessed right. The Grande Mademoiselle was
not sleeping. Since the King's verdict she had taken to
her bed, taking nothing but broth and flooding her
pillow with tears. Her companions and a few loyal
friends tried to comfort her in vain.

"He should be there," she would scream, pointing to
the empty place beside her in the bed that Lauzun was
to have occupied. "He should be *there!* Oh, I'm going
to die, ladies, I'm going to die."

The sight of a similar despair was an easy pretext for
Angélique to give vent to the tears she had kept back
for two days now. She burst into sobs.

Mademoiselle de Montpensier was moved to see her
share her sorrow so, and clasped her to her bosom.

They stayed together that way till morning, talking
about Lauzun and the King's cruelty, holding each other's
hands and weeping like fountains.

chapter 21

*W*HEN Angélique finished explaining to Colbert that Baktiari Bey did not want to meet the King because he had not been received with enough pageantry, the minister raised his arms to the heavens.

"And all I do is scold the King for his expensive tastes and his extravagance!"

When he heard this, Louis XIV laughed heartily.

"You see, Colbert, old man, your lectures are sometimes unjustified. Spending money recklessly for Versailles is not such a bad investment as you seem to think. That way I make the palace so extraordinary that it arouses everyone's curiosity and makes us the envy of even the most distant nations. I have longed to see those nations in its halls, each dressed in the fashion of his own country, comparing all these splendors to their own, as they prepare to meet the great prince whose reputation has allured them. If I may tell you my thoughts, we ought to be humble so far as we ourselves are concerned, but at the same time proud and jealous of the position we occupy."

The day on which the Persian embassy arrived at the golden gates of Versailles, thousands of potted plants from the greenhouses had been set out along the terraces so that the wintry lawns looked like summery meadows. The floor of the great hall was completely covered with rose petals and orange blossoms.

Baktiari Bey's progress led him past silver-gilt vessels and masterpieces of the goldsmith's art displayed in his honor. He was taken on a tour of the entire palace, whose gold and crystal stood comparison with the pleasure domes of the Arabian Nights. The tour ended in the Baths, where a gigantic tub of purple marble designed for the King convinced the Persian that the French did not neglect their ablutions so much as he had been led to believe. The thousand-odd fountains in the park completely convinced him.

It was a day of triumph for Angélique. Everywhere and always she took precedence, for Baktiari Bey, perhaps with intentional mischief, neglected the Queen and the other ladies and addressed all his remarks to her.

The silk treaty was signed in a very friendly atmosphere.

Exhausted from all the excitement of the reception, Angélique returned to Paris. But when she arrived at her hôtel, a dirt-stained royal messenger was on the steps waiting for her.

"Thank heaven, I've caught up with you, Madame. The King sent me after you."

He handed Angélique a note which commanded her to return to Versailles with all speed.

"Can't I wait till tomorrow?"

"The King himself said 'with all speed,' and instructed me to escort you back, no matter what the hour."

"The Saint-Honoré gate will be closed."

"I have a passport that will get it opened."

"We'll be attacked by robbers."

"I am armed," the man said. "I have two pistols in my saddle holsters, and my sword."

It was a command from the King, and there was nothing for her to do but obey it. Angélique wrapped her cloak about her and set out once more.

When they arrived the palace rose out of the night like a blue monster against the pale pink and gray dawn sky. In the window of the King's conference chamber a torch glistened like a pearl in the sea-depths of the marble courtyard, still flooded with darkness. Angélique shivered as she followed the messenger through the empty hallways and past Swiss guards drowsing here and there at their posts.

But there were many people with the King: Colbert; de Lionne, drawn and haggard from sleeplessness; the King's confessor, Bossuet, whose eloquence pleased the King to the extent that he frequently asked his advice and wanted to add him to his Court; Louvois, his face as grim as if he had witnessed a catastrophe; the Chevalier de Lorraine, and a few extras whose faces reflected the atmosphere of controversy. They were all standing before His Majesty, and it looked as if they had been there in conference with him a good part of the night, for the candles were almost burnt out.

When Angélique was announced, they all stopped talking. The King asked her to sit. After what seemed like an endless silence, during which the King kept examining the letter in front of him to conceal his expression, he finally spoke:

"Our Persian ambassador has ended his visit in a strange way, Madame. Baktiari Bey has headed south, but he has sent me an urgent message concerning you and . . . Here, read it yourself."

The message which had doubtless been translated and painstakingly transcribed by the Armenian Agobian, thanked the King once more for his splendid entertainment and his kindness. Then there followed an exact enumeration acknowledging the gifts His Majesty, Louis XIV, the greatest monarch of the West, had sent the Shah of Persia via the ambassador:

- 1 silver-gilt service engraved with fleur-de-lis
- 2 gold clocks which told the date and the season
- 1 dozen pocket watches engraved with fleur-de-lis
- 2 large Gobelins tapestries
- 1 onyx die for a royal seal, engraved with the Persian emblem of a lion and a rising sun.
- 2 large portraits of the King and the Queen in their robes of state
- 20 lengths of fine linen
- 1 charcoal brazier made of gold-plated iron, with two bellows worked with an iron string
- 3 cases of silver cannonballs for warming the bath of the Shah of Shahs
- 6 cases of gewgaws, called "Temple jewels," for the Shah to give his servants or toss to the people
- 3 pots of geraniums to be replanted in Persian soil
- 1 saddle of Lyons leather with a silver halter

But His Majesty had omitted from all these gifts the precious turquoise His Excellency expected as a reward for faithfully discharging his mission. There followed a description of the turquoise, so detailed that anyone could see a woman was meant and that the woman was none other than Angélique.

Baktiari Bey thought the customs of the West would not permit him to leave before he had tested in turn the good will of the possessor of such a rare treasure. But now the treaties were signed to the satisfaction of all, and of the French King in particular, why was not the "charming Marquise," the "star of the Court of France," the "most intelligent woman in the world," the "lily of Versailles," among the last gifts Monsieur de Lorraine and the Marquis de Tercy had brought him as he was leaving? He had thought discretion might have led her to wait until nightfall to join him with all her baggage and vehicles, and so he had started out. But at the first halting place he suspected he had been tricked. Were they treating him like a donkey with a carrot held before its nose to get him across a rickety bridge? Was the sovereign of the West two-faced? Was his trickery as great as his greed? Would he consider the treaty just another game? Go back on his word? . . .

The long list of questions left no doubt about the mood that had motivated Baktiari Bey to write the letter, or of the likely possibility that he would discredit the French to his master and undo all the good that had been achieved.

"Well?" said Angélique.

"Yes, well indeed," the King mimicked. "Will you be so good as to tell me what shameless conduct you dared indulge in at Suresnes for such a disgraceful proposal to be made us?"

"My conduct, Sire, was that of a woman sent to a potentate to flatter him, not to say seduce him, so as to wheedle him into being favorably inclined to our points of view, and thus serve the King."

"Are you insinuating that I encouraged you to prostitute yourself to achieve results?"

"Your Majesty's intention was quite clear to me."

"How can you be so foolish? A woman of intelligence
and character like you has twenty different ways of
pacifying a prince, without acting like a whore . . . But
you had to become the mistress of this hot-tempered
barbarian, this infidel enemy of your Church. Did you?
Answer me!"

Angélique bit her lip to hide a smile, and cast her eyes
over the assemblage. "Sire, your question embarrasses me
before all these gentlemen. Permit me to say that this is
a subject for the ears of my confessor alone."

The King half rose, his eyes flashing. Bossuet intervened, rising to his full Burgundian height and raising
his Bishop's hand authoritatively.

"Sire, allow me to remind you that only a priest has the
right to know the secrets of a person's soul."

"So has the King, Monsieur Bossuet, when the actions
of his subjects involve his government. Baktiari Bey has
provoked my displeasure by his effrontery, but it must
be admitted that when a man, Persian or not, is led
on . . ."

"He was not, Sire," said Angélique firmly.

"I am glad to hear it," said the King. He sat down
with obvious relief.

Bossuet emphatically declared that whatever might
have happened in the past, it was the present that was
important. The question amounted to this: how to soothe
the temper of Baktiari Bey without granting his demands?

Everyone began to offer his own opinion. Tercy
thought the ambassador should be arrested and thrown
into prison, and the Shah of Persia informed that his
his envoy had died in France of a quartan fever. Colbert
almost grabbed him by the throat. Soldiers like him had
no notion whatever of the importance of trade in the
economy of a nation! Like Tercy, Lionne thought there
was no need of getting uneasy about those distant Mohammedans. But Bossuet and the Jesuit combined their
eloquence to demonstrate that the future of the Church
in the Orient depended on the success of the embassy.
Finally Angélique suggested there was only one way to
tell Baktiari Bey his request was refused without his

taking it as a personal insult, and that was for the King
to write he was extremely sorry he could not grant his
dear and noble friend's request, but Madame du Plessis
was a *"sultana-bachi,"* and therefore the ambassador
would surely understand how impossible it was for his
desires to be fulfilled.

"What does *'sultana-bachi'* mean?"

"The favorite wife of the sultan, Sire, chosen by him
above all others, to whom he entrusts the direction of his
harem and whom he frequently asks to share his responsibilities as a ruler."

"If that is what the title means, don't you think Baktiari Bey would be correct in calling my attention to
the fact that in the West the Queen represents the
sultana—what d'ye call it—*bachi?*"

"Your Majesty's objection is well taken, but you
may rest easy. Often in the Orient a prince finds it
obligatory, for dynastic reasons, to marry a princess of
royal blood whom he himself has not chosen. This does
not prevent him from raising another to the rank of
favorite, and it is she who has the power."

"Strange custom," said the King. "But since you tell
me there is no other way . . ."

All that was left was to compose the letter. Colbert
wanted to do this himself. He read it aloud:

". . . Ask me for any other woman of my kingdom, and
she shall be yours," he ended. "The youngest, the loveliest, the fairest—you have merely to choose."

"Easy now, Monsieur Colbert," said the King, "or you
will get me involved in an unsavory business."

"Sire, Your Majesty should understand that you cannot
flatly refuse him without offering him some compensation for what he has lost to his great disappointment."

"My word, I never thought of that. I guess you are
right."

Everyone was glad to see the King come out of the
conference with a happy expression on his face. For the
greater part of the day the Court had been expecting a
political explosion, at the very least a declaration of
war. To satisfy their curiosity, the King told with great
humor about the final demands of the Persian am-

bassador. But he did not mention the name of Angélique, only said the Oriental prince had been so taken
with the beauty of the French women that he wanted a
real flesh and blood memento of them.

". . . More flesh than blood," Brienne added, laughing
at his own joke.

"The difficulty was in choosing such a souvenir," the
King went on to say. "I thought I would entrust the
selection to Monsieur de Lauzun, he is such an expert in
such matters."

Péguilin waves his hands gracefully. "An easy assignment, Sire. Our Court is full of pleasing whores
. . ." He chucked Madame de Montespan under the chin.
"Why wouldn't this one do? She has already proved how
well she can please a prince."

"Fresh!" fumed the Marquise, slapping his hand away.

"Then how about that one," Péguilin went on, pointing to the Princess of Monaco, who had been one of his
own mistresses. "She seems likely to me. Perhaps this
will prove to be the only chance she hasn't taken. From
a pageboy on up . . . even women."

The King interrupted him. "Watch your language,
sir."

"Why, Sire, when no one watches his conduct?"

"It looks to me as if Péguilin were getting ready for
another little visit to the Bastille," Madame de Choisy
whispered to Angélique. "But he did make a good answer. What is all this scandal about the Persian ambassador? It looks as if you were mixed up in it."

"I'll tell you bit by bit at Saint-Germain," Angélique
said, deliberately omitting to tell the Duchess that she
was returning straight to Paris.

With a great din of cracking whips and grinding of
axles and whinnying, the coaches got into line. For a
few days now Versailles' gilded gates would be shut as
well as its tall windows which now were reflecting a
sunset as crimson as the evening before.

As he passed, Lionne stuck his head out of the window of his coach. "You can brag about making me the
goat in this damfool business. The King has assigned
me the task of finding the . . . compensation for the

Persian ambassador. What will my wife say? Well, I saw a little actress in Molière's company, intelligent and quite ambitious. I don't think it will be hard to persuade her."

"All's well that ends well," said Angélique with a wan smile.

She was having a terrible time keeping her eyes open, for she had been running to and fro for exactly twenty-four hours without stopping. The very thought of getting back into her coach and traveling over the road from Versailles to Paris again turned her stomach.

Her coachman was waiting for her in the courtyard, his hat in his hand. With great dignity he informed Madame la Marquise that this was the last time he would have the honor of driving her. He had always done his job well, but God was not pleased with sheer stupidity, and he was getting old. He ended by saying that to his great regret he must leave the service of Madame la Marquise.

chapter 22

*T*HE beggars were waiting in the back room of the
kitchen. As she tried a white apron around her waist,
Angélique reminded herself that she had too long neglected her duty as a noblewoman, such as giving alms
with her own hands once a week. With her crazy zig-
zagging between Paris and the Court with its continual
fêtes, her visits to the Hôtel de Beautreillis had become infrequent. Now she needed some opportunity to
check her accounts.

Roger ran the establishment well. Barbe was there to
take care of Charles-Henri. The Abbé de Lesdiguières
and Malbrant were there for Florimond whom they followed to Court. But her own business affairs and those
of the Plessis-Bellière family were getting into a terrible
mess.

She went to visit David Chaillou, who kept a tight rein
on the chocolate shops of the city and managed them very
well. She also went to see the men responsible for her
imports from the "isles."

When she returned she found the maids and the
Gilandon girls preparing gifts for the poor, for this was
the day for almsgiving at the Hôtel de Beautreillis. It
would last into the evening. Angélique herself carried
the baskets of round loaves, and Anne-Marie Gilandon
followed her with a basket of bandages and medicines.
The winter day shed its gray light on the faces of the
poor, some sitting on benches or stools, others standing
along the wall. They had already drunk a big bowl of
soup.

First she distributed the bread. To the mothers she
recognized she added a little ham or a sausage which
would last their families several days. There were some
new faces. Possibly some of the old-timers had got tired

of coming since they had not seen her for so long. Even
beggars have feelings.

She got down on her knees to wash the feet of a woman
with an ulcerated leg who was holding a fretful child on
her lap. The woman's face was hard and grim, and her
lips were set in a manner Angélique seemed to recall.

"Did you want to ask me something?"

The woman hesitated. A dog many beatings have
taught to cringe can sometimes look defiant. She held
out the child stiffly. Angélique examined it. It had
fresh sores at the base of its neck, two of which were
suppurating.

"This must be taken care of."

The woman shook her head emphatically. An old
cripple named Stale Bread came to her assistance.

"She wants the King to touch it. You know the King.
Tell her how to go about it."

With her fingertip Angélique dreamily stroked the
child's forehead. It had a funny little nose and the eyes
of a frightened squirrel. Have the King touch it? Why
not? Since Clovis, the first Christian king of the Franks,
this gift of healing scrofula had been handed down
to his successors. God had transmitted to them this
power with the holy chrism that the miraculous dove
had brought from heaven in a glass phial on the day of
the first coronation. The legend was that when Leonicet,
a squire of Clovis, caught scrofula, Clovis saw in a vision
an angel who told him to touch his servant's neck.
When he did so, he experienced the joy of healing
his faithful servant Leonicet. Ever since then the Kings
of France, as heirs of this remarkable gift, had been
besieged by poor folk covered with sores. No sovereign
had ever neglected this duty, Louis XIV less than some.
Almost every Sunday, at Versailles or Saint-Germain, or
every time he came to Paris, he received the sick. In one
year he touched more than fifteen hundred, and was said
to have worked many cures.

Angélique said she thought one had to speak to the
King's doctor, as it was he and his assistants who ex-
amined the sick before they were presented to the King.
A cart would take them to Versailles, where the ceremony

was held most often. She advised the woman to come to see her the following week. In the meantime she would speak to Vallet, the King's doctor, who was present at His Majesty's evening meal every day.

The beggars who had been listening to the conversation, implored her in turn. "Lady, we want to be touched by the King too. Lady, intercede for us."

She promised them she would do her best. Meanwhile she dressed the child's sores with compresses of a green liquid that her own doctor had recommended.

Old Stale Bread was a regular. For years he had been coming to the Hôtel de Beautreillis for Angélique to dress his ulcers and wash his feet. He saw no use in it all, but he let her do it because she insisted. Mumbling in his tangled gray beard about his pilgrimages, for he did not wish to be thought a vulgar beggar, he would tell her about all the trips he had made to holy shrines and show her the cockleshells in his hat and the rosaries he had brought back, and the bell at the end of his pilgrim's staff.

These trips had not taken him much out of the Ile-de-France, but he knew every one of the castles in it, even the smallest, in which as an experienced beggar he knew how to get a handout. Since the King did not like living in Paris, the great nobles were building everywhere, wishing to emulate their master in constructing lavish residences, laying out parks, cutting avenues through the forests, planting orange groves and installing hundreds of fountains. That was all to the good for Stale Bread. Limping, whining, begging, like Saint Roch with his starveling yellow dog always trailing along, he wandered up and down the roads and took advantage of the ceaseless traffic of wagons and carts bringing construction materials to get a lift.

Stale Bread judged the great by their kitchens. It was a point of view as valid as any other, and Angélique liked to hear him run on.

"What story have you for me today, Stale Bread?"

"This morning," the old cripple said, "I was coming back from Versailles on foot. A little walking is good for anyone. Suddenly my mutt started barking, and a robber

came out of the woods. I needed just one look at him to
say to myself, 'That's a bandit.' But do you think I was
scared? Not a bit! He came up to me and he said: 'You've
got bread to eat. Give me a piece and I'll give you some
gold.' 'Show it to me first,' I said. He took out two gold
pieces. I gave him all my bread for it. Then he asked me
the way to Paris. 'It just happens I'm going there too.'
A wine-seller was going by with empty barrels in his cart,
and he was glad to take us both along. We got to talking
on the ride, and I told him I knew everyone in Paris,
especially the nobility and all the great establishments.
'I would like to go to Madame du Plessis-Bellière's,' he
said. 'It just happens I'm going there too.' 'She is my only
friend,' he said."

Angélique stopped in the middle of her bandaging.
"You're making this up, Stale Bread. I don't have any
friends among the robbers of the forest."

"I'm just telling you what he said. If you don't believe
me, ask him. He's here."

"Where?"

"Over there in the corner. He's a little scared, I guess.
He doesn't seem to want anyone to look him square in
the face."

The person he pointed out did indeed seem to be
hiding. He was leaning his face against a post. Angélique had not noticed him when she was handing out
bread. His lean body was wrapped in a tattered cloak
the edge of which he had drawn over the lower part of
his face. His appearance did not inspire her with confidence. She got up and went straight over to him. Then
she suddenly recognized him in a burst of fear and joy.
It was Rakoczy.

"You!" she exclaimed.

She seized him by the shoulders and felt the thinness
of his body through the cloak. "Where did you come
from?"

"That old fellow told you, from the woods."

His dark eyes were sunken, but they still burned with
their old fire, and his lips were pale against the tangle
of his beard. She realized that more than a month had
gone by since the Russian delegation had visited Ver-

sailles. Heavens, it was not possible! In the dead of
winter!

"Don't stir," she said. "I am going to take care of you."

As soon as the visit of the poor came to an end, she
took the Hungarian prince into a comfortable room next
to the Florentine bath. Rakoczy tried to make a joke of
it all. He straightened up, draping his rags about him
with a devil-may-care attitude, and inquired after her
health as if he had just met her in the King's antechamber. But as soon as he had bathed and shaved, he
sank on to the bed and fell into a deep sleep.

Angélique summoned her steward. "Roger," she said,
"the man I have just been with is our guest. I can't
tell you his name, but understand that we owe him a
secure place of refuge."

"Madame may count on my secrecy."

"Yours, yes, but the staff is large. Roger, I want you
to make all my people understand—from the little stableboy Jeannot up to your bookkeeper—that they are to
make no more of this man than if he were invisible.
They have never seen him. He does not exist!"

"I understand, Madame."

"You are also to tell them that if he goes out of here
safe and sound, I will give them all a reward. But if
anything happens to him under my roof . . ." Angélique clenched her fists and her eyes were flashing. ". . .
I swear I will dismiss you all. Everyone, from the lowest
to the highest, do you understand? Is that clear?"

Roger bowed. His long service with Madame du Plessis had taught him that she always meant what she said.
His own opinion was that a good servant who knew his
place should be blind, deaf, and, if possible, dumb, and
he tried to inculcate the servants he was responsible for
with the same ideal. He said he would pledge their
silence and that none of them would let the glory of
idle gossip outweigh the advantages of serving Madame.

She felt reassured on this point. But to shelter Rakoczy
was something else again. To help him escape and get
across the frontier was still another. She did not know
what orders Louis XIV might have issued concerning the

revolutionary. She sketched several plans, estimating the money and the friends she could rely on to make this difficult undertaking turn out well. She was still deep in her plans when the little clock in her room chimed the hour of eleven.

As she rose to prepare for bed she almost screamed. Rakoczy was standing in the door to her room. Angélique recovered herself.

"How do you feel?"

"Wonderful."

The Hungarian stretched his long thin body which hardly filled the clothes that plump Roger had loaned him. "I feel better for just getting rid of my beard. I kept thinking I was turning into a Russian."

"Shh," she said, laughing. "People don't talk about ropes in the house of a man who's been hanged."

Suddenly she shivered, remembering how once she had tried to rescue the Gutter Poet. She had not succeeded; the King's police had been stronger than she. The Gutter Poet had been hanged in the Place de Grève. But now she had other means at her disposal. She was rich and influential. She would succeed this time.

"Are you still hungry?"

"I'll always be hungry," he sighed, patting his hollow stomach. "I think I'll be hungry right up till my last gasp."

She took him into the next room where she had had a table set with him in mind. Gold candlesticks were lit at either end. On a golden platter lay a huge roast turkey stuffed with chestnuts and garnished with baked apples. Beside it were covered dishes of hot and cold vegetables, an eel stew, salads, and a golden bowl full of fruit. To honor the poor fellow after his sojourn in the forest, Angélique had had the table laid with some of her gold service, of which she was very proud. Besides the platter, the candlesticks and the bowl, she had set out two priceless antique goblets and ewers.

Rakoczy uttered a wild cry of delight, meant more for the golden skin of the turkey than for the goblets and plates. He dashed to the table and began to wolf down the food. It was not till he had torn off and devoured the two wings and a drumstick that he motioned Angélique peremptorily to sit down opposite him.

"You eat too," he said with his mouth full.

She laughed at him sympathetically, and filled his goblet with burgundy. Then she poured herself some and sat down as he had directed. There was no question of her getting even a morsel of turkey; the signs pointed to Rakoczy's eating it all. His sharp white teeth sank into the tender meat with obvious pleasure, and cracked the bones easily. Rakoczy wiped his hands, took a drink, uncovered the dishes and heaped his plate, gobbled that up, and after another goblet of wine, returned to the carcase of the turkey. His sparkling black eyes rose toward Angélique.

"You are beautiful," he said between mouthfuls. "All the time I was roaming the forest I could see you in front of me—a vision of light and comfort . . . the most beautiful woman . . . the tenderest . . ."

"Were you hiding in the forest all this time?"

The prince began to feel full. He licked his fingers and stroked his long mustache which he arranged to droop over the corners of his mouth. It might have been due to the candlelight, but his skin seemed to have yellowed, making him seem more of an Asiatic than ever, what with his slanting eyes. But their dancing, mocking glints robbed them of Oriental mystery. He tossed back his long glossy black hair, curled like a gypsy's.

"Yes. Where else could I go? The forest was the only refuge open to me around Versailles. I had the luck to find a marsh which led to a pond where I splashed around for a long time, and that made the hounds on my trail lose my scent. I could hear them baying and the shouts of the lackeys. . . . To be a quarry is not very pleasant. But I had Hospadar, my pony. He didn't want to get out of the water, even though icicles were forming on his mane, for he knew we would be lost if we did. Toward evening we could tell that our followers had given up and gone home."

Angélique filled his glass. "But how did you exist? Where did you take shelter?"

"I happened on an abandoned woodcutter's hut. I lit

a fire. After staying there a couple of days I started
wandering again. Just as we were about to collapse I
glimpsed a little hamlet in a clearing. That night I crept
into it and stole a lamb that kept me in food for quite
a while. Hospadar ate moss and berries. He is a horse
from the tundras. At night I would go into the hamlet
and steal more food, and in the daytime I burrowed
under a lean-to I built with the knife I always carry
under my clothes. The people in the hamlet weren't
disturbed by the smoke they sometimes saw, and they
blamed the wolves for the stolen animals. The wolves?
Some came prowling around our shelter, but I drove
them off with flaming brands. One day I decided to go
farther southward and try to get out of the forest into
some region where no one had heard of us. But . . .
how can I explain it . . . the forest is a harsh reality for
a man from the steppes. There was no wind, no odor
to guide me, only the snow and the fog that shrouded
every dawn and every twilight. The forest is a closed
world, like a dream palace. . . . One day I came to a hill
from which I could see the forest stretching all around
me like the sea. Nothing but trees or the vast empty
spaces where the swamps were. . . . It was like a desert
. . . and in the center was an island all white and red
. . . made by the hand of man. I saw I had come back
to where I started from. It was Versailles!"

He stopped and his head drooped. For the first time he
seemed crushed by his failure.

"We stayed for a while looking at it while the wind
whipped at us. Then I knew that I could never escape
the man who had built all that—Versailles. A lawn of
many colors stretched from the base of the palace and
I could see flowers of red and purple and blue and yellow
on the outskirts of the wintry woods."

"They *were* flowers," said Angélique. "It was the reception for the Persian ambassador."

"I thought it must be a mirage brought on by hunger.
I was beaten, utterly discouraged, for I saw then what
I had long suspected, that your king is the greatest in
the world."

"But you dared defy him right to his face. What a

mad thing to do! What an insult! Your dagger at the very feet of the King, before the whole Court of Versailles!"

Rakoczy leaned across the table with a smile. "An insult for an insult. Didn't you like my gesture just a little?"

"Perhaps. But see where it led you. Your cause itself will suffer."

"That is true. Alas, our Oriental ancestors bequeathed us their drive but none of their prudence. When it is easier to die than to submit, then is the time for bold gestures and great deeds. I have not finished my combat in the arena against the tyranny of kings. Then I suddenly thought of you." He shook his head tenderly. "Only a woman can be trusted. Men have often surrendered those who have asked their protection. Women, never. I got the idea of coming to you, and so here I am. I would like to take refuge in Holland, which is also a republic that paid dearly for its freedom. It welcomes political refugees."

"What did you do with Hospadar?"

"I could not come out of the forest with him. He would betray me. Everyone used to point at the little Hun horse. I couldn't leave him in the forest to the wolves. . . . I cut his throat with my knife."

"No!" Angélique exclaimed, her eyes filling with tears.

Rakoczy drained the golden goblet in front of him, set it down, and stepped slowly over to her. Half-sitting on the table he leaned down and looked at her closely.

"In my homeland," he said solemnly, "I have seen soldiers toss children into the flames right before their mothers' eyes. I have seen them strung up on tree branches by their feet, while their mothers stood below watching their agony and hearing their screams for the rest of their lives. That was in the repression under the King of Hungary assisted by the Emperor of Germany. That's why I seized a torch and lit fires of my own. What is the death of a faithful horse in comparison with that? Don't waste your sympathy. I told you I had no more than my horse and my dagger. That is no longer true. Now I have nothing."

Angélique shook her head. She could not speak. Jumping up, she went to her writing desk, took out the casket containing his dagger studded with turquoises and gave it to him. His face lit up.

"So it fell into your hands! Ah, God was good to send you to me as a guiding star in this land. Here is a token of triumph. Why are you weeping, my beautiful angel?"

"I don't know. It all seems so cruel and inevitable."

Through her tears his face seemed like that of a sacrificial victim. Then she saw his hand close around the dagger. He had found a weapon he had learned to use, and that he would use again. He slipped it into his belt.

"Nothing is inevitable in this world," he said, "except the struggle of a man to live in peace with his soul."

He stretched himself, spreading his legs and extending his arms with deep satisfaction. After his incredible physical hardships he needed only a few hours' rest to recover the strength and agility of a wild beast waiting to spring.

She thought he reminded her of someone, less in his face than in his lanky figure which seemed to have steel springs.

"For the moment my soul is in retreat," Rakoczy said, grinning like a wolf. "I am aware only of the needs of my body."

"Are you still hungry?"

"Yes . . . for you."

He made his bright, penetrating eyes sink into hers.

"So you have demonstrated," she said, smiling.

"My words are as real as my deeds. The love I bear you is rooted deep within me—in my arms, my legs, my whole body. If I touched you I would warm you."

"But I am not cold."

"Yes, you are. Very cold. I can sense how lonely and cold your heart is, and I could hear your sobs from faraway. Come to me."

He embraced her without violence but with a strength that left her weak. His lips roved from her throat to the tender spot behind her ear. It was impossible for her to resist him. Their hair entwined. She felt his mustache tickling her bosom as he kissed her breasts, bending over them as if he were sucking a cool draught from a woodland spring. An almost painful feeling surged through her, constricting her throat and making her hands tremble. Each passing moment welded her tighter to his hard frame. When he let her go, she staggered dizzily, as if she had no gravity. His eyes spoke his demand.

Angélique left the room and went to her own chamber. She began to rip off her clothes, tearing frenziedly at her stiff stays, letting her heavy skirts fall around her feet. She felt her body quivering warmly under her lace chemise. Kneeling on her bed, she undid her hair. A bright, primitive passion flooded her undimmed by any consideration. He had lost everything. She would not mince matters with him. She let her hair stream down her bare back, relishing its delicious touch, ran her fingers through it, spread it out as her head tilted back and her eyes closed.

From the doorway Rakoczy was watching her.

The amber light of an oil vigil lamp in the niche at the head of her bed lit on the curves of her well-fleshed thighs. He could see them quivering. It revived the glints of her lovely auburn hair that fell like a cloak of water over her sleek shoulders and on to her upturned breasts. Her necklace of pearls was still about her neck.

She watched him come toward her with half-closed eyes. Suddenly she knew who it was he reminded her of —her first husband, the Comte de Peyrac who had been burned alive in the Place de Grève. He was just a little shorter and did not limp.

She stretched forth her arms to him, calling him to her with a sigh. He leaped forward and took her once more into his arms. Resistless, yielding, she surrendered completely to his soft caresses. Exquisite, untrammeled pleasure swept over her.

"How good a man is!" she thought.

For three nights she slept snuggled close to his long male body. The bed was warm, the curtains pulled close. She would revel in the newly rediscovered delight of having someone beside her and cling to him until sleep overcame her. Then when her sleep grew lighter, toward morning she would grope for his hand and stroke his soft hair. If he were no longer there, she quailed at the thought of being once more alone. She never asked herself why she loved him. What did it matter?

He would be wide awake at once, like a man used to being on the alert. Then his face would startle her for a moment, as if she were a woman of a conquered town awaking in the invader's bed. But he would put his arms around her and she would yield her nakedness to him as he caressed her tightening breasts. He had been surprised that anyone so beautiful and reserved as she could live alone so long. Now he discovered that she could fondle him passionately, that her capacity for love was inexhaustible, that she begged for love and accepted it with a sort of fascinating shyness.

"I am always learning something new about you," he murmured into her ear. "I thought you were too strong, too cold, too intelligent to be so physical. But you have everything. Come with me, be my wife."

"I have two children."

"We will take them with us. We will make them into horsemen of the steppes, true heroes."

Angélique tried to imagine her cherubic Charles-Henri as a martyr to the cause of Hungary. She laughed, tossing her hair carelessly over her silky shoulders. Rakoczy clasped her to him voraciously.

"How beautiful you are! I cannot live without you. When I am away from you my strength drains from me as from a wound. You cannot leave me now." Then suddenly, listening, his face darkened.

He sat up. "Who is there?"

He ripped back the curtains of the bed. At the far end of the room a door was opening, revealing Péguilin de Lauzun on the threshold. Behind him billowed the great white plumes of the King's musketeers.

The Marquis advanced. He saluted Rakoczy with his sword.

"Prince," he said with all courtesy, "in the name of the King, I arrest you."

After a moment of silence, the Hungarian got out of bed without embarrassment and bowed to him.

"My cloak is on the back of that chair," he said calmly. "Will you be so good as to hand it to me. As soon as I am dressed, I will go with you, sir."

Angélique wondered whether she could be dreaming. This was the very thing that had haunted her dreams for three nights. She was so astounded she never thought of the shameless disarray she presented.

Lauzun ogled her facetiously, and blew her a kiss. Then, resuming his formality, he said: "Madame, in the name of the King I arrest you."

There was a knock on the door of her cell and someone tiptoed in. Angélique was frowning over her worm-eaten embroidery frame and did not look up; it would be just another of the nuns bringing her some weak broth in that humble way they had of keeping their eyes lowered and their gestures servile. She rubbed her hands together to get the stiffness out of them caused by the dampness of the room, took up her embroidery needle again, and concentrated on her work.

A burst of laughter close to her ear made her jump. The young nun who had just come in was indulging herself to her heart's content.

"Marie-Agnès!" Angélique exclaimed.

"Oh, my poor Angélique. If you only knew how funny you look as a prisoner condemned to do embroidery!"

"I like embroidering . . . but in other surroundings, naturally. How do you happen to be here, Marie-Agnès? Who let you in?"

"I did not have to be let in. I live here. You are in my very own convent."

"Is this the Carmelites of Mont Sainte-Geneviève?"

"It is indeed. Bless the luck that brought us together. I didn't know until this morning the name of the great lady we had been ordered to be jailors for, and then the Mother Superior immediately gave me permission to visit you. Of course, I'll do anything I can to help you."

"I don't know what you can do for me, I'm sorry to say," Angélique said ruefully. "The three days I've been here I've noticed that the strictest kind of orders must have been given about me. The nuns who bring me food are as deaf-and-dumb as the little half-wit who sweeps up the room. I asked to see the Mother Superior, and I am still waiting for her to come."

"It's not easy for us to comply with His Majesty's explicit orders when he sends us a mangy sheep we want to keep from the rest of the flock."

"Thank you for the compliment."

"It's the way we describe you among ourselves. We are sheep without a blemish." Her green eyes, so like her sister's, sparkled in her pale face which was thin and drawn from fasting. "You are here to do penance for your many great sins against morality."

"Sheer hypocrisy! If I'm here for being immoral, then it's high time all the ladies of the Court were put under lock and key."

"But you were denounced by the Brotherhood of the Holy Sacrament."

Angélique stared at her sister.

"Don't you know," Marie-Agnès continued, "that good Brotherhood wants to abolish licentiousness everywhere. They give the King information about the private life of his subjects. They have spies everywhere, and hardly let people—how shall I say it?—sleep in peace."

"Are you trying to tell me I have servants in my house paid by the Brotherhood of the Holy Sacrament to inform them about my private life?"

"That's right. You are no better off in that respect than all the other people in the Court and in the city too."

Brooding, Angélique took a few stitches with the red wool she was using.

"So that's how the King knew I was hiding Rakoczy. Marie-Agnès, can you tell me who took it upon himself to betray me to the King?"

"Possibly I can. We have all sorts of noble names among our sisters and they know loads of secrets."

She came back the following day with a smug smile pregnant with promises of information.

"Well, I found out. In all likelihood you have Madame de Choisy to thank for snatching you out of the clutches of the devil."

"Madame de Choisy!"

"That's the one. For a long time she has been worried about the state of your soul. Search your memory. Who was so eager to recommend a companion or a lackey to you?"

"Good Lord!" Angélique groaned. "Not one, but half a dozen. The whole household of my children is made up of Madame de Choisy's protégés."

Marie-Agnès laughed till she was out of breath. "How naive you are, my poor Angélique! I always thought you were much too pure in heart to be at Court."

"How was I to know anyone was so interested in saving my soul?"

"They are interested in everything. That's the test of human devotion. God needs uncompromising soldiers, and that's the secret of the Brotherhood. They'll stop at nothing to save a soul. The purity of their motives justifies what to less complicated minds would appear downright treachery."

"Don't tell me you're on their side," Angélique flared, "or I shall never speak to you again so long as I live."

The nun smiled smugly again, then lowered her eyes and grew serious. "God alone can judge," she said.

She promised again that she would do everything she could to keep her sister informed of what fate awaited her. It was not impossible for her to intervene in her behalf. Everything was in the hands of the Brotherhood of the Holy Sacrament, but the Mother Superior of the Carmelites had considerable influence over certain members of that committee of pious laymen.

"Don't forget there's a bit of politics involved in this," Angélique reminded her. "Rakoczy was a foreign revolutionary and . . ."

"That doesn't make a bit of difference. In the eyes of those fanatics a lover is a lover. Whoever he is doesn't matter . . . unless he is the King, of course. Perhaps he is the one who will rescue you in the end."

As she went out, her black veil floated behind her provocatively. Days passed. Then Angélique had an un-expected visit from Solignac. He revived painful mem-ories, but since from the very first he spoke of the King's clemency so far as she was concerned, and gave her some hope of being set at liberty, she listened to him with patience. He talked for a long time. She had to undergo a regular sermon on the temptations of the flesh which seemed to her quite out of proportion to the three un-lucky nights she had spend in Rakoczy's arms. What had happened to him? She hadn't let herself think much about his fate in order not to lose courage herself.

"Do you come to me in the name of the King?" she asked when he had finally ended his discourse.

"Of course, Madame. His Majesty's decision alone could make me take such a step. In our opinion you need a longer time to meditate on . . .'"

"And what does His Majesty intend to do about me?"

"You are at liberty," Solignac said, pursing his lips. "That is—and let us understand each other—you are free to leave this convent and go back to your Hôtel de Beautreillis. But under no circumstances may you return to Court without having been previously invited."

"Have I lost all my posts?"

"That's another matter. I scarcely need add that the life you lead while awaiting such an invitation must be exemplary. You must conduct yourself in a manner be-yond criticism."

"By whom?" said Angélique trenchantly.

Solignac did not deign to answer her. He arose pa-tronizingly. Angélique threaded a needle and resumed her embroidery.

"Well, Madame," Solignac said in surprise, "didn't you hear what I just told you?"

"What was that, sir?"

"That you are free."

"Thank you, sir."

"I am prepared to escort you to the door of your home."

"Thank you very much, sir. But what need is there for me to hurry? I am not unhappy here, and I shall enter into my freedom when I wish and as I wish. Please thank His Majesty for me. I am most grateful to you. Bless you!"

Quite out of countenance by her suave protestations, Solignac bowed and took his leave.

Angélique took with her only those things she could carry. She could send for the rest the next day. She had not been able to bring much with her when she was arrested. She wanted to return on foot to convince herself that she was actually free again. Fortunately, the bad joke had not lasted long, but she didn't want to have it repeated too often. To live in the shadow of committing a false move that might mean spending the rest of her days behind bars, did not appeal to her.

"Why is the Brotherhood of the Holy Sacrament so relentless toward me?" she asked Marie-Agnès, whom she summoned to say goodbye to her. "Haven't they enough to do with greater sinners than I? Now that you have opened my eyes, I can see I have been spied on continually and all kinds of traps have been set for me. It was Madame de Choisy who told me the King had ordered me out of the palace at Fontainebleau. I found out later he had never given such an order, and I had almost committed a fatal mistake in leaving. What I don't see is how they can be so eager to harm people who have done nothing to them."

"There's something about you that arouses the hatred of prudish people," Marie-Agnès said thoughtfully. She was talking to her sister through a wooden lattice, as the nuns were not permitted to converse without that barrier to intimacy. "What did Monsieur de Solignac advise you to do?" she asked again.

"Go home and live there in an exemplary fashion far from the pleasures of the Court."

"Then do just the opposite—at least so far as the first part of that injunction is concerned. Go back to Versailles just as soon as you can and demand to see the King."

"But if those orders were genuine, I'll run the risk of enraging His Majesty."

"You can take the risk," said Marie-Agnès flippantly. "There isn't a soul who doesn't know the King is mad about you. Actually his anger is only his way of expressing his royal jealousy, and a Madame de Choisy or a Solignac has just stirred it up. Take your proper place again. They say you're the apple on the top of the tree for the Sun King, and that your virtue has even resisted his assaults on it. But you have to go off and sleep with an outlaw who hasn't a penny and whom the police of the entire kingdom are looking for. You've fooled the King, and you've fooled the fanatics, and you've fooled your whole world in a shameless fashion. In short, you've ruined everything."

"Marie-Agnès, your perception astonishes me. You think I'm a fool and you're right. If only I had you with me at Court to give me advice! But you stick to your trade and leave all your rivals breathless trying to keep up with you, or scratched by your sharp nails. I can't understand what you are doing as a Carmelite. When you wanted to take the veil I was convinced it was only a passing fancy. But you stuck to it. Every time I see you or listen to you, I am dumbfounded to see you in this nun's habit."

"Why are you dumbfounded?" She lifted her head. The yellow light of a thick candle shining in the corner of the room illumined her wide-open eyes. "I had a child, you recall, Angélique. I have been a mother, and it was you who kept me from dying as a result. But what happened to my child, my son? I left him with the witch Monvoisin. Sometimes I think of that innocent little body, my own flesh and blood, possibly sacrificed on the altar of the Devil by the secret magicians of Paris. I know what they do in their Black Masses. People come to them for help in love or power or money, for those they want to see dead and for the honors they hope to get, and that hideous travesty of the Mass gets it for them. I think of my baby . . . they have pierced his heart with a long needle to draw off his blood and mix it with offal to make a foul parody of the Blessed Host. When-

ever I think of that, I think that if I could ever do more
to expiate my crime than enter a cloister, I would do it."

Angélique shuddered as she walked down the street
from Mont Sainte-Geneviève. There were street-lights
now in Paris. La Reynie, the new chief of police, had
determined, they said, to make Paris a clean, well-lighted
city where honest women could walk abroad after nightfall. Here and there wide lanterns topped with a cock,
the symbol of watchfulness, spread their reassuring ru-
tilant glow.

But when, thought Angélique, would La Reynie ever
dispel the thick night of hatred and crime that covered
the city? She thought of that world which for years had
possessed her with all its temptations, its pleasures, its
horrors. Which would win, the forces of light or of
darkness? Would not the fire of Heaven destroy this
wicked city because there could be found no just soul
within it? Her sister's final confidence had evoked a fear
that stifled her. She felt menaced on all sides.

A few of her faithful servants welcomed her at the
Hôtel de Beautreillis. The others had fled. By the disorder and the desertion in her home she could measure
the damage from the hurricane of royal disfavor. For the
first time she was worried about Florimond. Barbe told
her they had had no news of the boy. All she knew was
that he had left his post as page at Versailles.

"Are you sure?" Angélique asked in terror.

Would they attack Florimond next?

"Swordthrust" Malbrant and the Abbé des Lesdiguières were nowhere to be found. The Gilandon girls
had left the place.

"So much for them! I am sure it was those minxes who
betrayed me."

Charles-Henri gazed at his mother out of big blue eyes.
She wanted to take him on her lap and hug him as the
only thing of value she had left in the world, but she
refused to weaken. The sight of the child depressed
her. Why bring children into the world to double your
woes by seeing them suffer through your own fault?

She preferred to shut herself up in her room and apply
herself to the bottle of plum brandy which would help

distract her from her misery of soul and give her strength to face the coming struggle.

A little later, half-drunk, she knelt at the foot of her bed.

"Oh God, if the fire of Heaven strikes this city, have pity on me. Help me. Lead me to those green pastures where my lover waits for me."

chapter 23

VERSAILLES was bathed in light. The warmth and springtime glow of an April day wrapped the palace in that rosy-golden vapor that belongs only to lands which know the joy of *dolce far niente*.

"How lovely Versailles is!" Angélique said to herself in a rapture of enthusiasm.

Her spirits had revived; her anguish of soul was gone. At Versailles one had to believe in the mercy of God and in that of the King who had built this marvel. But one thing was sure, Solignac had not been wrong in telling Angélique she was banished from the Court until re-invited. She had succeeded, however, in getting a message through to Bontemps, and when he joined her near the pool of Clagny he confirmed the shocking ban.

"For some days His Majesty could not even bear to hear your name, and we had to be careful not to mention you in front of him. You greatly offended him, Madame. I think you know how."

"I'm pining away, Bontemps. Can't I see the King?"

"You must be out of your mind, Madame. I just told you he can't stand the merest mention of you."

"But if he would see me, Bontemps, if you were to help me see him, don't you know what it would mean for you . . . haven't you just an inkling?"

The Chief Valet of the Bedchamber rubbed the end of his nose as he thought it over. He knew his master's nature better than the King's confessor did, and he also knew how far he could go without displeasing him.

"Of course, Madame, I will do my best to persuade His Majesty to meet you in secret. If you get him to forgive you, he will forgive me."

He advised her to wait in the Grotto of Thetis, which

was deserted that day because all the Court was on the bank of the Grand Canal where a fleet of miniature galleys was being launched.

"The boats will drift down toward Trianon, and the King can leave without attracting attention. Furthermore, he can get to the Grotto of Thetis without passing the palace. But I can't say when this will be. You'll have to be patient, Madame."

"I will be. The Grotto is a delightful place to wait, and at least I won't suffer from the heat there. Monsieur Bontemps, I shall never forget what you have done for me today."

The valet bowed. He understood her meaning and hoped he could play a winning card. He had never been able to endure Madame de Montespan.

The Grotto of Thetis, one of the most unusual sights of Versailles, had been hewn in a granite cliff to the north of the palace. Angélique entered by one of its three gates. The sun's rays gilded the bas-relief of Apollo plunging into the sea in his chariot, symbolizing the sun going to rest in the realm of Thetis at the end of the day. The interior was like a dream-palace. The pillars were of rough-hewn stone, and in niches faced with mother-of-pearl tritons blew their conch-shell horns, while shell-framed mirrors that created enormous perspectives reflected them to infinity.

Angélique sat on the edge of a large scallop-shell of jasper. Around her graceful sea-nymphs held dripping candelabra aloft, whose six branches imitating seaweed spouted jets of iridescent water. Hundreds of birds fluttered among the rosy mists of the vaulted roof, giving the grotto the sound of a grove. At first these seemed to be real, as did their songs, but a closer look revealed that their wings were of silver and their bodies of mother-of-pearl so that they resembled the birds of an underwater paradise. They were Francinet's latest invention. A water organ was so placed that its tones echoed throughout the grotto from one side to the other.

Angélique beguiled the time by listening to the music and picking out the innumerable details of the beauty that surrounded her. Here art and mechanical skill had reached a peak of perfection, and it was easy to see why the King liked this unusually tasteful spot. On fine days he loved to bring the ladies of the Court here to listen to chamber music. The previous year he had brought the Prince of Tuscany here for a repast of fruits and jams.

Angélique let her fingers trail in the crystal clear water. She didn't want to think. It was useless and perhaps unlucky to prepare a speech in advance only to find it wanting when the time came to use it. She would trust to the spur of the moment. But as the hours dragged by, she became more and more anxious.

It was the King she was to meet. The awe he could inspire in her buffeted her like gusts of an icy wind, chilling her to the marrow. Sometimes when she looked at him, so calm and solemn and yet so friendly, she could be terrified by the majesty she perceived behind his mask of an ordinary mortal. This sensation returned to her now as a kind of paralyzing fear, and if he had spoken to her at that moment, she would have stammered a reply like everyone else struck dumb by the royal presence. She remembered seeing on a battlefield in Flanders a rough non-commissioned officer covered with scars and medals turn pale at suddenly finding himself in the presence of Louis XIV and his suite, and quite incapable of uttering anything but incoherent grunts to the questions the King so gently asked him.

"If I panic, I'll be lost," she said to herself. "I must not be afraid. Fear means defeat. Still the King holds my fate in his hands."

She shuddered, thinking that she heard a step behind her on the mosaic floor. But no one was there. She looked toward the main entrance that opened on the sinking sun, tinting the afternoon with pink. Above the lintel was the emblem of the King on a background of flaxen-colored shells. The monogram was made of tiny pearl-like shells. The crown above it was decorated with mother-of-pearl fleur-de-lis outlined in amber which shone like gold in the half-light.

Angélique could not take her eyes off that emblem. She felt a presence near her, but she hesitated to turn around. When at last she did so, she rose as she saw the

King, then remained hypnotized to the point that she forgot to curtsy.

The King had entered by one of the hidden doors of the grotto which opened on the north terraces and was used by servants when there was a reception there. He was clad in a suit of purple taffeta, modestly embroidered, and set off by exquisite lace at his throat and his wrists. His expression did not bode well.

"Well, Madame," he said, "aren't you afraid of my anger? Didn't you understand what I told Monsieur de Solignac to convey to you? Do you want a scandal? Must I remind you before witnesses that your presence at Court is not required? Do you know that I have lost all patience? Well, answer me!"

The questions were like a hail of bullets.

"I wanted to *see* you, Sire," Angélique answered.

What man beholding her before him in the golden shadows of the Grotto of Thetis with such a disturbingly mysterious look in her emerald eyes could resist her charms? The King was not one to remain long insensible to them. He saw that her feelings were not feigned, that she was trembling all over. His mask of severity suddenly crumbled.

"Why . . . oh, why did you do that?" he exclaimed almost sadly. "Such an unworthy betrayal . . ."

"Sire, an outlaw sought refuge with me. Let women act according to the dictates of their heart and not according to the soulless principles of politics. Whatever his crime was, he was a poor wretch who was dying of hunger."

"It is indeed a matter of politics. What do I care how much you sheltered him and fed him and helped him escape! But you made him your lover as well. You acted like a prostitute."

"Those are harsh words, Sire. I remember Your Majesty was once more forgiving when Monsieur de Lauzun at Fontainebleau was the cause of a painful incident between my husband and him, and I was then more to blame than now."

"We have come a long way since then," said the King. "I don't want . . . I don't want you to give to others what you will not give me."

He began to pace up and down, touching the pearly birds and the puffy-cheeked tritons. With the simple words of a jealous man he was confessing his bitterness, his disappointment, his defeat, and in spite of his reputation for concealing his thoughts, was about to reveal his intentions.

"I wanted to be patient. I wanted to prick the bubble of your vanity and your ambition. I hoped you would learn to know me better and that your heart would eventually be stirred . . . somehow. I looked for ways to make you mine, and when I saw that haste displeased you I was content to let time go by. Now it has been years, yes, years since I first conceived a passion for you, since the day I first saw you as the Goddess of Spring. But you maintained your inverted snobbery, your disregard for conventional behavior . . . You came here, you presented yourself before your King without being invited . . . Ah, how beautiful and bold you were! I knew you were going to be mine and that I would desire you to the point of madness, and to conquer you seemed so easy. But the tricks you used to rebuff me—I don't know what they were. I saw myself routed on all sides. Your kisses were neither promises nor confessions. Your confidences, your smiles, your serious words were no more than traps into which I was the only one to fall. I have suffered cruelly from not being able to take you in my arms, from not daring to do so lest you would escape me farther. . . . What good has all my patience, all my care, done? Now look at how you despise me still by giving yourself to an abominable savage from the Carpathians. How could I forgive you for that? . . . Why are you shaking so? Are you cold?"

"No. Afraid."

"Of me?"

"Of your power, Sire."

"I am sorry." He put his hands gently on her waist. "Do not be afraid. You are the only person whose fear of me hurts me. I should like you to find joy in me, happiness, pleasure. What would I not give to see you smile? I have searched in vain for something that might satisfy you. Don't tremble, my love, I shall not hurt you.

I cannot. This month gone by has been a hell for me. Everywhere I sought your eyes. And I could not stop thinking of you in the arms of that Rakoczy. Oh, how I have wanted to kill him!"

"What have you done with him, Sire?"

"So it's his fate that worries you, is it?" he grinned. "So it's for his sake you have the courage to present yourself before me? Well, relax. Your Rakoczy is not even in prison. See how unfairly you judge me. I have loaded him with favors. I have granted him everything he has wanted to get from me for a long time. He has gone back to Hungary with his pockets full of gold to sow disorder there between the German Emperor and the King of Hungary and the Ukrainians. That suits my plans, for I have no need whatever for a coalition in Central Europe just now. Everything has turned out for the best."

Of all he had been saying Angélique caught just one sentence: "He has gone back to Hungary." She was shocked. She could not tell whether her attachment to Rakoczy was very deep, but never for a moment had she dreamed that she might not see him again. Now he had returned to that distant land so wild and far away it seemed to be on another planet. The King had abruptly swept him clean out of her life, and she would never see him again.

She wanted to scream with rage. She wanted to see Rakoczy again. He was her lover, clean and sincere and ardent. She needed him. No one had the right to direct the lives of others this way as if they were marionettes. Her anger made her see red.

"At least you gave him plenty of money," she cried, "so that he can fight kings and chase them out, and deliver his people from the tyrants that oppress them and play with their lives as if they were puppets, so that he can give them the freedom to think, to breathe, to love . . ."

"Shut up!" The King had grasped her shoulders in a vise-like grip. "Shut up!" Then his voice grew calm. "I entreat you not to insult me, my love. I could not forgive you for that. Don't show me your hatred. You cut me to the quick. You don't have to say things that will only drive us apart. We ought to come closer to each other, Angélique. So be still. Come."

He led her to the edge of a marble pool where the water glimmered like a pearl. She was panting. Her teeth were clamped, her throat tight. The King's strength subdued her. He was stroking her forehead, as she loved him to do, and mastering her.

"I beg you, don't give way to nerves. Madame du Plessis-Bellière would never forgive you for that."

With a quick sob she yielded to him. Tired and broken in spirit, she leaned her head against him as he stood by her. He dominated her. The setting sun quickened the red and gold tints of his hair. Never before had she known how overpowering his strength could be. She realized now that ever since that first morning when, like a lark before a bird-charmer, she had come to Versailles to be crowned Goddess of Spring, she had unknowingly been in the King's hands. Possibly the most stubborn animal he had ever tamed, yes, but he had succeeded. He had always shown the patience, the stealth and the unruffled calm of a great wild beast lying in wait for his prey. He sat beside her, pressing her warmly to him, speaking tenderly.

"What a strange love ours is, Angélique!"

"Is it only a question of love?"

"For me, yes. If it is not love, then what is it?" he said passionately. "Angélique . . . how that name haunts my memory! When my work lets me, I close my eyes. A dizziness comes over me and your name springs to my lips . . . Angélique! I have never known such torment so to distract me from my work. Sometimes I am frightened by this love I have allowed to penetrate my soul. It causes me a faintness like a wound of which I fear I shall never be healed. You alone can heal me. I dream . . . yes, sometimes I do dream . . . of the night I shall hold your warm, sweet-smelling flesh close to mine, not knowing what look is in your eyes . . . And I dream of things more precious still, and that part of you which is beyond price. I dream of your smile—so light, so friendly, so complex—beaming on me from among the throng on some great day when an embassy arrives and I am only the King dragging my heavy robe and scepter down the Hall of Mirrors . . . of a look from you that will approve my designs . . . of a frown that will prove your jealousy . . . of ordinary, tender things I shall never know."

"Haven't your mistresses already taught you them?"

"They were my mistresses, not my friends. That was the way I wanted it. Now it is something else . . ."

He gazed at her with a look in which was not desire alone but another sentiment compounded of tenderness and admiration and devotion, an expression so unusual for the King that she could not tear her eyes from his. She saw him clearly now as a solitary man yearning toward her from the top of a mountain. Ardently, silently they questioned each other with their eyes. The rustling of the water-organ mingling its fluty voice with the sound of the water in a rustic symphony enveloped them like an ethereal promise of happiness. Angélique feared to succumb. Turning her head away, she broke the spell.

"What has happened between us, Angélique? What has come between us? What is this barrier I sense in you, which I storm in vain?"

She put her hand to her forehead and tried to laugh. "I don't know. Pride perhaps, or fear. I haven't the things I need for that hard task of being a royal mistress."

"Hard task? What a cruel way of speaking you have!"

"I'm sorry, Sire. But let me speak frankly while there is yet time. To be always dazzling, to be always dissembling, to bear the weight of jealousy and intrigue and . . . Your Majesty's infidelity, that is not for me. To be something one tosses aside like a toy no longer fun to play with takes more ambition, or more love. It broke Mademoiselle de la Vallière, and I am not so thick-skinned as Madame de Montespan." She rose abruptly. "Stay faithful to her, Sire. She has a strength to match yours, not I. Don't tempt me any more."

"Are you tempted?"

He wrapped her in his arms and buried his face in her

golden hair. "Your fears are groundless, my lovely. . . .
You know me only on the surface. For what other
woman would I have been so forgiving? The soft ones
are whining ninnies. The ambitious have to be beaten
down lest they devour me. But you . . . you were born
to be a *sultana-bachi,* as that dark prince said who
wished to carry you away with him. The one who can
dominate a king. I accept the title. I bow. I love you in
a hundred different ways—for your weakness, for your
sadness I would so like to dispel, for your spendor I
would so like to possess, for your intelligence which con-
founds me but which I need as much as I need precious
things of gold and marble about me, almost more beautiful in their perfection than one should have near one,
as a token of wealth and strength. You have given me
what I lacked—confidence."

He had taken her face in his hands and was raising
her to him as if he never tired of trying to plumb her
mystery.

"I expect everything from you, and I know that if you
consented to love me, you would not deceive me. But
so long as you are not mine, so long as I do not hear
your voice moaning in a swoon of love, I am afraid. I
fear you waiting to trap me in sly deception. That is
why I want to hasten the hour of your surrender. For
then I shall have nothing to fear, neither you nor the
whole earth. . . . Have you ever imagined that, Angé-
gelique . . . You and I together . . . What could we
not do? What conquests could we not undertake? What
glories could we not expect? . . . You and I together . . .
We would be invincible."

She did not answer. It was as if a mighty wind had
shaken her to her very foundations. She kept her eyes
closed and offered the King only her pale, pale face in
which he could decipher nothing. He understood that
the moment of grace had passed. He sighed.

"You don't want to answer without thinking? That is
only wise. And you don't like my having stopped you, I
can see. Well, hothead, I grant you another week of
penitence to calm your resentment and reflect on my
words in solitude. So back to your hôtel in Paris until

next Sunday. Then Versailles shall see you once more, lovelier than ever, more beloved if that is possible, and more triumphant over my heart in spite of your guilty straying. Alas, you have taught me that great as a king may be, he cannot command love, only loyalty, not even equal desire. But I shall be patient. I shall not despair. Another day will come when we shall embark for Cythera. Yes, my darling, there shall come a day when I shall lead you into Trianon. I have had built there a little porcelain pagoda to love you in, far from the din, far from their intrigues that frighten you, with only the flowers and the trees to know we are there. You shall be the first to use it. Every stone, every object has been chosen for you. Do not protest. Leave me only hope. I know how to wait."

Holding her by the hand, he led her to the entrance of the grotto.

"Sire, may I ask you for news of my son?"

The King's face darkened. "Ah, that's one more worry your turbulent family has caused me. I have had to remove the little page from his post."

"Because of my fall from grace?"

"By no means. I had no intention of making him suffer for that. But his conduct displeased me. Twice he pretended that Duchesne, my head steward, wanted to poison me, that's all. He pretended he had seen him put a powder in my food and he accused him of it noisily. From the fire in his eyes and the distinctness of his voice I knew he had inherited his mother's boldness. 'Sire, do not eat that dish and do not drink that wine,' he said loudly and clearly just after the test had been made. 'Monsieur Duchesne has put poison into it.' "

"Oh dear," Angélique sighed disconsolately. "Sire, I don't know how to tell you how embarrassed I am. The boy is very high-strung and imaginative."

"The second time he pulled the prank, I had to be firm. I did not want to punish too severely a boy I was interested in because of my fondness for you. Monsieur was there. He found the boy amusing and wanted to engage him. I gave him permission. Your boy is now at Saint-Cloud, where my brother has just taken up his springtime residence."

Angélique turned all the colors of the rainbow. "You let my son go to that sewer!"

"Madame!" thundered the King. "Another of your intolerable expressions!" Then he softened and began to laugh. "But that's the way you are, nothing can change you. Come, don't exaggerate the dangers that threaten your boy in that, I agree, rather immoral establishment. His tutor, the abbé, follows him everywhere, and so does his squire. I wanted to please you. I am sorry I have succeeded so poorly. Of course, you will want to go to Saint-Cloud, so merely ask me for permission and anything else I can do for you."

"Sire, let me go to Saint-Cloud."

"I will do more. I shall give you a message for Madame so that she will receive you and keep you with her a day or so. Then you can visit your son at leisure."

"Sire, you are too generous."

"Only too loving. Do not forget that again, Madame, and do not toy with my heart."

Florimond's eyes looked straight into hers.

"I swear I am not lying, Mother. Monsieur Duchesne is poisoning the King. I have seen him several times. He puts a white powder under his fingernail and flicks it into His Majesty's goblet between the time he tastes the wine himself and the time he hands it to the King."

"Come, come, my boy, such a thing is impossible. Besides the King has suffered no ill effects from this so-called poisoning."

"I don't know about that. Perhaps it's a slow-working poison."

"Florimond, you don't know what you're saying. A child should not speak about such serious matters. Don't forget the King is surrounded by devoted servants."

"Who doesn't know that?" Florimond said.

He looked at his mother with the same sympathetic condescension as Marie-Agnès had done. For an hour she had striven to get him to admit he had been making the story up. She felt on the verge of an emotional crisis. She certainly was not equipped to bring up such an imaginative child. He had already grown away from her. Now he was going his own way self-confidently, and she had too many cares of her own to attend to him properly.

"But who could have put such an idea into your head that the King was being poisoned?"

"Everyone talks about poison," he said frankly. "The other day the Duchesse de Vitry asked me to carry her train. She was going to Monvoisin's in Paris. I listened at the keyhole while she consulted the old witch. Well, she asked for poison to slip into her old husband's soup, and also a powder to attract the love of Monsieur de Vivonne. The Marquis de Cossac's page told me his master had gone to ask for the secret of winning at cards, and at the same time for some poison for his brother the Comte de Clermont-Ledève whose heir he is. And," Florimond finished with a flourish, "the Comte de Clermont-Ledève died a week ago."

"My child, don't you know what harm you can do yourself by retailing these slanders so freely?" said Angélique, trying to keep her patience. "No one will want a page in his service who gossips so at random."

"But I am not gossiping," shouted Florimond, stamping his red heel on the floor. "I'm trying to tell you, but I think . . . yes, I really think you must be dumb." He turned away with a gesture of wounded dignity, and stared out the window at the blue sky to conceal his trembling lip. He was too old to cry, but tears of frustration welled into his eyes just the same.

Angélique did not know what tack to try next. There was something about the boy she could not fathom. He was surely lying unnecessarily and with vexing assurance, but for what purpose? In despair she turned to the Abbé de Lesdiguières and blamed him.

"This boy needs a spanking. I don't think much of your discipline."

The young priest turned red up to the edge of his wig. "Madame, I do my best. Through his job Flori-

mond has come into contact with certain secrets he
thinks he knows the answer to . . ."

"Teach him at least to keep them," Angélique said
drily.

As he began to stammer, she remembered he was one
of Madame de Choisy's protégés. To what extent had he
spied on her and betrayed her?

Florimond had mastered his tears. He said he had to
go for a walk with the little princesses and asked to be
allowed to leave. He went out by the window in a gait
he tried to make dignified, but as soon as he had crossed
the terrace at the entrance steps, he broke into a run.
They could hear him singing. He was like a butterfly
intoxicated with the lovely spring day. The park at
Saint-Cloud with its endless lawns was full of the chirp-
ing of treetoads.

"What do you think of all this, Monsieur de Lesdiguières?"

"Madame, I have never caught Florimond in a lie."

"You want to defend your pupil, of course, but in
doing so you will spoil your sense of evaluation . . ."

"Who doesn't know that?" said the abbé, using
Florimond's exrpession. He clasped his hands tightly together in a gesture of anxiety. "At Court even the greatest shows of loyalty are open to suspicion. We are surrounded by spies . . ."

"You should know a great deal about spies, Monsieur
Abbé, since you were paid by Madame de Choisy to
snoop on me and betray me."

The abbé turned pale as death. His girlish eyes
widened. He began to shake and finally fell on his knees.
"Pardon, Madame. It is true. Madame de Choisy put me
in your household to spy on you, but I did not betray
you. I take my oath on that. I would never have done
you the slightest wrong, Madame, not you, never!"

Angélique got up and went to look out the window.

"Believe me, Madame," the young man begged again.

"All right, I believe you," she said tiredly. "But tell
me, then, who did denounce me to the Brotherhood of
the Holy Sacrament? Was it 'Swordthrust' Malbrant? It's
not the sort of role for him."

"No, Madame. Your squire is a good man. Madame de Choisy placed him with you to help his family which is an honorable one in its province."

"What about the Gilandon girls?"

The abbé hesitated. He was still on his knees.

"I know Marie-Anne went to see her benefactress a few days before your arrest."

"Then it was she. What a louse of an ingrate! You are doing well in your profession, Abbé. I don't doubt if you keep on you'll be a bishop some day."

"It's not easy to live, Madame," the abbé murmured softly. "Think of what I owe Madame de Choisy. I was the youngest in a family of twelve children, and the fourth boy. There was not always enough to eat in our castle. I was drawn to the Church because I like to study and do good. Madame de Choisy paid for me to go to seminary for several years. When she got me a place in the world she told me to report all the immorality I observed so that I could combat the forces of evil. I found it a noble and inspiring duty. But when I entered your household, Madame . . ."

Still on his knees, he looked at her with such spaniel eyes that she took pity on the romantic passion she had aroused in his frank and open heart.

He was of that breed of petty nobility who grow up in crumbling old castles without a penny to make a career for themselves, and have nothing to offer but what they do possess—their souls and their bodies. That was the kind that Monsieur, the King's brother, made the prey of his unnatural desires. It was better for a younger son of a good family to hire out to Virtue. This reflection led her to other concerns.

"Get up," she snapped. "I forgive you because I think you are sincere."

"I am devoted to you, Madame, and I love Florimond like a brother. Are you going to separate us?"

"No. In spite of everything, I feel easier when I know he is with you. But Monsieur's circle is the last place I would choose for him. No one knows how depraved that prince's tastes are and those who surround him. A lively, pretty boy like Florimond is not safe there."

"That is quite true, Madame," said the abbé, who had got to his feet and was unobtrusively dusting off his knees. "I have already fought a duel with Antoine Maurel, Sieur de Volone, who it perhaps the biggest rogue of them all—thief, blasphemer, atheist, sodomite. He trains and sells boys as if they were horses; he carries on his trade in the boxes at the Opera. His eye lit on Florimond and he tried to seduce him, but I interfered. So we fought a duel. Maurel resigned after I wounded him in the arm. I also dueled with the Comte de Beuvron and the Marquis d'Effiat. I made it clear that the boy was a protégé of the King's and that I would complain to His Majesty if he suffered the slightest harm. Everyone knows you are his mother and that your influence with the King is not to be sneezed at. Finally I worked it that he was appointed companion to the two little princesses, and so he has been somewhat removed from that strange society. Oh, Madame, I have had to accustom my eyes and ears to plenty of things around here. At Monsieur's rising they talked about boys the way a bunch of young bloods might talk about girls. The women are the worst because you can't fight a duel with them. Mesdames de Blanzac, d'Espiney de Melun, and de Grancy all haunt me like mythological monsters, and I don't know how to get rid of them."

"Don't tell me they're after Florimond too."

"No, it's I they want."

"Oh, you poor thing," exclaimed Angélique, not knowing whether to laugh at him or pity him. "My poor little abbé, what a task you've taken on. I absolutely must get you out of here."

"Don't worry, Madame. I know that Florimond has to have a career and he can only get ahead in a prince's household. I try to protect him and strengthen his character and keep him from getting cynical by shielding him from too much depravity. Everything is possible when the soul is strong and when God's help is sought. That's the real meaning of my function as his tutor, isn't it?"

"It certainly is, but you did not have to agree to bring him here."

"It is very hard to go against the King's decisions,

Madame. It seemed to me that the dangers he would encounter here might be less than those that lay in wait for
him at Versailles."

"What do you mean?"

The abbé looked around him cautiously, then came
over to her. "I am sure two attempts were made on his
life."

"Now you're really out of your head, my boy," said
Angélique shrugging her shoulders violently. "You are
obsessed to the point of delirium with the notion that
your pupil is being persecuted. Who would want to
take the life of a child of that age, the youngest and the
most famous in the whole Court?"

"A page whose clear little voice sometimes tells embarrassing truths a bit too loudly."

"I don't want to hear any more. I an certain you are
out of your head. You've been hearing too many ghost
stories, and believing them. Duchesne has the reputation of an honorable man."

"Don't all those who live at Court have an honorable
reputation, Madame? Who would dare label anyone else
there a scoundrel or a criminal? How unseemly that
would be!"

"You are painting everything too dark. I don't doubt
you are Florimond's guardian angel, but I would like
you to apply yourself to subduing his imagination and
your own at the same time. For the time being I am not
going to believe Master Florimond, the two hundredth
and last page of the King's Wine Service. It's absurd."

"Not believe a page who is your own son, Madame?
Oh, Madame, I beg you, don't turn your back on those
who are unquestionably loyal to you. Don't you know
you have many enemies? How they would like to trip
you into some hidden pit! Don't leave a stone unturned
in protecting yourself. If anything happened to you, I
would die of grief."

"You are not lacking in eloquence, little abbé," Angélique said kindly. "I must recommend you to Monsieur
Bossuet. A little inspiration never hurts a sermon. I
think you may turn out to be someone, and I'll do my
best to help you."

"Oh, Madame, is this the way you have let yourself lapse into the cynicism of the Court ladies?"

"I am no cynic, my boy. But I would like to see you with both feet on the ground a little more."

The Abbé de Lesdiguières opened his mouth to make one last protest, but the arrival of someone in the room where they were talking interrupted him. He bowed and went in search of his pupil.

Angélique went back into the drawing rooms. The doors were wide open to let in the fresh spring air. In the distance one could see Paris.

As the King had advised her to do, Madame sent her majordomo to ask Madame du Plessis to stay at Saint-Cloud until the following day. Angélique accepted listlessly. In spite of all its charm and luxury, Monsieur's Court was too ambiguous and disquieting. The Prince's women were as disreputable as his catamites. Angélique encountered there all the persons she had deliberately avoided at Versailles. Bold and handsome women, for the most part extremely wicked and even worse than wicked, amused Monsieur with their quarrels and intrigues, and he lapped up all their vulgar gossip like a concierge. He was not unintelligent and he had shown that he was courageous in military campaigns, but he had been so perverted that he inevitably relapsed into completely idle ways and vices.

Angélique tried to spot that unblest Prince of Sodom, "handsome as an angel in a painting," the Chevalier de Lorraine, who for years had been Monsieur's favorite and had in fact become the master of the Palais Royal and of Saint-Cloud. She was surprised at not finding him. She asked Lady Gordon, a Scotswoman she liked and a member of Madame's suite, what the story was.

"What? Don't you know? Where have you been? Lorraine is in disgrace. First he was put in prison for a while, then sent into exile to Rome. It's a great victory for Madame. For years she has fought to get the better of her worst enemy, and now at last the King has listened to her."

She offered Angélique the hospitality for the night of the antechamber where she slept with the other Maids of Honor, and there she told her the whole story of the last skirmish in which Madame had won the victory she had so long despaired of. Lorraine had been arrested right in the Prince's bedroom by the Comte d'Ayan in spite of the fact that it was surrounded by Monsieur's bodyguards. Monsieur had wept and howled with despair, and had dragged Madame off to Villers-Cotterêts to get her out of the way. Ever since, things had begun to improve a little. Monsieur still wept a good deal, but Madame's position was unassailable because the King was on her side.

Angélique went to sleep with her ears ringing with the scabrous details. She worried about Florimond, and she had the feeling that she was being menaced by a thousand different things slithering around her like serpents.

At daybreak she was awakened by a gentle knocking at the door against which she was lying. When she opened it, there stood Madame, wrapped in a long gauze scarf and smiling at her.

"It's you I wanted to see, Madame du Plessis. Will you go for a walk with me?"

"I am at Your Royal Highness' command," Angélique replied.

They descended the staircase of the silent palace in which the guards were drowsing against their halberds. Angélique thought of the castle of the Sleeping Beauty.

Dawn was breaking over the dewy lawns of the park. In the distance Paris lurked behind the morning mists. It was so chilly that Angélique was thankful she had brought along a cloak.

"I love to walk in the early morning like this," the Princess said, stepping along at a brisk pace. "I don't sleep well. I read most of the night, and just as I thought I could finally doze off, the daylight aroused me. Do you like to read?"

Angélique confessed she rarely found time for literature.

"Even in prison?" asked Henriette d'Angleterre with a knowing laugh.

But she was not being malicious, she was just disenchanted.

"I know so few persons here who like to read. Take my brother-in-law, the King. He doesn't like it if a novelist or a playwright fails to give him a first edition of his work, but he has no intention of reading a word of it. But I read from taste. I should like to write too. Shall we sit down?"

They sat on a marble bench in a circular spot where several paths converged. The Princess had hardly changed at all since the time Angélique used to go to her card parties at the Louvre. She was small and had an elfin grace. Her porcelain skin made her seem more delicate than her Bourbon and Hapsburg relatives, whose gross manners and ignorance she quite openly criticized. She ate like a bird and slept even less, and her interest in art and letters was genuine. She had been the first to encourage Molière, and now she was beginning to patronize the fastidious Racine. Although she had a certain admiration for the Princess' intelligence, Angélique found her too bizarre. She made everyone feel rather earnest, and the very things that might have made her attractive elsewhere only wove a net of isolation about her here. This she was not aware of, but it pained her none the less, and gave her blue eyes a distracted look.

"Madame," she began after a moment of silence, "I come to you because you are said to be a very rich woman, as well as an obliging and discreet one. Could you lend me four thousand *pistoles?*"

Angélique needed all her aplomb to keep from falling over backward.

"I need that much to prepare for my trip to England," Princess Henriette continued. "I am riddled with debts. I've already pawned part of my jewels, and it's no use my pleading poverty before the King. Still it is for his sake that I am going to England. He has entrusted me with a mission of the highest importance—to prevent my brother Charles from joining the new alliance between the Dutch, the Spanish and the Germans. I should be brilliant and seductive so as to make France popular in every possible way, and that won't be easy if I have to appear in a dress too tight to sit down in. That's a manner of speaking, of course, as I'm sure you understand, my dear. You know what these embassies are like. You have to squander money like water for bribes and good will and signatures. If I appear stingy, I won't succeed, and succeed I must."

As she talked her cheeks had reddened, yet she concealed her embarrassment with her easy manner of speaking. It was this embarrassment, so uncustomary for her, that inclined Angélique to be generous.

"I hope Your Highness will forgive me for not being able to give you all you ask. I would have a good deal of trouble raising four thousand _pistoles_ so quickly, but I can promise you three thousand for sure."

"My dear, what a comfort you are to me!" Madame exclaimed. Apparently she had not hoped for so much. "You can be sure I will repay you as soon as I return. My brother is fond of me, and he will certainly give me gifts. If you only knew how important this is for me! I promised the King I would succeed. I owe it to him to do so, for he has paid me in advance."

She took Angélique's hands and squeezed them in appreciation. Hers were cold and thin. She was on the verge of tears from nervousness.

"If I failed, it would be a terrible blow. I got the Chevalier de Lorraine exiled only in exchange for this. If I fail, he will return. I would not be able to endure it if that monster were to run my household again. I am no angel by any means, but his influence over Monsieur and his followers has gone beyond the limit of endurance. I can't stand it. His antipathy for us women has reached the point of actual hatred—all the work of that Chevalier de Lorraine. Once I thought I could get around him. I sensed the danger in him. If I had been richer then, perhaps I would have succeeded, but Monsieur offered him enormous sums, and perquisites that the King gladly granted. I couldn't match them. Like a rapist who doesn't care what he does so long as he gets what he wants, he laid hold of Monsieur and robbed him of shame and money."

Angélique did not try to stop her flow of words. She could see that the Princess was in a highly nervous state. She must have been frantic about this loan and dubious of getting it up to the last moment. Her closest friends were more accustomed to intrigue and debauchery than to generosity.

"Will you promise I can have the money before I leave?" she asked anxiously.

"I give you my word, Your Highness. I will have to consult my business manager, but a week from today three thousand *pistoles* will be in your hands."

"How good you are! You restore my faith. I didn't know where to turn for help. Monsieur has been spiteful to me since the Chevalier's exile. He treats me like the worst of his . . . creatures."

She continued her confidences in bits and pieces. Doubtless she would later be sorry for it, for experience had taught her that she always trusted the wrong person. She would tell herself that Madame du Plessis was either dangerous or a fool. But for the moment she was having the rare experience of finding a friendly ear into which to pour her troubles. She was telling Angélique now about the struggle she had carried on for years to get away from her household and even her house and from the filth they were mired in. Everything had gone wrong from the very start. She should never have married Monsieur.

"He is jealous of my intelligence, and my fear that no one likes me or even thinks well of me will haunt me the rest of my days."

She had hoped to be Queen of France, but she did not say so. This was one of the heavy grievances she bore Monsieur—that he was not his brother. The way in which she spoke of the King was full of bitterness.

"If he weren't so afraid my brother Charles would make this alliance, I would never have got a thing from him. My tears, my shame, my grief, mean nothing to him. He doesn't care about his brother's degradation."

"Are you sure, Your Royal Highness, that you are not exaggerating? The King surely can't like to see . . ."

"Oh yes, I know him well. It's rather to the advantage

of a man on the throne to see those nearest to him by
birth sink lower and lower into vice. That way his own
grandeur and strength of character seem all the greater.
My husband's pets are no threat to the royal power. All
they need is gold and gifts and lucrative sinecures.
The King gives them out freely. Lorraine got everything
he wanted from him. He is sure of Monsieur's loyalty.
The King has no fear that he will turn into an insurrec-
tionist like their uncle Gaston d'Orléans. But this time
I spoke up. Because he needed me he had to give me
what I wanted. I recalled to him that I am the daughter
of a king, and that if I were maltreated I had a brother
who is a king too, and he would avenge me."

She sighed deeply, and put her hand over her heart
to still its throbbing.

"I shall win in the end, and yet I can't help being
afraid. I am surrounded by so much hatred. Several times
Monsieur has threatened to poison me."

Angélique jumped. "Madame, you must not give way to
such morbid thoughts."

"I don't know whether they are morbid or just plain
looking at the facts. People die easily these days."

Angélique thought of Florimond and the exhorta-
tions of the Abbé de Lesdiguières, and fear rose in
her like an icy serpent.

"If Your Highness is convinced, you must work hard
to protect yourself. Tell the police your suspicions
and get protection from them."

Madame looked at her as if she had said the most incongruous thing possible. Then she burst into laughter.

"You astonish me with the simple ideas you have.
The police? Do you mean those bullies Le Reynie bosses
around, like Desgrez who was ordered to arrest my counselor Cosnac, Bishop of Valence? Don't be silly, my dear,
I know them only too well. They are not going to stick
their long red noses into our affairs."

She arose and smoothed down her ice-blue gown of
grosgrain silk. Small as she was, she carried herself like a
queen. She seemed taller than Angélique, though she
was shorter.

"Remember we have no other recourse at Court but

to defend ourselves alone or . . . die," she said calmly.

They walked back in silence. The green lawns of the park were like velvet, and the breeze wafted to them the fragrance of the blossoming trees. There was none of the formality of Versailles here. Madame had designed it all in the English fashion, perhaps the only taste she and Monsieur had in common. When the King came to Saint-Cloud, he was offended by what he called "this disorder."

There was a melancholy smile on the Princess' lips. Nothing could distract her from the fear that haunted her days.

"If you only knew," she said, "how gladly I would stay in England, and never, never come back here!"

chapter 24

"MADAME," demanded the beggars, "Madame, when are we going to the King so he can touch our sores?"

They were crowding into the Hôtel de Beautreillis. With Angélique as their intermediary they thought themselves as good as cured already. She promised them that the following Sunday they could take part in the ceremony. She knew the steps she would have to take, but she was so busy with her own preparations for returning to Court that she decided to go to Madame Scarron to ask her to take her little troop of beggars to the King's doctor.

She recalled that she had not seen the young widow for some time. The last time . . . why, it was during the great fêtes at Versailles in 1668. Two years! What had happened to Françoise since then? Angélique was full of remorse as she stopped her sedan chair before the door of the modest house in which Madame Scarron had been hiding her poverty for years.

She knocked on the door in vain, but from little signs she was sure there was someone in the house. Perhaps it was only a maid, but if so, why didn't she come to the door? Finally Angélique gave up. At the next cross-street a jam of coaches made her bearers stop. Unconsciously Angélique looked back up the street they had just left. Somewhat to her surprise she saw the door of Madame Scarron's house open and the young widow herself step out. She wore a mask and was wrapped up in a dark cloak, but Angélique easily recognized her.

"This is too much," she exclaimed as she jumped out of her sedan chair.

She told the lackeys to go back to the Hôtel de Beautreillis without her. Putting her hood over her head, she started out after Madame Scarron. The widow walked rapidly in spite of the two heavy baskets she was carrying. There was something mysterious about her, and Angélique decided to trail her without catching up with her. As she came to the Cité, Madame Scarron went to the steps of the Palace and hired one of the plain wheelchairs drawn by one man and called "vinaigrettes."

After waiting a moment, Angélique decided to continue on foot, as a vinaigrette never moved very fast. Later she regretted this decision. She thought she would never stop walking. She crossed the Seine and started down an endless street which eventually turned into a sunken road that terminated out in the country near Vaugirard. Angélique had to slow down and so lost sight of the vehicle for a while. She was disappointed to see the vinaigrette turn out of a lane and head back empty.

She would not have it said that she had come this far in vain. She ran behind the porter and slipped him an *écu*. For such a regal tip he had no hesitation in pointing out to her the house where he had left his passenger.

It was one of the new houses that were being built in increasing numbers in the suburbs between the truck-farmers' rows of cabbages and the sheepfolds. Angélique lifted the bronze knocker. After a long wait she saw a hand open the peep-hole, and a maid's voice asked what she wanted.

"I should like to see Madame Scarron."

"There's no Madame Scarron here. I don't know anyone by that name." She shut the peep-hole.

Angélique's curiosity was aroused by all this mystery. "My dear," she said, "you don't know me if you think I'm going to give up."

There was only one way to make Françoise show herself and she was going to use it.

She beat a tattoo on the door with all her might until the peep-hole opened again.

"I tell you there is no Madame Scarron here," the servant shouted.

"In that case, tell her I am here on behalf of the King."

The hand behind the bars hesitated, then after a long moment chains rattled, bolts were shot and the door creaked open. She squeezed through into the house. Françoise Scarron was leaning over the railing at the top of the staircase with an anxious expression on her face.

"Angélique! For heaven's sake, what's wrong?"

"You don't seem very glad to see me. I have had a dreadful time catching up with you. How are you?"

She went up the stairs and kissed her friend enthusiastically, but Françoise was wary.

"So the King sent you? Why you? Has something been changed since his last instructions?"

"I don't think so," said Angélique. "This is a strange way for you to act. Are you annoyed with me because I haven't been to see you for so long? Let me explain why. Can't we go in and sit down?"

"No! No!" Madame Scarron said quickly blocking the way, her arms spread out across the door of the room Angélique wanted to enter. "No. Tell me first."

"Now, Françoise, we can't just stand here on the stairs. What's happened to you? You aren't the same woman I used to know. If you are in trouble, never think I wouldn't help you."

Madame Scarron did not seem to hear her. "What exactly did the King say to you?"

"The King has nothing to do with it, Françoise, I confess. I wanted to see you and just used his name as a kind of Open Sesame."

Madame Scarron covered her face with her hands. "Oh Lord, this is frightful! You to come here! I am ruined . . ." Observing that the servants in the entrance hall were looking at them with curiosity, she ended by shoving Angélique into the little living room. "Well, come in. Now, where were we . . . ?"

The first thing Angélique noticed was a cradle near the window that seemed to have an occupant. She went over it to and saw a baby only a few months old smiling happily.

"So that's your secret, my poor Françoise! He's sweet, and you shouldn't have been uneasy on my account. You can depend on me to keep your secret."

So the stubborn virtue of the young widow had at last yielded! She owed all her success in life to her reputation, and yet here she was in quite an embarrassing situation.

"You must have had a dreadful time. Why didn't you tell your friends? We would have helped you."

Françoise Scarron shook her head and smiled wanly. "No, Angélique, it's not at all what you think. Take a good look at that baby, and you will see."

The baby looked up at her with sapphire blue eyes which, as a matter of fact, did seem familiar to her. "Eyes as blue as the sea," she thought. Suddenly it dawned on her—this was the child of Madame de Montespan and the King.

"That's right," said Madame Scarron, wagging her head. "You see what a spot I am in. If it hadn't been the King himself who asked me, I would never have done it. I have to take care of this baby in such utter secrecy that no one will ever suspect he exists. The Marquis de Montespan could claim him by law, as he is quite capable of doing. You can see what a scandal that would make. So, I'm no longer alive . . ."

She drew Angélique down beside her on a sofa. Now that her initial annoyance was over, she wanted the comfort of someone to talk to. She explained how Louvois had recommended her to the King when, as soon as the royal bastard was born, the question arose of who could take care of him well and discreetly. According to law, the child belonged to the husband of Madame de Montespan, since she and the King were married each to another person. Pardaillan, being the person he was, could well be feared. So it was a question not only of bringing up the child but of hiding his origins and guarding him with the greatest possible care. The job required complete loyalty, intelligence, and shrewdness. When Madame Scarron was sounded out, she accepted.

"The King was a little hesitant about me. I don't think he likes me, he has seen me so often. But Louvois

and Athenais insisted. Athenais and I have been thick
for ever so long. She knows what she can expect from
me, and I would have been ungrateful to refuse her after
all she has done for me. Ever since, I have lived as apart
from the world as if I had taken the veil. If only I
had found peace as well! But I have to see to the house
here, supervise the nurse, the cradle rocker, the servants, none of whom know who I am or whose the child
is. And all the while I have to keep putting in an appearance here and there, and living at home so that
no one will suspect what I'm doing. I go in at one door,
and out at another in secret, and when I go to visit my
friends I take the precaution of being bled first so that
I won't blush at lying in answer to the questions I'm
asked. I hope God will forgive me. Lying is the least
of the sacrifices the service of the King demands."

She talked with the good humor with which she had
always made light of her woes. Angélique gathered that
at heart she was rather pleased with her own importance. In spite of its hazards, the post was an enviable
one and gave her a front seat in the life of the King.

The baby whimpered and Françoise got up to see
to it. She smoothed its blankets and pillow in the same
house-wifely way she did everything. Like many women
who live alone and remote from the world of children,
her feelings about her "baby" were not very spontaneous.
She had never known what it was to play with a baby
and leave its tiresome moments to the nurse. But it was
easy to see that this child would get from her everything
it needed for the development of its body, its mind, and
its soul. She was the perfect governess.

"He could be healthier," she said to Angélique. "You
see, he was born with a slightly twisted foot, and they're
afraid he may grow up with a limp. I mentioned it to
the King's doctor, who is also in on the secret, and he
said he thought the waters at Bérèges might prevent
such a deformity. So in the summer I must take him
there. You can see how my job doesn't leave me a free
moment, and what's more it will get worse before it gets
better. Soon I'll have two to be responsible for."

"So the rumors that Madame de Montespan is pregnant again are true?"

"Alas!"

"Why alas?"

"Athenais was in despair when she told me."

"She ought to rejoice. Isn't it a new and unmistakable proof of the King's favor toward her?"

"Alas!" Madame Scarron said again, staring at Angélique, until she had to turn her eyes away.

Françoise lowered her own eyes. There was a silence in the room.

"She is in a frightful state," said the widow. "She comes here every now and then, not to see her baby, but to confide in me and spill all her worries. At Versailles she has to keep smiling all the time. It is no secret that the King's affections are straying." She looked Angélique straight in the face. "And that he is in love with you, Angélique."

Angélique tried to shrug it off. "It's no secret to anyone that the King had me arrested and thrown into prison. That's a fine proof of his love!"

Madame Scarron wagged her head. She would have liked to hear more, but just then the wheels of a coach screeched to a stop outside. Someone rapped impatiently at the door, and a moment later Athenais' imperious tones resounded in the entrance hall. Françoise turned white. She tried to get Angélique to hide in a wardrobe, but Angélique refused. The house was small and had no curtained alcoves.

"Don't be silly. What are you afraid of? I'll explain why I'm here. War has never been declared between us."

She withdrew a little as Madame de Montespan entered swathed in veils. She hurled her fan and her purse on a table, and then a box of lozenges, her gloves and even her watch.

"This is too much," she said. "I have just found out he met her the other day in the Grotto of Thetis."

Then she turned and saw Angélique. Apparently the image of her rival was clearly etched in her mind, because for several seconds she thought she was having an hallucination. Angélique took advantage of the pause to launch her offensive.

"I must apologize to you over and over again, Athenais. I didn't know when I came here that I was intruding into your house. I wanted to see Françoise, whose goings and comings intrigued me so I followed her here."

Madame de Montespan had turned purple. Her eyes were flashing with the fire of unspoken rage.

"You must believe me," Angélique insisted, "when I tell you Madame Scarron did everything to keep me from finding out your secret. He is in good hands. I am the only one to blame."

"Oh, I believe you," exclaimed Athenais with a burst of harsh laughter. "Françoise isn't such a fool as to perpetrate such a blunder knowingly."

She sank into an armchair and stretched out her pink satin slippers. "Take these off for me," she said to Françoise. "They're killing me."

Madame Scarron got down on her knees to remove them.

"Ask them to bring me a basin of warm benzoin water."

Then her gaze returned to the intruder. "As for you, I know you and your sanctimonious touch-me-not attitude. Nosey as a concierge, spying everywhere, too mean to pay a lackey to do your dirty work for you! Your former profession of procuress that you practiced in your chocolate shop sticks out all over you."

Angélique turned on her heel and started for the door. If Athenais were going in for insults right at the start, it would be better to break with her. Angélique was not afraid of her, but she had a morbid horror of scenes with women who accuse you to your face truly or falsely with words that leave a venomous sting behind.

"Stay!"

Athenais' imperious voice stopped her. It was hard for anyone to resist a Mortemart in that mood. Angélique herself felt that Athenais was making a slave of her, but she returned. If Athenais wanted to cross swords, she would fight too. Calmly she waited, her impenetrable

green eyes falling on the Marquise de Montespan, one of
whose silk stockings Madame Scarron had just finished
doughnutting off. There was a trace of scorn in Angélique's eyes, and in her attitude the self-possessed dis-
interest of a person concerned only with her own affairs.

Madame de Montespan's flaming cheeks had faded. She
knew it would do her no good to humiliate her rival. She
changed her tone.

" 'What in-com-par-able dig-ni-ty Madame du Plessis-
Bellière has,' " she said mockingly. " 'Just like a queen.
Not to mention that mysterious quality of hers that
seems to distinguish her.' That's how the King speaks
of you. 'Have you noticed,' he says to me, 'how seldom
she smiles? Yet she can be as gay as a child. Ah, the
Court is a sad place!' The Court a sad place! That's
the kind of inanities you make the King say. That's
how you have seduced him by your detached air, your
lack of sophistication, your turned-up nose. 'Her mys-
teriousness,' I once said to him, 'comes from her misfortunes before she married du Plessis when she had
to sell her charms in unspeakable dens.' Do you know
what he did? He slapped me." She burst into hysterical
laughter. "It was a fine time for him to slap me. The
very next day they found you in bed with that Asiatic
bandit with the long mustache. Oh, how I laughed!"

The royal infant suddenly woke up and began to howl.
Madame Scarron took him out of the cradle and carried
him off to his nurse. When she returned, Madame de Montespan was weeping hot tears into her handkerchief, her
hysterical laughter having turned into hysterical crying.

"It's too late," she sobbed. "I thought that would be
the end of his love for you, but his love survived it. He
was only punishing himself in punishing you, and I
just had to bear the brunt of his foul humor. I had to
believe the affairs of state could not go on without you.
'I would have liked to ask Madame du Plessis' advice,'
he would say. That's what I couldn't bear. He has no
use for a woman's advice. He takes infinite pains to see
that no one can possibly accuse him of doing anything
because a woman advised him or asked him to. When he
grants me a favor—an advancement for some one or other

of my protégés—he does it as if he were giving me a
jewel to pay me for being his mistress, not because he
trusts my judgment. But *she* . . . SHE! He asks her advice on questions of *international* politics." Madame de
Montespan shrieked as if that last adjective were the
crowning blow. "He treats her like a man."

"That ought to be some reassurance to you," said Angélique.

"No! You are the only woman he has ever treated that
way."

"Nonsense! Didn't Madame just get assigned to an important diplomatic mission in England?"

"Madame is the daughter of a King and the sister of
Charles II. Besides, even if the King did employ her and
is grateful to her for undertaking the project, he has
nothing but loathing for her. Madame just thinks she
has regained his friendship and perhaps even his love by
this means, but she is sadly mistaken. The King uses
her, yes, but he despises her more and more for being so
intelligent. He doesn't like intelligence in women."

Madame Scarron interrupted in an attempt to sweet-
en the atmosphere. "What man does like intelligence in
a woman?" she sighed. "My dear, dear friends, you're
arguing about nothing. Like any other man, the King
likes variety. Let him follow his whim, it's a common
one. With one he likes to chat, and with another, to sit
in silence. You are in an enviable position, Athenais, and
I wouldn't make light of it if I were you. Whenever you
try to get everything, you risk losing everything, and
someday you'll wake up quite surprised to find the King
has forsaken you . . . for a third charmer you haven't
foreseen."

"That's right," Angélique said. "Don't forget, Françoise, you're the one the King is fated to marry some
day, as the witch predicted. And we, Athenais and I,
will find ourselves with our noses out of joint." She put
on her cloak in preparation for leaving. "Don't forget
that, Madame. We were friends once."

Athenais de Montespan sprang up like a jack-in-the-
box. She leaped after Angélique and seized her by the
wrists.

"Don't think what I just said is an admission of defeat or that I leave the field to you. The King is mine. He belongs to me. You shall never have him! I'll tear his love for you out of his heart by the roots. And if I can't do that, I'll tear you out, yes, right out of the land of the living. He is not the sort of man to keep on loving a ghost."

She sunk her nails into Angélique's arm. The pain aroused Angélique's smoldering hatred. She had often seen in others how destructive that emotion could be, how it ate away at them like an acid, but at that moment she had never hated anyone so much in her life. All her loathing for Madame de Montespan began to flow out of her like seething lava, and she conceived for her a profoundly bitter disgust that transformed itself into rage. Freeing one of her arms, she struck the King's mistress full in the face with all her strength. Athenais shrieked.

Madame Scarron threw herself between them. "Stop!" she said. "You are disgracing yourselves, ladies. Remember you both come from the same province. All three of us are from Poitou."

Her voice was surprisingly commanding, and she dominated them with the calm, wise dignity that shone in her level black eyes. Angélique never could tell why that allusion to their common birthplace should have so deflated their anger. She withdrew and shakily descended the stairs. The nails of the Fury had left deep purple crescents on her flesh, which were beginning to ooze blood. She stopped in the vestibule to dab at them. Madame Scarron caught up with her there. She was too much a diplomat to let go so unceremoniously the woman who perhaps tomorrow would be the new favorite at Versailles.

"She hates you, Angélique," she whispered. "Take good care of yourself. I am on your side, you know."

"A madwoman!" Angélique kept telling herself to calm her nerves.

But it was worse than that. She knew perfectly well that Athenais was no madwoman, but quite in control of her senses and capable of anything. Now she was hated, something she had never been before. By Philippe, perhaps, when he was struggling against the attraction she held for him, but that was not the smothering hatred which was surrounding her now like poison flowers. And in the wind that blew over the sandy hillocks of Vaugirard she seemed to hear the plaintive voice of her little lost page:

> The Queen has had a nosegay made
> Of the fairest lilies in the glade.
> The Marquise sniffed their fragrance sweet,
> And fell down dead at the Queen's feet.

chapter 25

*A*FTER Mass the following Sunday the King went to touch the scrofulous. The parade proceeded from the chapel to the Salon of Diana, down the Great Gallery, across the Salon of Peace and into the gardens. The infirm, accompanied by long-robed doctors and some almoners, were waiting at the foot of the stairs to the Orangerie.

Angélique followed with the ladies. By some stroke of luck Madame de Montespan was not present, nor was the Queen. Mademoiselle de la Vallière sidled up to her and told her how glad she was to see her again. The pathetic ex-mistress was keeping her hopes up just as long as any hope was possible. No one could mistake the smiles and looks the King gave Madame du Plessis-Bellière, and the whole Court knew that her disgrace had been followed immediately by restoration to favor.

After two hours the rumor got around that refreshments were waiting in the Grove of Marais. Everyone cut across the lawn to the Royal Avenue.

Angélique saw Madame de Montespan advancing under a parasol of pink and blue satin edged with gold and silver lace that her little Negro was carrying behind her. She was full of smiles for everyone as she invited them to follow her to her favorite grove. She herself had designed it and supervised its construction.

All the Queen's lap dogs bounded down the staircase by the Fountain of Latona yapping happily. Behind them came the sad-faced, ugly dwarfs. Then the Queen, sad-faced and ugly too. She was out of temper because she had no parasol like Madame de Montespan's to shield her from the sun. Presently the King joined Angélique.

The Queen's dwarfs began stamping out a grotesque

sarabande under the leadership of Barcarole, winding
among the courtiers who were either delighted or
shocked at the travesty. Their hoarse shouts and their
cackling laughter drowned out the music of the violins.

The King looked at Angélique beside him as if he
were hypnotized.

"To behold you is sometimes joy, sometimes torture.
When I see the veins pulse in your snow-white throat I
want to put my lips to it, lay my forehead against it.
Everything in me cries out for the warmth of your presence. Your absence is like an icy shroud to me. I need
your stillness, your voice, your strength. Yet I long madly
to see you weaken. How I should like to see you sleeping
beside me, tears pearling your lashes, vanquished in our
tender combat! And to see you awake with ardor renewed and bubbling out of you like cool water from a
woodland spring as the dawn caresses your cheek with
its rosy fingers. You blush so easily people think you are
susceptible, but you are really as hard as a diamond. I
have loved so long your hidden violence that now I
shudder to think that some day it will tear you from my
grasp, . . . my heart, my soul!"

A violent bump interrupted them. Angélique's dish
flew out of her hands as she was carrying it to her
mouth, and shattered into a thousand pieces. The sherbet spilled on the ground, staining her blue gown with
streaks of the many-colored dessert. Barcarole had mis-
judged his distance in leaping and had jostled her elbow.

"A plague on these shrimps!" exclaimed the King
furiously. He grabbed his walking stick and whacked the
back of the awkward dwarf, who scuttered away squawk-
ing like a seagull. When the Queen rose to his defense,
the King put her in her place sharply. One of the dogs
dashed to lap up the remains of the sherbet.

Twenty ladies present rushed to help Angélique
sponge the spots off her gown, or brought her napkins
and water. Her glory today had been too dazzling. Then
everyone suddenly remembered that the sun would
soon go down and left the shade to return to the lawns
and enjoy the daylight while it lasted.

The little dog was writhing in agony on the ground when Barcarole came back to the deserted spot. He summoned Angélique and bent over to examine the animal's convulsions.

"You see? Now I hope you will understand, Marquise of the Angels. I hope you will get it through your head somehow. He's going to croak from eating the dessert that was intended for you. Of course it would not have had such a ghastly effect on you. By now you would have just begun to feel sick, but you would have spent a horrible night, and in the morning you would have been dead."

"Barcarole, it's inconceivable, what you say. The King's punishment has unsettled your reason."

"So you don't understand?" said the dwarf. "You fool, didn't you see the dog eat your sherbet?"

"No, I was too busy with my dress. The dog might be dying of something else, so far as that goes."

"You don't believe me because you don't want to believe me."

"But who would want to take my life?"

"What a question! For one, the woman whose place you have taken in the King's affections. Do you think she has any love for you?"

"Madame de Montespan? That's impossible, Barcarole. She is cold and wicked and likes to spread scandal, but she would never go that far."

"Why not? Whatever she gets her claws on she keeps tight hold of."

He picked up the dog which has just given its last gasp, and threw it deep into the bushes.

"Duchesne was the one who did it. Naaman, the little Negro, told me. She confides in him as she thinks that because he has a funny accent he can't understand French. He sleeps on a cushion in the corner of her room and she pays no more attention to him than to a dog. Yesterday he was in her room when she received Duchesne. She is his bad angel. It was she who got him his post as the King's steward. Naaman heard them mention your name and listened because he knows you. You were his first owner and he loved Florimond, who used to play with him here at Versailles and give him candy. She told Duchesne: 'It must come to a stop tomorrow. You'll find an opportunity during the fête to bring her a drink into which you have dropped something.' Then she gave him a phial. Duchesne asked: 'Did La Voisin prepare this?' and Montespan said: 'Yes, and anything she makes is pretty effective.' Naaman didn't know who La Voisin is, but I do. La Voisin was my patroness. Oh, she knows plenty of ways to send people into the other world."

Angélique's thoughts whirled in her brain like the scattered pieces of a difficult puzzle.

"If you are right, then Florimond was not lying. Do you think she would also try to poison the King? What would be her purpose?"

The dwarf looked doubtful. "Poison him? I don't think so. But she has had powders La Voisin gave her put into his food to cast a spell on him. They had no effect whatever on the King, either good or bad. Now we had better scram out of here before Duchesne comes back with his fags."

Outside the dusky grove night was spreading over the copper sky. Coolly murmuring water trickled from the urns supported by cloven-hoofed bronze satyrs placed here and there along the walk. Barcarole trotted along beside Angélique like a misshapen shadow.

"What are you going to do now, Marquise?"

"I don't know."

"I hope you're going to go all-out."

"What do you mean by that?"

"Defend yourself the same way. An eye for an eye and a tooth for a tooth, as they say. You can slip the Montespan a blackspot in her soup, since that's her style. A few rusty knives wielded by the brotherhood some dark night on the Pont-Neuf will do for Duchesne. All you have to do is give the order."

Angélique kept silent. The evening mists were making her shiver. She did not want to believe him yet.

"There's nothing else to do, Marquise," whispered Barcarole. "Unless you want to give it all up. She is going to keep the King, and on the honor of the Mortemarts, as she says, the devil himself will help her!"

Several days later a fête brought the royal family together at Versailles. The household of Monsieur and that of Madame added a note of domesticity to the festivities. Florimond, accompanied by his tutor, greeted his mother while she was talking to the King by the Latona Fountain. The boy was perfectly at ease with the great, for he knew his pleasant face framed in brown curls, and his innocent smile, could disarm them. He was dressed in a crimson velvet suit and black stockings with gold cloches. He bowed to the King and kissed his mother's hand.

"So this is the deserter?" said the King kindly. "Do you like your new job, my boy?"

"Sire, Monsieur's household is pleasant, but I prefer Versailles."

"I admire your frankness. What do you miss most about Versailles?"

"Your majesty's presence . . . and the fountains."

It was a happy choice. Nothing was dearer to the heart of Louis XIV than his fountains and the admiration they aroused. And flattery was not displeasing to him, even from the lips of a thirteen-year-old.

"You shall see them again. I will tend to it when you have learned not to tell lies."

"Learned to keep still, perhaps," Florimond said, "but not to lie, because I never have lied."

Angélique and the Abbé de Lesdiguières, who was discreetly standing a few steps away, showed signs of anxiety, for the King was frowning at the boy looking up at him so proudly.

"The boy does not look much like you, but he is obviously your child from the way he can cope with things when he wants to. Your relationship might be suspected if it were not for that chin of his that proclaims he is yours. Of the whole Court only you and he could look at the King that way."

"I beg Your Majesty's pardon."

"Why? You are not sorry for him or for yourself. But, what the devil! I don't know what to think of this business. They say truth is found in the mouths of babes, so why should I doubt it. I must question Duchesne. He was recommended to me by Madame de Montespan, but no man knows him well."

Angélique later recalled that at the very time the King was talking a lackey was kneeling to offer him a basket of fruit, not for his use—for the King never ate unless surrounded by his household officers—but for him to admire. The King praised the beauty of the big red, green and russet-skinned apples, the honey-colored pears, the dawn-tinted peaches. Then they were taken away to be displayed on the long tables covered with such dazzlingly white clothes that they looked like arctic snowfields. The weather was just right for the kind of entertainment that had been arranged for the day, and the evening was so mild that the courtiers crowded on the lawns and terraces near the palace. It was then while she was looking at the golden cross cast over the fields by the sunset that Angélique felt a little hand grab her skirt.

"Ma'm! Ma'm Plessis!"

She looked down to discover Naaman, the little Negro page, in his peacock-blue jacket, turban and full trousers. Even in the dim light she could see the whites of his eyes rolling like billiard balls.

"Ma'm! You boy dyin'! You boy dyin'!"

His accent was so thick she did not grasp his meaning.

"M'sieu Florimond! He vessick, vessick. Die!"

When she heard Florimond's name she grabbed the page and shook him.

"What's the matter with Florimond? Speak up!"

"Dunno, ma'm, dunno. E'yone sca'd 'bout he!"

Angélique started off at a run for the North Terrace where she had seen the Abbé de Lesdiguières a little while before. He was still there by one of the big marble vases filled with geraniums, bearing up heroically under the teasings of Madame de Garmont and Madame de Montbazen.

"Abbé," she shouted, "where is Florimond?"

"He just went by, Madame. He told me he had to do something in the kitchen and would be back presently. You know how he loves to run errands and make himself useful."

"No, no!" said Naaman, shaking his turban with its long aigrettes. "*He* say: 'I get rid dat Florimond you know how. We be quiet now. He no tattle no mo.' "

"Did you hear what he said? The boy will never talk any more?" Angélique screamed, shaking the abbé. "For the love of God, tell me where he went!"

"I—I—he told me," the abbé stammered, "the kitchens . . . he was going by the Diana staircase to get there quicker . . ."

Naaman howled like a monkey caught in a trap and stuck out his pink tongue toward the palace. He raised his hands with his fingers spread melodramatically.

"De Di'na stai'case? Oh, ve'y bad, ve'y bad!"

He broke away and ran as fast as his legs could carry him toward the palace. Angélique and the abbé followed him. Her maternal instincts gave wings to her feet, and in spite of her heavy dress, her high-heeled slippers and the page who kept tripping over her train, she kept up with them and got there just as they started quizzing a guard in the vestibule of the South Wing apartment.

"A little page dressed in red?" said the guard. "Yes, I saw him go by just a minute ago. I was surprised because hardly anyone goes this way since the stairs were torn up for the enlargements."

"But . . . But . . ." the abbé stammered, "beforehand . . . when we used to live here, the Diana staircase was often used. You could go up it to a balcony from which the South stairs led down to the kitchens."

"Not any more. They've torn down a whole wall to enlarge the wing. The Diana staircase is out of use. There is nothing but scaffolding at the top."

"Florimond did not know. Florimond did not know," the abbé kept repeating like an automaton.

"You don't mean the boy went up there?" the guard exclaimed with an oath. "I shouted at him to stop, but he was running too fast."

Already Naaman, the abbé and Angélique were off

again. The Diana staircase loomed before them into a darkness so deep they could only guess at the scaffolding at the top. The workmen had already quit. It was toward that dark maze of unknown pitfalls that Florimond had run. Angélique started up, her legs dissolving under her.

"Wait," shouted the guard. "Wait till I get my tinderbox. You'll fall into the hole. There is a catwalk, but you have to know how to find it."

Angélique groped her way forward among the beams and the heaps of fallen plaster until the guard caught up with them.

"Stop!" he called. "Look!"

The flame of his tinderbox revealed only two feet away a yawning chasm two stories deep.

"They've taken away the catwalk!" the guard said.

Angélique's knees buckled under her as she leaned over the dark abyss that had swallowed up her child.

"Florimond!"

Her voice seemed to come from someone else. A draught blew the dank air of the cavernous gulf up into her face. The echo of the huge palace was her only answer.

"Florimond!"

The guard tried to pierce the darkness with his feeble flame. "I can't see a thing. If he fell, he must still be down there. We've got to get rope and ladders and torches. Father, hold her so she won't fall too. Don't stay there. We'll go for help."

Haggard with anxiety she staggered down the accursed stairs.

"They've killed my boy . . . My pride and joy . . . The little tattler will never talk again . . . Florimond didn't know . . ."

The guard and the abbé helped her to a bench in the dark vestibule. The two Negro pages were howling like birds of ill omen.

A maid carrying a six-branched candelabra appeared from a corridor running perpendicular to the courtyard.

"Are you ill, Madame? I have some smelling salts with me."

"Her son has fallen off the scaffolding," the guard said. "Stay here with your candles. I'm going for help."

Angélique stood up suddenly. "Listen!"

Her voice was enough to hush up the pages. Then from far off they could hear someone running, running in little red heels. Florimond suddenly emerged at full tilt from the same corridor as the maid. He would have passed without seeing them if the guard had not had the presence of mind to bar his way with his halberd.

"Let me go! Let me by!" Florimond shouted. "I'm late bringing what Monsieur de Caraport sent me for in the kitchen."

"Stop, Florimond," shouted the Abbé de Lesdiguières, trying to hold him with his shaking hands. "That staircase is dangerous. You'll be killed if . . ."

He turned deathly white and sank onto the bench beside Angélique. For a moment it had seemed Florimond would dash to his death right before their eyes. But the guard had him tightly by the collar.

"Take it easy, you little monkey! Didn't they just tell you it was dangerous?"

"But I'm late!"

"You're never late when you risk death. Take it easy, son, and thank the Blessed Virgin and your good angel."

Still out of breath, Florimond explained what had happened. Just as he had got to where they now were he had run into the Duc d'Anjou, the King's third and youngest child, only a year and a half old, all decked out in his gold lace and pearl cap and a lace collar and the great ribbon of Saint Louis pinned across his black velvet dress. He had escaped from his nurses and was wandering through the labyrinth of his palace with an apple in his hand like a little lost god.

Always obliging, Florimond had picked up the royal baby and carried him back to his nursery quite a distance away in the apartments of the Dauphin and his sister. At the very time that Angélique was almost fainting as she leaned over the brink of the cavernous pit, Florimond was receiving the heartfelt thanks of the prince's nurses and governesses. Then as they were bless-

ing themselves for being spared, he was off like the wind
to finish his errand.

Angélique took him on her lap and hugged him to
her. She could hardly make sense.

"If he had left me too, after Cantor, I would have
died. Everything that held me to you, my love, would
be gone. Oh, when will you come back to rescue me?"

She did not even know whom she was talking to, so
hysterical was she. Never would she forget the mocking
sweetness of that twilight at Versailles when the little
black hands of a slave had tugged at her gown: "Ma'm,
you boy dyin' . . ."

She looked around for Naaman, but he had disappeared. Now that Master Florimond was safe and sound,
he had gone back to his mistress, the "other one."
Doubtless he'd get a slap from her jeweled hand for
being away so long.

The maid had gone for some wine and glasses. Angélique forced herself to drink a little, even though her
throat was still tight from worry.

"You have a drink too, you others," she said. "Drink,
my good soldier. Without you and your tinderbox we
might all be at the bottom of the pit."

The guard tossed off at one gulp the glass she gave
him. "I won't refuse, for I'm on the safe side too. What
I don't understand is how the catwalk got taken
away. I'll have to tell my captain to report it to the
supervisor."

Angélique slipped him and the maid three gold
pieces each. Then, holding Florimond tightly by the
hand, and followed by the abbé and her page, she went
to her own apartment. There she collapsed again.

"They wanted to kill my son!" was all she could think
of.

"Florimond, who sent you on an errand to the
kitchens?"

"Monsieur de Caraport, an officer of the King's Table
Service. I know him well."

Angélique put her hand to her damp forehead. "Will
I ever know the truth?"

In the next room she heard René de Lesdiguières telling "Swordthrust" Malbrant about the incident.

"Did that Monsieur de Caraport tell you the Diana stairway was dangerous and that no one had used it for a long time?"

"No."

"He must have warned you, but you weren't listening."

"No, that's not so," Florimond protested angrily. "He even said, 'Go by the Diana staircase. You know the way. It's the shortest way to the kitchens.'"

I wish I knew if he's fibbing to get out of it, Angélique thought. She could not get rid of the obsession that someone wanted to kill her son. "The catwalk has been taken away . . ." What should she do? What was she to think?

In her doubt and danger all she had to guide her were literal-minded servants, like the little Negro and the dwarf. The whole petty world of Versailles groveling in the shadow of the great seemed to rise up before her to mutter: "Take care!" She was tempted to trust that animal instinct.

"What must I do?" she asked Malbrant, who was a man of some experience even though he was only a squire. His white hair gave him an air of wisdom that must have taken him some time to acquire. He knitted his bushy eyebrows while he listened to the abbé's report.

"We ought to go back to Saint-Cloud, Madame. The boy has some protection in Monsieur's establishment."

Angélique smiled listlessly. "Who would have thought there would come a day . . . " Well, that's that. I think you're right."

"The main thing is not to let him fall into Duchesne's clutches again."

"You think that's where the trouble came from?"

"I'd stake my right hand on it. Let him wait. Some day I'll catch him and skin him alive."

Florimond was just beginning to understand that an attempt had been made on his life. He was proud as a peacock.

"It's all because I told the King I didn't lie about Duchesne. Picard, the lackey who was offering him the fruit, must have heard me and told Duchesne."

"But it was Caraport who sent you to the kitchens."

"Caraport obeys Duchesne. So that old Duchesne is scared of me!"

"When will you ever learn you just can't say things at random?" Angélique demanded. Now after smothering him with kisses she was having difficulty to keep from slapping him. "Don't you realize you could have broken every bone in your body if you had fallen off that scaffolding?"

"I'd just be dead," Florimond said philosophically. "Hell, that happens to everyone. I would have been with Cantor by now." Then after a moment's thought he said: "No, Cantor is not dead."

Thérèse and Javotte came in with the dress Angélique was to wear to the ball.

"Take him away," Angélique told his tutor. "My nerves are so frazzled I don't know what I'm doing. Watch over him and don't leave his side for a minute."

The boy had hardly left with the abbé and the squire than she wanted them back.

"I'm losing my mind. If I only knew for sure . . ."

She asked Thérèse to pour her a glass of brandy, but then she hesitated to drink it. What if it were poisoned? Nevertheless she drained it down and then things seemed clearer.

"If I knew for sure, then I would take action."

Barcarole's hints came back to her. To get rid of Duchesne would be an easy matter, which Malbrant could take care of, or else some hired assassins. If she had one of Madame de Montespan's servants on her side, she could at least know ahead of time what dangers threatened her. She thought of Desoeillet, whom Athenais trusted implicitly, but who was a venal enough girl she had once caught cheating at cards.

Thanks to another glass of brandy she was able to dance and appear on the top of the wave, but much later after the Queen's supper party, when she came back to her apartment, her sense of fear returned and became almost unbearable. It seemed to her that she was not alone in her room. She turned her head and almost shrieked with terror. Two black eyes were staring at her from behind a wardrobe, and a shrunken figure tiptoed out like a cat stalking a mouse.

"Barcarole!"

The dwarf was looking at her with an intense, almost cruel expression on his face.

"The magician is here at Versailles with his partner," he whispered hoarsely. "Come on, sister, there are things you ought to know if you care about your life."

She followed him out the secret door that Bontemps had shown her. Barcarole had no candle, but he could see in the dark like an animal. Angélique kept stumbling and bumping into the walls of the narrow secret corridor. She had to stoop, and grope with her hands before her. She felt as if she were buried alive.

"Here we are," Barcarole said.

She heard his fingernails scratching on the wall in search of something.

"Sister, because you are one of us, I will show you something. But be careful. Whatever happens and whatever you hear or see, don't make a sound."

"You can depend on me."

"Even if you should see a crime? A crime more horrible than any you could imagine?"

"I won't flinch."

"If you do, it means death for you and me both."

There was an almost inaudible click, and then the frame of a door was outlined in light. Angélique fixed her eyes on the barely opened crack. At first she could not make anything out. Then little by little she distinguished the furnishings of a room in which three big wax candles were burning. Then she heard chanting like that in church. Shadows flitted about. Squatting on his heels not far from her was a man chanting in a singsong voice like a tipsy sacristan. He held a missal and was swaying backward and forward. Through the steam that rose from kettles bubbling on chafing dishes she saw a tall man advance toward them. Angélique felt an icy sweat drip down her neck.

Never, she thought, have I seen a more terrifying human being.

It was a priest, for he was wearing a sort of white chasuble embroidered with black fir-apples. In spite of his springy walk, he was of a great age which showed in a sort of inner corruption expressed by the color of his face, which was like wine-lees, and in the purplish veins that webbed his features. He seemed a half-decomposed cadaver raised from a grave and daring to mingle with the living again. The hollow sonority of his voice cracked into a senile quaver that nonetheless gave him a weird kind of authority. One eye was completely gone, but he squinted out of the other with an intensity that seemed to miss nothing and could penetrate into the deepest secrets.

Angélique recognized the witch Catherine Monvoisin among the women kneeling before him. Then she sensed what the scene before her meant. Half-swooning, she leaned against the wall. Barcarole grabbed her hand and squeezed it hard.

"Come now, don't be afraid. They can't know you are here."

"The Devil knows it," she stammered through chattering teeth.

"The Devil is gone. See, the ceremony is almost over."

Another woman advanced and knelt. When she raised her veil, Angélique saw it was Madame de Montespan. She was so astounded she forgot her fear. How could the intelligent, haughty Athenais sully her beautiful body in this sinister travesty!

The priest held out a book to her. The Marquise laid her white hands on it. Her rings glittered. Like a halting schoolgirl, she repeated a prayer.

"In the name of Ashtaroth and Asmodeus, lords of friendship, I ask the friendship of the King and the Dauphin, and that I may keep it always. May the Queen be sterile. May the King leave her bed and board for me. May all my rivals perish . . ."

Angélique hardly recognized her, so distracted she looked, so enthralled by her passion for meandering into this horrible adventure whose true meaning she had not grasped.

The bluish vapors, tinged with the acrid odor of incense, thickened, then drifted into thin clouds that raveled out over the celebrants, giving them the misty look of faces seen in a dream. The psalms-singer fell silent. He had closed his book and was scratching himself as he waited for the congregation to depart.

Madame de Montespan asked him: "Have you the shift?"

"That's right, the shift!" said La Voisin rising. "We took great pains not to forget that, not after all you paid us. I know you'll say it's a lovely piece of work. I gave it to my daughter. Margot, bring the basket here."

A girl of about twelve appeared out of the haze and set down a basket from which she extracted with great care a nightgown of pink voile embroidered with silver threads.

"Be careful not to hold it too long," her mother said. "Use the plane-tree leaves I brought."

Angélique stuffed her hand into her mouth. From her hiding place she recognized one of her favorite nightgowns there in the hands of the girl.

Thérèse!" someone called.

Angélique's maid appeared with the supercilious look on her swarthy face of a fool who has been raised to an important position.

"Take this, my girl," said La Voisin, "and handle it with caution. Here, I'll give you some plane-tree leaves to protect yourself. Don't shut the basket, Margot, we've got to put you know what into it."

She went to the other end of the room and returned with a little bundle of white linen on which stains of blood were raying out.

Angélique squeezed her eyelids together and clasped her hands tightly against her breast to keep from crying out in horror: "Murderers! Foul, monstrous murderers!" She hadn't the strength to look any more, but she could hear them bustling about in the sacristy blowing out the candles and clinking the silver vases together.

The cracked, sepulchral voice of the priest said: "See that the watchmen don't look into the basket."

"No danger," cackled La Voisin. "After all the precautions I've taken, the guards will be bowing and scraping to me instead."

Suddenly there was total silence. Angélique opened her eyes in darkness. Barcarole had shut the door.

"I guess you know enough about that now, since you could hardly stand any more of it. Let's be on our way before we run into that rat of a Bontemps. He snoops around all night long like a weasel."

Back in Angélique's apartment he stood a-tiptoe to reach the decanter of plum brandy. He poured two glasses.

"Drink this. You're positively green. You aren't so used to it as I am. Lord, I worked for two years as a porter in La Voisin's house. I know her well. I know all of them. She's not a bad sort. She knows a lot, especially about chiromancy and physiognomy. She's been studying them since she was nine years old. She told me the people who come to get their palms read inevitably say they want to get rid of someone. At first she used to answer they would die when God pleased, but then they would tell her that she wasn't very clever, and so she changed her ways and got rich. Ha-ha!"

Barcarole smacked his lips and poured himself another glass of brandy.

"What worries me is that shift. It's yours, eh?"

"Yes."

"I thought so. Seeing your maid Thérèse at that witches' sabbath put a bug in my ear. Sure as shooting, Montespan wants to get rid of you. She has paid La Voisin to make one of her special medicines for you. It wasn't so long ago, I know, that she went to the Auvergne and to Normandie to learn the secrets of poisoning without a trace."

"Now I've been warned I can escape the trap, and I know whom to ask for advice too." She drank her second glass of brandy assiduously. "Who was the priest?"

"Abbé Guibourg from the parish of Saint-Marcel in

Saint-Denis. He's the one who sacrifices babies so that their blood can be drunk."

"Stop it!" Angélique shouted with all her might.

"La Voisin has an oven at her house in which she must have burned up at least two thousand stillborn children or sacrificed ones."

"Stop it! Be still!"

"Nice people, aren't they, Marquise, these high and mighty, and they have nice friends too, eh? The one chanting psalms near us was Lesage, the 'great author' of sorcery. Madame de la Roche-Guyon is the godmother of his daughter. He-he-he!"

"Shut up!" Angélique shouted. She picked up a figurine from the mantel and hurled it at him. It broke against the wall. Barcarole turned a somersault and headed for the door still chuckling. She heard his ribald laughter disappear down the passageway.

When Thérèse came to her room the next night, carrying the pink nightgown, Angélique was in a negligee at her dressing table. She watched the maid in her mirror as she spread the shift carefully on the bed, fluffed up the pillows and turned down the covers for the night.

"Thérèse!"

"Madame Marquise?"

"Thérèse, you know I am very pleased with your work . . ."

The girl fidgeted with a silly smile on her face. "Madame la Marquise makes me very happy."

"I should like to make you a little present. You deserve one. I am going to give you that nightgown you just brought me. It will just suit you. Take it."

Angélique turned back to her mirror. There was a deathly hush in the room. She saw the reflection of the girl's ashen face, and had proof enough. Suddenly she rose up in anger.

"Take it," she said in a terrible voice, her teeth set. "Take it!" She marched over to the maid, her emerald eyes flashing like lightning. "Don't you want to take it?

Well, I know why. Open your hands, you accursed wretch!"

Thérèse dropped the plane-trees leaves which she had crumpled up in her hands to hide them.

"The leaves! The plane-tree leaves!" shouted Angélique, crushing them under her foot.

She struck the girl with the full force of her arm, twice, three times, making her head wobble.

"Get out! Go to your master, the Devil!"

With a dreadful groan Thérèse went out, her face buried in her arms.

Angélique was trembling in every muscle. A few moments later Javotte brought in a tray of supper, and found her standing in the middle of the room staring about her unseeingly. Silently the girl set the pot of jam, the rolls and the pitcher of lemonade on the table.

"Javotte," Angélique said suddenly, "haven't you always loved David Chaillou?"

The girl blushed, and her soft gray eyes opened wide. "It's been a long time since I've seen him, Madame."

"But you always were in love with him, weren't you?"

"Yes. But he probably wouldn't even look at me now, Madame. He has become an important person with his restaurant and chocolate shop. They say he's going to marry the daughter of a notary."

"Why does he have to do that, the fool? He needs a woman like you. You shall marry him."

"I am not rich enough for him, Madame."

"You shall be, Javotte. I will give you a dowry of four hundred *livres* a year, and a complete trousseau. You will have two dozen sheets, Cambrai underwear, damask tablecloths. You will be such a good match that he is going to take another look at your pink cheeks and your pretty nose. I know he always liked them."

The maid looked at her in astonishment. "You will do all that for me, Madame?"

"Why shouldn't I? You fed my children when that nurse was letting them die of starvation." She put her arms around the graceful shoulders of the girl and felt the comforting warmth of her young body pressing against her own.

"Have you been a good girl, Javotte?"

"I've done my best, Madame. I have prayed to the Blessed Virgin. But you know how it is here with all these fresh lackeys around, and the fine gentlemen making eyes at you. It's been hard sometimes. I've let them kiss me, for sure, but I never committed any sin."

Angélique hugged her tighter, admiring the courage of this orphan adrift in the corruption of Versailles.

"Go now, my child. Tomorrow I am going back to Paris to see David Chaillou. Soon you will be married to him."

"Can I help Madame undress?" Javotte asked, moving toward the pink nightgown.

"No, leave that alone. Run along now, I want to be alone."

Javotte went out obediently, but not without a sidelong glance at the decanter of brandy to see how empty it might be. For some time the Marquise had been leaving very little in it.

chapter 26

*T*HE very next day Angélique was returning in
her coach from Paris to Saint-Germain. A cab had turned
over in a ditch, and as Angélique drew near she recognized the girl waiting in the briars by the roadside as
one of Madame de Montespan's suite, Mademoiselle
Desoeillet. She stopped and waved at her in a friendly
way.

"Oh, Madame, what a mess I am in!" the girl exclaimed. "Madame de Montespan sent me on an urgent
errand, and she'll be furious at my being late, and yet
here I've been stuck for a whole half hour. That fool
coachman didn't see a big rock in the middle of the
road."

"Were you going to Paris?"

"Yes . . . that is, half-way. I was to meet a person at
the Bois-Sec crossroad who would give me a message
for Madame de Montespan. Now I'm so late the person
will probably have gone. Madame de Montespan will be
terribly out of temper."

"Get in. I'll have the horses turn around."

"Madame, you are too kind."

"I can't leave you in this fix. I'm glad to do Athenais
a favor."

Mademoiselle Desoeillet gathered up her skirts and
seated herself respectfully on the edge of the coach seat.
She seemed worried. She was quite a pretty girl with that
certain boldness Madame de Montespan managed somehow to instill in all her suite. Her attendants were
known for their fine speech, their wit and their good
taste. She trained the women in her own image—always
at ease and always unscrupulous.

Angélique watched the girl out of the corner of her
eye. She had already thought of allying herself with one

of her enemy's companions and especially with this same Desoeillet, whose weak character she had previously noted. She was a tricky, conscienceless girl, and it took a trained eye to catch her at her game; but Angélique's experiences in the Court of Miracles had taught her all the devices of cheats. Mademoiselle Desoeillet undoubtedly was familiar with them too.

"Ah, here we are!" said the girl, sticking her head out the window of the coach. "The Lord be praised, the urchin is still there."

Angélique ordered the coachman to stop. Out of the green forest screen a twelve-year-old girl who had been waiting in the shade of the trees advanced toward the coach. She was simply dressed and wore a white bonnet. She handed a little package to Mademoiselle Desoeillet, who whispered something to her and then took out her purse. Angélique could see the gold coins through its mesh, and calculated to the last *écu* how much it contained. The total made her raise her eyebrows.

"What can be in that package to make it cost so much?" she asked, eyeing it through her quizzing glass as Mademoiselle Desoeillet stowed it away in her big bag. She thought she detected a bottle.

"We can go on now, Madame," the girl said, visibly relieved to have accomplished her errand so easily.

While the coach was turning around in the junction of the two roads, Angélique stole another look at the girl in the white bonnet who was disappearing again into the forest.

"Where have I seen that child before?" she thought uneasily.

She kept still for a moment while the coach was getting under way again for Saint-Germain. The more time went by the more she believed she could turn this occasion to her advantage. Suddenly she uttered a little cry.

"What's the matter, Madame?" asked Mademoiselle Desoeillet.

"Nothing at all, just a pin that came unfastened."

"Can I help you?"

"No, thanks, it's nothing."

Angélique turned from red to pale and back again, as suddenly she remembered the face of the urchin girl. She had seen it before in the light of two candles on a sinister occasion. It was La Voisin's daughter, the one who was carrying "the basket."

"Can't I help you, Madame?" the girl insisted.

"Well, yes, I guess so, if you could help me unfasten my skirt."

The girl did so, and Angélique thanked her. "You are very kind. You know, I have often admired your cleverness as a wardrobe mistress for my friend Athenais ... and your patience too."

Mademoiselle smiled a reply. Angélique wondered whether she knew about her mistress' evil plans. Who knows, perhaps she had right in her bag the poison that was destined for Madame du Plessis-Bellière, with whom she was now getting on so well. Fate has a wry sense of humor. What good did it do to laugh up one's sleeve? But she would lose nothing by waiting!

"What I most admire about you is your skill at cards," Angélique went on subtly. "I was watching you last Monday when you beat the Duc de Chaulnes. The poor man will never get over it. Where did you learn to cheat so cleverly?"

The sugary smile of Mademoiselle Desoeillet vanished. It was her turn to change from red to white and back again.

"What are you saying, Madame?" she faltered. "Cheat? I? Why, it's impossible. I would never allow myself . . ."

"Neither would I, my dear," said Angélique, deliberately emphasizing the tartness of her familiarity.

She took the girl's hand and turned it over to examine the ends of her fingers. "Your fingertips have such delicate skin I can guess what you use them for. I have seen you file them with a piece of whaleskin to make them sensitive enough to detect the markings on the cards you play with. They're marked in such a way that only hands like yours can recognize them. The Duc de Chaulnes' tough hands would be hard put to find anything suspicious . . . unless someone called it to his attention."

The girl's veneer cracked, and she became just a little adventuress seeing her castles in the air crumble. She knew that at Court the only thing no one took lightly and that could lead to ruin was dishonesty at cards. The Duc de Chaulnes was already put out at having lost over a thousand *livres* to such a young girl of humble origin, and would never endure the insult of having been cheated. If her tricks were uncovered, the guilty girl would be ignominiously banned from the Court.

Angélique tried to keep her from getting on her knees on the floor of the coach to entreat her.

"Madame, you saw me. You could ruin me."

"Get up. What good would it do me to ruin you? You're a clever little cheat. It takes eyes like mine to spot you, and I think you can go on winning for some time to come . . . that is, of course, if I keep my eyes closed."

The girl turned all the colors of the rainbow. "Madame, what can I do for you?"

She had dropped her "Mortemart" accent, and her voice was now definitely common. Angélique looked out the window coldly. The girl began to cry and told her her life story. She was the illegitimate daughter of a great nobleman whose name she did not know. An intermediary had seen to her education. Her mother had been a chambermaid, and had wound up as the proprietress of a gambling house, whence the other side of her education. Shuttled between a convent boarding school and the good training of a cardsharp, she had learned how to use her quick-wittedness, her prettiness and her scraps of refinement to get people of good society interested in her and willing to help her along. Athenais, who was a past master at recognizing characters of her ilk, had attached her to her suite. Now she was at Court, but that had not wholly prevented her from relapsing into her old habits. There was card-playing . . .

"You know what happens when that catches up with you. I can't afford to lose, I'm too poor. And every time I don't cheat, I lose. I am crushed with debts now. What I won from the Duc de Chaulnes the other day will just allow me to pay off enough to keep going, and I don't dare go to Madame de Montespan. She has already paid for me too often, and she has told me that some day she is going to get tired of it."

"How much do you owe?"

She rolled up her eyes as she figured. Angélique tossed a purse into her lap. Mademoiselle Desoeillet took it with trembling hands, and the color came back into her cheeks.

"Madame," she repeated. "What can I do for you?"

Angélique nodded toward the bag. "Show me what you've got in there."

After considerable hesitation Desoeillet took out a dark-colored bottle.

"Do you know whom this brew is intended for?" Angélique asked after looking at it a moment.

"Madame, what do you mean?"

"Maybe you don't know, but I think your mistress has tried to poison me twice. What would keep her from trying a third time? And, what's more, I recognized that little girl who sold it to you as the daughter of Monvoisin, the witch."

Mademoiselle Desoeillet looked around her in terror. At last she said she knew nothing about it. Madame de Montespan ordered her to go for medicine secretly compounded by sorceresses, but she didn't know why.

"Well, you try to find out," said Angélique sharply, "for I am counting on you to warn me from now on of all dangers that lurk for me. Keep your ears open and keep me informed of all you can overhear about me."

She kept twisting the phial in her fingers. Mademoiselle Desoeillet put her hand out timidly to recover it.

"Oh no, I think I'll keep it."

"Madame, that's impossible. What will my mistress say when I come back without it? She will blame La Voisin and whatever explanation I make will end up being discredited. What if she finds out I was with you in your coach?"

"That's true. Still, I need some proof. You are going to help me," she said, digging her nails into the girl's wrist, "or, I promise you I will destroy your life. You will be banished, ruined, despised by all, and it won't take me long to do it."

The unfortunate Mademoiselle Desoeillet was looking for some way to excuse her disloyalty.

"I think I know something . . ."

"Yes, what do you know?"

"The medicine I was sent for is innocuous. As a matter of fact, it is intended for the King. Madame de Montespan also goes to La Voisin for philtres that will rekindle the flame of his love for her."

"Which Duchesne pours into his goblet."

"So you know everything, Madame? How frightful! Madame de Montespan told us she thought you were a witch. I heard her. She was in a towering rage. She told Duchesne: 'Either that woman is a witch, or La Voisin has fooled us. Perhaps she has even betrayed us to her, if the other one has paid her more . . .' I know she was talking about you. 'It won't last long, though,' she said to Duchesne. It was this very morning. She had sent us all away because she wanted to talk in great privacy, only . . ."

"You were listening at the keyhole."

"Yes, Madame."

"What did you hear?"

"At first I couldn't make much out. Then little by little my mistress kept raising her voice, she was so angry. It was then I heard her say: 'Either that woman is a witch, or La Voisin has fooled us. All the attempts have failed. She must have been warned somehow. Who warned her? It's got to stop. You go to La Voisin and tell her the joke has gone on long enough. I pay her a lot. Either she finds something that will work, or she will be the one to do the paying. I'll write her myself. That will put the fear of God into her.'

"She sat down at her desk and wrote out a note she gave to Duchesne for La Voisin. 'Show her this note. After she has read it, and is convinced how angry I am, burn the paper in the flame of a candle. Don't leave until she has given you what we need. Wait, I have a handkerchief here that belongs to you know who. The page who picked it up gave it to me, thinking it was mine. I haven't been able to get to any of her maids since Thérèse shot out of here as if the devil were chasing her. Also, she has very few servants and no followers. She's a strange woman. I don't know what the King sees in her, except her beauty, obviously.' She was talking about you, Madame."

"So I gather. And when is Duchesne going to meet La Voisin?"

"Tonight."

"When? Where?"

"At midnight, at the Golden Horn tavern, a secluded place between the walls of Paris and Saint-Denis. La Voisin will walk there from her house in Villeneuve. It isn't far."

"Well, you have been of use to me, my girl. I shall try to forget for a while that you have very sensitive finger-tips. Here we are at Saint-Germain. We're going to get out here, but I don't want anyone to see us together. Put on a little powder and rouge, you look fearfully pale."

Hastily Mademoiselle Desoeillet tried to repair her shattered appearance. Stammering her thanks and vowing loyalty, she jumped out of the coach and took to her heels.

Angélique brooded as she watched her disappear like a pink butterfly in the springtime sunlight. Then she recovered herself and stuck her head out the window of the coach.

"To Paris!" she shouted to the coachman.

When she had changed into a thick skirt and a corduroy jacket and tied up her hair in a black satin kerchief like a shop girl, she asked for "Swordthrust" Malbrant to come to her. She had already sent to Saint-Cloud to get him back, even at the risk of leaving Florimond to the abbé and the dubious protection of Monsieur's Court.

When he came to her apartment and saw only a simply dressed woman, he was astonished to hear her speak with the familiar tones of the Marquise du Plessis-Bellière.

"Malbrant, I want you to come along with me."

"You certainly are well disguised, Madame."

"Where I'm going it wouldn't look well for me to

show up in full regalia. I see you have your sword. Well, take a rapier and a pistol too. Then go find Flipot. Wait for me in the alley behind the hôtel. I'll come out to meet you by the door from the garden."

"As you say, Madame."

A little later, riding behind Malbrant, Angélique arrived in the outskirts of the suburb of Saint-Denis. Flipot had accompanied them on foot. They stopped in front of the dark inn of the Three Comrades.

"Leave your horse here, Swordthrust, and give the innkeeper an *écu* to watch it. Otherwise we might never be able to get back. Horses disappear easily hereabouts."

The squire did as she bade him, and followed her. He asked no questions, just chewed the ends of his mustache and grumbled about the uneven paving blocks and the mud which still lingered in the cracks between the cobblestones of the dirty alleys in spite of the warm sun.

Perhaps this district was not so strange to the old gladiator. During his salad days he might well have had an adventure or two around there.

Not far from where they were was the red-painted wooden statue of the Father Eternal, the protector of beggars, in its niche on top of a pile of refuse. Flipot made his devotions joyously. He felt at home here.

Deep in his improbable palace of mud and crumbling stone was the Grand Coesre, Wood-Bottom, enthroned as usual in his cripple's bowl. His henchmen were numerous enough to take him about whenever he wanted to go, in a broken-down chair whose flowered upholstery and gilding were almost hidden under a layer of filth. But Wood-Bottom seldom liked to stir. The darkness of his abode was so dense that even in full daylight the oil vigil lamps were kept burning. Wood-Bottom liked it that way. He loathed the light and he hated to be uncomfortable. It was not easy to get to him. At least twenty times visitors would be stopped by gallows-birds asking what the hell they were doing there. Flipot gave the password.

Finally Angélique stood in his presence. She had a

bulging purse she intended to give him, but Wood-Bottom only looked at her scornfully.

"Not too soon," he said. "Not too soon!"

"You don't seem very glad to see me, Wood-Bottom. Haven't I always sent you what you needed? Haven't the servants always brought you a roast suckling pig at New Year's and a turkey and three barrels of wine for mid-Lent?"

"Servants! Servants! Do I have to see those asses! Do you think I have nothing better to do than peck at food and have soup sent me and chew on meat? I've got enough money to have a feast if I want one, just as I always had. But you don't come here very often. Too busy being a wicked beauty, eh? There are plenty of girls—who don't know what respect is."

The king of the beggars was sorely vexed. He accused Angélique less of thinking herself above him than of neglecting him. He could see nothing strange in a great Court lady's coming through twenty-inch-deep mud and filth and risking her life among the vagrants to see him. He wouldn't have thought it strange to see the King of France's coach stop before his outlandish hovel to pay him a visit. Among kings, isn't there . . .

He was King of the Pennies and he knew the power of his fearful sovereignty.

"You could come to terms with La Reynie if he'd let you. What does he mean surrounding us with his policemen? Who wants police around? The police are all right for dumb rich people, because if you're dumb you have to be honest. But we have to work hard. How else would we live? Prison? The rope? Hang you, lock you up. To the galleys with all thieves! The public hospital for beggars! What then? He wants to exterminate us, that damned La Reynie."

He went on with a great string of grievances. The great days of the Court of Miracles had come to an end when La Reynie had become lieutenant of police and stuck lighted lanterns around Paris.

"Who's that?" he said at last, pointing to Malbrant with his pipestem. "Who's that?"

"A friend. You can trust him. He's called 'Sword-

thrust.' I need him for a little play I'm staging, but he
can't act it out all by himself. I need three or four
more."

"Who know how to play a farce . . . with a sword or a
club? They can be found."

She told him her plan. A man had a rendezvous with
the sorceress Monvoisin to bring her a letter in a tavern
behind the ramparts of Villeneuve. They'd have to wait
till he left his assignation with the witch. Then the
bullies lurking outside could spring on him. . . .

"And gluurrkl" said Wood-Bottom, pointing to his
throat.

"No, I don't want any blood. No crime. I only want
him to speak up and confess. Malbrant will take care of
that."

The squire came over to her, his gray eyes alert.
"What's the name of this man?"

"Duchesne, the First Steward of the Wine Service. You
know him."

Malbrant beat his chest with satisfaction. "There's
one job I'll be glad to do. I've wanted to say a few
things to him for a long time now."

"That isn't all. I need an accomplice in La Voisin's
house, someone to go with her to the meeting and be
there when Duchesne gives her the letter. Someone especially quick with his hands so that he can get hold of
the paper before it burns in the candle."

"That can be found," said Wood-Bottom.

He had a fellow named Jack-o-lantern called, a pale
redhaired ragamuffin who had no equal for picking
pockets and concealing his loot in his sleeves. But his
red hair made him easily recognized, and after a good
many sojourns in the Chatelet prison and a few sessions
on the rack which had left him with a twisted leg so
that he limped, he found it hard to make a living. To
snitch a letter right out from under the eyes and
noses of a whole audience would be child's play for
him.

"I need that letter," Angélique said. "I'll pay for it in
gold."

The difficulty of meeting La Voisin and accompany-

ing her to so secret a rendezvous was not insurmountable
to the thieves. They had plenty of accomplices right in
her very house. There was Picard, who worked as her
lackey, and the Cossack, who was in love with her daughter. Through them Jack-o-lantern could easily get himself
hired to carry her torch or her bag. Even though she
now moved in high society, the sorceress still kept one
foot in the underworld. She knew how useful it was to
have the Great Coesre as an ally.

"She mustn't catch on, is that it?" said Wood-Bottom
giving Angélique an understanding look. "We don't
squeal here. If anyone does—death! We have no use for
stoolpigeons." He heaved up his huge torso, encased in
a military tunic with gold braid, and leaned on his
hairy fists like a gorilla, which he rather resembled with
his lumpy face and fierce look. "The power of the vagabonds is eternal," he trumpeted. "Old La Reynie will
never put an end to it. It will always spring to live again
in the gutters."

Angélique wrapped her cape around her. She felt
herself growing faint. In the light of the smoky oil
lamps the face of the Great Coesre under his ostrich-
plumed hat seemed to her to bear the brand of Cain.
Great red faces were thronging around her, bearded
faces too, among which the wan face of Jack-o-lantern
stood out in contrast.

She knew most of the bullies Wood-Bottom had summoned from among his bodyguards—Peony, the perpetual
drunkard; Rat Poison, the Spaniard; several others
whose names she had forgotten; and a newcomer called
Death's Head, whose whole jaws were exposed, for the
Brotherhood of the Holy Sacrament had cut off his lips
for blasphemy. Indeed, she was not trembling because of
fear, for she had learned the rules of the game and could
communicate with this ugly world.

The underworld never pardoned a traitor, and never
betrayed its own people. On top or on the bottom the
"brothers" and "sisters" who had demonstrated their
loyalty and bound themselves to the society of Paris
thieves by the oath of the vagabonds, would always have
access to the assistance of their fellow-members. If they

were poor, a kettle of soup was always available to them;
if they were powerful, swords would be drawn against
their enemies.

The bond was indestructible. Barcarole was proof
of this. Wood-Bottom would not forsake him. No, Angélique was not afraid of them. Their wolfish cruelty
terrified her less than that of certain far more refined
persons she could name; their stinking sores revolted her
less than the fine raiment that concealed loathsome
villainy. But as she listened to the thundering voice of
the Great Coesre, she remembered some dreadful experiences. Angélique was suffering the dizziness of one
standing on the brink of a precipice from which she
might fall to her doom, a feeling of being hurled from
the sumptuous heights to which she had arrived into
the bottomless despair of hell.

"So one always has to come back here," she thought.

It seemed to her that she would always carry with her
in the folds of her cape the ineradicable stench of the
misery of her past. All the perfumes of the world, all
the diamonds in the world, all the glory of the King's
favor would never expunge it.

When Angélique returned home she sat down at her
desk. Her visit to Saint-Denis had shown her more clearly
than she had imagined what would be done that night
in Villeneuve. All the details had been attended to, and
there was nothing more to do but wait and try not to
think. About ten o'clock Malbrant came to her. He wore
a gray visor-mask and was wrapped in a cloak the color
of a stone wall. She spoke softly to him as if she might
be overheard in the silence of her handsome room where
once she had received Rakoczy's love.

"You know as well as I do what I want to get out of
Duchesne. That's why I chose you. Let him reveal the
plans of the woman who sent him, and give the names
of the people who are trying to do me harm . . . but
above all, get the letter. Watch at the window of the
inn. If he makes any sign of weakening before Jack-o-
lantern has a chance to filch it, burst in with your men.

Also try to get the mixtures, the poisons La Voisin will give him."

She waited.

Two hours after midnight she heard the distant creaking of the little secret door by which Malbrant had left the hôtel, then his heavy quick military step on the flagstones of the vestibule.

He entered and laid some objects on the table near her. She saw a handkerchief, a phial, a leather pouch, and a little square of paper—the letter.

Madame de Montespan's handwriting leaped out at her and a wild feeling of triumph thrilled her. The words of the letter were overpoweringly dreadful:

". . . You have deceived me," wrote the noble Marquise in her flowing hand distinguished by its highly original spelling, for her education had been rather neglected. "The person is still alive and the King grows fonder of her every day. Your promises are not worth the money I have paid you—more than a thousand *écus* up to now for medicines which bring neither love nor death. Just remember that I can ruin your reputation and turn the whole Court against you. Entrust what is necessary to my messenger. This time you had better be successful."

"Wonderful! Wonderful!" shouted Angélique. "Ha! So this time you had better be successful, yes, my fine Athenais. And in fact I will succeed. All your arms won't be worth much against my hands."

At the bottom of the page there was a red spot that was turning brown. Angélique touched it and found it moist. She forgot her excitement and looked at her squire.

"What about Duchesne? What did you do with him? Where is he?"

Malbrant turned his head away. "If the current is strong, he must be almost out to sea by now."

"Malbrant, what did you do? I told you I didn't want any crime committed."

"It's always better to get rid of a corpse before it begins to stink," he said, his eyes still lowered. Then suddenly he looked her full in the face. "Listen, Madame," he said, "listen to me. What I am about to say to you may seem strange coming from an old weather-beaten good-for-nothing like me. But I am fond of your son. All my life I have done nothing but stupid, useless things insofar as both myself and others were concerned. Weapons are all I know anything about because of having handled them. But how to fill my purse I do not know. I was getting old, my body was wearing out, and Madame de Choisy, who knew my sainted aunt, my pious sister and my priestly brother, said to me: 'Malbrant, you bad boy, what would you say to teaching two rich nobleman's sons how to use a sword in exchange for good bed and board?' I said to myself, 'Why not? Let your old scars heal a little, Malbrant.' And so I entered your service, Madame, and that of your children. Perhaps I have some children of my own. It's likely, but that's not the point, I admit. With Florimond it was different. I doubt that you know him so well as I, Madame, even if you are his mother. That boy was born with a sword in his hand. He handles one like Saint Michael himself. When an old hand like me sees that talent, that power, that gift—ah, well . . . Then it was that I began to think of how I had wasted my life and of how alone I am in the world, Madame. In that little boy I saw the son I perhaps have never had—whom I shall never know at any rate—and whom I shall never be able to teach to wield a sword. There are things like that you don't know you have inside you, but they're the ones that make you want to live. That Duchesne wanted to kill Florimond."

Angélique shut her eyes. She felt faint.

"Up to now," the squire went on, "no one could say for sure. But now it is certain. He confessed it, blurted it out when we held his feet in the fire: 'Yes, I did want to get rid of that little louse,' he cried. 'He's ruined me in the eyes of the King by arousing his suspicions . . . he's spoiled all my hopes. Madame de Montespan has threatened to have me fired for not being subtler.' "

"So it's true that he put powders in the King's wine?"

"The favorite instructed him to. It's all true. And he threatened to kill Florimond if the boy betrayed him. He

put the poison in the sherbet that was intended for you.
The Montespan went to La Voisin for a means of killing
you. Caraport, one of the King's stewards, was their
accomplice. It was he who sent the child on an errand to
the kitchens by way of the scaffolding. 'Scaffoldings
ninety feet high,' as I yelled at him, 'ninety feet up
from the stone pavement in the dark! Well, it's your
turn to fall down them now, you beast who would take
the life of a child!' "

Malbrant stopped and wiped his face. He stared at
Angélique who was looking straight ahead of her.

"I had to get rid of that stinking carrion," he repeated in a low voice. "He wasn't very pretty to look at.
What good would it have done to leave him alive? Just
one more enemy for you. There are enough as it is, I
think. When you start something like this, Madame,
you've got to see it through to the bitter end."

"I know."

"The others agreed with me. There was no other
way to finish the job. My good companions did their
work well. Jack-o-lantern made a deal with La Voisin's
lackey to get himself the job of carrying her torch. He
pretended to be deaf and dumb. She kept him with her
during the rendezvous. Everything went as planned. She
said she did not want to go to the meeting place
alone. She wanted a deaf and dumb fellow who could
wield a knife. So Jack-o-lantern showed up and she took
him along. We kept watch outside. Soon I saw things
begin to go wrong between La Voisin and Duchesne.
They couldn't find the letter. Then the fun began. La
Voisin stalked out without demanding her payment.
Jack-o-lantern pretended to defend her for the sake of the
farce. Then we got busy with the man. It was not easy—
he was tough to handle. But finally we got him down
and got the handkerchief, the bottle, the little bag in
which the magic powders are, I guess, and lastly the
secrets I just told you."

"Good!"

Angélique opened a drawer of her desk and took out
a purse of gold pieces.

"This is for you, Malbrant. You did a good job."

The squire stowed it away immediately. "I never say no to money. Thank you, Madame. But believe me when I say that some day I will do it for nothing. The little abbé knows that. We asked each other what we should do. You are all alone, aren't you? You were right to confide in me."

Angélique's head bowed. The time had come for buying accomplices and paying for silence, and it would last the rest of her life. Between her and this adventurer whom she knew so little there would always be the screams of the murdered Duchesne, the plop of a body thrown into the Seine.

"My silence? I have kept it for people who deserved it less than you. Even the end of a bottle doesn't remind me of what I want to forget."

"I thank you, Malbrant. Tomorrow I will send you back to Saint-Denis with the money I agreed to pay. Then you will go to Saint-Cloud. I want Florimond under your protection. Now you may leave. Sleep well."

He bowed like a musketeer, as he well knew how to do. But before shutting the door behind him he looked back at her with mingled fear and admiration. Not that she frightened him. Quite the contrary. He was afraid for her. He was afraid to see her weaken. There are some persons who could walk on heaps of corpses without turning a hair. He knew plenty like that. "The other woman," for example. But this one was different, well though she knew how to fight.

chapter 27

*T*HE King had not yet come out of Mass when Angélique mingled with the throng of courtiers awaiting Their Majesties in the Salon of Mercury at Versailles, where they had arrived the night before.

She hoped her absence had not been noticed in the change of residence from Saint-Germain to Versailles. She got there at an early hour after concealing with carefully applied make-up the ravages of the previous night's fatigue and mental anguish. She was beginning to acquire the remarkable resilience of all sophisticates, the ability to change roles like actors without any effort, and to appear after a sleepless night and four hours of coach travel with a dazzling smile and a fresh complexion. She bowed to people to right and left, and inquired after many. Thus she learned the details of the full dress expedition into Flanders to see Madame off on her visit to her brother Charles II of England. Several of the gossips were surprised to discover that Angélique had not gone too. They said that Madame would return soon and that her negotiations were off to a good start. The amply proportioned Mademoiselle de Querouaille, whom the Princess had taken along in her suite, would not be the least effectual of means to convince the young Charles II that he should avoid the triple alliance and extend a friendly hand to his brother-in-law Louis XIV. There was considerable laughter about whether Mademoiselle de Querouaille's fine features would surpass her plump figure in the eyes of the English. But Madame knew her brother's taste in women well. Apparently he preferred quantity to quality.

The Stewards of the King's Table passed by, carrying silver-gilt pots of jams and dishes of fresh fruit for what was called the King's hunting snack. Angélique heard one of them remark on the absence of Duchesne. She drifted away from the groups of courtiers and leaned on a window sill of the Great Hall. It was a beautiful day. The lawns showed the effects of the thousand rakes the gardeners had applied to their surface. She recalled the first morning she had ever seen them, with Barcarole beside her, when day was breaking over Versailles and there was only one person in the world a menace to her.

Tossing her head, and with a stately gait, she passed through the Great Hall toward the South Wing. After opening several doors she arrived at an apartment that also looked out on the terraces.

Madame de Montespan was at the dressing table in her gorgeous boudoir. Her ladies-in-waiting were gabbing around her, but they fell silent when they saw Angélique.

"Good morning, Athenais dear," Angélique said gaily.

The favorite wheeled around on her embroidered silk stool. "Oh, yes," she said. "What can I do for you, my dear?"

There was a time when each had tried to surpass the other in the farce of their armed truce. Now neither took the trouble to pretend, even in public. Athenais de Montespan's blue eyes surveyed her rival. There was not the shadow of a doubt in her mind that this sudden affability was a disguise for something.

Angélique spread her skirts on a little sofa upholstered in the same material as the dressing-table stool and the chairs. The furniture was indeed lovely, but its blue tints clashed with the greenish gold of the walls. She would have to have that changed.

"I have some interesting news for you."

"Really?"

Mademoiselle Desoellet turned pale. The big tortoise-shell comb set with pearls that she was fixing in her mistress's hair shook in her hands. The other girls looked at her wonderingly. Madame de Montespan turned back to her looking glass.

"Well, we are waiting," she said coldly.

"There are too many people here. Only you need to hear this."

"You want me to send my ladies away? That's impossible."

"Perhaps. Let's say it would be preferable."

Madame de Montespan wheeled around. She saw in Angélique's face something she had never expected to find there. She hesitated.

"I'm not made up yet, and my hair isn't done. The King will be waiting for me to accompany him on his walk through the gardens."

"Don't worry. I can look after your hair and you can be putting on your powder meanwhile," Angélique said.

She moved behind Madame de Montespan and skillfully attacked her heavy braids of hair the color of ripe wheat.

"I'm going to do it in Binet's latest style. It will suit you to a T. Give me that, my child," she said to Mademoiselle Desoeillet, as she took the comb from her hands.

Athenais dismissed her suite. "Run along, ladies!"

Angélique slowly undid the braids and spread out like a cape the long, delicately perfumed locks, separated them into two with the comb, and then with a sure touch twisted one hank around the crown of Athenais' head. What a wonderful effect it had! Her own hair seemed dark next to the pure gold of her rival's. Lucifer before his fall must have had hair like this.

"Please hand me a couple of pins."

In the looking glass Madame de Montespan was keeping an eye on her rival. Angélique was still lovelier and more dangerously so, because her beauty was so out of the ordinary. Her smooth durable complexion withstood those enemies of pink-and-whiteness—pimples and broken veins. She always seemed to be powdered, so clear was her skin, and her little nose showed none of the effects of wine tippling and rich food. Her complexion set off her green eyes the way gold mountings add to the luster of precious stones. Her hair, perhaps less blond than Madame de Montespan's, was redeemed by its natural waviness and its rich glossy glints.

"No man could ever look at that hair and not want to stroke it," Athenais had once said in a fit of jealousy.

Angélique did not take her eyes off her enemy, whose looks she could see in the mirror. She bent to whisper in her ear: "Duchesne died last night at an assassin's hand."

With a certain admiration she noted that Madame de Montespan hardly moved a muscle, merely went on looking almost insolently calm.

"Hmm," she said, "no one has told me yet."

"No one knows it yet, except me. Would you like to hear how it happened?"

She kept on separating the glossy locks and rolling them one by one over an ivory rod.

"He was coming out of Monvoisin's house. He had brought her a message, and in return had got from her a little sack and a phial. No one will ever know that . . . unless you let it out. Pay attention, my dear, you are getting your rouge on crooked."

"You swine!" said Montespan between her teeth. "You whore! You filth! How dare . . . how dare you do that!"

"What about you?"

Angélique tossed the comb and the ivory rod on to the dressing table. Her hands seized the smooth, white, rather fleshy shoulders that the King so loved to kiss, and dug her nails into them as her anger flared.

"What didn't you dare! You wanted to kill my son."

They were both breathing hard as their eyes met in the mirror.

"You wanted me to die a horrible, shameful death. You called down on my head all the curses of the Devil himself. But the Devil has turned on you now. Listen carefully. Duchesne is dead. He will never blab. No one need ever know where he went last night and what he was after and who wrote the letter he delivered to La Voisin."

Madame de Montespan suddenly weakened. "The letter!" she said in a different voice. "Didn't he burn the letter?"

"No!" She recited softly: " 'The person is still alive and the King grows fonder of her every day. Your

promises are not worth the money I have paid you—
more than a thousand *écus* up to now for medicines
which bring neither love nor death . . .' "

Athenais had turned white, but she reacted with the
pitiless energy that had always kept her going. She tore
away from Angélique's grip proudly.

"Let me go, you Gorgon. You're killing me."

Angélique took up the comb again, while Madame
de Montespan reached for a puff and dabbed clouds of
powder over her bruised shoulders.

"What do I have to do to get that letter back from
you?"

"I will never give it to you," said Angélique. "Do you
think I'm that much of a fool? That letter and the
baubles I described to you are in the hands of an agent
of the law. Forgive me if I don't tell you his name. But
remember he often has an opportunity to get to the
King. Now, if you'll please hand me those pearl-headed
hairpins, I'll fix your chignon."

Madame de Montespan gave them to her.

"On the day I die," Angélique continued, "the sad
news of the sudden and inexplicable end of Madame du
Plessis-Bellière will no sooner have reached the ears of
that agent than he will have gone to the King and
shown him the objects and the letter I have given into
his safekeeping. I don't imagine His Majesty will have
any trouble recognizing your handwriting and your faultless spelling."

The favorite was making no more attempt to dissemble. She seemed to be choking, for her chest was
heaving with spasms. Her feverish hands kept opening
boxes and bottles as she streaked make-up over her forehead and cheeks and eyelids.

"What if I don't let you blackmail me?" she exclaimed suddenly. "What if I'd risk everything to see you
dead?" She stood up, clenching her fists, almost breathing flames of hatred. *"Dead!"* she repeated. "That's the
only thing I care about—to see you dead! If you live,
you will take the King away from me. I know that. Or
else the King will take you. It amounts to the same
thing. He craves you desperately. Your coquettish re-

fusals of his desires work in his blood and rob him of reason. I don't matter any more. Soon he will come to hate me, because he wants to see you in my place, here, in this apartment he had made for me. Since my fall is certain whether you are dead or alive, I at least want you dead, dead, dead!"

Angélique heard her out impassively. "There's a certain difference between a temporary fall from favor, which would at least make the King show you some regard and which would leave you—who knows?—the hope of sometime regaining his affection, and the horror he would feel toward you when he was informed of your crimes, not to mention the exile or the imprisonment to which he would condemn you for the rest of your days. I'm sure a Mortemart knows the right choice to make between those alternatives."

Athenais was wringing her hands. Her display of rage and her impotency had made her appear rather naive. "The hope of regaining his affections," she echoed. "No. If you ever win him, it will be for life. I know that. You know him as well as I do. I was master of his senses, but you are master of his heart. And, believe me, it's something to be master of the heart of a man who doesn't hesitate to admit it."

She looked at her rival as if she were seeing her for the first time, perceiving in her calm, dangerous beauty a weapon she had not suspected before.

"I am not strong enough," she said.

Angélique shrugged her shoulders. "Don't play the victim, Athenais. It's not the part for you. Just sit down again and let me finish your hair."

"Don't touch me!"

"But this hair-style is quite becoming to you, Athenais. It would be a pity to leave it done up on one side and hanging loose on the other."

In desperation Athenais handed her the comb as she would to a servant. "All right, finish. And be quick about it!"

Angélique twisted a long golden lock around her finger, and arranged it so that it trailed gracefully down her pearly neck. As she glanced into the mirror to see how it looked, she met the stormy eyes of her enemy. She had won, but for how long?

"Leave me the King," said Athenais suddenly. "Leave me the King. You do not love him."

"Do you?"

"He belongs to me. I was made to be Queen."

Angélique rolled up two more locks and pinned them over the temples like wood shavings. Binet could not have done better.

"My dear Athenais," she said as she finished, "it's no use for you to appeal to my finer feelings, for I have none so far as you are concerned. I will make a bargain with you. Either you leave me alone and stop plotting against my life, in which case you can trust me to say nothing about your relations with sorceresses and demons; or else you can keep on with your vindictiveness and continue to store up bolts of lightning that will be unleashed upon you and annihilate you. Don't think you can get around these facts by trying to do me harm in some other way like undermining my reputation, or ruining my credit, or harassing me with little underhanded attacks to make my life miserable. I shall always know where these are coming from, and I won't have to wait for death to relieve me of you. You say the King loves me. Just think what his wrath will be when he finds out you tried to do me in. The agent of the law who has my secrets in his keeping tested in person the nightdress you sent me. He will bear witness before the King to the injuries you wanted to do me. One more bit of advice, my dear. Your hair looks lovely, but your make-up is smeared. It's in ruins. If I were you, I'd start all over again."

As soon as Angélique left, Madame de Montespan's girls trooped back solicitously, and formed a circle about their mistress' dressing table.

"Madame, you are crying."

"Yes, you fools. Can't you see how dreadful my make-up looks?"

Stifling her sobs, she looked in the mirror at her bleary face, tear-streaked with red and white and black. She

heaved a deep sigh. "She's right, the swine," she muttered. "It is a ruin. I'd better start all over again."

No one missed the new look on Madame du Plessis-
Bellière's face as she appeared for the King's walk
through the gardens. She was radiant, and the way she
carried her head was almost intimidating. Everyone
began to feel as Madame de Montespan had recently felt.
It was as if they had been deceived. The little Marquise
had indeed quite a collection of masks. Those who had
thought she was being very cautious about remaining in
favor now could see that she was not going to be another
La Vallière. Those who were betting that Madame de
Montespan would get rid of "the hick" now felt their
confidence falter in the face of the haughty looks she
gave them and the way she smiled at the King. The
King's attitude sealed their defeat. He made no pretense
at having eyes for anyone but her.

Madame de Montespan was absent. No one took ex
ception to it, but found it quite natural for Angé
lique to be walking at the King's side down the path
to the grove and colonnade of Minerva, and then on
their return to the palace via the Fountain Walk.

The King called her into his conference chamber, as
he often did when he needed her advice on some matter
of trade he was discussing with his ministers. This time
she noticed that the room was empty. As soon as the door
closed behind them he took her in his arms.

"My beauty," he said, "I can't go on like this! When
will you stop torturing me? This morning you had me
completely in your power. I could see nothing but you.
You were my sun, my star I never reach, the cool
spring from which I could not drink. Your glory suffused
me and your perfume was all the air I breathed, and yet
I could not lay my hand on you. Why? Why so cruel?"
He was burning with desire he could no longer control.
"Don't think you can go on playing with me like this
much longer. You'll have to end by yielding to me, even
if I have force you to."

His steel-like muscles were bruising her as they flattened her against his stone-hard chest.

"You might make me your enemy," she said.

"I am not so sure of that. I was wrong to think your heart would awaken to me if I were patient. You are not ruled by your emotions. You want to know your master before you obey his orders. Only after he has won you over will you be loyal to him. Only when I have penetrated your flesh will I have penetrated your heart." He added plaintively: "Ah, how the secrets of your body torment me!"

Angélique felt dizzy from her head to her toes. "I can't go on like this either," she said to herself, sinking into a kind of exhaustion.

"When you are mine," the King was saying, "when I have won you either by your consent or by force, I know you will never leave me, for we two were made for each other and to rule the world, even as Adam and Eve were."

"So Madame de Montespan said with a certain assurance," Angélique remarked with a thin smile.

"Madame de Montespan! What is she thinking of? What hold does she have on me? Does she think I am blind? That I'm not aware of her wicked heart, her concierge-like spying, her boundless tiresome pride? I know her for what she is—beautiful and sometimes diverting. Does her presence intimidate you? I tell you I would sweep out of your way anyone you did not like. If you asked me now to get rid of Madame de Montespan, she would be out of the palace by tomorrow."

Angélique pretended to take this humorously. "All this display of power frightens me a little, Sire."

"You have nothing to fear. I would give you my scepter. I know it would be in worthy hands. You see, again you have succeeded in checking my violence and again I trust in your wisdom to choose the day and the hour when you will favor me. I will let time take care of overcoming your apprehensions so far as I am concerned. Now, don't you think we could arrive at some understanding between us?"

His voice was supplicating, and he kept holding her hands in his.

"Yes, I think so, Sire."

"Then some day, my beauty, we will set sail for

Cythera—the isle of love . . . Some day . . . promise me."
  Between his kisses she murmured, "I promise."
  Some day she would kneel before him and say, "Here
am . . ." And she would lay her forehead in his roya
hands. She knew that she was inescapably set on tha
course toward that time. Now she had got rid of th
dangers that threatened her life, the attainment of thi
love weighed on her and inspired her with alternat
fear and triumph. Would it be tomorrow? Or later? Th
answer was hers to make, and yet she was leaving it t
fate.

chapter 28

ANGELIQUE spent three days in Paris going over some business with Colbert. She was coming back to her house after being with him till quite late one evening. In front of the Hôtel de Beautreillis was the outline of a beggar limping along in the bluish darkness of the moonless June night. As she approached the door she saw it was Stale Bread.

"Go to Saint-Cloud! Go to Saint-Cloud!" he said in his hoarse voice.

She tried to open her door but he prevented her.

"Go to Saint-Cloud, I tell you. Something's going on there. I've just come from there in a wine cart. There's an entertainment there tonight. So go on . . ."

"I wasn't invited to Saint-Cloud, Stale Bread."

"Someone else is there who wasn't invited either. . . . Death. . . . And it is in his honor the party is being given. Go see for yourself . . ."

Angélique suddenly thought of Florimond. Her blood ran cold.

"What's going on? What do you know?"

But the old vagabond had moved off, grumbling.

Angélique shrieked to the coachman to take her to Saint-Cloud. She had a new coachman now, who had worked for the Duchess de Chevreuse and was more philosophical than his predecessor had been. He merely remarked that to travel through the woods at that hour of the night was to invite danger. Without getting out of the coach she had three of her footmen awakened and also Roger, her steward. They armed themselves and mounted their horses to protect the coach which was turning in the direction of the Saint-Honoré gate.

The treetoads sounded like sleighbells jingling in the darkness of the park. Angélique's nerves were

jumpy anyway, and the sound aggravated them. She pu
her hands over her ears to shut it out. As they rounded
a bend in the avenue the country house of Monsieur
d'Orléans loomed before them, its windows winking as
the torches passed behind them. There were plenty of
coaches parked on the terrace, and the great gates were
wide open.

Something was indeed going on, but it was no fête.

Trembling with anxiety, she jumped out of the
coach and ran to the entrance. There was no page there
to take her cloak or ask what she wanted at this late
hour. But the foyer was full of confused people rushing
to and fro and talking in whispers. Angélique caught
sight of Madame Gordon-Huntley.

"What's going on?" she called to her.

The Scotswoman made a vague, distracted gesture.
"Madame is dying." She disappeared behind a tapestry.

Angélique grabbed a lackey by the arm. "Madame dying? It's impossible. She was in perfect health yesterday.
I saw her dancing at Versailles."

"The same today. At four o'clock Her Highness was
laughing and chatting merrily. Then she drank a cup
of coffee and immediately was seized with pains."

Madame Desbordes, one of the Princess' ladies-in-waiting, was stretched out on a sofa sniffing smelling salts.
She had just been revived from a swoon.

"It's the sixth time since this afternoon, the poor
woman," said Madame de Gamaches.

"But what is the matter? Did she drink the same cup
of coffee?"

"No, but she made it. She was accused of causing the
terrible accident."

Madame Desbordes was gradually recovering her
senses. She began to scream hysterically.

"Get control of yourself," Madame de Gamaches begged
her, "you aren't guilty of anything. Try to remember if
you boiled the water. I brought it in, and Madame
Gordon gave it to her in her own special cup."

But the pathetic lady in waiting could not seem to
understand. She kept wailing, "Madame is dead! Madame
is dead!"

"We all know that," said Angélique. "Did Madame see a doctor?"

"All of them," brayed Madame Desbordes. "The King sent his own. They are all here. Everybody is here. Mademoiselle is here. Monsieur is here. The Queen . . ."

"Oh, for heaven's sake!" Madame de Gamaches interrupted her. She too was getting hysterical.

While they were trying to extract some information, Monsieur himself appeared out of Madame's apartments, accompanied by Mademoiselle de Montpensier.

"Cousin," she was saying vigorously, "you must remember that Madame is dying. Talk to her about God . . ."

"Her confessor is with her," Philippe d'Orléans protested gently.

He casually adjusted the folds of his jabot. Of all those present he certainly appeared the least upset, but he was at the mercy of the Grande Mademoiselle's insistence, and had to listen to her. She shrugged her shoulders in fury.

"Her confessor! I'd be in a sorry state if I had to appear before God with no preparation but that nobody's. Her confessor indeed! You had to send him around in a coach so that the public could see she had one. His only recommendation is that he has one of the handsomest beards in the country, that's all. But when death . . . Have you ever thought of what it means to die, cousin?"

Monsieur was contemplating his fingernails. He sighed listlessly.

"Well, you do know your time will come too," exclaimed Mademoiselle, bursting into sobs. "Then will be the time for you to study your fingernails. Ah, my poor darling," she said as she caught sight of Angélique, and beckoned her to her.

She sank on to a bench. "If you could only see this affecting sight! All these people buzzing around Madame, chattering and prating as if they were at a play. Her confessor doesn't know how to do more than stroke his beard and mumble platitudes . . ."

"Calm yourself, cousin," said Philippe d'Orléans sympathetically. "Let's see now, whom can we find to be with Madame during her last hours who would look well in the Gazette? Ah, I have it—Father Bossuet. Madame sometimes liked to talk with him, and he is the Dauphin's religious advisor. I'll send for him."

He gave orders accordingly.

"But there's no time to lose. Who knows whether Madame will still be alive by the time Monsieur Bossuet gets here? Isn't there anyone here at Saint-Cloud?"

"My goodness, can't you be satisfied?"

One of the Maids of Honor recommended Father Feuillet, a canon of Saint-Cloud, who had a certain reputation.

"And an evil character too," the King's brother snapped. "Call him if you want, but I shall have none of him. I have already said my farewells to Madame."

He pirouetted on his high heels and went toward the staircase with his gentlemen attendants. Florimond, who was among them, saw his mother and ran over to kiss her hand.

"It's a sorry business, isn't it, Mother?" he said. "Madame was poisoned."

"For the love of heaven, Florimond, stop talking about poison."

"But she certainly was poisoned. I know she was. Everyone says so and I was there myself. Monsieur wanted to go to Paris, and we had gone down into the courtyard with him. Just then Madame de Mecklenburg arrived. Monsieur greeted her and went with her to see Madame, who also came to meet her. It was right then Madame Gordon gave her the cup of iced coffee she always had that time of day. As soon as she drank it, she put her hand to her side and moaned: 'Ah, what a pain in my side! Oh, it's terrible. I can't stand it.' Her cheeks had been pink, but they turned deathly white. 'Help me away,' she said. 'I can't stand up any longer.' She was walking all bent over. I saw her myself."

"The page is right," confirmed one of the younger of Madame's suite. "As soon as Madame got into bed, she told us she was sure she had been poisoned and asked for an antidote. Monsieur's First Valet of the Bedchamber brought her some snake oil, but her pains were so great it only seemed to increase them. It must have been some terrible new poison."

The Grande Mademoiselle butted in. "Don't talk so foolishly. Who indeed would have wanted to poison a lovely woman like Madame? She had no enemies."

They shut up, but continued no less to think about it, including Mademoiselle de Montpensier. One name was on everyone's lips—that of Madame's own husband, or else of his exiled favorite. Mademoiselle went to greet Father Feuillet, who had just been announced.

"If it hadn't been for me, Father, the poor princess would have gone to meet her Maker like an heretic. Come along, I'll show you the way."

Madame de Gamaches whispered why Monsieur did not like Father Feuillet. He was a strict, uncompromising priest, to whom one could well apply that verse from the Psalms: "I will speak of thy testimonies also before kings, and will not be ashamed." Once he was asked to lunch during Lent here at the King's brother's house. Monsieur took a little cracker and asked him: "This is not breaking fast, is it?" "Eat a whole ox, but be Christian," the priest replied.

The girl clucked her tongue. A commotion coming from the Princess's apartments brought the women to attention as they foresaw what might have happened.

The King was leaving with his doctors. The Queen followed him, dabbing at her nose and eyes with her handkerchief. Then came the Comtesse de Soissons, Mademoiselle de la Vallière, Madame de Montespan and Mademoiselle de Montpensier. As he passed, the King saw Angélique. He stopped in his tracks and oblivious to the looks that followed them took her into an alcove.

"My sister-in-law is dying," he said.

His face showed his grief and how upset he was, and his eyes seemed to be asking for consolation.

"Is there no hope, then, Sire? What do the doctors . . . ?"

"The doctors said for hours that it was only a temporary discomfort. Then they all suddenly lost their heads and didn't know what to do. I tried to get them into some sort of rationality. I am no doctor, but I could think of thirty remedies for them to try. They said all we had to do was wait. They're asses!" He turned a dark look on the pointed hats of the practitioners huddled together in consultation.

"How could such a thing have happened? Madame was in excellent health. She came back from England so happy . . ."

He looked at her penetratingly without speaking and she could see in his eyes the terrible suspicion that lurked in his mind. She bowed her head, not knowing quite what to say. She would have loved to take his hand, but she did not dare.

"I would like to ask a favor of you, Angélique," he whispered. "Stay here until . . . until the end, and then come to Versailles to consult with me. You will come, won't you? I need you . . . my darling."

"I will come, Sire."

Louis XIV heaved a great sigh. "Now I must go. Princes must not look upon death. That's a rule. When I myself come to die, my family will desert the palace and I shall be quite alone. . . . I'm glad Madame has that highly respected Father Feuillet with her. It's no time now for the wit of courtiers and the assurances of worldly confessors. Ah, here comes Monsieur Bossuet. Madame will be very glad to have him."

He went to meet the Bishop and talked with him a minute. Then the royal family departed, and Bossuet entered the bedroom of the dying woman. From without came the sound of coach doors slamming, and horses pawing the pavement.

Angélique sat on a bench to wait. Florimond was darting hither and thither like any other child in a tense situation that does not involve him. He told her that Monsieur had gone to bed and was sound asleep. A little before midnight Madame de la Fayette, who had been at the Princess' side, came to tell Angélique that Madame knew she was at Saint-Cloud and wished to see her.

The room was full of people, but the presence of

Bossuet and Father Feuillet had imposed a sort of propriety on the atmosphere. Everyone was talking in
whispers. The two ecclesiastics moved away from the
head of the bed to make room for Angélique. At first
she thought it must be someone else lying there, so
changed was Madame. Her unfastened nightdress revealed her shrunken body, so thin that she already
looked like the skeleton she so soon would be. Her
cheekbones stuck out, and her nose was pinched. There
were dark circles under her eyes, and her whole face
was twisted with her agonies.

"Madame," whispered Angélique, "how you must be
suffering! I can't bear it to see you in such pain."

"You are sweet to say so. Everyone else tells me I'm
exaggerating my pain. If I were not a good Christian, I
would kill myself rather than try to bear it." She was
breathing with difficulty, but she went on. "Still, it is
good for me to suffer. Otherwise I would have nothing
to offer God but an empty, misspent life. Madame du
Plessis, I am so glad you came. I have not forgotten the
favor you did me and the debt I owe you. I brought
back from England . . ."

She beckoned feebly to Montague, the English ambassador, who came over to the bedside. The Princess
spoke to him in English, but Angélique gathered that
she was directing him to pay Angélique the three
thousand *pistoles* she owed her.

The ambassador was crushed, for he knew what despair the death of his beloved sister Ninette would cause
his master Charles II. He proceeded to ask the dying
woman if she suspected foul play, for he had heard and
understood the word "poison" which was being bandied
about, as it was the same in both languages. Father
Feuillet interrupted:

"Madame, you must not accuse anyone. Offer your
death as a sacrifice to God."

The Princess nodded. Her eyes closed. For a long moment she was silent. Angélique started to withdraw,
but the icy hand of Henriette of England still clasped
her own, and she could not pull it away. Madame opened

her eyes again, her blue eyes swimming, but she fixed
them on Angélique with an undivided attention that
was full of wisdom.

"The King was here," she said. "With him were
Madame de Soissons, Mademoiselle de la Vallière and
Madame de Montespan . . ."

"I know," Angélique said.

Madame fell silent. She kept looking at her intently.
Suddenly it occurred to Angélique that Madame had
loved the King too. Their flirtation had become so
serious that to avert the suspicions of the Queen Mother,
who was still alive then, they had conceived the plan of
making one of Madame's ladies-in-waiting a screen for
them. This was none other than Louise de la Vallière.
Then the haughty princess had been dethroned by her
humble follower. Her pride would not allow her to
mourn except in private and in the arms of her best
friend, Madame de Montespan . . . who now had taken
her place in turn. She had just now seen by her bedside
the King and his three mistresses, the two former ones
and the present one, in a strange recurrence of her
dream of ambitious love that she had followed so in
vain and that had brought her such a humiliating
defeat.

"Yes," Angélique said softly.

She smiled a little poignantly. Madame had not had
the qualifications, but her defeat had not made her
vindictive and she had always been gracious and ex-
troverted and intelligent. Too intelligent. Now she was
dying surrounded by hostility or at best indifference.

Her eyes dimmed. In a barely audible voice she murmured: "I could wish, for his sake, that he might fall in
love with you . . . *you* . . . because . . ."

She was unable to finish the sentence. Her hand fell
on the coverlet. Angélique withdrew and left the room
to return to her bench outside. As she waited she forced
herself to pray. About two o'clock in the morning
Bossuet left the Princess and sat down beside her to
take a little food. A footman brought him a cup of
chocolate.

Florimond, still darting about like a swallow, whis-

pered to Angélique that the death rattle was in Madame's throat. Bossuet set down his cup and returned to
her bedside.

Then Madame Gordon-Huntley emerged to shout:
"Madame is dead!"

As she had promised the King, Angélique immediately
prepared to go to Versailles. She would have liked to take
Florimond along, to get him out of the way of the funeral
preparations, but she found him sitting on a chest in the
foyer holding the hand of a nine-year-old girl.

"This is the little Mademoiselle," he told her. "No
one is paying any attention to her, so I thought I ought to
keep her company. She doesn't realize yet that her
mother is dead. When she does know, she will cry. I ought
to stay here to comfort her."

Angélique gave him her blessing, and stroked his
curly hair. A good vassal shares the sorrow of his lord
and stands by him in trouble. She herself was going to
her King. With tears in her eyes she kissed the little
princess, who as a matter of fact did not seem much
disturbed over the loss of a mother she had hardly
known and who had paid her little attention.

Other vehicles were rolling over the road to Versailles.
Angélique ordered her coachman to pass them at full
speed. When she arrived at the palace, it was still the
dead of night. She was admitted to the King's conference room where he was waiting.

"Well?"

"It's all over, Sire. Madame is dead."

He bowed his head to conceal his feelings.

"Do you think she was poisoned?" he asked finally.

Angélique made a vague gesture.

"Everyone thinks so," the King went on. "But you
have a level head. Tell me what you think."

"Madame had long been afraid she might die of
poison. She confided that to me."

"So she was afraid. Of whom? Did she ever mention
any names?"

"She knew the Chevalier de Lorraine hated her and
would never forgive her for her part in his exile."

"Any others? Tell me, please. If you don't tell me, who else will?"

"Madame said that Monsieur had often threatened her when he was in a rage."

The King sighed deeply. "If my brother . . ." He lifted his head. "I have ordered the Steward of the Table at Saint-Cloud, Maurel, to be brought here. I doubt he will be long in coming. Wait, I think I hear him now. I should like you present at the interview. Hide behind that tapestry."

Angélique slipped behind the curtain he pointed to to her. The door opened and Maurel, led in by Bontemps and a Lieutenant of the Guard, entered. He was a coarse-featured man, not lacking in arrogance in spite of his professional air of servility. In spite of being under arrest he appeared calm. The King signaled his valet to stay. The lieutenant departed.

"Look at me," said the King soberly to Maurel. "Your life will be spared if you tell me the truth."

"Sire, I will tell you the absolute truth."

"Don't forget that promise. If you renege on it, torture is ready and waiting for you. It's up to you whether you wish to leave this palace alive or dead."

"Sire," the man replied calmly, "after your sacred words, I would be a fool to lie."

"Good! Now answer me. Did Madame die of poison?"

"Yes, Sire."

"Who poisoned her?"

"The Marquis d'Effiat and I."

The King flinched. "Who assigned you that fearful duty? And from whom did you get the poison?"

"The Chevalier de Lorraine was the originator and prime instigator of the plot. He sent us from Rome the venomous drug I prepared and that d'Effiat put in Her Royal Highness's drink."

The King's voice suddenly fell. "What about my brother . . . ?" he said, trying to get control of his voice. "Did he have any knowledge of this conspiracy?"

"No, Sire."

"Will you take your oath on that?"

"Sire, I will swear before God that I was the guilty

one . . . Monsieur did not know the plot . . . we could not count on him . . . he would have exposed us."

Louis XIV drew himself up. "That's all I need to know. Now, go, wretched man. I will spare your life, but get out of my kingdom. If you ever cross its frontiers again, you will be a dead man."

Maurel left with Bontemps. The King rose and left his place behind his work table.

"Angélique!"

His voice was that of a wounded man calling for aid. She ran to him. He pressed her so hard against his breast she thought he would crush her to death. She felt his forehead on her shoulder.

"Angélique, my angel!"

"I am with you."

"What a horrible thing!" he muttered. "What vile, treacherous minds!"

Still he did not know everything. Some day he would. He would stand alone in the midst of a sea of shame and unthinkable crime.

"Don't leave me alone."

"I am with you."

"Wherever I look, I can find no one to confide in."

"I am with you."

At last he seemed to understand. Raising her head, he gazed at her a long time. Then he asked her timidly:

"Do you mean it, Angélique? You will never leave me again?"

"No."

"You will be my faithful friend? You will be mine?"

She nodded. Gently she lifted his hand to her face.

"Do you really mean it?" he repeated. "Oh, it's like . . ."

He tried to find a word for his rapture. The dawning day was casting its rosy light on the edge of the draperies.

"Like the dawn . . . a token of life, of strength . . . that is what you have given me on this terrible night when death has struck. Oh, my soul's joy . . . you will be mine! Mine! I shall possess the treasure . . ."

He clutched her with violent passion. She felt his strength passing into her, and like him believed their

union would make them insuperable before the world.
Her enemies were fleeing, the demons returning to hell.
The long struggle was over and the problem solved.
Their weary spirits were finding a sudden revivifying
peace.

Bontemps was rapping at the door. "Sire, it's time."

Angélique struggled to free herself, but he held her
close.

"Sire, it's time," she echoed.

"Yes, I must become a King again. I'm so afraid that
if I let you go I'll lose you again."

She shook her head with a sad little smile. She was
tired. The anguish of the night had made her eyelids
droop. Her disordered hair made her look like an exhausted lover.

"I love you," the King said. "Oh, how I love you, my
angel. Never leave me!"

After the customary celebration of the King's rising,
the courtiers as usual went to Mass with him. He took
his place with an impassive face. There was stifled
sobbing among the congregation. Bossuet slowly ascended the pulpit. In the golden light streaming through
the windows he lifted his rugged, ruddy face, and
stood erect in his black cassock and lace surplice. He let
a long silence reign. Then his hand fell to his side as his
booming voice rose to the high vault of the chapel.

"O night of disaster! O night of terror, echoing with
the thunderclaps of this dreadful news: Madame is dead!
Madame is dead! . . . Madame has passed from morning
unto evening as a flower of the fields. In the morning she
bloomed with all the graces you know so well. In the
evening, drooped . . . How great is God's diligence. In
nine short hours, the work was done. . . . Oh, vanity of
vanities . . ."

chapter 29

*A*NCHORED in the marina among the moving shallops and beside two small English warships, a Neapolitan felucca and a Biscay galley, the great vessel was swaying like a butterfly balancing on a blade of grass.

It was a miniature frigate, equipped with small bronze cannons, on each of which shone the golden cock surrounded with fleur-de-lis, garlands, shells and sea gods. The ropes were of apricot and crimson silk, the hangings of brocade fringed with gold and silver. From the masts and spars, which were painted red and blue, floated pennons in a gay symphony of colors, and everywhere the arms and emblems of the King sparkled in gold.

Louis XIV was rendering this jewel of a ship the homage of his Court. One foot on the gilded gangplank, he turned toward his ladies. Who would be chosen to lead the procession from the meadows of Trianon? In his suit of peacock blue, the King looked as radiant as the cloudless day. He smiled and extended his hand to Angélique. Before the eyes of the entire Court she ascended the gangplank and settled herself under the brocaded canopy. The King sat beside her.

After them the other guests took their places on the Grand Vessel. Madame de Montespan was not among them. She was presiding over the company assigned to the Grand Galley, an honor which did not deceive her and made her pale with rage. The Queen was on the Neapolitan felucca. The rest of the courtiers were in shallops. The King's musicians embarked on a barge hung with red and white damask.

To the sound of violins and oboes the little armada glided over the glassy surface of the Grand Canal. The cruise seemed all too short. Dark clouds began to pile up in the deep blue sky.

491

"A storm is gathering," Angélique remarked in an attempt to disguise her apprehension in commonplace conversation.

"Do you think we'll be shipwrecked?" asked the King, looking at her devotedly.

"Perhaps . . ."

The group disembarked on the green lawns where marquees had been set up over buffets laden with delicacies. They danced, they chatted, they played games. In the game of blind man's buff Angélique was blindfolded and whirled around by Monsieur de Saint-Aignan to make her lose her sense of direction. When he let her go and tiptoed away she felt abandoned in the stillness about her.

"Don't leave me," she cried laughing.

She waited a moment to sense the rustling around her. Then someone crept up behind her and snatched off the blindfold.

"Oh," she exclaimed, blinking.

She was no longer in the meadow where the Court was playing—she could still hear the laughter—but on the edge of a thicket. At the top of a rise built of three flower-covered terraces a little palace she had never seen before was in the process of construction. It was made of white porcelain. Before it was a row of pink marble columns. Acacia trees surrounded it, perfuming the air with their intoxicating scent.

"This is Trianon," said the King.

He held her close to him. With his arm around her waist he led her up to the pagoda.

"We had to see this together, didn't we, Angélique?" he said in a low voice. "We had to end here."

She felt his masterful hands quiver on her side. He had never been able completely to overcome his timidity with women. No sooner had he completed a conquest than fright overtook him.

"My beautiful love! My lovely one!"

Angélique no longer resisted him. The little pleasure dome offered her a refuge of silence. The power that led her on she could not repulse. Nothing now could break this magic circle of love and solitude and shade.

A glass door opened for them. The interior was furnished with brocade pieces of exquisite taste and workmanship. Angélique was too excited to notice more than that it was ravishingly beautiful and that there was a huge curtained bed in an alcove.

"I'm afraid," she whispered.

"There is nothing to fear, my love."

Leaning her head on his shoulder, she let him take her lips, unfasten her bodice, find the soft globes of her breasts, thrill to the touch of her warm secret places. Gently he pulled her along, as if wounded by the violence of his passion.

"Come! Come!" he begged her softly.

His sensuality was primitively savage. A tempestuous torrent swept him toward this woman he desired. In comparison with his composure as a monarch this blind passion was overwhelming.

Angélique leaned against the bed and opened her eyes. The King was giving himself to her without any reservation, and she felt rather strong and motherly as she took him in her arms and soothed the torments of his flesh with her gentle caresses.

There was a flash of lightning. Her body grew tense, and her eyes stared into the gloom that had descended over them.

"The storm," she muttered.

A distant rumble pierced the silence. The King saw how troubled she looked.

"It's nothing. What are you afraid of?"

But he found her body restive in his arms. She eluded him and ran to the window, where she leaned her burning forehead against the cool panes of glass.

"Now what?" he asked. "This time it can't be modesty. Your delays have indicated a barrier I have long suspected. There is a man between us."

"Yes."

"His name?"

She turned toward him, her fists clenched, and her eyes flaming.

"Joffrey de Peyrac, my husband, whom you had burned at the stake."

Slowly she raised her hands to her face. Her mouth was open as if she were gasping for breath.

"Joffrey de Peyrac," she repeated.

Her legs gave way and she sank to her knees, babbling incoherently. "What have you done with that sweet singer, that genius, that great lame clown who held all Toulouse under the spell of his innocent magic? How could I ever forget Toulouse, where they sing and curse and scatter flowers and maledictions. Toulouse, that most cruel and gracious of cities, the city of Joffrey de Peyrac whom you had burned alive in the Place de Grève . . ."

There was naught before her eyes but that flaming pyre in the evening of a winter's day—nothing but the flames and the night. A sob escaped her.

"They threw his ashes into the Seine. His children have no name. His castles were razed. His friends turned against him. His enemies forgot him. Nothing remains of the Palace of Gay Learning, where life was so happy and bright. All that you took, but you shall not get everything. You shall not have me. I am still his wife!"

The rain was streaming down outside. The storm was at its height.

"Perhaps you do not remember," she continued, "that a man is a man after all, even for a monarch as omnipotent as you. Now he is dust, his ashes scattered to the winds. But I remember and I always shall. I went to the Louvre to entreat you for his life, but you drove me away. You knew he was guiltless, but you wanted to see him burned. Because you were afraid of his influence in Languedoc. Because he was richer than you. Because he would not cringe before you. You bribed the judges to condemn him. You had murdered the only witness who could have saved him. You let him be tortured. You let him die. And I—you left me abandoned in wretched poverty with my two children. How could I ever forget that!"

She was racked with sobs, but the tears would not come. The King looked as if he had been struck by lightning.

The minutes ticked past interminably. Should he speak

or be still? Neither words nor silence could wipe out the past. It was the past that separated them from each other like an insurmountable wall.

When the sun came out, the King glanced toward his gardens. With a measured step he strode to the seat where he had left his hat and put it on. Then he turned to Angélique.

"Come, Madame. The Court is waiting for us."

She did not budge.

"Come," he insisted. "We must not be late. We have talked too much."

She shook her head. "Not too much. It had to be said."

Broken in spirit as she felt, she made a great effort to imitate the dignity of the King. She stepped before a mirror to repair her hair and fasten her gown. How empty she felt!

Their steps echoed in the colonnade of marble. Side by side they walked, yet strangers they would be from henceforth and forever.

That night there was a ball, a late supper, cards. Angélique kept asking herself whether she should flee, or wait for a sign from the King. It was impossible that he would continue as he had done. But when and how would he react to this new turn of events?

The morning returned, and the hours went by amid new pleasures. The King did not appear. He was working. Angélique was the center of attention. Her disappearance the previous evening at the same time as the King's had not passed unnoticed, and had seemed significant to everyone. Madame de Montespan had left Versailles to conceal her fury. Angélique forgot the dangers her rival had put in her path, now that she was confronted with a more immediate one. If the King disgraced her, what would become of Florimond and little Charles-Henri?

She accepted an invitation to play cards and lost a thousand *pistoles* in one hour. This stroke of bad luck seemed symbolic of the mess she had made of her life. In repulsing the King's love she had played her trump card and lost. One thousand *pistoles!* That's what came of living with a dice box in your hands. She had no love for gambling, but hardly a day went by at Court when she was not asked to take part in a game. That's how some people were reduced to begging for favors or sinecures to fill their lean purses. From one debt to another they passed their time in being ruined and in recouping their losses, pawning their jewels to be present on some Court expedition, replenishing their wardrobes so as to shine at a ball, writing petitions.

It was high time for her to chafe at the way Court life could confiscate a fortune since she was going to leave Versailles. She was sure of that now. These would be her last hours there.

As she stood by one of the windows of the Grand Gallery she recalled again the morning she had stood there were Barcarole watching the park awake, gazing at the palace of which she would have some day been queen. At the end of the Royal Avenue she could glimpse the masts, the sails and the ropes of the little fleet that seemed to beckon her to faraway fabulous ports.

Bontemps found her there, lost in her reverie. He whispered that the King wanted to see her and was waiting for her. The hour had struck!

The King was calm as usual. She could detect no trace of the emotion that agitated him when he saw her come in. But he knew that there would be played out now a drama whose last act was of infinite importance to him. Never had he yearned more avidly for a victory. Never had he felt so sure in advance that he would meet with defeat. "She will go away," he thought, "and my heart will turn to ashes."

"Madame," he said when she sat down, "yesterday you made many grievous and unjust accusations against me. I have spent a good part of the night and today reviewing the records of that trial, and have pieced it all together again. It is true that many of the details were no longer in my memory, but I had not forgotten the affair itself. Like most of the peremptory acts I had to perform at the start of my reign, that one remained deeply etched in my memory. It was a difficult game of chess in which my crown and my power were the stakes."

"My husband never threatened your crown or your power. It was jealousy alone . . ."

"Don't start saying things against me again," he said. "And let's stop quarreling over the premises of the problem right now. Yes, the Comte de Peyrac did threaten my crown and my power because he was one of the greatest of my vassals. The great have been and still remain my worst enemies. Angélique, you're no fool. Anger hasn't robbed you entirely of your good sense. I'm not giving you excuses, but reasons for changing your opinion. I must explain to you how things stood then. There were terrible insurrections throughout the kingdom both before and after I attained my majority— a foreign war in which these civil conflicts made France lose many of her advantages. A prince of the blood, my own uncle Gaston d'Orléans, was at the head of my foes, a very powerful man. The Prince de Condé had allied himself to him, and there were many conspiracies against the throne. The members of the Parlement were in revolt against their King. In my Court there were few who served me with disinterested loyalty, and that made my most apparently submissive subjects more to be feared than the insurgents. The only loyal ones were my mistrusted and slandered mother, and Cardinal Mazarin, who was universally hated. Besides, they were two foreigners. The Cardinal was an Italian, as you know. My mother had remained very Spanish in her sentiments and her customs. Even the best-intentioned of the French hardly endured their way of living. You can guess what the less well-intentioned made of it. In the midst of all that here was I, a child, invested with an overwhelming authority, but knowing I was too weak to wield it and that I was threatened from every quarter."

"You were not a child when you had my husband arrested."

"Stop being so stubborn, for heaven's sake. Are you going to be like all other women, incapable of seeing a problem in its entirety? However painful for you the consequences of the arrest and execution of the Comte de Peyrac, it was only a tiny detail in the panorama of rebellion and struggle that I am trying to depict for you."

"The Comte de Peyrac was my husband, and his fate, you must admit, is a more important detail to me than all your panorama."

"History shall be written in terms of Madame de Peyrac's opinions," said the King ironically, "even though my panorama is the whole world."

"Madame de Peyrac is not concerned with the history of the whole world," she snapped back savagely.

The King half rose to stare at her as she sat there with the fire of revolt in her cheeks, and smiled a little sadly.

"Some evening not so long ago, in this very room, you placed your hands in mine and renewed your oath as a vassal of the King of France. I have heard those words many times and seen them followed by the same betrayals and desertions. The breed of great lords will always be ready to toss their proud heads in revenge and rebellion against a master they think too hard on them. That's why I keep them all here at Versailles, right under my eyes. That lances the boil and drains off the evil fluids. I have no illusions, not even about you. So," said Louis XIV, "I have always perceived in you, in spite of the attraction you have for me, something utterly indifferent so far as I was concerned."

After a moment of thought, he continued. "I am not asking you to pity the young king in distress I was then. I do not promise to inspire respect and obedience. Between my former helplessness and my present power I have traveled a long hard road. I have seen my Parlement raise an army against me, and Turenne take command of it; the Duke de Beaufort and the Prince de Condé organize the Fronde; the Duchesse de Chevreuse intrigue to bring the armies of the Archduke of Austria and the Duc de Lorraine to Paris. I have seen Condé, after being my savior, slam the door behind him muttering low threats. Mazarin had him arrested. Then his sister the Duchesse de Longueville roused Normandie, and the Princesse de Condé, Guyenne; while the Duch

esse de Chevreuse was inviting the Spaniards to invade
France. I have seen my prime minister in flight; the
French fighting among themselves under the walls of
Paris; my cousin the Grande Mademoiselle directing the
cannons of the Bastille to be turned on my troops. Grant
me at least the extenuating circumstance of having been
brought up in a school of total distrust and treason. I
have learned how to forget it when I had to, but not the
lessons I learned from those bitter times."

Angélique sat with folded hands as he talked. Her
eyes were not on him. He felt her lack of attention, and
it hurt him more than all the troubles he had undergone.

"Why are you pleading with me?" she said. "What
good will it do?"

"To protect my reputation! The incomplete information you have about the occurrences that motivated me
have led you to draw false, insulting conclusions about
your King. A king who would abuse his power to satisfy
base desires is hardly worthy of the sacred title he received from God Himself and from his own great ancestors. To ruin the life of a man for no other reason
than envy and jealousy is a reprehensible act, inconceivable on the part of a true sovereign. To do the
same under the conviction that the execution of one will
spare the exhausted people greater troubles yet is an
act of wisdom and foresight."

"How had my husband threatened the peace of your
kingdom?"

"By his presence alone."

"By his presence alone?"

"Here me out! At last I achieved my majority. It was
not like a simple person's arrival at that stage when he
starts to manage his own affairs. I was fifteen years old.
I knew only the weight of the burden, not my own
strength. I kept my courage up by telling myself I had
not been put and kept on the throne without the ability
to find means of accomplishing the good work I was
determined to do. These means were given me. The
first act of my majority was to have Cardinal de Retz
arrested. That way I began to run my own household.
In a few years I had sealed the fate of those who for so

long had been embroiled in mine. My uncle Gaston
d'Orléans was exiled to Treyes. Others were pardoned,
among them Beaufort and La Rochefoucauld. The Prince
de Condé went over to the Spaniards, and I condemned him to death for contumacy. When I was about
to be married, the Spaniards negotiated a pardon for
him, which I granted him. Time passed. Other cares
demanded my attention, among them the preponderance
of more and more great ladies in the affairs of my Comptroller Fouquet. Another was the opposition of a province that for years had been the rival fief of the Ile-de-
France, Aquitaine. You were then its queen, my darling.
People kept talking of the wonders of Toulouse and
how your beauty revived memories of the lovely Eleanor
of Aquitaine. I was not unaware that the customs of that
province are so different as to render it almost a foreign
country. Cruelly punished during the Albigensian Crusade, later and for a long time subject to the English
and almost wholly given over to heretical beliefs, it
would support only with constraint the protectorship
of the Crown of France. The Count of Toulouse's very
title marked him as an unworthy vassal, regardless
of what his personal character might have been—or that
of any other man with the same title. He was a person
of lofty intelligence, an eccentric and charming character, rich, influential, and scholarly. Once I had seen
him I became obsessed with anxiety. Yes, he was richer
than I, and that I could not have, or in our day and age
money is more powerful than power, and sooner or later
he was going to match his power against mine.

"From then on I had only one plan—to destroy that
force which was growing beyond my grasp, creating by
my very side another state, perhaps soon to be another
kingdom. Believe me when I tell you that in the first
place I never wanted to attack the man himself, only
diminish his prerogatives and reduce his power. But
the more I studied the case, the more I discovered a
defect in my plan to let the Comte de Peyrac live, which
permitted me to entrust to another the difficult business
of a king who was vigilantly guarding his throne. Your
husband had an enemy. I shall never know why, but

Fouquet, the all-powerful Fouquet, had sworn his annihilation."

Angélique was wringing her hands as she listened to him, suffering to the very depths of her heart, reviving the past that had swallowed up her happiness. She shook her head. Her forehead was damp.

"I have done you wrong, my love," said the King. "My poor darling!"

He fell silent, overwhelmed for a moment by the weight of a destiny that after ranging them against each other as deadly foes had brought them to the verge of passion. He heaved a great sigh.

"From then on I entrusted the whole business to Fouquet," he continued. "I was sure he would do it well, and he did. He knew how to use for his own weaselly ends the vindictiveness of the Archbishop of Toulouse. I admit it was fascinating for me to watch his strategy. He too had money and influence, and was not far from thinking himself the master of the country. Patience! I thought. His turn would come and I wouldn't be unhappy when it did. Meanwhile I watched him reduce my enemies by the same subtle procedures I would later use to demolish him. Now that I have read over the records of the trial I can better understand why you are so indignant. You spoke of the murder of one of the witnesses for the defense, Father Kirchner. Alas, it's all too true. Everything was in the hands of Fouquet and his agents, and Fouquet wanted the Comte de Peyrac to die. It was indeed going too far. When he did that, I stepped in . . ."

The King brooded for a moment.

"You came to the Louvre to entreat me. I remember that, as well as I do the day I first saw you here so dazzlingly beautiful in your golden dress. Don't think I am entirely forgetful. I have a rather good memory for faces, and your eyes are not easy to forget. When, years later, you appeared at Versailles I recognized you at once. I had always known who you were, but you were introduced as the wife of your second husband the Marquis du Plessis-Bellière, and you seemed anxious to have no mention made of your past. I thought then I was granting your wish in accepting the amnesty you offered me. Was I wrong?"

"No, Sire. I thank you for it," said Angélique sadly.

"Should I have known then that already you had in mind such an exquisitely cruel revenge? To make me pay with the agony of my heart, as you are doing now, for the torments the King had inflicted on you before?"

"No, Sire, no. Don't think me capable of such meanness, and so useless to boot."

The King smiled wanly. "How well I recognize you in that remark. Vengeance is futile, as a matter of fact, and you are not a woman to waste your energies in a vain pursuit. But you achieved it nonetheless. You have hurt me, have punished me, a hundred times over."

Angélique looked away. "What power have I over destiny?" she said faintly. "I should have liked to—yes, I admit it—should have liked to forget. I loved life so. I was too young, I thought, to remain faithful to a dead man. The future was smiling on me and luring me on. But now the years have gone by, and I am still helpless in the face of one fact. He was my husband. I loved him with all my being, and you had him burned alive on the Place de Grève."

"No," said the King.

"He burned on the pyre," Angélique repeated savagely. "Whether you wanted him to or not. All my life I shall hear the crackling of the fagots consuming him by your orders."

"No," repeated Louis as if he were hitting the boards of the floor with his walking stick.

This time she heard him. She looked at him distractedly.

"No," said the King for the third time. "He was not burned. It was not he who was consumed at the stake on that January day in 1661, but the corpse of a condemned murderer which was substituted by my orders. By my orders," he shouted, *"by my orders!* At the last minute Joffrey de Peyrac was saved from his ignominious fate. I took pains to instruct the executioner myself of my plan, as well as how to keep the matter a dark secret, for I had no intention of granting him a spectacular pardon. Even though I wished to save Joffrey de Peyrac, I was not saving the Count of Toulouse. The secret nature of my plan created a thousand difficulties. The result was a scheme which was made possible by the existence of a shop on the Place de Grève. It had a cellar that was connected with the Seine by a subterranean tunnel. The morning of the execution my masked agents took up their positions there and brought the corpse in a white shroud. Then the cortège arrived. The executioner took his supposed victim into the shop for a drink, and the substitution was made out of sight of the crowd. While the flames were consuming a nameless hooded corpse, the Comte de Peyrac was spirited away through the tunnel to the Seine, where a boat was waiting for him."

The King knitted his brows as she looked at him with a stunned expression on her deathly white face.

"I have not said whether or not he is still alive. Banish that hope, Madame. The Count is dead, quite dead, but not in the way for which you hold me responsible. He was responsible for his own death. I gave him his life but not his liberty. My musketeers took him to a fortress in which he was imprisoned. But one night he escaped. It was foolish of him. He was not strong enough to swim the river, and he drowned. His body was washed up on the riverbank some days later and was identified.

"Here are the documents that attest to what I have just told you—the reports of the Lieutenant of the Musketeers and others telling of his escape and the identification of his body . . . Good Lord! Don't look at me so blankly. Can I believe you still love him now? One can't still be in love with a man long since disappeared from your life, and dead too. Ah, but that's a woman's way, always clinging to dreams. Have you never thought of the slow march of time? If you found him again now you would not recognize him any more than he would recognize you. You have become a different woman, just as he would have become a different man. I can't imagine you so lacking in logic . . ."

"Love is always lacking in logic, Sire. May I ask you a favor? Give me the document that tells of his imprisonment and his escape."

"What do you want to do with it?"

"Read it at leisure to appease my sorrow."

"I am not fooled by you. You have some new game in mind. Listen to me carefully—I forbid you, do you understand, I forbid you to leave Paris until I give you permission on pain of incurring my wrath."

Angélique lowered her head, clutching the file of papers to her breast like a treasure.

"Let me examine them, Sire. I promise to return them to you in a few days."

"Very well. But take good care of them. It is your right, since I was the first to tell you the story. I only hope your perusal of them will convince you that the past cannot be recaptured. You will weep and moan, but then you will return to reasonableness. Perhaps the experience will be good for you."

She seemed absent-minded. Her long lashes cast their shadows on her cheeks.

"What a woman you are!" he murmured. "You have your childish side, and yet you are a stubborn lover with a power to love as inexhaustible as the sea itself. If only you had not been made for me, alas! Go to your dreams, my darling. Farewell."

Angélique left him, forgetting to curtsy and without noticing that he had risen and was holding out his hands to her as her name died on his lips.

"Angélique!"

It was twilight as she crossed the park. She had felt the need of a walk to calm her nerves. She still kept the papers clutched to her as she walked, talking to herself. Those who passed her thought she must be either crazy or drunk, but that did not keep them from bowing low to Madame du Plessis-Bellière, the new favorite. She did not see them any more than she saw the trees or the statues or the flowers. She walked rapidly in her search for solitude and quiet. Finally she stopped by a little pool where bubbles of water were floating on the dark surface. She was out of breath because her heart was beating so irregularly.

She sat down on a marble bench, intending to read the documents the King had given her, but the light was too dim. She lifted her eyes to the heavens where the great trees gently tossed their crests.

The intuition that sleeps in every woman's heart awoke a sureness in her. Since he had not died at the stake, he might still be alive. If fate had snatched him so miraculously from the flames, would it not also restore him to her, not deprive him of life four years afterward by some trick? She would never be able to believe that part of it. Somewhere in this vast world he must be. He was waiting for her, and she would walk barefoot, if need be, over every inch of ground, known and unknown, until she found him. They had taken him away from her, but his life was not over. The day would come when she would reach him, fall upon him weeping, be joined into one with him again. She recalled neither his face nor his voice, not even his name, but she stretched forth her arms toward him across the gulf of the long dark years. Her eyes sought the darkening heavens against which the treetops swayed like seaweed in the breezes of the night. With a delirious exaltation she cried: "He is not dead! HE IS NOT DEAD!"

ABOUT THE AUTHORS

ANN and SERGE GOLON, actually husband and wife, collaborate to write the novels which bear the name of Sergeanne Golon. Serge Golon acquired a background as an engineer, prospector, chemist and geologist prior to turning full time to writing. Ann Golon, the daughter of a French naval officer, became a journalist. The pair met while pursuing their separate careers in darkest Africa and married shortly thereafter. Since their return to France in 1952, they have devoted themselves largely to recording the adventures of their fascinating heroine, Angélique, who has become one of the world's most famous fictional personages.